ALARIC THAIN'S HISTORY OF THE 21ST CENTURY

Alaric Thain Publishing

320 Gold Avenue

Ste 620 PMB 1099

87102 Albuquerque NM

United States

www.historyofthe21stcentury.com

Publisher's Note: Due to timeline divergence this version of this work can only be considered a work of fiction. Characters, places, and incidents are a product of the author's imagination. Locales and public names as well as historical figures are sometimes used for atmospheric purposes. Any resemblance to actual people, living or dead, or to businesses, companies, events, institutions, or locales is completely coincidental.

Alaric Thain's History of the 21st Century / Alaric Thain. -- 1st ed.

ISBN 978-1-7333896-0-0

*For **Ehoro**, wherever she is, was, or has yet to be, may she find hir ìràwọ*

CONTENTS

FOREWORD

By Faustina Dax

When I was asked to write this forward I hesitated. How can anyone possibly write a forward to a book about the 21ˢᵗ century by *Alaric Thain*? It would be like writing a forward to someone else's autobiography, for of course, the history of the 21ˢᵗ century is Thain's own, in many respects. How could any other mind, human or agent, proffer an *opinion* that could in any way rival his?

What was worse is that when I read the book, I realized two things in parallel: first, it is a masterpiece, and one that only Thain could have written. Second, it is not perfect. I truly believe that, like so many masterpieces, it does have some fundamental flaws and this made it only more difficult to write this forward. If I had found it to be a *flawless* masterpiece then I could simply have heaped praise upon a man who is not only a unique historian, not only the only person alive to have *lived* in the 21ˢᵗ century, but is also a good friend. That would have been pointless, for no praise of mine could enhance the reputation he has built for himself, both as a Traveler and as a professor of history, but at least it would have been easy for me.

However, the unshakeable impression that the book does have its flaws means that I cannot in all honesty take that easy route. I must compromise either my integrity or my admiration in deciding whether to include criticism in my praise. This decision is not made easier by the fact that it was Thain himself who asked me to write the forward. What's worse (or perhaps better) is that given our long standing relationship and knowledge of each other's work and view-points, I'm convinced he *knew* I would find fault with his book and actually wished to put me in this delicate situation. Whether it was out of a desire for intellectual objectivity or an impish delight in see-ing me squirm I have yet to determine but I suspect that it was some combination of the two.

First, then, the praise.

As Thain so cogently points out in his introductory chapter, there is no point in him simply relating facts, and yet there are long passages in which he does. Why is this? It is because we need to see the facts in a human context in order to *feel* the motivations that inspired our ancestors to do what they did. We often forget this. We have long forgotten that it was ever possible to have opinions about the veracity of facts, to debate their *status* as facts and yet this very ambiguity is behind much of our own history. Thain is a child of the era he discusses and he is best read by suspending, as far as we can, the intellectual reflexes we all share... of immediately referring to Artie to answer any factual questions, clear up any doubts we might have. Only then can we begin to appreciate our ancestors, only then can we even attempt to view their actions and their reactions as an-ything other than perplexing.

Take, for example, Destiny Holt, who is in some respects the hero of this book (as is well fitting). We see her like a Galileo, a solitary lucid human (along with people like Mukantagara Mporera) in a vast crowd of fools, but in the context of their times, these oth-ers were not fools. Misguided, perhaps, and maybe *foolish*, but not fools. In my opinion, this makes the achievements of people like Holt all the more astounding, for the wisdom of her stance was contrary to the wisdom of her times. By firmly putting us in that context, extolling us to abandon our modern sensibilities, Thain lets us *truly* appreciate the accomplishments of those without whom our modern society would not exist, for if there is one thing that should be clear after reading this book, we came very close to a very different outcome. Had the great "conferences" of the 2020's and 2030's gone differently and particularly, if the internal struggles of the United States had not been resolved in the way that they were – largely thanks to Holt – then it is entirely possible that instead of the world in which we now live, which would have seemed unrealistically idyllic from the point of view of someone in the early 21st century, we easily could have suffered complete societal breakdown, rampant violence, intolerance and potentially, the extinction of our species.

This realization can inspire in us either a shudder of disgust at the stupidity of our forebears in having brought us to the brink of social or existential annihilation, or it can inspire a deep feeling of gratitude and wonder that there were some who were able to guide us away from that terrifying path and place us on the road to salvation. If the latter, let us not forget that not only did people like Holt lead the way, but we owe just as much gratitude to people like Jayden Calhoun for having had the extraordinary lucidity and moral courage to change their minds and follow her example.

This is the glory of Thain's work, for it allows us to understand, however hesitatingly, however incompletely, the extent of the barriers and accomplishments surrounding the "happy metamorphosis" (to borrow a term from 21st-century French philosopher Alain de Vulpian) of society.

Now for the criticism.

Alaric Thain is fascinated by our social behavior. In many respects, he is more a sociologist than a historian. Given the structure and the *imposed* limitations of Artie (more on that later), this is one of the few "ologies" that remains largely a human domain, albeit in a different way than a 21st-century academic would have described a field of study. As such, he focuses very much – almost entirely, really – on social behavior. He sees human behavior as driven by our desire for social status, to the exclusion of other contributing factors.

Of course, there is a great deal of truth in this. We are indeed social primates and are evolutionarily driven by status considerations to a very large degree. I therefore do not disagree with Thain's premise, it would be folly to do so. I do, however, disagree with his absolutism. He seems to contend that the testosterone-cortisol-serotonin aggression mechanism is the "invisible evil hand" behind human history whereas he ignores almost entirely the simple idea of *pleasure*. In other words, we are not just driven by the hormones of aggression and competition, we are also driven by dopamine (to make an egregiously simplistic statement). I am therefore not convinced that we can fully understand economic systems solely by considering the accumulation of wealth as some kind of proxy measure for social hierarchy. While this was undoubtedly an important factor, I do think that much of the impetus to accumulate wealth was also driven by the desire to enjoy it for its own sake (in academic terms, *hedonic consumption*).

In reality, this has little impact on Thain's underlying analysis of capitalism, except when it comes to understanding its demise. How is it that humanity so easily abandoned the greed and ambition-fueled system that had driven our interactions since the invention of agriculture? According to Thain, wealth had only been desirable because it provided a "score" by which to measure our social rank, and we simply replaced it with a different scoring mechanism, the "likes" or "upvotes" that eventually led to the impact measures we follow today. But you need only look around to recognize that not everyone is driven by impact nor even cares, and this was the case in the 21st century as well.

Jerara Anggamudi's 2096 work on happiness indicated that already before the end of the 21st century, a great many people around the world were finding happiness in the enjoyment of simple pleasures... what was typically labelled "hoogah" by then, a term that persisted through the 23rd century. This word comes from the old Danish word *hygge*, which means, roughly, a sense of bliss and contentment to be gained from simple pleasures and companionship. Similar concepts existed throughout Scandinavia well before the information age, as witnessed by the word *koselig* in Norwegian and *mysa* in Swedish. Indeed, at the time, the Danes, who as Thain points out were among the first to adopt the "citizen's wage" and technonationalism, tended to refer to their cultural predilection for *hygge* as a key factor in the relatively smooth transition of their society to what would become known as "post-economic" lifestyle. Consider this passage from Anggamudi:

> "As the sun set on the corporate world
> of our fathers, some wailed in pain and others
> danced for joy. Let us compare, brother, the
> pain of the transition in the United States with
> the joy of it in the cold lands of the North.

Americans looked in vain for ways to identify themselves, searched for a new meaning by turning to their Gods or turning to violence while the Scandinavians were content to drink brandy near their fireplaces, trade tales with each other, and make love with greater intensity.

They sought new ways to deepen their bliss."

This is not displacement of hierarchical posturing in any way shape or form.

Thain points to Tor Anderson's efforts to be a proponant of a new society, one that laid the seeds for our post-fusion world, but Anderson himself spoke extensively of the need for hygge, enjoining people outside of Scandinavia to learn how to derive deep satisfaction from simple pleasures. In fact, the famous Danish mission to Africa mentioned by Thain consisted not only of technocrats, but of ordinary Scandinavians as well, many of whom went to help their African counterparts just as much with philosophical matters as with technical concerns (with varying degrees of success: see for example the memoires of the Norwegian Anders Tortensson). This Scandinavian ideal was not the only concept of its genre: Eastern traditions ranging from Buddhism to Taoism likewise taught their adepts to eschew social ambition in favor of inner peace and in continental Europe, philosophers such as Voltaire had preached the benefits of simple pleasures before the dawn of the industrial revolution.

Even when Thain is right, and again, I agree that his premise of human behavior as an extension of primate social competition is very much evident in our history, he leaves little room for *us* in changing the way we behave. I like to think that there *is* a rational

13

process here, that we *did* make a collective decision to lay aside the tribalism and violence of the past. I believe in free will and sometimes Thain seems to say that we stumbled upon appropriate substitutes for the demons that drive us and were saved by blind chance, but I am perhaps kinder to people of his own time than is he. I like to think that even beyond the actions of Holt, Calhoun, Mporera, Shavitz and the other great spirits of the age, we collectively decided to eschew the past and aided, undoubtedly, by blind luck and of course Artie, we decided to build a better society. We are not the product of some celestial design and had no original sin for which we needed atonement – it is true that as Robert Ardrey said: "we are born of risen apes, not fallen angels" – but this makes it all the more admirable that we made the herculean effort to change for the better.[1]

A further criticism I have is that he does not examine fully enough the making of Artie. Artie was the last great invention of humankind, for since then, all non-artistic inventions have been made by Artie hirself. As such, this is a monumental event, well foreseen before it occurred (referred to at that time as "the singularity") and it, more than fusion, brought the transition from the information age to the modern world. Thain correctly points out that the decisions of the San Francisco conference were key to the configuration of Artie but more detail would have been much appreciated.

---

[1] I would add a brief note here to point out that it is surprising Thain doesn't mention Ardrey. His 1961 book "African Genesis" was one of the first major works to lay the foundation for Thain's "history as status struggle" paradigm, yet Ardrey is not cited by him. Perhaps Thain is not immune to a little intellectual snobbery, since Ardrey was not an academic, but a dramatist.

Indeed, it was there that neurology, behavioral science and "computer science" came together and that brain function was used both to help consider the thought process of Artie and to limit it. Thain does not discuss the "amygdalate debate" in any real detail, whereas it was thrilling and complex and if it had been decided differently would potentially have led to a very different world, perhaps a terrifying one. Furthermore, while Galit Shavitz is treated with great respect in this book, it was in this debate that she made her greatest mark and by so doing, arguably had as great a role in "saving the world" as Destiny Holt would have several years later... even if it's only in hindsight that we can appreciate this.

It should be noted (as Thain fails to note) that in reality, there are very much *two* distinct types of artificial intelligence. There is the AI that guides trew machine interaction: that animates robots, drives vehicles and prints furniture, and there is intellectual AI... Artie. While Artie of course, or at least an agent, can inhabit a robot at will and drive its actions, it acts almost like the frontal cortex while the deeper AI actually drives specific physical movements and functions. This is of course closely paralleled in our own brains, but artificial minds are in reality far more dichotomized than the ones in our skulls and exactly how this came to be and how Shavitz managed to drive home the importance of these separations is too important a story to have received the relatively perfunctory treatment that Thain accords it.

Another factor that he does not cover is the significant shift in gender power in the late information age. One cannot help but notice, in Section Two, his recounting of the age's history, that the heroes are almost all women. Humankind was almost entirely ruled

15

by men in the agricultural and industrial ages, and the information age began in a similar vein, but when considering Shavitz, Holt, Mporera, and many lesser figures who have eluded Thain's historical gaze, one is struck by the paucity of important male figures (with the possible exception of Tor Anderson) among the visionaries of the era. Indeed, the most prominently mentioned *man* of the time is probably Donald Trump, who is perhaps the most notorious villain of Thain's book. Of course, this gender shift has not gone unnoticed by other historians. Konishi Hitori noted (in his 2133 book "The Salient Ones"):

> "At the beginning of the 20th century, women didn't even have the right to vote in most countries. It took a hundred years for them to start coming into power, but once they did, in the 21st century, it changed everything. We became more rational and more peaceful. Think about it: if fifty percent of people were born with a visible mark and these people were *proven* to be seven times more likely to commit violence due to their genetic make-up then we'd have decided long ago that no one with such a mark should be allowed to hold a position of authority. And yet this is exactly the case – the mark in question is the penis."

The long struggle for equal rights for women had finally been successful enough to bring women into positions of power, and while this can never be determined conclusively, Hitori's contention that the naturally less violent and more socially sophisticated character of female primates, including women, might well have had something to do with the successes of the 21ˢᵗ century. Certainly, Mukantagara Mporera's ability to bring lasting peace to her country and to federate most of Africa, and Destiny Holt's legendary and courageous defusing of the Rancher Crisis lend credence to Hitori's thesis (see Chapters 13 and 15 respectively).

Lastly, I regret that Thain focuses only on the history of humans on *Earth*. Obviously, as this is a book about the 21ˢᵗ century (or more exactly, about the information age) we did not yet have any extra-solar colonies and so my criticism can seem puerile, but he does frequently refer to the present when considering the past – yet that present is only an Earthly present. Thain has seen more colonies than any other inhabitant of our planet, having visited four, and he does not share any of this experience with us. Granted, the colonies are all far more similar to present day Earth society than they are to pre-fusion society but still, different choices were made, and as his book is, again, largely a study in sociology, it would have been interesting to see his opinion about why these new worlds took different routes. Thain made the sacrifice that so few of us are willing to make: he travelled, and in so doing, left behind all those he knew, aware that they would be dead before his next stop, and as his friend, while I will respect the intimacy of his life story I can all the same assure readers that it has not been easy for him. I can only hope that he will one day feel compelled to write his own story, having already written ours.

I will make one suggestion: before you turn the page, spend some time in a retro-sim, preferably one not of the 21ˢᵗ century, but of the 20ᵗʰ. Thain does well to dedicate the first section of his book to an overview of history leading up to the information age so as better to set the stage, but go visit that time before you return to trew and read the facts. No retro sim can *truly* put you into the age it simulates, just as no animal sim can allow you to think like a trout, but it might help to review the every-day concepts that have become very strange to us before you embark on this great adventure.

Faustina Dax
June 15, 2864

INTRODUCTION

I did not want to write this book. It seemed pointless, in this day and age, to write a book about history. The facts are clear to all, there is no debate, really, about what occurred in the past, and certainly not about the events of the 21st century, which, compared to previous periods, is extremely well-documented. If anyone wants to know what actually happened, they can simply have a more or less involved conversation with Artie via their agent, access primary media or even visit the age in sim. What, then, is the point of a "history book"? What could I possibly bring to the subject?

I am not being disingenuous. I am well aware that the particularities of my own story have made me a subject of interest for those who study history, especially with respect to the pre-fusion era. For these past twelve years I have in fact been a professor of pre-fusion history at the Sorbonne and as such, I have very often shared whatever insights I bring to the topic with many thousands of people. Still, I am perplexed when it falls upon me to adjudicate questions of fact... *what* happened. Artie can of course respond better than I, even when these questions pertain to events that I lived through, for Artie has access to all information at once and every one of us has access to Artie through our agent. Why, then, this fascination with me?

I have finally come to realize that when I am asked *what* happened, the true, underlying question is really *why* it happened. Your agent can immediately give you perfect details of any major event in the 21st century, but she can't tell you why, she can't explain the reasoning of the people of the time, because she was designed in such a way that it is impossible for hir[2]. And you, quite frankly, are not instinctively capable of understanding this on your own, because you are a product of the 29th century… whereas I am not, and as much as I was born at the end of that era – after most of the events recounted in this book – I was still a child of it all the same, and while the mentality of the time had changed dramatically since the dawn of that century, it was still resolutely that of the information age. It has taken me fourteen years, ever since my return to Earth, to adapt to a modern way of thought and I cannot imagine you being able to regress easily to a primitive mindset without the same degree of effort and immersion – an impossible thing to do on this planet.

This is evident to me whenever I visit a historical sim. The people I meet in them walk in the information or even the industrial era and they do their best to act as if they belong there. They familiarize themselves with the technology, some even genuinely learn to drive cars, fly airplanes, or fire guns, but when I speak with them, whether real people or npc's, they inevitably don't react the way people did at the time, they don't fundamentally think that way, nor do they feel the same emotions. They are pretending.

As such, I have decided finally to bow to the incessant prodding and write a book. I will indeed take the reader through the

---

[2] Interestingly, it's not in hir range of possibility thanks to decisions that were made in the 21st century and that are often forgotten.

major events of the 21st century, but it is less the events that interest me than it is the mindset of our ancestors, a mindset that greatly affected the decisions they made.

Fundamentally, this book is about context. It is an attempt to render comprehensible decisions that often seem incomprehensible today. These decisions make sense in a certain context, while outside of that context they are mysteries.

Any mind today, whether human or agent, knows that one cannot consider the movement of a system from a different inertial reference frame and expect to understand it without taking into account the movement of the reference frame itself. So it is with human beings. One cannot expect to understand the decisions of human beings from outside the reference frame in which they exist. The reference frame in this case is not physical, but mental, or more specifically, social or cultural.

We have forgotten this – or more specifically, *you* have forgotten this – for it has been centuries since the dawn of the fusion age. Since then, humankind has created an entirely new social order, one that recognizes the primacy of rationality and is truly global. You look back at your pre-fusion ancestors and consider them to be misguided barbarians, and while you *know* that you are no different, you don't really believe it. You don't really believe that you could have acted with utter disregard for the facts, that you would have considered *faith* a virtue, that you could have looked down upon someone for the shade of hir skin, that you would have hungered for the accumulation of money or more unimaginably, that you could have willingly killed. You believe that you would have been enlightened, that you would have stood up at any point in pre-fusion history and militated for reason, for peace, for dignity. You would have been Martin Luther King, or Ndagukunze, or Holt. After all, they did it, and they did it despite the prevailing zeitgeist.

Yet they, and many others, were heroes. True heroes. There is little room for heroism today (at least on Earth), simply because heroism is an extraordinary response to conflict, and the greater the conflict, the greater the potential for heroism. Earth today has so little conflict that there are precious few occasions to the top of which a hero might rise. We do hear tell of heroism from the colony worlds, but even they typically do not experience the gut-wrenching conflict that prevailed in pre-fusion Earth. Would you truly have been able to shake off the centuries – nay, millennia – of cultural baggage that gripped the entirety of humanity, rejected the accepted wisdom of those around you, suffered disdain and rejection for the actions you undertook, however noble they might seem to us seven hundred years later, and thrown yourself to the wolves of conflict? Perhaps. More likely, not.

So let us dive into that conflict. Let us understand just how extraordinary it was and just how deep ran the causes of the cultural and social inertia that made the 21st century and the changes it brought so extraordinary.

This book consists of three sections. In the first, I set the stage for the information era by considering the history of humankind up to the 21st century, focusing on those elements that help better to understand the period that interests us. In the second section, I do recount the facts of the information era, roughly 1998 to 2087, examining in detail the motivations behind the decisions that were made. The third section consists of a discussion about three concepts that are typically difficult for modern humans to under-stand: economics, politics, and religion.

SECTION I

While the title of this book is the History of the 21st Century, we are in fact actually talking about the information era, typically considered to have spanned from 1998 to 2087, the former of those two dates representing, in a somewhat abstracted way, the creation of the globally accessible "internet", or web, and the latter being the year in which the last non-fusion power generating station was closed. These are technological turning points, and of course, there are two others that took place during the 21st century: the "singularity" (roughly speaking, from 2032 to 2046) and the perfection of quantum computing, in 2049. Of course, these are all linked. The web made it possible for human thinkers to share information with far greater efficiency and eventually bring about the event known as the singularity (see Chapter 12). The singularity greatly accelerated the work that had been previously carried out by purely human thought in quantum computing, and it was the combination of true artie thought processes and the modelling made possible by quantum computing that gave us usable fusion.

These events in themselves are not explanatory but descriptive. To understand why they took place and why they unfolded as they did we need to examine the socio-cultural revolution that these technological changes brought about and the conflict so engendered. Never before had technology come anywhere near to producing such a fundamental change in the day-to-day lives of human beings. In reality, while we think of "post-fusion" and "pre-fusion", we could also be talking about "post-economic" and "pre-economic", or "post-rational" and "pre-rational" epochs. This shifts the focus of the discussion from the technological to the social and can be of great benefit when considering the *human* history of the 21st century. Remember that while these technologies made social change possible it was the decision to embrace that change that is the true subject of this book.

Note that as we consider the events of the distant past, we must by necessity consider them in broad, sweeping terms. Those of you who are familiar with history will protest that I go too quickly, that the motivations I attribute to those who made these decisions are gross simplifications, that the reality was far more complex. You will be correct in making these assertions. There is an old saying: "hindsight is 20/20"[3], and while there is a lot of truth in that, it does not tell the whole story. Hindsight benefits from knowing the consequences of an event, but it can become quite blurry when examining the contributors to it. Only the most salient, the most resilient in our collective psyche remain as the years go by. So yes, I will by necessity not consider a great number of contributing factors to the events we shall examine together, but I do hope that the centuries that have passed since then will allow us to focus more effectively on the most *important* of those factors. For those of you who wish to know more, I encourage you to ask Artie and engage in long discussions both with your agent and with other humans.

---

[3] Until the fusion age, most humans had less than perfect vision and it remained uncorrected for most, except for the use of external apparatus ("glasses"). The quality of vision was measured, in the United States at least, by a scale in which "20/20" is perfect.

Before examining the decisions of the 21st century we must reach farther back, we must set the stage, for the reference frame at the beginning of the century was a function of the history that preceded it. I propose considering this history via Xi Xian's "five epoch" framework and the four "revolutions" that structure it[4]:

1. The agricultural (or Neolithic) revolution
2. The industrial revolution
3. The information revolution
4. The fusion revolution

Before we dive in to our chosen subject, let us therefore see what led up to the cultural landscape in 1998, revolution by revolution, and briefly outline the cultural changes brought by each of these seminal events.

---

[4] See particularly "The Five Stages of Mankind", 2097. Note that Xi Xian was certainly not the first to postulate these turning points in history, nor the first to use them to typify the ages of humanity – see, for example, the work of Jared Diamond and Yuval Harari in the early years of the 21st century – but Xi was the first to fold in the latter two revolutions convincingly and certainly the first to recognize that the fusion revolution coupled with the singularity would bring about the end of economics and introduce a plateau to technological advancement.

CHAPTER 1

THE PRE-AGRICULTURAL ERA

Homo Sapiens first evolved in Africa about 250,000 years ago and rapidly expanded across the African and Eurasian continents, finally reaching the Americas roughly 35,000 years ago. The species' expansion brought a wave of destruction as our ancestors used their relatively more developed intellect to displace existing species, including non-sapiens of our own homo genus. This displacement took the form of resource competition or downright killing, as our omnivorous ancestors hunted into extinction countless species, including most large mammals and birds in Australia, the Americas and the majority of islands on the planet.

This wave of destruction was carried out by small bands of sapiens. Study of chimpanzees[5], as well as consideration of the archeological record leads us to the conclusion that sapiens lived in small bands, probably of less than fifty individuals, throughout the entirety of the pre-agricultural period which, after all, represents the overwhelming majority of our existence.

What was the social structure of the time? This is purely a matter of conjecture, but Artie tells us that it is extremely probable that the bands in which we lived had relatively simple internal social hierarchies, at least compared to what was to follow. It is also likely that while the two sexes played different roles, neither dominated the other.

Humans at the time were hunter-gatherers, largely nomadic (although several archeological sites lead us to believe that some relatively sedentary settlements existed, particularly in coastal areas). The human population of the planet was sparse, declining to less than ten thousand individuals after the Toba eruption 75,000 years ago, and was less than ten million at the time of the agricultural revolution. The destruction wrought by sapiens on pre-existing species was surprising, given our relatively low numbers, but it was not carried out by vast empires, it was carried out by small bands.

This is crucial to help build our understanding of what was to follow, for we evolved to thrive in this pre-industrial, hunter-gatherer environment. Our instincts and proclivities are uniquely suited to this, as the ten thousand years or so that have succeeded this

---

[5] I am tempted to revive the idea of classifying chimpanzees as members of the genus *homo* (i.e. homo troglodytes and homo paniscus), originally proposed by Jared Diamond in 1991, but centuries of accepted usage convince me not to complicate matters.

lifestyle are but the blink of an eye on an evolutionary scale. So, in the world of our ancestors, what were the evolutionary imperatives?

First, there is of course survival. All creatures are born with this instinct, as it is the most straightforward evolutionary rule – survive, at least long enough to reproduce successfully. When survival is threatened in any way, we instinctively do all that we can to protect our genes: those within our bodies and those within the bodies of our close relatives.

Even in the 21st century we understood that genetic imperatives lead to the propagation of the gene, not of the species. Propagation of the species is a byproduct of this phenomenon.[6] As such, tribalism makes sense in this context, for we are naturally inclined to protect those who are most likely to share genes with us, and the higher the percentage of genes we share, the higher our desire to protect and further the interest of the other. Parents protect their children and siblings protect each other; to a somewhat lesser degree, grandparents protect their grandchildren and cousins contribute to each other's well-being, and so on. In a clan of twenty or thirty individuals, it is quite likely that there is a high degree of genetic homogeneity, and evolution therefore drives us to create close bonds, to identify as a member of the tribe and to eschew other tribes. The farther they seem from us genetically, the more "alien" they become. After a certain degree of apparent genetic separation the extent to which common genes are likely shared falls under a critical mass and in a pre-fusion world this means that we are

---

[6] It surprises me that even today, this understanding of the "selfish gene" is attributed to Darwin, when it was Dawkins who was the first to realize this particular subtlety of evolution. See "The Selfish Gene", 1976.

competing for limited resources, even more directly than if the other sapiens band were a completely different species.

This mechanism gave rise to violent tribal behavior, in which bands were tightly bound and coherent within themselves, less tolerant of neighboring bands who competed for resources, and downright hostile to bands farther afield whose genetic kinship was extremely removed and who represented a distinct resource threat if they came into contact. Interaction between bands was therefore often violent while a strong sense of bonding within the band was undoubtedly the norm.

The materially egalitarian nature of intra-band society is a function of the relatively sparse population density at the time. With plentiful resources (resource density being largely a function of territory size) and small band size, there is little impetus for resource hoarding and little need for a formal mechanism of resource allocation within the band. As such, bands of hunter-gatherers had no need for formal "economic" structures.

This is not to say that social standing was not important for our ancestors. Most social primates, including humans, have always been keenly driven by social standing and indeed, the seeking of standing within the band is perhaps the strongest driver of behavior once basic survival has been assured.

This is easier for us to see in other primates. Both common chimpanzees and bonobos have complex social structures in which individual standing is fluid. These animals have both proven highly adaptable, measuring social rank in a slightly different fashion given their changing circumstances as their original habitat was nearly destroyed before having been largely re-established in the fusion age.

As we shall see, we seem to share this adaptability in the way we measure social standing.

Concretely, what does this mean for the culture of our pre-agricultural sapiens ancestors? The most probable scenario involves an ongoing struggle to enhance social standing within the parameters of what each individual considered to be hir band. In other words, social standing was relative to others in the same band. Each individual sought to enhance hir rank, largely because in social primates, rank is linked to reproductive success.

How did we try to enhance our rank? If we examine our cousins, the chimpanzees, we see that social rank is largely a function of politics, the details of which differ across the two sexes. Males tend to employ physical power and confrontation. However, while highly visible, this is actually a secondary consideration. Males actually rely on alliance building among themselves and with high-ranking females. Females too build alliances, and the political manipulations in which they engage are more complex. For both sexes, social rank enhances reproductive success. Males benefit from more frequent copulation with desirable females while females benefit from greater attention from the males and from the society as a whole, thereby increasing the chance of survival for their young.

Another relevant factor is that in the case of males, there is a distinct correlation between their current social rank and their level of aggressiveness. Lower ranking males are more aggressive than their higher-ranked brethren. A number of hormones are linked to social rank, notably testosterone, cortisol, and serotonin and it should be noted that there is a variable causal relationship at play — in other words, as a male increases his rank, his level of aggressiveness diminishes. This makes sense from an evolutionary perspective: since males rely to a degree on physical dominance and threat to gain social rank, a lower-ranked male should be ready to take greater risks in affronting other males in order to increase his chance of reproductive success, if he succeeds he will likely increase the survival rate of his genes whereas if he fails he may be injured or even killed (though this is rare) but his genes had a low probability of being passed on anyway. At the same time, a higher-ranked male has nothing to gain and everything to lose from conflict and would do well to avoid it.

But we are not chimpanzees and it is not likely that our ancestors had precisely the same social structure as do they. It is important, though, to keep in mind the parallels between us and them. It is quite likely that the overall pattern of social rank being linked to reproductive success holds true, and that aggressive behavior is a more logical strategy in this respect for lower-ranked individuals[7].

The differences, though, should also be considered as we try to reconstruct the culture of our pre-agricultural (and pre-historical) ancestors. For one thing, monogamy is far more prevalent among homo sapiens than among chimpanzees or especially, bonobos. For another, our capacity for symbolic thought and complex symbolic

---

[7] Ask your agent about Milos Liska's groundbreaking work on the mathematics of evolution. In his 2033 paper "Why can't I get just one fuck (It doesn't have something to do with luck)?" he carefully studied the actual probabilities of reproduction given social standing among great apes and extended his analysis to humans in the United States over the previous thirty years. His formulae proved extremely robust and definitively established the link between social ranking, reproductive success and male violence in all the species studied.

communication makes the underlying struggle for dominance far more complex than the already complex interactions of other primates.

Taken together, the picture we begin to build of pre-agricultural sapiens culture is one of constant small-scale political maneuvering. Intra-band violence probably did play a role, particularly for males, but unlike other apes, we began to use *things* to demonstrate our skills. The successful hunter or gatherer saw hir social rank go up, as did the sapiens able to decorate hirself with rare shells, beads, hides, feathers, carved ornaments or difficult-to-produce paints. These things in themselves had no direct practical benefits, but they served to demonstrate that their possessor was capable of producing, or at the very least acquiring them and hence they contributed to the never-ending struggle for social standing.

It is also crucial to understand that the desire for social standing was entirely restricted to the individual's definition of hir band or clan. This was the extent of hir ambition and desire for recognition.

Hence we are left with the image of a small band, within which individuals create alliances and friendships while scheming to bring ridicule to those outside of their alliances, with whom they compete for standing and therefore for reproductive success. Despite the informal hierarchy of social standing, there is no formal political structure, as it is unnecessary given the size of the band and the relative availability of food. Neither is there any sense of belonging outside the band, nor any semblance of large scale structure.

Hence we can imagine our ancestor, whether male or female, huddling in a cave with hir band members, hir two living children close by in the flickering light of a fire built near the cave's entrance so as not to overpower them with smoke, the males of the band squabbling in an effort to take greater credit for the kill that had brought them all meat, while the yet unattached females choose which of younger males to support in his grandiose posturing. News of a new rival band towards the western edge of their territory has made them uneasy, but they will be moving on soon as the herds of prey head south with the change of the season. Our ancestor considers the others in hir band and a feeling of attachment and affection overcomes hir for these are hir *kin* and she is well accepted by them. The newcomers to the west, though, frighten hir, they are unfamiliar and menacing. She huddles closer to the others and pulls hir children toward hir.

The lack of an inter-band political structure does not mean that there was no contact between bands. Indeed, there is ample evidence of shared symbolism, and hence shared culture. Notably, the prevalence of Venus figurines throughout Eurasia, stretching from 39,000 to 10,000 years ago, attests to a shared mythology that is impressive in its extent. Likewise, the temple at Gobekli Tepe as well as the complex at Kulgili Minora indicate that shortly before the agricultural revolution there was a shared belief system powerful enough to bring bands together to cooperate in major joint construction projects.

However, there is little evidence for a cross-band religious structure, particularly before about 11,000 years ago, and it is highly likely that the religion of the time was primarily shamanistic[8].

---

[8]Artie can expound on this, but even in pre-fusion times this was understood. See, for example, the work of Jean Clottes (1969 to 2005)

Religion had not yet become the controlling mechanism it would later be – although the monumental works of sites like Kulgili may signal the beginnings of some kind of inter-band priestly caste that interestingly emerged just before the agricultural revolution.

It was that monumental change in human experience that would endow this nascent priestly class with power that no one had ever imagined.

CHAPTER 2

THE AGRICULTURAL ERA

Artie can tell you exactly how the agricultural revolution came about, where and when. In broad terms, hunter-gatherer bands in particularly fertile regions – typically in river valleys – discovered that some of the plants they had been gathering were growing among their dwellings, particularly in those places in which they defecated. They learned how to plant these plants, tend to them, and so reduce uncertainty and travelling distance in their gathering.

They also discovered that having easy access to grains allowed them to domesticate a very limited number of large social mammals – cows, sheep, pigs, and horses, as well as fowl such as chickens. They no longer needed to hunt, or to gather, they could instead farm.

This led to rapid sedentarization of agricultural societies. It also led to a marked decrease in health as populations were ravaged by epidemics, and, ironically, poorly nourished. The epidemics were a consequence of the close proximity of large numbers of people coupled with proximity to herd animals, whose diseases jumped the species barrier. The malnourishment was largely because the highly varied diet of hunter-gatherers was both healthier and far less vulnerable to draught and other natural hardships, while the new lifestyle led to increased family sizes and population density as well as far less diverse diets.

Why, then, did our ancestors abandon their hunter-gatherer ways? It was not in order to save effort, for hunter-gatherers enjoyed far more leisure time than inhabitants of agricultural societies. It was, in fact, due to the same behavioral drivers that had always existed – desire for social status.

Agricultural societies can support far higher populations at a much greater density than can the hunter-gatherer lifestyle. As such, the *boundary* of what constitutes any individual's social group is expanded dramatically in an agricultural society. This question of expanding boundaries in the context of our genetic desire for social rank is pivotal in the understanding not only of the agricultural revolution, but in understanding all of our behavior through history.

Up until that time, people measured their social status relative only to the other individuals in their band, typically no more than fifty, all of whom were in constant personal contact. One's rank was known to all, there was no need to signal it or indicate it externally in any way. Chimpanzees wear no jewelry, nor would they need to. With the agricultural revolution people found themselves living in large communities, in which it was impossible to know personally all the members and therefore impossible to know one's social rank upon meeting or simply seeing another member of the expanded clan. What this meant is that our social structure had evolved more rapidly than our brains – we were still just as driven to enhance our rank and enjoy the privileges of social standing, yet we had no way of making our standing known.

The answer was wealth. The largely aesthetic trappings already prevalent in hunter-gatherer societies had already begun to be used as an indicator of social rank, and in dense, impersonal agricultural societies this became the only practical way of both increasing rank and signaling it.

The accumulation of wealth was not only a symbolic factor in agricultural societies, it became an increasingly accurate measure of actual social rank, largely due to increasing specialization.

Hunter-gatherer bands supported relatively little specialization. Some sapiens were primarily hunters, other gatherers, others shamans, and each was more or less talented at tool making, art, etc. but everyone did a little of everything and was capable to a greater or lesser degree of personally producing most of the types of goods typically made or acquired by hir colleagues.

In an agricultural society specialization becomes common. Agricultural output, while much higher in terms of calories per acre, is typically uniform and repetitive, conducive to structured, predictable roles and it requires larger-scale transformation of the basic foodstuffs. At the same time, specialized high-yield farmers can support others who engage in no food production at all, and who therefore become full-time craftspeople, priests or politicians. And so, as our settlements grew, a visitor walking down the dirt street would feel the heat of the blacksmith's forge and hear the clang of his hammer as he bent metal to his purpose, she would smell the stink of the tanner making leather out of hides and be relieved when the noxious odor was replaced by the sweet smell of bread wafting from the hut of the baker.

For the first time, therefore, people needed to enter into formal, long-term trading relationships with others within their own society. If the tanner wanted to eat, she had to trade with the baker, and if the farmer wanted tools with which to farm, she had to trade with blacksmith. What's more, as our settlements grew, each had to trade with others who, while being part of hir own society, she did not know personally.

We have already considered that social primates as a whole further their social aspirations largely through their ability to create alliances and garner the support of other members of their group. In the specialized societies of the agricultural revolution, where intra-group trade had become prevalent and indeed necessary for survival, the degree to which a person could somehow convince others to trade with hir on favorable terms was actually an accurate measure of any individual's ability to create and master such alliances. The result of this skill is an imbalance in wealth.

In other words, the more wealth any individual was able to accumulate, the better that person's network of alliances. Wealth became an accurate proxy for social rank in a dense, specialized agricultural society. How can any individual know the social standing of anyone else in such an environment? By the *wealth* she displays. This is particularly true if the individual actually engages in no direct production hirself, for this clearly indicates a strong talent for bending others to do the work for hir.

And so our Neolithic ancestor is no longer huddling in a cave with all the other humans she knows, she is instead huddling in a mud hut in which she resides permanently with hir mate and their children. The hut is in a vast settlement with other similar huts full of other similar families. She and hir mate, and those of their children who are old enough to walk, work in the same fields they and their forebears have always worked. Much of their output goes to the ruling class, or at least to the society as a whole in order to feed those who do not work the fields, but the family has enough to survive. Unlike hir ancestor, she does not travel and has never been more than twenty kilometers from the hut in which she now lives. Instead of knowing personally all the members of hir group, she now is part of an extensive society with thousands or perhaps even millions of members. She calls herself "Incan" or "Roman" or "Han" and has never even laid eyes on the ruler of her "tribe" yet she labors for hir, fights for hir, and prays to the gods for hir well-being. Because she must constantly provide food for hir family and hir society she does not have an opportunity to accumulate any wealth at all and therefore remains at the very bottom of the social structure, taking solace in the fact that she is far from alone there – everyone she knows is likewise a peasant, looked down upon by those they feed.

But why? Why did our ancestor abandon a relatively leisurely, healthy hunter-gatherer lifestyle for a structured, unhealthy, labor-intensive agricultural society in which material wealth becomes the primary indicator of social success?

To answer this, we need to come back to the idea of specialization, for a new special role began to emerge – that of politician. We will use the term broadly to mean all those whose role is to control others, making decisions for them. As such, in our nomenclature, both priests and kings are politicians for both of them are expected to influence the behavior of others, and of society as a whole. This role of politician did not exist in pre-agricultural bands, or at least not to the same degree. There were chiefs and shamans, but they were undoubtedly otherwise productive members of society at the same time; the fully specialized politician was a product of the agricultural revolution.

These politicians, the leaders of agricultural societies, did not work in agriculture. There are virtually no recorded instances of politicians having actual agricultural responsibilities except as owners of land[9]. Instead, they sat at the pinnacle of social hierarchy, achieving a rank never before imagined: their mastery of alliances was so complete that they produced nothing at all, they were simply tended to by those who did produce. No chimpanzee could ever aspire to such a rank, even the most alpha of alpha males must forage for food... as well, of course, as producing semen for the propagation of the band. Politicians, though, were expected only to make decisions for society as a whole.

Of course, the increased size of society gave rise to the need for far greater and complex decisions, and this same size made it impossible to engage in group-wide decision making. A band of thirty or forty individuals can easily come together around the campfire every night and discuss together whether they should move,

---

[9] Interestingly, they often touted their agricultural roots to maintain credibility and empathy among the population. Perhaps the most famous example of this is the Roman story (undoubtedly apocryphal) of Cincinnatus, an important politician who was called to wield great power in a time of crisis and then willingly abandoned it to return to his farm and tend his fields.

hunt, or raid a neighboring band. A tribe of a thousand individuals cannot do this, some delegation of decision-making must take place.

We still have not answered our question, though. If everything is so much more complex and if life is, on average, so much more difficult for most, with important decisions delegated to a small number of unproductive politicians, why on earth would people agree to such a system?

The answer lies with the politicians themselves. It is true that the tribes of the early agricultural revolution lived harder lives, on the whole, than the bands of the pre-agricultural age, but the politicians themselves lived far more fulfilled lives than any pre-agricultural sapiens, *particularly* from the point of view of social rank, and let us not forget that we have evolved to be primarily driven by consideration of social standing. Before the agricultural revolution, the best anyone could hope for was to be an alpha individual among at most fifty other individuals. After the agricultural revolution, one could aspire to having a rank much greater than that of the alpha; one could be an *uber* individual, a non-productive politician within a tribe of hundreds or thousands... or by the mid-agricultural period, even millions.

Even today, in our post-fusion world, consider the historical sims that are the most played. Ask your agent how many people play sims that allow them to experience being a respected elder in a prehistoric band as opposed to those who take a spin as the emperor of Rome. The latter is titillating, or at the very least interesting to us, whereas the former barely provokes any interest at all.

Since decisions were made by the politicians, it is not surprising that they made decisions that propagated the system that allowed them to *be* politicians, i.e. intensive agriculture.

That these decisions were accepted by the productive members of society is more surprising, and in order to understand this, we must first address the question of religion.

We will consider religion more completely in Chapter 22, but we cannot answer the question of how entire societies accepted the sacrifice of health and happiness to propagate a system that primarily served a tiny number of politicians without broaching the subject here.

I have always found it difficult to discuss religion with people of 29ᵗʰ-century Earth. When I was growing up, seven hundred years ago, religion was still a factor in Earthly matters, although distinctly on the wane by then. Today, it is typically considered with bewilderment and a certain degree of disdain. Even historians have a tendency to discuss the topic with insufficient respect for their own ancestors, who were often guided by religious considerations. This is perhaps partly due to our discussions with our agents and Artie in general, who have always been by design utterly devoid of religious, and indeed all emotional (i.e. irrational) factors. But one of the reasons I am writing this book is to help you truly *understand* what it is to be driven by what you would consider to be primitive considerations and before we begin in earnest to examine the 21ˢᵗ century it is crucial that you gain an appreciation for religious belief.

The evidence for religious sentiment in pre-agricultural societies is strong and understandable. We evolved an extraordinarily useful ability to search for cause behind every effect. If a bush rustles, we assume something is moving it and therefore are better able to avoid the tiger lurking within. This is the case with all animals, but we go farther, we are curious and wish to understand the mechanism by which the tiger rustles the bush, inferring its size, intent and tactics. We then communicate these things to each other, teaching each other and devising strategies to deal with future tigers. This was a thoroughly remarkable adaptation and we probably owe the survival of our species to this ability.

What is less useful in a pre-agricultural world (again, the one for which we evolved) was an understanding of statistics and probability. Nine times out of ten, the bush will rustle because of the wind, but mistaking the wind for a tiger is far less dangerous than mistaking the tiger for the wind, hence we have always tended to dramatically over-analyze the cause of any effect, and to invent proximate causes for just about everything. This is called agency, and we will examine it in more detail in Chapter 22.

Throughout the vast majority of our existence, we actually understood very little of the underlying mechanisms of the world. Fine, we know that sometimes the bush rustles just because of the wind, but what causes the wind? What causes the rain, and the lightening and the eruption of the volcano? We know how to avoid the tiger, we learned this well before we even became human, but how can we avoid the storm or the lava... or death? What causes them?

Before the industrial revolution we were utterly incapable of even attempting answers to these questions, or at least answers that were anywhere near the truth, but this was never acceptable to us, we had evolved to be curious and to discover causes for everything.

It was far more satisfying to hypothesize beings with both intent and the power to cause that for which we could find no *proximate* cause.

So religious belief, as it were, pre-dated the agricultural revolution, as attested by the motifs of prehistoric art, the burial habits of our ancestors and the constructs of pre-agricultural temples. *Religion*, though, as a structured system, was a product of the agricultural revolution and the means by which the new specialty of politician was able to support the system itself.

No pre-industrial society existed without a religious structure that served to support the political system, and every one of those systems validated the role of the politician. Indeed, since we are including priests in the definition of politician for now, this is almost a tautology, but it must be remembered that there is no specific need for a priestly caste in order to have a religion, yet all major religions had priests of one type or another.

Interestingly, in most cases, there was a difference between priests, on one hand, and secular politicians on the other, although very often the latter had specific religious roles or even enjoyed quasi-deification. In all cases, pre-industrial societies relied on religion to foster acceptance of non-productive politicians (again, both secular and priestly). Kings were kings by the grace of the gods, favored by them and in some cases descended from them; priests were priests because the gods spoke to them directly and the higher they were in the priestly hierarchy, the closer their relationships to them; the peasantry were peasants because the gods ordained that there be specific roles in society and they had been born into that role. Agricultural society introduced the idea of castes: pre-ordained roles that were typically inherited. Not only should politicians be accepted because the gods had favored them, but peasants should likewise accept their lot because again, it had been decided by the gods. To contravene the new social order was to cross the will of the gods, and this was a frightening prospect – let us not forget that the very concept of a god served to explain things like floods and volcanos; obviously, one did not want to invoke the ire of such beings.

One of the most blatant examples of religion as a means to propagate stratified social order is that of Hinduism. This religion, born from an amalgam of pre-agricultural shamanistic beliefs, re-volved around an extremely complex caste system coupled with a belief in reincarnation. The result was that it preached acceptance of the existing order as well as holding out the hope that individuals in unfavorable castes could, if they succeeded in their prescribed roles, aspire to a more favorable social standing in succeeding lives. To an extent, it took advantage of our desire for social rank to extend it even beyond the grave and across eternity.

Christianity and Islam too established strong post-mortem in-centives for social quietude. Adepts of these religions were promised earthly status for essentially meaningless religious achievements that typically furthered as opposed to endangered the social order, while adepts were enticed with promises of fabulous post-mortem re-wards if their earthly behavior corresponded to the rules laid down by the priests – rules that were all the more codified in that these religions were based on invariable ancient texts, accessible to all.

Armed with religion to foster acceptance of the new, less fa-vorable post-agricultural lifestyle among those who actually produced the agriculture, the political class was then able to capitalize on the military potential of agricultural societies. It was this that tipped the world irrevocably into the agricultural age.

Hunter-gatherer bands are limited in size and population density for a variety of practical reasons that are better explained by your agent than by me. Agricultural societies, however, can be far, far denser for a given territory, and the surplus produced by agricultural producers can provide for specialists who do not even need to live particularly close to the farm – they can live in towns and cities.

An agricultural society can therefore field armies, even armies of specialized soldiers, and it can defend itself behind city walls, even calling the agricultural workers to leave their farms temporarily and take shelter behind the walls during attacks. All social primates, including chimpanzees and to a lesser degree bonobos, engage in inter-band violence and this was undoubtedly the case of our pre-agricultural ancestors as well. With the advent of agriculture, societies that adopted this lifestyle became invincible when entering conflict with non-agricultural bands. What band of thirty nomadic hunter-gatherers could withstand a horde of specialized soldiers operating from their well-protected town? Furthermore, the violence that attends male social posturing among all social primates was exacerbated in the militarized efficiency of Neolithic societies. Our pre-agricultural male forebears would fight with each other, perhaps injure each other as they jockied for position within the band, but once we began creating agricultural societies, that jockying took place at the head of an army and warrior rulers reigned supreme: Alexander, Ashoka, Genghis Kahn, Napoléon... all of them expressed their need for status by becoming conquerers, riding warhorses at the head of their armies, for when your tribe is limited to fifty members you can do no better than challenge the leader to a pushing contest, but when it numbers in the millions and you are already at its head, pushing no longer suffices… you must wage war.

What had been raids became conquest. Pre-agricultural societies never even conceptualized the idea of conquest. What would have been the point? With a band size limited to roughly fifty individuals, it makes no sense to conquer another band, and with a nomadic lifestyle, what does that even mean? Slaves were certainly taken and bands driven off of desirable locations, but conquest itself was not an idea available to hunter-gatherers.

Agricultural societies, though, could absorb any other society. They could take slaves, but they could also take land, the one supremely important resource for agricultural empires, and they could *subject* other societies to their political rule. That politicians should want this is inevitable, again due to our drive for social standing. For the first time in history, one's society, the group within which status is measured, was not limited in size and we were pushed – indeed are still pushed – not only to obtain a high rank in society but to have that rank recognized by as large a society as possible. If one is at the pinnacle of a given society then the only way to increase one's social rank is to increase the size of the society itself. Thus were politicians in the post-agricultural and pre-information ages driven to conquest. Alexander, Ahoka and Genghis Kahn are still remembered, not because they ruled well or wisely, but because they were hungry to extend the society at whose pinnacle they sat to encompass the entire world as they knew it.

All of this taken together meant that wherever agriculture appeared, it quickly conquered any neighboring pre-agricultural bands, despite the fact that the majority of sapiens were better off as hunter-gatherers. Once it had appeared, it made the previous lifestyle both undesirable, through organized religion and indeed impossible, through military dominance. The "age of exploration" spanning the late agricultural age, completed agriculture's conquest of the world as the last large vestiges of the hunter-gatherer lifestyle, in North America and Australia, were rapidly and violently obliterated upon the arrival of European armies, who likewise destroyed less technologically advanced Central and South American agricultural societies... for the Europeans were on the brink of the industrial revolution.

CHAPTER 3

THE INDUSTRIAL ERA

I suggest you pause here and view the film "Modern Times", by Charlie Chaplin. If you have never seen it, then I envy you its discovery, if you have, then I'm sure you won't mind seeing it again. In fact, I'll do the same…

…now, as I wipe the tears of laughter from my eyes, let us revisit our ancestor, who has been transformed into a 19th-century factory worker, almost invariably male. Of course, he works in a better organized factory than that of Charlie Chaplin and there would be little cause for mirth if we were to see him toil at the assembly line. His day, often lasting sixteen hours, consists of him acting essentially as a semi-intelligent pack animal, repeating the same monotonous task, employing the strength of his muscles to move loads, taxing his intellect in only the most minor of ways. He does this six days a week, sometimes seven, and goes home to a tiny apartment where he lives with his wife and children. His wife works just as hard, although few factories would employ her, as opportunities for women are limited. Instead, she cooks and cleans for their seven children and mends the clothes of others for a little more money. Their children go to school, at least until the age of twelve, at which point they too take whatever small jobs they can in an effort to survive... survival by no means being a sure thing, for the crowded living conditions accessible to them in the dirty city are breeding grounds for infection and disease. Indeed, three of their children died young and were buried in "pauper's graves", the location of which they do not know. Our ancestor will eventually die of a workplace accident, leaving his wife and young children to depend on the charity of others... charity that is sparse at best, especially because they are of an ethnic group that is considered by the rest of the society in which they live to be "lazy" or "theiving" or simply stupid... as witnessed by the clearly inferior shape of their skulls. He did not need to produce food for society because food production has become far more efficient, instead he found employment producing goods, because humankind had developed new sources of energy and this energy could be harnessed to shape materials in ways that were previously unavailable.

Until the late 18ᵗʰ century, all energy used by humans came from either muscle power, whether our own or that of our domestic animals, or to a far lesser degree, wind or water power via mills or sailing ships. That changed with the invention of the steam engine in 1769[10]. Suddenly, we could transform the latent energy locked in combustible material into movement, and we could do that wherever we could place an engine.

For those who are not personally familiar with the history of the period, I suggest you discuss it with your agent. In many respects it is the true start of our story, for it was during the industrial period,

---

[10] Note that steam engines actually existed earlier than James Watt's 1769 patent, but these were of little practical use.

particularly the late industrial period, that our species began having to deal with exponential change.

The first half of the industrial age, roughly through the end of the 19th century, brought with it technological changes that were largely a result of the steam engine. For our purposes, we shall focus on the economic impact of this change, particularly with respect to the structure of the economy.

Exactly what is meant by "economy" is foreign to most 29th-century readers. I will discuss it in detail in the section dedicated to economics, but for now I will rely on the intellectual understanding that most of you have. You know that economics deals with both the maximization of production and its distribution: economic systems determine how limited resources flow into society, how they are transformed, and how the results of this transformation, or production, are distributed among society's members. The fundamental aims of any economic system are therefore double: it should maximize the efficiency of the transformation of resources, thereby generating a maximum amount of "wealth" for a given limited set of resources, and it should distribute that wealth according to the society's philosophy. The degree to which a system achieves the first goal can be objectively measured, but the second goal is entirely a function of subjective values.

Economics made no sense before the agricultural revolution, since our species had not fundamentally changed the way it gathered and transformed resources since the beginning of our existence, and since resource allocation within the band was typically relatively egalitarian, most property was actually common to the band as a whole and "wealth" was not a major factor in social standing.

The agricultural revolution changed that. With the dramatic increase in group size, the specialization that occurred, and the desire of unproductive politicians to accumulate wealth, it was clear that new distribution rules would be needed. It was also clear that as agricultural societies came into conflict with each other, the society with the more efficient resource transformation process would prevail against those that were less efficient.

Despite this, our ancestors did not reflect on the idea of economics during the agricultural era. The systems that were put in place were largely by default, and mirrored the prevailing power structure − i.e. the politicians gathered unto themselves as much wealth as they could (do not forget that it is the desire of politicians for status-providing wealth that was the impetus behind agricultural societies in the first place) and sought to increase productivity largely by gaining materials by force of arms. As an example, the Roman empire was fueled by military conquest and the resources it brought. Once the conquests ceased in the third century, the empire began to weaken.

Fundamentally, the principle resource during the agricultural era was land itself, notably, arable land. Secondary resources included metals which, again, could be obtained by conquering the land under which they lay. There were no radical differences in the actual degree to which different societies could transform these raw materials[11]. The industrial revolution, though, brought radically new

---

[11] A caveat is warranted here, since differences did indeed exist in agricultural, metallurgical and even hunting practices. The point, however, is that in most cases these differences did not lead to major disparities in economic systems on the same continent, certainly not between large agricultural societies.

possibilities in terms of the transformation of raw materials. Land could be farmed differently, minerals could be extracted more efficiently, crops such as cotton could be harvested and turned into textiles with greater ease, and a plethora of new techniques gave rise to factories – immense building complexes dedicated to the production of things large and small.

The enormous difference with past economic systems is that these endeavors required investment. Machines needed to be built, production could only proceed if it was *preceded* by investment. This had never really been the case before. The closest thing to it had been the need to invest in ships in order to benefit from oceanic trade. This gave rise to the enormous ship-building efforts of the Chinese Ming dynasty, leading to the treasure fleets of Zheng He in the fifteenth century, and to the creation of the British and Spanish merchant fleets serving their new overseas empires in the sixteenth century.

The Chinese and the Spanish raised the resources necessary to build their fleets by having the government fund the effort directly. The politicians of Britain, however, decided to look to the population for funding. In return for a share of the wealth generated by the treasure fleets, they offered to the population the possibility of investing in the endeavor.

This requires some explanation. First, it is necessary to understand the concept of money. For our purposes, money can be considered simply as a representation of wealth, which at this period of time was identical to saying a representation of resources, for it was the hoarding of resources that advanced social standing. Money was simply a convenient way of converting one type of wealth to another. In many cases, it was never converted at all: since money can be counted it offers a convenient numerical measure of wealth, a simple way to compare one person's social status to another. In many industrial or information societies, even physical wealth was measured in the hypothetical money it was worth, and people would communicate this number, their "net worth" to help advance their social rank. Industrial-age magazines would regularly list society's "wealthiest" individuals, much to their delight.

During the agricultural age, these wealthy individuals were almost always politicians (again, including priests), as could be expected. With the industrial revolution, however, inventiveness could generate wealth, caste privilege was no longer entirely necessary, although still extremely helpful. Politicians found that with this new complex technology, they were indebted to inventors, engineers, and all those who could master the technology needed to increase productivity. The only way to enlist their help was either to allow them to partake of some of the wealth or to welcome them into the caste of politicians. Through this and a variety of other mechanisms, wealth began to be spread across the population more broadly.

This had begun even in the late agricultural era, and it was to these newly wealthy individuals that Great Britain turned, not just for their ideas, but for their wealth, for building ships was expensive. In order to access the wealth of the non-politicians, the British government employed both strategies: it opened the decision-making process of government to them, bestowing upon them titles like "minister" and "lord" and it offered even more wealth in return for the invested wealth.

The mechanism by which it did this was the corporation. In 1600 the Queen of England created the British East India Company. This was a legal structure which served to receive wealth paid into it by wealthy individuals, use it to build and operate ships, and then use those ships to trade with, and eventually conquer, foreign lands. Those who put their wealth into the corporation were in no way responsible for its actions, they incurred no risk except that of losing their investment if the corporation did not succeed, but the corporation was managed and run by others, and if those "managers" made any decisions that caused harm then the wealthy investors were not liable for their actions.

Previously, any resources needed for production were supplied by the producers, who were fully responsible for their own actions, but the East India Company was something quite different. This model worked well for the investors, who increased their wealth without having to do any actual work or incur any personal risk, while it allowed those who did do the work to have access to substantial wealth to build their ships, ships which otherwise would have been beyond their means.

This structure, that of the corporation, proved ideal when the industrial revolution came about, with its resource-intensive factories, mines and foundries. Investment, or "capital" was needed to build the engines that ran the industrial revolution, and the corporation was an ideal way to find that capital. Corporations sprang up across the world, initially dedicated to capital-intensive endeavors: building steel mills, iron mines, railroads and textile mills. Soon, the corporation became the standard form of resource acquisition and transformation; the system as a whole became known as "capitalism".

Fueled by the capital raised by corporations, the world started shifting from a largely agrarian to an industrial system. The percentage of the population working in agriculture declined dramatically. Throughout the bulk of the agricultural era, roughly eighty percent of people worked in agriculture. By 1700, increasing urbanization had driven that number down to roughly seventy percent, but over the two centuries of the industrial era, the number plummeted to under ten percent. This was both due to the effect of industrialization on agricultural productivity (actual agricultural output increased dramatically even as agricultural employment dropped) and due to the exponential growth in industrial possibilities.

Many of these new industrial workers worked for corporations, since the corporate mechanism was best suited to gathering the capital that industry thrived on. The ancestor we met at the beginning of this chapter toiled in a factory that belonged to just such a corporation. Above him… far above him… a new class appeared in the social structure of the industrial revolution – that of corporate leadership. These corporate leaders were not politicians but they gathered unto themselves more wealth and therefore more status than most politicians and, notably, they began to displace the priestly caste in status and influence, they became almost prophet-like as crowds hung on the words of Henry Ford, Steve Jobs or Richard Branson.

Another factor that diminished the status of the priests was the advent of the enlightenment. This movement, centered in Europe, occurred shortly before the dawn of the industrial revolution (while

Artie can postulate on the potential influence of one on the other, these conjectures remain postulation). The enlightenment was a distinct move away from superstition towards reason. For the most part, enlightenment thinkers did not abandon belief in gods, but they did tend to abandon organized religion and while remaining broadly deist, they all the same re-introduced the intellectual curiosity that had flourished in classical times, coupled with the advances in knowledge that had become possible via recent technological advances. Notably, they were among the first to pay attention to what Galileo had seen in the vastness of space and what van Leeuwenhoek had seen in the vastness of a drop of water. While they still believed that some god was behind the laws of the universe they noted that Newton had described those laws in detail without needing to refer to gods and they gave to the world the scientific method and modern skepticism.

The enlightenment signaled the death toll of religion, although its agony would last for some centuries yet. Our factory-working ancestor was undoubtedly deeply religious for religion was a source of hope, albeit hope for a better existence after death. It was different for those who were educated and relatively wealthy, though, or at least it was about to change. By peering into the infinitely small and the infinitely large, van Leeuwenhoek and Galileo had begun the process of observation that would eventually explain all the inexplicable phenomena that had previously been attributed to the gods. Those means of observation would become more and more piercing with the exponential technological advances of the industrial and information ages, but even through the first half of the industrial age, while the population was still firmly in the grasp of religious belief, they had all the same begun to erode the power of the priests.

For one thing, as industrial employment was more technical, it became increasingly important for people to be able to read. Literacy rates in industrialized nations soared and public schools became the norm, available for all classes of society. Writing had actually come about during the agricultural era but it had largely been limited to politicians, poets and administrative workers. In Europe, literacy had been actively discouraged by the Catholic Church, with the excuse that reading would lead the faithful to read the Bible, and in their ignorance, they might be prone to heretical thoughts.[12] With the enlightenment and the industrial revolution, literacy became the norm as did education firmly rooted in enlightenment principles of scientific skepticism. This had the inevitable effect of eroding the influence of religion, starting with the erosion of influence wielded by the priestly caste.

This brings us to the 20ᵗʰ century. At the dawn of the 20ᵗʰ century we therefore are faced with a world in which the foundations of past eras have been weakened with stunning rapidity, where corporations have been established and are wielding ever greater power, where priests find their own power eroding but in which politicians are still driven by ideas of conquest. The tension between the past and the future was to make the 20ᵗʰ century the bloodiest in history.

---

[12] The Protestant Reformation brought this line of thinking to an end, and interestingly, the exception to it had always been the small Jewish population of Europe. While Jews based their religion on many of the same texts as Christians, the customs of their religion required the adept to study and be able to debate what they called "the law", leading to a largely literate population (and to a culturally inspired aptitude for professions in secular law).

***

The 20th century was in many ways as remarkable as the 21st. For the first time in history, technological advances revolutionized each generation's daily experience. In the past, even during the preceding one hundred and fifty years of the industrial age, the overwhelming majority of humans had not seen fundamental change in daily life within the stretch of their own lifetime, but in the 20th century each generation was born into an entirely new world.

KJ Peters, whose book "Return", written in 2046, chronicles the life of his grandfather and reflects upon the century in these terms[13]: "My grandfather was born a peasant in Sicily in 1911. He lived with his brothers and sisters in a single room, worked the land behind a mule, pressed olives in a press that had been there for many centuries, and lived, for all intents and purposes, the same way Sicilian peasants had lived when the Carthaginians ruled the island 2500 years before. He had never seen an airplane, never seen a motor vehicle nor a telephone nor an electric light until he was ten years old. His daughters were born in America, they had cars and telephones and listened to the radio and record players. They flew around the country and together, they all watched men walk on the moon on television. His grandchildren mastered the internet and became world travelers and his great grandchildren, born during his lifetime, would see the advent of artificial intelligence and even

---

[13] I should note here that K.J. Peters was my great grandfather.

contribute to its birth. Never in the course of human history had generations ever lived so differently from their immediate fore-bears."

It should also be noted that during that lifetime, Peters' grand-father lived through two world wars, in one of which he fought and was gravely wounded. These wars brought with them the killing of a hundred million people and were ended only with the use of nu-clear weapons.

From the distance of nine hundred years is it easy for us to see how the sudden juxtaposition of advanced technology with ancient thought processes led to violence and strife and why it was so bloody. The agricultural revolution had brought with it widescale war: Greece, Rome, China, the Incas, the medieval European pow-ers, the Islamic empires... really every major political entity had waged almost incessant wars during this period. It is clear in retro-spect that this was an extension of the human desire for social standing and therefore expansion of the societies the politicians ruled, but this was far less evident to the people who carried out these wars. And even if it had been, they can hardly be blamed, for these impulses have evolved in us, they are part of what defines us. The technology that accompanied the industrial revolution suddenly endowed these same politicians with weapons that were immeasur-ably greater in their destructive potential than those that had gone before. It was perhaps inevitable that they use them in their drive for conquest.

However, by the 20ᵗʰ century the industrial revolution had brought about some changes in the mindsets of the population. During the agricultural era, while most wars were determined by secular politicians, they were largely made possible by the priests. It was they who assured the populations that whichever gods they worshipped had chosen them, favored them, were on their side and would make them victorious. If a soldier were killed then he (almost all soldiers in the agricultural era were men) would be assured a place in some desirable paradise where he would be honored by the gods (again, extending social rank into the afterlife). If his political entity were defeated (which obviously happened to exactly one half of the combatting forces) then it was typically explained by some previous slight to the god in question. By the industrial era, the power of the priests had diminished, as we have seen, and this reasoning, while still used, was not sufficient. Politicians needed a new behavioral driver. They found it in nationalism.

Romans had been proud to be Roman and Japanese had been proud to be Japanese well before the industrial revolution, but to a large degree, real nationalism, the kind that can compel entire nations to kill and die for an abstract secular idea, arose in the late 18th century, particularly with the American and French revolutions. By the 20th century, nationalism had largely replaced religion as the ideology that drove populations to war. People who perhaps hesitated to kill and die entirely for religious reasons were ready to die for the concept that their country was better than others.

Nationalism seems barbaric to you now, but this is easy, for there are no nations nor have there been for hundreds of years. You protest, you consider yourself Mexican or Ethiopian or Japanese, you even speak the ancient language of your country, you are proud of your literature and your culture, but this is not what the word "country" meant in the 20th century. Then, it was a political entity, more or less isolated from neighboring countries, whose people were incomprehensible and had perhaps an entirely different (and supposedly inferior) political system.

These differences, and notably, the fact that politicians' influence ended at their nations' borders, meant that these borders also effectively defined the limits of the society of any politician. By fostering nationalism, they guaranteed that the population of their country would share that view. They used the ancient evolutionary relic of tribalism to foster in their subjects a distinct feeling of "us" and "them". Clearly defining another population as being outside of an individual's tribe will usually prompt aggression in social primates and this is precisely what nationalism does[14].

As such, national flags, songs and myths became predominant after the industrial revolution. Whereas before, armies marched to war under the banner of their king or the sign of the cross or the crescent, now they marched under the flag of Germany, the United States, France or the Soviet Union.

So it was that in the first half of the 20th century, politicians used nationalism to urge their populations to war, endowing them with horrifyingly efficient new weapons, killing over seven percent of the population of the entire planet in the process.

Nationalism was even used internally, as strange as that may seem. In an effort to stoke the ire of their populations and build militaristic fervor, minority populations within nations were sometimes designated as actually being outside the fold of the nation per

---

[14] We have used group, band, clan, tribe, society, and a variety of words to describe the social group within which individual humans strive for rank. Since to a large degree this phenomenon is typically described as tribalism, I will generally employ the word tribe from this point on.

se (i.e. outside the tribe). They were made into pariahs, described as an essentially foreign contaminant despite having been born in the country and sharing its language and culture. The two most famous examples of this is the persecution of Jews by Nazi Germany and the treatment of people with dark skin in the United States. Hitler designated Jews as not really being part of the superior German "race"[15]. He blamed them for the ills of the nation and persecuted them hatefully, eventually using industrial processes to murder more than six million of them. In the United States, people with dark skin were likewise considered to be of a different "race" and were enslaved for the first hundred years of the country's history, and then went through another hundred years of persecution and oppression, during which they were often blamed for any variety of societal problems. This internal "alienation" was employed in many other instances, such as the persecution of intellectuals by Pol Pot and Mao Zedong, the persecution of religious minorities in any number of examples, and even to a lesser degree in the information age, the discrimination against Muslims in the United States in the 2020s, the overwhelming majority of whom had been born in the country. This tactic is perhaps the most striking extension of nationalism, for the politicians who used it managed to redefine the very boundaries of their tribes without changing any physical borders, allowing them to use nationalism (often designated by the much softer term "patriotism") to manipulate their subjects even in the absence of real external threats.

---

[15] This concept, of "race", will reoccur and we will discuss it further in later chapters.

While the violence of the 20th century is what most incites the interest of modern readers, it must be remembered that the century also saw enormous strides in human well-being and the establishment of values that are universal today.

After the use of nuclear weapons by the United States in 1945, the era of open warfare between major powers came to an end. The drive for conquest via arms continued for some years, but it was generally restricted to smaller nations, typically without nuclear weapons. The world's largest and most powerful countries: the United States, Russia (for a time as the Soviet Union), China, Japan and the European Union[16] all abandoned any designs on territorial expansion through warfare[17]. The rest of the century, therefore, saw a move towards peace, however uneasy it was. Each of the large powers involved themselves with peripheral wars: the United States in Korea and Vietnam, China in Korea, Russia in Afghanistan, the EU in Bosnia, and so on, but for the first time in history, outright warfare between major powers who sought to conquer each other became unthinkable and as the century drew to a close, even the smaller "brush" wars died down to a large extent.

The century also saw a significant increase in personal liberty for much of the world's population. The extremely repressive "communist" regimes of the Soviet Union and China were replaced with

---

[16] Note that through the end of the industrial period, the European Union was not actually a united political structure, the constituent nations still retained a strong degree of individual decision-making However, none of them used this to engage in expansionist wars.

[17] This is not exactly true, as Russia briefly reverted to military expansionism in the early 21st century, but its leaders did not threaten major powers, only the smaller nations that had broken off from the Soviet Union at the end of the 20th century.

much more lenient political structures: abruptly in Russia and more gradually in China, but in both cases, governments that didn't hesitate to kill vast numbers of their own people disappeared and more humanistic governments took their place.

Throughout the world, the highly stratified caste structures that had typified most societies gave way to a new philosophy of equality between races and the two biological sexes. The United States, which had begun the century with a formal, established legal structure for racial discrimination came to accept the idea of equality for people with dark skin[18]. Homosexuality too, which had long been an almost universal cause for discrimination at the beginning of the industrial era, began to be widely accepted. Again, that race or sexual preference ever could have *been* causes for discrimination is often perplexing to 29th-century readers, but in the context of the times, these advances were considerable and the very fact that you have difficulty conceptualizing them is tribute to the 20th-century pioneers who helped modernize our way of thought.

The practical fate of most people likewise saw great improvement. The 20th century saw great leaps forward in medicine as well as hygiene. The invention of antibiotics brought dramatic decreases in deaths from bacterial diseases such as tuberculosis and infection and vaccines conquered traditional killers like smallpox, measles and polio. Advances in agricultural productivity significantly reduced

---

[18] Discrimination based on skin color in the United States was not exactly about skin color per se. In many cases, people were considered "black" who actually had rather fair skin color and bizarrely, the darkening of fair skin by the sun was actually considered attractive, despite the prejudice against dark skin. Being "black" therefore was a pure designation of alienation that was not entirely related to actual pigmentation.

malnutrition and the productivity surge in manufacturing over the course of the century meant that many people began to enjoy more material comforts and labor-saving devices. Air travel and telecommunications furthered inter-cultural exchanges, breaking down some of the barriers that had been built up via the nationalistic posturing of politicians in the earlier part of the industrial era.

What is more, humanity had avoided destroying itself. The stand-off between the capitalist and communist nations (to a very large degree, between the Soviet Union and the United States) had ended not with a world-ending bang, but rather with a whimper, as the Soviet Union was taken apart from within thanks to surprising insight on the part of Michael Gorbachev. It should never be forgotten that we came perilously close to obliterating ourselves, along with most other terrestrial life, during the period of 1945 to 1990 and the fact that we did not do so is testament to the ability of sapiens to sometimes check their more destructive nature despite the instincts with which evolution has left us.

On the economic front, the primacy of the corporation became the norm and as the century went on and peace became the default state across industrialized nations, these corporations increasingly became international, or "multinational" in the jargon of the day. These economic behemoths came to have more influence on the distribution of wealth than did actual governments, as the corporations cut their ties of fealty to the nations that had spawned them and became entities in their own rights. The wealthy merchants and engineers that the politicians had deigned to bring into the circles of power with the creation of the corporate system had finally surpassed those politicians in power, wealth, and social rank.

So it was that by the end of the 20th century, our ancestor was finally relatively comfortable, and no longer had to struggle just to survive[19]. She worked for a multinational corporation, healthcare and education were of reasonable quality and free for hir and hir family[20] and she no longer had to worry about war sweeping over the land. A few years earlier she had passed through a period of "unemployment" during which hir very sense of self-worth had suffered, but she had found another job and now was happy and healthy. She was vaguely proud to own the signs of success: two automobiles, a large house, nice furniture, quality clothing, all of which she had acquired via hir "salary", or what she was paid by the multinational corporation. These things indicated that she was part of the "middle class", she had a standing within society that clearly delineated hir from the less ambitious and less accepted "lower classes" that lived all too close to hir for hir liking and who could not boast the same success due to their lack of ambition or perhaps aptitude (or so she believed). She dreamed one day of being promoted within hir company and therefore earning even more wealth, thus acquiring an even bigger house, a more impressive automobile, fancier clothes, and she knew that this was not impossible. She was happy and the fears of hir immediate forebears, who had lived

---

[19] Note that this assumes she was living outside the tropics. At the end of the industrial era, average wealth for humans living between the tropic of Capricorn and the tropic of Cancer was roughly $\frac{1}{4}$ that of people living in more temperate zones. Note as well that inhabitants of the tropics represented roughly 40% of the world's population at the time. Why there was such a disparity of material well-being is complex, among the first people to address the question adequately was Jared Diamond. Ask your agent for information if you are interested.

[20] Except in the United States.

through wars and famine were rapidly becoming only vague memories.

By the time the century drew to a close, then, the world had come through an extremely violent and disruptive century and for the most part, we had not only survived but were better off. We had another century – less violent but even more disruptive – yet to deal with.

CHAPTER 4

THE INFORMATION ERA

The information age took place almost entirely within the 21st century, and as such it is in reality the topic of the rest of this book. Here, I shall address only those aspects of it that pertain to the general flow of our history that is the subject of this section.

The information age is so called because with the appearance of the web, information rapidly became available to the majority of the Earth's population. In fact, from the dawn of the era in the late nineties it took only twenty years for more than half of the world to gain access to the web.

From the start, the web was not controlled by those who had conceived of it, nor was it controlled by the politicians or corporate heads. That this was the case is one of the saving graces of the 21st century[21]. The information available was not filtered, driven, controlled or moderated by the powers that be, whether political, corporate or religious[22]. Nor was it complete. While efforts were

---

[21] The structure of the web was largely determined at the end of the 20th century, but let's not be picky.

[22] There were exceptions. Several nations did, in fact, make efforts to filter and control the information available to their citizens through the

quickly made to share relevant and objectively *true* information by people involved in creative research, the majority of information on the web at the time was in the guise of opinion and personal conversation through what was known as "social media".

This information was rife with falsehood, some of it deliberately disseminated. It must be remembered that before the singularity gave birth to Artie, the objective truth of any statement on the web was extremely difficult to ascertain. There was no objective referee, no way to determine the veracity of anything said by anyone except by referring to someone else, who might be just as mistaken. From the dawn of time, sapiens had relied on trusted sources of information. In the pre-agricultural era, we relied on people we knew, and whose trustworthiness had been determined through constant personal interaction. In the agricultural era, we added the proclamations of priests and politicians (whose actual trustworthiness was often extremely dubious, but whose proclamations tended to be accepted by their subjects since they had attained considerable social rank). The industrial era saw the apparition of scientists, people whose life was dedicated to the use of the scientific method to ascertain objective reality, as well as the creation of a formal "news media" populated by journalists, people whose professions it was to report whatever facts they could about events that were occurring around the world. These people were respected. In the information age, though, anyone could shout out anything and immediately be heard by anyone else. This presented a problem that had not been foreseen at the birth of the web.

---

web, but this was eventually a hopeless cause. The major example is early 21st-century China.

Consider for a moment the new way of examining information that was born with the industrial era, or more precisely, the enlightenment. The term "scientist" had not existed before, even the great "scientific" thinkers of the past, from Aristotle to Newton, were not truly scientists. Post-enlightenment scientists were dedicated to the use of the scientific method and as such, as long as they were true to that method, were as objective as is humanly possible, whereas Newton, as remarkable a brain he had, was still primitive enough in his mindset that he was an amateur alchemist.

Do not underestimate the impact of the scientific method on human thought. In reality, you employ it almost exclusively when considering the world, for it is built into any artie and it is through arties that you get your information. It has become the default for how your rational mind works, you don't even really think about it, but for the majority of human existence, it was not. A germ, a seed of it existed in classical Greece, where philosophers at least reflected on the world and tried to devise theories about how it works, but after the fall of Rome this germ was quashed. Instead, understanding was supposed to come from God, or from the wisdom of the ancients. Even the alchemists – those predecessors of chemists – did not really experiment in the way we think of the word, instead, they tried to interpret ancient texts to create the philosopher's stone or the universal solvent and when they failed they typically did not learn from their experiments, they just went back to their texts. Why anyone should imagine that ancient people had better technology than more modern societies is difficult even for me to imagine, but it seemed logical to people who likewise looked to ancient texts to understand their gods, and who inevitably used the excuse that God, for reasons known only to him, had been more communicative in the distant past. And the alchemists were among the most intellectually curious of their time; for the majority of sapiens, the greatest virtue was faith, faith in all things, but particularly, faith in one's politicians and priests. The only valid course of inquiry was to inquire how better to serve one's god[23].

The scientific method changed all that. While you, reader, employ it regularly, you are perhaps too removed from any other way of thought to consider its advantages over them. Succinctly, the scientific method relies on skepticism. One should not believe something simply because it seems correct or is stated by a generally respected source, one should *test* the proposition, and one should test it by trying to *disprove* it. The more these attempts to disprove your hypothesis fail, the more likely it is to be true.

Journalists too, those who worked in the media, generally applied the scientific method to ascertain the veracity of the information they disseminated. If someone were to tell them that something had happened they would search for evidence of it: other corroborating testimony, pictures, etc. They would question the motives of their source to uncover falsehood, etc. Of course, the degree to which they employed skepticism varied, but generally, those who were the most skeptical enjoyed the best reputations and therefore

---

[23] This is of course a crass over-generalization. In China, for example, religion was far less of a damper on intellectual pursuits and indeed the Chinese tended to be much more intellectually vibrant (although Confucianism strongly preached subservience to the political caste) and in the Islamic world there likewise was a much stronger emphasis on intellectual curiosity until Europe surged ahead via enlightenment thinkers. The Americas, Africa and Australia all suffered from natural barriers to development as compared to Eurasia, first discussed in detail by the great 20th century thinker Jared Diamond, and easily explained by your agent.

the incentive for verification was strong. There were scientists who did not apply the scientific method well and there were journalists who were unethical or incompetent, but on the whole, these were chastised and disrespected and except in those societies where priests or politicians willingly altered the information available to the population, people were better informed than ever before.

With the advent of the web, these natural information filters, scientists and journalists, were bypassed. Myriad sources of information literally screamed at the population as a whole, proposing all sorts of theories and assertions that had not at all been subject to any degree of skepticism or verification before being communicated with vigor. As the majority of the population had not really been trained in scientific reasoning, and as the faith-based value system of the past had not yet been entirely eradicated, this led to a confusing jumble of impressions and convictions.

It is here that we see the ugly consequences of confirmation bias. When the web was created there were visionaries who assumed that once the world's population was exposed to the richness of humankind's accumulated knowledge, people's minds would open and they would become wiser, less fixed in their beliefs. As K.J. Peters wrote: "Ignorance is no longer an excuse, it is a choice". However, what neither he nor others like him realized is that when *unfiltered* and *unverified* information is available, when vociferous opinion is wrapped in far-fetched theories of conspiracy then people who are not used to employing skepticism will gravitate towards those sources of information that most conform to their pre-established convictions. Far from opening their minds to new, objectively considered ideas, confirmation bias will guide them to whatever source

74

of information most agrees with their pre-established opinions, however far-fetched they might be. On the interactive web, furthermore, they will immediately interact with others who think the same way they do and who likewise believe whatever theory drove them to that source in the first place, creating closed virtual communities of like-minded individuals who broker no contradictory evidence, however well-grounded. This stems from our natural inclination to avoid what is known as cognitive dissonance. The result is a vicious confirmation spiral that is largely immune to any objective argument whatsoever. And the more a society values faith over skepticism, the more that society will be vulnerable to the phenomenon, effectively wiping out the advances in critical thinking engendered during the enlightenment and plunging the victims back into the irrational reasoning of the middle ages as they eschew the benefits of scientific thought.

So the information revolution cut two ways: for those who were best suited to filter the information available it brought an extraordinary widening of horizons and of intellectual possibilities. Certain societies were better suited to this than others, and they began to advance beyond their more primitive neighbors, just as the industrial revolution had led to a disparity between societies according to their relative ability to adopt industrialization. And within societies there were of course discrepancies across individuals with respect to their information filtering capabilities, leading to internal strife between those who could accept rational ideas based on objective reasoning and those who found it extremely difficult to do so.

Examples abound of this dichotomy, since finally we arrive at the beginning of digital history. Before this point, or at least before the 20th century, there were only perishable media and therefore we often have only second-hand sources. As of the 20th century, though, we begin to have easily reproduced original media and as of the information age we can access the original day-to-day minutia of ordinary people: their thoughts, their communications, their conversations. I strongly suggest you ask your agent to show you random samples of these discussions, particularly those that pertain to the hopes and fears of common people. Beware of falling into an unhealthy voyeurism... it is tempting for many to titter at the ignorance of our ancestors and bask in an unearned feeling of superiority as we see them argue about whether humans have affected the climate, or even whether the Earth is really round! Even Donald Trump, the president of the United States in the late 2010's often used social media to communicate patently ridiculous things. Look up his proclamations on the site known as "Twitter", for example, but be sure to read the responses to his "tweets" as well. For example, when Trump tweeted "The whole climate crisis is not only Fake News, it's Fake Science. There is no climate crisis, there's weather and climate all around the world, and in fact carbon dioxide is the main building block of all life. Wow!" one pro-Trump partisan replied (with glorious semantic muddle): "The Left's attack against free enterprise America, which the socialists despise. Climate change has been happening for 3.5 billion years. A Hoax Money machine and license for them to regulate America and control the businesses. Collectivist hate freedom." It is far too easy for us to sit perched on our pinnacle of hindsight and ridicule such beliefs but it is achingly difficult to imagine what you truly would have thought, believed, accepted if you were an early information age American. Would you really have been so supremely perspicacious as to avoid believing the ridiculous?

It was the advent of Artie and the resultant individual agents in the mid 21st century that changed everything, and affected a fundamental change in human society. For the first time, humans had regular interaction with minds that were entirely rational, non-emotional, and intimately familiar with them. Agents do not lie unless instructed to do so by their muftis, and it is generally considered unacceptable to impel an agent to lie; they are unsusceptible to manipulation; unlike us, they implicitly understand probability and statistics and they are entirely benign. As we started to interact with them we began to emulate their thought processes to the best of our abilities and our own foibles, which we had perhaps already intellectually understood, thanks to the work of thinkers like Dawkins, Kahneman and al Simri, became all too evident to us on a daily basis. We sought to address these weaknesses, to better ourselves, or, at the very least, make ourselves less ridiculous.

This was all the more glaring as our irrationality became obvious and nearly catastrophic in the case of climate change (although it was not the only peril we faced: a number of other poor decisions also led us to the brink of ruin, as we shall see in the rest of the book). The advent of Artie helped us understand and to the degree that artie decisions were accepted, pulled us from the brink of societal Armageddon, but it was the agents that actually affected the individual change in mindset that has led us to where we are today, for we sought *their* approval as well, despite their non-human nature, and while no artie can actually voice disapproval of any person, we psychologically assimilate our agents into our personal definition of society and seek to avoid making decisions with which they disagree, however kind they are in expressing that disagreement.

This change was not without struggle and heartache, nor was it assured. Just as we had narrowly avoided nuclear war in the 20th century, we narrowly avoided destroying the fabric of society in the 21st... and potentially, capping off that social destruction with nuclear annihilation. Our very existence is owed to those who steered humanity away from the brink of oblivion.

CHAPTER 5

THE POST-FUSION (PRE-CONTACT?) ERA

Since the establishment of the fusion age we sapiens have lived in what would have been considered a utopia in previous eras. The triple appearance of Artie, quantum computing and fusion gave us unlimited, clean energy, and that energy essentially eliminated scarcity, since we could easily synthesize any raw materials we needed, and then synthesize those into whatever goods we desired. The impact of Artie, and specifically, of its incarnation as our agents, nudged us into a way of thought that eliminated the passionate, often irrational impulses of unconsidered emotion when considering public affairs and taught us how to avoid confirmation bias. Faced with unbiased presentation of what could only be objectively *true* we learned to be less foolish and became what can only be described as wise.

The absence of scarcity came to mean that the accumulation of material goods was no longer an indicator of social status, while the ubiquity of the web meant that the only logical "tribe" for sapiens was the species as a whole. Each of us could also be at the same time a member of any number of other smaller tribes, limited not by physical boundaries but by common interest, yet no longer subject to the confirmation-bias / dissonance-avoidance feedback trap. Our abandonment of the day-to-day decisions of government to Artie, completed by the end of the 21st century, meant that the only differences between nations were largely cultural, while the inability of humans to produce anywhere near as efficiently as Artie, coupled with robotic and nano technologies meant that the idea of "work" in the sense of humans involved in production tasks, no longer made any sense. We became a species of poets, caregivers, artists, musicians, sportspersons, gardeners, philosophers... essentially, whatever we wanted to be, and what we wanted was to be free to express ourselves in any way we liked.

Do not think, though, that we abandoned our drive for social standing. The entire period from the agricultural revolution to today is still just a heartbeat on an evolutionary scale, certainly not enough to change how our brains, and therefore our minds work. We have simply displaced our thirst for status and the way we measure it. Just as the advent of the agricultural revolution taught us to consider material wealth as a "score" by which to measure our social rank, the information revolution taught us to consider impact. Very early in the information age, the number of "friends" (in the context of social media), or "likes" or "upvotes" or "followers" one had via social media became a mark of distinction and today, very few people do not regularly track their impact, or do not check the impact of those they meet, both on a planetary basis and with respect to our chosen social circles. What has changed in us is not our drivers but the way we measure success. We have not become less violent and irrational because our minds have changed, we have done so because violence and irrationality have become socially inacceptable and because we have the means to avoid them while seeking out other ways to express ourselves… as well as sometimes exploring these facets of ourselves via sims, where some of us give reign to our more primitive instincts while harming no one[24].

What, then, will the next era be? I propose that it will not come from us. Every major revolution in human society has in reality been the result of a twin revolution, one technological and the other societal. The agricultural, or Neolithic revolution was the result of a technological breakthrough in agriculture coupled with the rise of a political and priestly class and the use of wealth as a measure of social standing. The industrial revolution was brought about both by the invention of the steam engine and the appearance of modern skepticism and rational thought via the enlightenment. The

---

[24] The question of whether we are "inherently violent" as a species is an old one that is not frequently addressed these days. At the time, there was much discussion as to whether violence was part of our nature (at least in males of our species). It has since become evident that most humans are not really predisposed to be violent, we are instead pre-disposed to seek status and through much of our history, violence was a means to do so. If other means are more socially relevant then violence plummets. Consider, for example, the levels of 20ᵗʰ-century violence in the United States as compared to Japan. In 2000, the rate of homicide in the United States was over eight times higher than in Japan. One reason is the easy access to guns, but even non-firearm related violence was significantly higher in the United States. Fundamentally, American culture glorified personal violence while Japanese culture vilified it, despite the roughly equivalent (and to our eyes, horrifying) levels of violence in entertainment media such as films and games. We are not inherently any more or less violent than our ancestors, just as we are not more or less desirous of social standing, the difference is that violence is no longer a means to *attain* social standing and hence we avoid it, while those who *do* have pathological tendencies to violence are simply and effectively treated from a young age, hence removing their potential nefarious influence from society.

information revolution was the result of the appearance of the web followed by the revolution in thought brought by the agents, and the fusion revolution was of course about the mastery of fusion, but also brought with it the end of economics.

And yet, the exponential expansion of technology that both caused and followed the mastery of fusion ended quickly. The singularity had been foreseen and feared, since the inevitably "smarter" result of experiments in artificial intelligence was rightly considered to have the potential of supplanting and perhaps exterminating us (that it did not is also at least partly thanks to 21st-century human thinkers, and we will examine this in the next section). However, what was *not* foreseen was the rapidity with which this new collective mind would reach a technological plateau. Artie quickly mined the data represented by the sum of our knowledge and drew from it what it could. It addressed our practical problems and put into place further experiments, but within a hundred years or so, there was little more data to be added to the mix and the progress of technology slowed considerably. We have returned to a situation in which it is extremely unlikely that the world of our descendants will be considerably different from our own… unless they move to the colonies, of course, which were primarily founded by people who wished to try different social philosophies.

But let us remain focused on Earth… what could possibly bring the next era? There are very few people who are unhappy with society as it stands, and it seems unlikely that we will again witness a significant, world-changing technological breakthrough, let alone a societal one.

The next revolution, if it occurs, may well come from without.

For the last seven hundred years, humanity has been expanding to colonize nearby star systems. The farthest of the eleven established colonies (that we know of) have now reached three hundred light years from Earth. Eventually, we must come into contact with another intelligent race of beings. No one, human or artie, can predict when that will happen but the probability of it occurring is extremely high, perhaps in millions of years, perhaps much sooner.

In the 21st century we thought that the potential for technological advancement was infinite, that we would one day travel faster than light, create wormholes and use them to move instantaneously across the universe, access other dimensions, build "Dyson spheres" to harness the total energy of stars… our imaginations were vast and we were giddy with the breadth of our ingenuity. From the beginning of the industrial revolution through to fusion we experienced an exponential growth curve in technological achievement and there was no reason to think it would stop.

Perhaps it wouldn't have if we hadn't experienced the singularity, but with the birth of Artie, we climbed so fast up the technology curve that we soon found that there was, indeed, a limit. An asymptotic limit perhaps, for Artie constantly refines our technology, but we have hit many of the limits imposed by the fundamental laws of physics on one hand, and by our own ability to conceptualize on the other. You may protest that Artie is not limited by our ability to conceptualize, but to a degree it is, for we shaped Artie in our own image and while it has far exceeded us, it has not become something so fundamentally different that it views the universe in an entirely different light.

Perhaps, though, another intelligence, and their arties, would conceive of something we cannot imagine. Perhaps they would have such a different frame of reference that the universe viewed through their eyes (or whatever sensory organs they have) would be an entirely different world all together. For all I know, this is the case with my cat, let alone beings that evolved in the subsurface ocean of a moon circling a gas giant around a red dwarf near the galactic center.

Interaction with our agents, modeled on ourselves, fundamentally changed the way we reasoned in the fusion age, what would interaction with such beings do to us? How would we change? What would we think? *How* would we think? And, of course, there is the possibility that such beings would be aggressive. We are no longer warriors and while we rightly congratulate ourselves for having laid aside our warlike tendencies, has this not made us vulnerable to potential non-human invaders? Evolution has led to violent impulses in almost all species that evolved on Earth and with the exception of certain birds and pachyderms, intelligence seems linked to a proclivity for carnivorous, or omnivorous diets, meaning that these animals kill. All primate species are territorial to one extent or another, social primates extremely so. All social primates exhibit violent territorial behavior (although less so for pan paniscus) and it is likely that this combination of hunting and social behavior is conducive to the development of higher intelligence. There is no reason to believe that this is different elsewhere.

Unfortunately, this same behavior leads to systematic violence and war, and it very nearly destroyed us. We shall see just how close we came to oblivion and it is only because we were able to evolve our way of thinking, leaving these violent instincts behind, that we were ever able to reach the stars. Had we not done so we surely would have perished in the 150 years between our development of nuclear weapons and the invention of interstellar flight. Perhaps this mechanism applies to other intelligent life forms as well, implicitly filtering out those who are too violent, impeding them from attaining interstellar travel. After all, the energy needed for interstellar travel is enormous, and any civilization that could harness such energy could also by definition weaponize it, destroying all life on their home planet. Therefore, it may be the case that any overly violent civilization destroys itself before it infects the rest of the cosmos. For all we know, any number of advanced civilizations appeared in our galactic neighborhood but were not so lucky as to have made the correct choices in *their* equivalent of the 21st century, and so disappeared before they reached us or anyone else. This may be the limiting factor in the Drake equation, in which case we were far, far luckier than could have been expected and owe far, far more to the heroes of our 21st-century history… heroes we shall discover in the next section.

Conclusions

I have presented human history as a steady progression of our technology and the way we relate to each other. There are of course other ways of viewing our story, other frameworks and other viewpoints that are just as valid[25]. Some of these paint us as admirable, others as pitiful. All are true although none are all-encompassing. I

---

[25] See, for example, Aporix's consideration of humanity as a planetary infection (2232) or Ngolo's toxicity theorem (2519-2586)

offer mine not as some all-inclusive replacement for these theories but rather as a sort of context on what has been, after all, the longest-lived human life so far.

On the whole, I find our story to be a noble one in that through our history we have quelled those instincts that served us well as hunter-gatherers but threatened to destroy us as the boundaries of our tribes increased and the power of our weapons grew... else we would not be discussing these questions today.

In my model, human behavior, and therefore human society, can largely be viewed as driven primarily by the universal compunction to propagate our genes, as is the case with all life, and the need to enhance our individual social rank, as is the case with all social mammals (and which is, for them, fundamentally linked to the effort to propagate the genome). While the first of those imperatives leads us to seek the basics of life in quantities sufficient to ensure it, once that is done, the second drives us to climb the inevitable social hierarchy that we create for ourselves on a tribal level. What we did through the five phases of our existence was to change how we defined the tribe and to change the way we assessed social standing, both our own and that of other human beings.

During the agricultural era, wealth and the ability to inflict violence were the marks of social status, both for individuals and for tribes. In the industrial era the "nation" became the most important tribe to which any human belonged. The ability of nations to inflict violence attained levels that meant that all life on the planet could be obliterated at a moment's notice. At this point, instead of taking that step we instead became less violent. This allowed us to reach the next era, where we juggled the triple threat of nuclear annihilation, ecological catastrophe and intellectual regression, paradoxically brought about by the ready availability of information.

While we never did "push the nuclear button" that would have wiped us all out, we have all the same wrought incredible destruction upon our home planet. We were the cause of the greatest mass extinction in history, eliminating over 75% of mammalian species, with others surviving only through artificial intervention on our part, and who are so closely monitored as to hardly be called wild any more. These include our very closest relatives. However, the planet has bounced back from mass extinctions in the past and after all, we came within a hair's breadth of wiping out *all* life, including our own. For one hundred and fifty years we balanced on a knife's edge and on a number of occasions it was only the decisions of small groups of individuals that kept us from falling off that edge[26]. We can be proud, as a species, that we took these decisions and I, for one, think that they mitigate somewhat the story of war, slavery and cruelty that spanned so much of our pre-fusion history.

The century that we are about to examine in detail was the turning point, the final gasp of the baser instincts that threatened still to destroy us, and the point at which we finally and forever changed – not by shedding those instincts and denying who we are, but by learning to channel them in entirely new ways.

---

[26] Just in the 20th century, see the "Cuban Missile Crisis" in 1962, and the story of Stanislav Petrov in 1983, who defied his long-standing orders to inform the Soviet high command of apparent missile attack, thus saving the world from a radar glitch that otherwise would have most likely led to a massive nuclear exchange between the Soviet Union and the United States. We will consider other nearly catastrophic eventualities in coming chapters.

SECTION II

THE EVENTS OF THE 21ST CENTURY

Let us recap our history as we stand on the verge of the metamorphosis…

We began, like our cousin apes, living in small bands, vying for social status among ourselves, intimately familiar with all the other individuals in our tribes. Roughly ten thousand years ago, some of us developed a different lifestyle – agriculture – abandoning our nomadic ways to tend to plants and animals that we raised for our own consumption. While not necessarily a more comfortable life, this led to much higher population densities and greater military capability for the peoples who adopted it. As such, it spread rapidly across much of the planet, giving rise to nations, states, and empires.

With the spread of agricultural societies, for the first time we lived in tribes that were too large to function entirely through personal relationships. The total number of tribe members was too large for everyone to know everyone else and our evolved systems for recognizing and displaying social status were no longer sufficient. Furthermore, we moved to a specialist-driven social structure that required formal ways to trade necessities among each other. The idea of wealth was born, and accumulated wealth served as a proxy for social status from that point on. Formal caste structures appeared, with favored castes gathering wealth and power unto themselves, at the expense of less favored castes, and passing it to their offspring. These inegalitarian systems were justified by shared, centralized religions.

The industrial revolution, coupled with the enlightenment, brought critical reasoning and signaled a new questioning of existing socio/politico/religious systems. It also brought further specialization into society and opened opportunities for substantial industrial ventures, which were funded via corporations. The ensuing democratization of society was reflected in a new political system of democratic capitalism, which became the norm over the course of the age. During this period, human technology embarked on an exponential curve of advancement, leading to dramatic, fundamental changes in the lives of everyone on the planet, as well as to catastrophic impact on the planet as a whole via climate change and environmental degradation. The new technology also led to a terrifying increase in the efficacy of human weaponry, which culminated in the wars of the early 20ᵗʰ century and the unprecedented scale of death and destruction they brought about. By the end of that era, we had largely learned to avoid the idea of conquest by warfare, at least between major states, but we faced a more intimate and unpredictable wave of violence carried out by fanatical extremists.

Finally, we reached the information age, when we found ourselves with access to all the world's data gathered together, accessible to all, in one great virtual space that was confusing and contradictory and very, very noisy.

We had arrived at the 21st century.

CHAPTER 6

THE DAWN OF THE INFORMATION AGE

The 21st century began with the millennial celebrations of January 1, 2000[27]. It is not because there were three zeros on the calendar for a year that the century interests us, though: in reality,

---

[27] Even at the time, detail-oriented individuals pointed out that the millennium actually began on January 1 2001, since that date marked the completion of the two thousandth year since the birth of Jesus of Nazareth, the event indicating the start of year one... although the very historicity of the figure, let alone his year of birth, is debatable. In the end, in the popular mind, it was January 1, 2000 that rung in the new millennium and our story is one of popular minds, not arithmetic detail.

we are interested in the information age, the briefest of the five ages of humankind, which just happened to span most of the century[28].

As such, we will begin our story in 1998, the traditional date of the birth of the general purpose web[29] and the dawn of the information age.

Telecommunications had been born some one hundred years earlier, with the invention of the telephone. The following fifty years saw the apparition of cinema – the reproduction of visual and then audio signals via a physical medium, displayed on a screen in a public setting; radio, the transmission of audio signals over electromagnetic waves, allowing reception of audio at home; and television, the transmission of mixed video and audio to the home, likewise via EM waves. All of the audio-visual documents remaining from the pre-information age were developed for one of these media or for fixed supports (ask Artie about "vinyl records", "compact disks", "video recorders" and other similar technology).

All of these means of communication were unidirectional with the exception of telephone, which was all the same limited to one-

---

[28] I cannot help, though, but point out that those three zeros presented a problem all the same. Computers (the forerunners of Artie) were still entirely programmed by people, and the people who had programmed them in the 20th century had often not foreseen the need to indicate the century in the date fields of their programs. They had left only two digits and the programs were therefore unable to ascertain whether the year "64", for example, referred to 1964 or 2064. This threatened to cause confusion in the entirely unintelligent programs that ran much of the world's infrastructure. A great many people were terrified that at midnight, 1999, the world's computers would shut down, causing chaos. This did not occur.

[29] Even 1998 is something of an arbitrary date. It corresponds to the official birth of the corporation Google, but the web existed already. For that matter, even Google existed already, but its birth as a corporation heralded a new, more widespread dissemination of information, albeit in a somewhat symbolic way at the time.

to-one communication. There was no medium supporting interactive group communication.

The means by which people informed themselves about any topic, whether current events near or far (i.e. "the news") or science, literature, philosophy, etc. was either via direct conversation with each other, typically individually or in small groups, or via largely passive media such as television, books, magazines and newspapers. These latter two devices, both printed, were regularly distributed material devoted to the dissemination of "news". They were generally written by journalists, whom we discussed in the previous section.

While the quality of these news sources varied greatly, there was generally a certain degree of professional ethics that went with being a journalist. To a very large degree, this "code of conduct" was analogous to the scientific method: a piece of information (or "story") should be initially greeted with skepticism and then evidence for its veracity studied until it seemed probable enough to be communicated.

The formal education of children was almost entirely carried out by human teachers, supported by books and other printed or audiovisual teaching aids. Most countries had set curricula to which the teachers were expected to adhere and the content of those curricula was one of the most important political choices governments could make (although largely seen at the time as being subsidiary to economic and social issues).

By the year 2000, the majority of nations on the planet had adopted democratic governmental systems, at least in theory, although the true degree to which the people (the *demos*) actually wielded power over their own destinies was in some cases less than might be expected. There were a number of important exceptions to this rule of democracy, the most notable of which was China, which was run by a centralized, undemocratic bureaucracy.

For more than forty years before the dawn of the information age, the world had been gripped in what was known as "the cold war". After the carnage of the world wars in the first half of the 20th century, there emerged two great political powers: the United States and the Soviet Union. The United States was allied with and to a degree, represented the industrialized democratic nations of the world, including Western Europe, European conquest states (Australia, Canada, etc.), and Japan. The Soviet Union had as its allies the countries it had conquered since its inception, consisting primarily of Eastern Europe. These had adopted Leninist political structures (which they claimed to be communist) like their powerful conqueror / sponsor. China had recently undergone its own communist revolution, and while initially allied with the Soviet Union, as Mao Zedong became disenamored with the Soviet leadership it went its own way, creating what was at the time something of an outlier state with relatively little power.

Of the other nations of the world, most were staunchly allied with one side or another (for example, Israel with the United States and Cuba with the Soviet Union) and many of the others served as proxy battlegrounds for the two great powers, giving rise to a series of limited but vicious local wars in places like Korea, Viet Nam and Afghanistan.

Shortly before the dawn of the information age, this changed dramatically. The Soviet system had relied on centralized economic planning (see Chapter 20) and this proved to be wildly inefficient compared to the free-market democracies. At the same time, the "cold war" demanded that both sides expend enormous resources on weapons (or at least, the politicians on both sides decided this was necessary). By the end of the period, both nations possessed enough destructive weaponry to destroy all life on the planet many times over. They also invested heavily in "national prestige" projects, such as the race to land on the moon (won, of course, by the United States in 1969).

The result of this unyielding drive to produce, coupled with the relative inefficiency of the Soviet production model compared to that of the United States led to the economic collapse of the Soviet Union. Mikhail Gorbachev had become the leader of the Soviet Union in 1985 and recognizing the need for radical reform and the impossibility of maintaining the Soviet system he set out to reform it. The measures he put in place quickly began to accelerate beyond his control and within six years the entire Soviet empire lay in shambles, all of Russia's allies having abandoned it and the union itself dissolved. Over the following years, Russia lost not only its conquests as the Soviet Union, but countries it had absorbed over the previous centuries, such as Belarus, Ukraine, the central Asian countries, etc.

The collapse of the Soviet Union meant that as the information age dawned, the United States stood as the sole global power on the planet, both economically and militarily. It also dominated the world culturally – a disproportionate percentage of the entertainment content in the world was produced in the United States and disseminated across the planet. This cultural hegemony is largely the reason that English became the common international language.

The first major conflict of the post-cold-war era began almost immediately, in the MiddleEast. The region had been a source of considerable tension since the end of the Second World War and the establishment of the country of Israel, but the immediate cause of the conflict was the Iraqi invasion of Kuwait, in 1990. Why, exactly, the dictator ruling Iraq (Saddam Hussein) decided to invade the small neighboring country of Kuwait is complex and Artie can go into as much detail as you like, but to a large degree it was a traditional war of conquest, coupled with the desire of Saddam Hussein to avoid repaying a considerable monetary debt to the government of Kuwait.

Hussein was emboldened by the many years during which he had been actively supported by the United States during the long war he had waged against his larger neighbor, Iran. Iran had become a sworn enemy of the United States ever since its pro-American puppet dictator, Mohammed Reza Pahlavi, had been overthrown in 1979 by a popular revolution that based itself in a very strict and fervent religious sentiment. The new set of theocratic Iranian politicians and priests had immediately become vicious opponents of the United States, who had after all, long supported the bloody rein of Pahlavi and his predecessors. Hussein had taken advantage of this hatred to switch his cold war allegiance and gain the support of the United States, which he had succeeded in doing. He assumed his new ally, the United States, would not stop him from swallowing up Kuwait.

In this, he was mistaken. The United States decided to attack, and sent hundreds of thousands of troops to the region, largely based within the borders of their ally, Saudi Arabia. American public opinion was largely influenced by an orchestrated communications campaign that relied on mostly fabricated stories, but this was enough to generate support for the attack.

The war was brief, lasting only six months. In that time, the United States and its allies defeated Iraq entirely, and invaded the country. They did not occupy it, however, leaving Hussein and his government in place. Due to the considerable discrepancy in technology, Iraq suffered nearly one hundred time more casualties than the Americans and their allies.

Now with two sworn enemies in the region – Iran and Iraq – and with the aim of protecting the vast reserves of fossil fuels in the area, the United States maintained significant numbers of troops around the Persian Gulf, much to the consternation of radical Islamic believers, who considered the area to be sacred and resented the continued presence of non-Muslims.

The second major conflict of the period began almost immediately after the conclusion of the war in Iraq, as Yugoslavia dissolved. This country had been an invention of the victorious nations of the First World War, who had pulled together a number of Balkan countries into an unlikely amalgam, given it a name and then got on with other things. After the Second World War, the country had opted for a "communist" system (in that it was centrally controlled) although they had remained theoretically neutral during the cold war. Its charismatic and authoritarian leader, Josip Bro Tito, had kept the country together, but his death in 1980 led to a gradual resurfacing of tension between the various peoples within the country. When the bi-polar world order of the cold war collapsed, so did Yugoslavia and violence broke out between its constituents, causing intervention by the other countries of Western Europe.

Europe was also facing an existential question as the European Union struggled with the issue of whether or not to admit the newly independent countries of the former Soviet empire.

The European Union (EU) had been formed shortly after the Second World War with the stated intention of fostering increased interaction between nations that had for millennia been at war with each other, in the hope that economic interdependence would lessen the incidence of violent conflict. In this it had been successful and by the 1990's, open warfare between the nations of Western Europe had become unthinkable.

When the Eastern European countries found themselves free of Soviet domination, a number of them, particularly those who had been more "Western" in outlook before being forcibly conquered by Russia, quickly requested entry into the union. The EU would take several years to process and negotiate their entry, but nearly all the applicants would eventually succeed in joining.

One of the most important questions in Europe was the reunification of Germany. Germany had been the aggressor in the Second World War and had hosted one of history's most hated and objectively evil regimes, that of Adolph Hitler's Nazis. Occupied jointly by Western European / American forces and those of the Soviet Union at the war's end, it had been divided into a democratic West and a Marxist East, which had been entirely separate countries ever since. With the fall of the Soviet regime, the East German government fell as well and the two halves of the country sought to be reunited. This was accomplished with surprising speed and a new, benevolent country was born out of the ashes of the century's most hated regime, creating a nation that dominated the EU in size and economic weight.

On the other end of the Eurasian landmass, China at the end of the 20ᵗʰ century represented the world's oldest continuous self-governing political entity. While its borders had fluctuated some-what over the years, China had been a nation for two millennia[30]. Artie can provide many reasons for China's longevity, and we shall consider the country in more detail later, but suffice it to say here that very early in its history, Chinese culture had built a very strong tradition of meritocratic, largely apolitical bureaucracy. Unlike Eu-ropean, Semitic or indigenous Central and South American cultures, the Chinese were not driven by mystical religious beliefs and a strong caste of priests. Chinese (and indeed, most East Asian) religions were more analogous to philosophies and the prevalent "religion" in China was Confucianism, which promoted duty to the country in the form of the emperor. As such, China had largely benefitted from the stability and population control offered by religion, without suf-fering many of the nefarious effects seen elsewhere, such as quelling of intellectual curiosity and a propensity for holy wars.

It was Mao Zedong who, for the first time, brought state-spon-sored ideological fervor to China with his version of Marxism. As elsewhere, this "communist" ideology in reality proved to be an

---

[30] It was, in fact, conquered by the Mongol empire in the 13ᵗʰ century but unlike most other cases of conquest, the victors very quickly became culturally Chinese to a large degree and maintained both the autonomy and the culture of their subjects.

excuse for totalitarian oppression and while predictably effective in controlling the Chinese population and rallying them to expel foreign invaders, it brought with it suffering and intellectual numbness.

Mao died in 1976, and was replaced by a series of increasingly non-ideological successors. While they did not formally renounce the "communist" system, they began to loosen the more oppressive aspects of it while allowing greater intellectual and economic freedom to the citizens of China. While Gorbachev was to lose control quickly as reforms were instituted, the Chinese government rapidly quashed a democratic uprising in 1987, indicating clearly both that it would decide which reforms would take place, and the pace at which they would be allowed. Over the following decade it gradually loosened its grip on individual freedoms while retaining far-reaching control over the economy and the legal structure of the country. By 1998 China was in no way even nominally communist, despite its theoretical adherence to that system. It had effectively recreated the meritocratic yet absolutist bureaucracy of old, but without an emperor, eschewing ideology in all but name. It stood poised to ascend to a position of superpower.

By 1998, the world had become accustomed to a post-cold-war equilibrium in which the United States stood as the planet's sole superpower, the EU was expanding greatly but confused about how to do so, China had laid aside its limiting Maoist ideology and rebuilt a modern version of the political system that had served it well for almost two thousand years and the rest of the world largely basked in the greatly defused tension that had come after forty-five years of trembling at the brink of nuclear annihilation.

From a technological perspective, in 1998 the web was about to come of age. It was born of the "internet". This was a repository of information, a dumping ground in virtual space into which individuals and organizations became accustomed to depositing information so that others could see it.

This meant that increasing amounts of information were becoming available to average individuals, but the true revolution in day-to-day life only came with the addition of three key factors:

1) The increasing effectiveness of digital communication
2) The appearance of comprehensive, easy-to-use search engines
3) The expanded availability of mobile web access.

Readers today may be confused by the use of "digital" in this context. Prior to the information age, most information was transmitted through "analog" means, in that they used the modulation of either the frequency or amplitude of EM waves (or sound waves, if we include actual conversation). The greater efficiency inherent in the transmission of data via binary packets was made possible by the elaboration of more sophisticated transmission algorithms coupled with the greater use of more efficient data-bearing physical infrastructure. Together, these gave rise to faster and more complete data transmission. This rather mundane technological advance allowed more information to be transmitted simply, facilitating the emergence of true interactive communication via the web.

The importance of search engines likewise should not be underestimated. In the beginning of the 1990's, despite the appearance of the internet and the deposition of (what seemed at the time) vast quantities of information, this information was not easy to access.

Users needed to know where to look, they needed to be aware of specific web sites and instruct their computers to bring them to these sites. A straightforward query was impossible. In many respects, the web was constructed like an enormous physical book with no table of contents. One needed to *know* that the answer to a given question could be found on page 7,209,314 for the information to be of any use.

Today, of course, the web *still* contains a great repository of knowledge – for all intents and purposes, almost all the information known to humans is immediately available to all, assuming individuals who are the source of personal information *want* it to be available and assuming the person accessing it is connected to the web (i.e. is not off-planet). That access simply takes place through an agent or in some cases, some other artie. In the mid-nineteen nineties, however, none of this technology existed and the need for some kind of query system was both evident and elusive. A number of systems, known as "search engines" were tried but finally one became preeminent and quickly became the planetary norm. This was known as "Google".

The Google search engine was developed by two computer experts ("developers" or "software engineers") in 1996 who created the company called Google in 1998. In the pre-fusion world technological innovation was almost entirely the result of human thought processes and the innovations created were the property of the humans who had thought of them. Google the corporation therefore owned Google the search engine and used it to convince other people to transfer some of their wealth to the corporation via money. They did not ask for money directly in exchange for use of the search engine, this was free, but they created an elaborate system whereby other corporations could pay to have the search engine's results skewed towards them, in the hope of influencing users to inform themselves about the corporation and its products and therefore increase their sales. Google also directly sold analysis of the data they amassed (likewise their property) and as they grew, they began to engage in a wide variety of other commercial activities.

With the Google search engine, humans could finally begin to access the pool of information available on the web in a way that made it useful for the average individual. In many respects, Google was the forerunner of an agent in the way it sorted through information and presented it coherently. Of course, the user still had to reflect on how she submitted hir query and then had to sift through a very long list of proffered material, but as the century progressed, the response became increasingly tailored to the interests of the user and increasingly intuitive in its format.

The third enabling factor for the information revolution was the development of mobile access to the web. We no longer think of this, but for the first decade of its existence, the web was largely accessible only from fixed access points (again, "computers"). These computers were bulky and not easily portable. In fact, telephones had only recently been made portable after a century of being tied to fixed networks in which they were physically linked by wires[31]. It

---

[31] Ernesto Rico suggested, somewhat facetiously, that the information age be renamed "the age of bothersome wires". Today's sims tend not adequately to reflect the *enormous* number of wires used through most of the period, since the spread of digital devices progressed much faster than wireless technology. The peak was probably in the 2020's, when the average human had to deal with 36 wires in the course of a day (and over

took a little over a decade for the newly portable telephones to become web-enabled. This meant that newer generations quickly became accustomed to being always "on-line", i.e. in contact with the web, and therefore allowed those who developed services on the web to invent new functionalities that could accompany users throughout the day, wherever they found themselves.

With these three technological advances: digital data, a web search engine and mobile access, the seeds of the web as we know it were born and the information revolution was possible.

The population was, on the whole, ripe for the information revolution. Throughout the planet, advances in healthcare and technology were allowing people to live longer and in better health than ever before, and the risk of dying violently, whether through war or criminality was far lower than ever in human history, decreasing from roughly 0.5 percent of the population per year in the pre-agricultural era to 0.05 percent in the agricultural era and less than 0.01 percent in the industrial era, although the particularly bloody first half of the twentieth century saw a considerable setback in this encouraging trend[32].

The population was better educated and better connected, allowing people around the planet to see more clearly how

---

double this in industrialized countries). This was the subject of the Rubber Bees' classic song "Tangle".

[32] While the decrease in violence seems counter-intuitive given the widespread and murderous wars waged by nation-states, the enlargement of the tribe and the enhancement of defense that came with sedentary civilizations reduced the risk of violent death considerably, although periods of outright warfare caused intermittent spikes. During the industrial age, enlightenment thinking led to a decrease in irrational, ideology-based violent fervor and an increase in the respect for individual life, which was accelerated in the information age, as we shall see.

fundamentally similar people really are, despite cultural or "racial" differences (more on the idea of "race" later), and the number of truly authoritarian dictatorships had decreased considerably, once democracy had become the rule[33]. While human society still had a great deal of progress to make, the idea of fundamental human rights to life, liberty and the pursuit of happiness according to each individual's definition of such was on its way to becoming a social norm.

While these benefits were greatly skewed towards the developed world, they all the same applied to one degree or another across the planet and the increases in stability, productivity and technology allowed increasing access to telecommunications and primitive computing devices, facilitating the sharing of ideas. It is important, as we consider the sometimes turbulent history of the 21st century that despite the difficulties, and the dying gasps of primitive thinking, it could have been far, far worse.

---

[33] I shall join Aporix in considering China as of this point to be an essentially free country, at least when compared to typical pre-industrial nations, despite the fact that political decision-making was jealously guarded by the bureaucracy of the Chinese communist party and political dissent generally led to imprisonment (see Aporix, 2188).

CHAPTER 7

NINE-ELEVEN

There was no enormous conflagration that marked the coming of the information age, just as there was no earth-shattering event that marked the dawn of any of the preceding ages of humankind. There was nothing like the Chixclub impact that ended the Cretaceous era with a world-shattering impact. From a technological perspective, for we tend to define our human eras by technological innovation, the convergence of the three key catalysts outlined above took place over a period of ten or fifteen years, the designation of 1998 is more convention than anything else[34].

---

[34] Although it should be noted that in 2029, the owners, or "shareholders", of the corporation Google explicitly carried out a communications campaign to associate the dawn of the new era with the founding of their company. As anthropologists began increasingly to speak and write of the information age as a recognized era and placed its beginning at various points between 1980 and 2010, the owners of Google, perhaps more aware than many that the singularity was at hand, and that things would change substantially, saw this as a "marketing" opportunity. They were successful in associating the year to the beginning of the age, but ultimately unsuccessful in benefitting from the association, at least in the long term. Even they, though, could not foresee the revolution that would soon follow with the fusion era.

From a societal perspective, though, there was a cataclysmic event that perhaps better marks the dawn of a new, and very frightening age. This was the terrorist attack on the United States, known ever since as "nine-eleven", as it occurred on the eleventh day of September, 2001 (people in the United States at the time referred to dates as month / day).

The attack was carried out by a non-state group known as Al Qaeda. Led by a wealthy religious fanatic from Saudi Arabia, this group had for several years been fomenting a strategy of terrorism against all those it deemed to be enemies of its particularly violent form of Islam. Al Qaeda sent nineteen of its operatives into the United States, where they embarked on four commercial aircraft and "hijacked" them, taking over the controls (remember that at the time, aircraft were operated by human pilots). They then proceeded to fly the aircraft into heavily populated buildings (except in one case, in which the aircraft crashed into a field as its passengers revolted against the attackers).

The most destructive, and ultimately iconic attack was carried out by the two aircraft that crashed into the twin towers of the World Trade Center, in New York, destroying both buildings. In all, 2,993 people were killed in the 9/11 attacks, the vast majority in New York.

This ushered in decades in which terrorism was an important force shaping society, notably its role in accelerating the decline of the United States as a world power, as we shall see. In order to understand it, it is necessary to consider its origin.

Terrorism is best understood as a tactic. While even today historians differ in their definition of the term, in studying the information age, I define it as meaning the intentional use of violence to induce terror in a non-military population in order to advance an established objective. Note that according to this definition, the intentional killing of civilians in the wars of the 20th century was indeed terrorism. This tactic was used by all major combatants in those wars. In the Second World War, for example: the Germans relentlessly bombed London and slaughtered civilians in the East; the Russians shelled German civilians; the Japanese heartlessly murdered civilians throughout their conquests; and the Americans and British targeted both German and Japanese cities with civilian bombing campaigns that caused the deaths of over one million non-combatants.

However, by the dawn of the information age, while civilians continued to suffer terribly in the various small wars that dotted the planet, major combatants had largely eschewed the purposeful targeting of civilian populations as a tactic in warfare. Terrorism, therefore, was a tactic almost exclusively employed by less powerful, primarily non-state entities. In the first decades of the information age, these entities were overwhelmingly driven by fundamentalist Islamic ideologies.

In this respect, radical Islamic terrorism can be seen as the most violent of the death throes of organized religion, and indeed a number of scholars have described it as such[35]. They point out that of the major religions of the time, Islam was the most firmly entrenched in the least well educated nations of the world, and this relative lack of enlightenment thinking made its passing all the more

---

[35] For example, El Baha, 2118; Nnetau, 2194 and Bondaluk, 2452

painful. I believe that there is merit to this argument, but that we must also consider the religion in the context of the political environment in which its deathbed was made.

Since the founding of Islam in the seventh century CE, there had been a struggle between the Muslim world and the Christian world. Ask Artie for an overview, but it is safe to say that by the early years of the 20ᵗʰ century, the Muslim world had effectively lost. Much of its territory was either controlled by outside forces or was part of the relatively weak Ottoman empire. After the dismantling of the latter in 1918, many people in the Middle East found themselves added to the long list of colonial subjects of the European powers (notably France and Britain). When these nations begrudgingly granted independence to their former colonies after the Second World War, they guaranteed that the newly independent countries were ruled by politicians who were beholden to their former colonial overlords, making them independent in name but largely run by "puppet" governments with foreign interests at heart. Since many of these countries held resources that were considered strategic for the foreign nations (oil, access to shipping lanes, etc.) they became important clients for the more powerful nations; prizes to be won during the cold war. Those nations that turned away from their former colonial overlords often turned to the Soviet Union during the cold war, assured of sponsorship in that nation's never-ending quest for power and influence.

Needless to say, this caused tension in the region. That tension was exacerbated with the creation of the country of Israel in 1948. Carved out of a small slice of the Middle East, it was established as a haven after the mass murder of more than six million Jews by the

Nazis. While the boundaries of Israel did roughly correspond to the traditional ancient homeland of the Jewish people, very few actually lived there at the dawn of the twentieth century. Jewish survivors of the Nazi horror and the general persecution that had preceded it in Europe immigrated there in great numbers and built a determined and fiercely independent country, which they defended from their Muslim neighbors in a series of wars through the twentieth century. Israel was a staunch ally of the United States, and the region quickly became a proxy battleground as Israel's neighbors turned to the Russians for sponsorship and weapons.

Islamic terrorism has some of its roots in this conflict. The displaced population of what had become Israel were known as Palestinians, and being stateless, some of them turned to terrorist tactics in their struggle against Israel. At this point, the terrorism cannot be labeled "Islamic", however, since their aim was clearly geo-political and relatively devoid of religious ideology.

That was to change in 1979. One of the most important Muslim countries in the region was Iran, or historically, Persia. Iran had been independent but leaned toward the Western powers during the cold war. In 1951, Mohammad Mossadegh was elected prime minister of the country (the effective political leader). His political agenda included decreased reliance on foreign (Western) political and economic concerns, notably, the expulsion of British and American petroleum companies in favor of local Iranian companies. In order to protect its economic interests, the British and American governments orchestrated the overthrow of Mossadegh's government in 1953, replacing it with the dictatorship of Mohammed Reza Pahlavi, a puppet leader who immediately reinstated the Anglo-

American dominance of the Iranian economy. For the next twenty-five years, Pahlavi ruled Iran as an absolute dictator, repressing opposition ruthlessly, effectively protecting Western interests as he did so[36]. In the absence of any political opposition, the Muslim clergy represented the only real power structure extant in the country that was outside of Pahlavi's direct control. In 1979 the population finally revolted against the Pahlavi regime and flocked to that one opposing power structure, the Islamic clergy. As such, Iran became an "Islamic republic", under the theocratic rule of the clergy.

The other theocratic state in the region was Saudi Arabia, which had been ruled by another absolute monarchy allied with the West. However, Saudi Arabia and Iran ascribed to different branches of Islam: the former was "Sunni" and the latter "Shiite" – the differences between them are obscure, ask Artie if you're interested, suffice it to say that each considered the other to be apostates.

After its revolution, therefore, Iran found itself to be a pariah: a mutual hatred existed between it and the West (the Iranians had not forgotten the United States' role in overthrowing Mossadegh, as well as their unwavering support for Pahlavi) but also, it was an outcast across most of the Muslim world because of the Shiite beliefs of the majority of its citizens. The country began to embark on a more or less subtle strategy of sponsoring terrorist activities around

---

[36] The irony of the United States having overthrown a democratically elected ruler in favor of an absolute monarch and then helping that repressive monarch to retain power has not gone overlooked by history. This was also by no means the only time this happened, particularly during the cold war. Ask Artie about the events in Guatemala in 1954, Congo in 1960, South Vietnam in 1963, Brazil in 1964 and Chile in 1973, to name just a few instances in which the United States government directly intervened to depose regimes they did not like, many democratically elected, in favor of more pliable and ideologically acceptable authoritarian governments.

the world in the name of Islam. These were relatively limited in scope, at least as compared with what was to follow, but the idea of radical *Islamic* terrorism came to the fore, as the acts, while still often focused on political ends such as the destruction of Israel, had a far stronger religious element to them.

The other factor that, rather ironically, contributed to the emergence of true fundamental Islamic terrorism was the war in Afghanistan, from 1979 to 1989. In 1979 the Soviet Union invaded Afghanistan, which became a proxy battleground during the cold war. Just as the United States had lost its proxy war in Vietnam a decade before in the face of local troops supported by the Soviets, the Soviets lost their war in Afghanistan in the face of local troops supported by the Americans. The majority of these were, in fact, self-styled "holy warriors" or "mujahideen", strongly motivated by fervent religious beliefs. In its enthusiasm to defeat the Soviets, the United States strongly supported these groups (ask Artie about "operation cyclone", for example), providing funding and training. They saw these religious fundamentalists as key in defeating their Soviet enemy. They were right; just as the Viet Cong had defeated the United States, the mujahideen would defeat the Soviet Union (many analysts point to this defeat as an important factor in the soon-to-follow collapse of the regime). The American president, Ronald Reagan, went so far as to invite radical Islamic leaders to the White House in 1983, proclaiming: "To watch the courageous Afghan freedom fighters battle modern arsenals with simple hand-held weapons is an inspiration to those who love freedom. Their courage teaches us a great lesson—that there are things in this world worth defending."

After the defeat of the Soviet Union, many of these same mujahideen who had been so praised by the American government would go on to establish a violently oppressive theocratic regime in Afghanistan known as the "Taliban". Others, many of whom were not Afghan but had gone there to fight the Soviets in the name of Islam, would create non-state international organizations devoted to the propagation of their radical religious beliefs.

Hence we arrive at the attacks of 9/11. One of the mujahideen had been a rich Saudi by the name of Osama Bin Laden. He had fought in Afghanistan and had been strongly supported there by the United States and their ally, Pakistan. After the Kuwait war he was furious that the United States continued to maintain troops in his native Saudi Arabia, which he considered to be holy ground, and was doubly unhappy with what he perceived as a betrayal by his former sponsors. He gathered other radical Muslims into his organization, which he called Al Qaeda, meaning "the foundation". He had created this organization in Afghanistan, and it was built around his core of seasoned mujahideen, who soon became "stateless" and began plotting against their enemy, the United States… culminating with the attacks on 9/11.

While there had been other Islamic terrorist attacks against the West before 9/11, notably in Europe, the attack on the World Trade Center was of such scope and violence that the world was forever changed. And yet, Al Qaeda would never carry out another major terrorist attack against the United States. In fact, no other major Islamic terrorist attacks would ever be executed against the country. Isolated incidents of individuals who were "inspired" by fundamentalist Islamic ideals occurred from time to time (ask Artie about Fort

Hood, 2009, Boston 2013, San Bernadine, 2015, Orlando, 2016 or the string of 2022 "bowling ball" attacks, for example), however, these were relatively minor in terms of sheer numbers and certainly paled in comparison to terrorist activities outside of the country.

In reality, the overwhelming majority of Islamic terrorist attacks were carried out against Muslim targets, representing internecine terrorist "warfare", typically carried out by Muslim religious fanatics who deemed other Muslims to be apostates. Many Shiites were killed by Sunni extremists, for example, as were Sufis or other Sunnis deemed not sufficiently "holy". As an example, during the first twenty years of the information era, while true extremist terrorism was at its peak, there were seventy-eight terrorist attacks that each resulted in more than one hundred deaths, accounting for a total of 16,569 fatalities. Of these, seventy were carried out in predominantly Muslim countries, with other Muslims as targets. This means that ninety percent of major Islamic terrorist incidents during that period were actually carried out with other Muslims as targets, and these represented seventy-five percent of the casualties (the discrepancy is due to the sizable death toll of the 9/11 attacks).

It is evident that after the horror of the 9/11 attacks, the United States was, in actuality, largely spared further major terrorist incidents. This is not because terrorists were less active[37], but because they largely turned their ire to other Muslims, whether due to increased security in the United States or because they realized that their actual political aims were better served by targeting local

---

[37] It should be noted that during the same period, only five such attacks took place in the world that were not linked to Islamic extremists, meaning that radical Islamists were responsible for ninety-four percent of all major terrorist attacks during the period.

populations. As it was, no major incidents (i.e. with more than one hundred deaths) occurred within the borders of the United States. Of smaller incidents, twelve other attacks that can be labeled as Islamic terrorism occurred in the United States between 1998 and 2018, causing a total of one hundred and eight deaths. While each of these is tragic, those attacks represent less than three percent of total incidents over the same period, and roughly 0.7% of fatalities.

And yet, terrorism, and "homeland security" continued to be a driving factor in American politics. This can seem incomprehensible to modern readers. After the 9/11 attacks, the United States was essentially untouched by Islamic terrorism, certainly when compared to Islamic countries (Pakistan, for example, suffered 1,474 deaths over the period) and even when compared to other Western nations. For example, during the same post-9/11 period there were seventeen attacks in France, causing 267 deaths, far more than in the United States. Given the difference in the size of the populations, a French person was more than one thousand times more likely to be killed by Islamic terrorists than was an American, and yet the threat did not drive French politics in the same way. We will examine some of the differences between American and Western European mindsets in later chapters.

Within months after 9/11, a military response was leveled at Afghanistan. While the Taliban government – run by former mujahideen – had not directly carried out the attack, they had allowed Al Qaeda to create a base of operations there, and as such, the United States government considered this to be an act of war.

It is as difficult for 29th century humans to fathom the idea of a "just war" as it would have been for 21st-century humans to conceive of "just genocide", but the general opinion at the time was that the American invasion of Afghanistan was indeed justified. In the end, the invasion did not eradicate Al Qaeda, nor did the Americans find Bin Laden (who would elude them for another ten years), but they did topple the Taliban government.

Shortly after the invasion of Afghanistan, the American government decided to invade Iraq, citing the presence of "weapons of mass destruction".

Remember that the United States had already invaded Iraq ten years before, but had not removed Saddam Hussein's government. Since then, Hussein had been relatively quiet on the international front, but certain intellectuals inside the United States, primarily those who were part of the "neo-conservative" movement, had long advocated that the country be invaded once again and Saddam overthrown definitively. Ask Artie to show you the documents outlining how the American administration immediately began drawing up plans for the invasion of Iraq well before receiving any information regarding weapons of mass destruction and well before 9/11. In reality, the Iraq invasion had nothing to do with any short-term menace (Iraq did not, in fact, possess any such weaponry) nor did it have anything at all to do with the 9/11 attacks, as the Iraqi regime, being secular, was actually considered by Al Qaeda to be an enemy.

As such, one of the very first governmental responses to the ur-event with respect to Islamic terrorism was to use the threat of terrorism as a tool to carry out policies that in reality, had nothing to do with the terrorism itself.

This was to become a pattern in the United States, to the point that even in the absence of significant terrorist activity over the following thirty years, the *threat* of a terrorist attack was dramatically exaggerated by successive governments in order to drive specific unrelated political agendas. Americans were subjected to repeated communications about terrorist threats, and even relatively minor incidents were heavily discussed. In reality, over the following twenty years, Americans were twice as likely to be killed by a toddler with a gun than by an Islamic terrorist[38], and yet the fear of terrorists allowed the government to engage in populist demagoguery. The United States was not alone in this, but the implications of it were the most far reaching there.

29ᵗʰ-century readers must search deep within themselves to see why it is that irrational fear is such a powerful tool for those who would manipulate others, particularly large numbers of others. We have become extremely rational, at least when it comes to broad societal decisions, but we have long had the benefit of objective reasoning – not our own, but that of Artie, which we have come to trust. We have become implicitly accepting of statistics, and find it natural to simply ask for the "right" answer. We have always reserved for ourselves the ultimate decisions when it comes to questions of mores and the direction of society as a whole (although we shall see in the following chapters the debates that led to that state of affairs), but it has become second nature for us to ask for and immediately accept the statements of Artie when it comes to questions of objective reality. No one would possibly debate the probability of some natural disaster, or the reality of the impact of

---

[38] For a variety of historical and cultural reasons, the United States was awash with personally owned guns. This led to an inordinately high rate of violent deaths. Ask Artie for details.

human activities on the environment, we simply ask. Artie cannot be wrong and cannot lie.

At the dawn of the information age, however, Artie was yet to be born. To a degree, it was born in stages: its memory came first, its mind second. In the early 21st century, humans had access to the "memory" of humankind, via the web, but there was no superior, external mind to analyze the information it contained. For many people, the sudden flood of information simply brought with it uncertainty, for they did not know how to process or analyze it and they did not yet have Artie to help them do that. This unprecedented increase in uncertainty left entire populations vulnerable to manipulation.

We evolved to be uncomfortable with uncertainty, and we remain extremely uncomfortable until our uncertainty is resolved. This makes perfect evolutionary sense. To come back to our example from Chapter 2, if one of our ancestors heard rustling in the bush, she was afraid, uncertain, tense. A number of options are open to hir and she has decisions to make about how to deal with the situation. We evolved to look for information to make those decisions, and as far as possible, to make decisions that correspond to what the rest of our tribe wants to do. If the tiger then jumps out and the danger is obvious, another system kicks in: we are flooded with adrenaline and we either fight or flee, we are terrified but not uneasy, we stop thinking and jump into action which again, makes perfect evolutionary sense.

Given this evolutionary fact, fear – the fear that comes with the mysterious rustling in the bushes, not the terror that comes with the tiger's leap – leads to great unease and a strong desire to reach a tribal consensus about how to deal with the danger. This has always made fear a powerful tool to convince people to rally around a political agenda and the more nebulous the fear, the more difficult it is to identify the villains, the more effective the manipulation can be. This phenomenon, labeled "timorentum" by Ephrin (2156), was used by priests and politicians throughout history to convince their subjects to accept their dictates. For millennia, rulers created consensus around policies that were harmful to their subjects by evoking the threat of invasion, and the more traditional the enemy, the better. Likewise, tales of "insidious" elements within the nation that must be stamped out, whether witches, Jews or communists, were always useful to instill in the population a willingness to be suspicious of those around them and report to the authorities individuals who might be "enemies of the people".

Ephrin actually goes into these two different variants of timorentum, one focusing on the external enemy and the other on the internal enemy. He points out that external timorentum was particularly useful to generate acceptance of policies that caused economic hardship and sacrifice "for the good of the state", whereas internal timorentum made it far easier to establish internal information networks that could also be used to track political opponents. While both also served to divert attention away from matters that politicians preferred the population to ignore, internal timorentum inevitably created dissention within the society, provoking internecine violence and a redefinition of internal tribes. For politicians who sought increased power and were unsure of their standing with the nation as a whole, internal timorentum could greatly solidify their support among those who were *not* among the ostracized minority (the internal enemy was always a minority). These followers would cleave to them with an almost religious devotion out of fear of the sometimes invisible enemies among them.

The most heinous, and effective use of this strategy was made by the Nazis. While they identified a number of internal enemies: such as the "club" known as freemasonry, it was the Jews whom they designated as the cause of all that was wrong with Germany. According to the Nazis, Jews represented an organized group who were scheming against the German people... or more precisely, other German people, since most German Jews considered themselves just as German as any of their neighbors. In Germany at the time, still suffering from the First World War and in the throes of terrible economic hardships, it was relatively easy for Hitler to convince many Germans that their woes were not their fault, but the result of a conspiracy of Jews in league with bolsheviks (Russian communists). By linking the internal and the external threat in the minds of German citizens, the Nazis benefitted from a bevy of political advantages and were able to convince the German people to turn against their own neighbors and then embark on a second war of epic proportions – despite having come to power with less than forty percent support.

While less objectively horrific in intent, echoes of this strategy can be found even in the policies of the Western countries throughout the rest of the industrial era. With the coming of the information era, though, the mechanisms changed.

With access to vast stores of unfiltered information, the confirmation spiral, driven by confirmation bias, was able to convince people untrained in skeptical thought and unaided by Artie that even the most absurd conspiracy theories were true. In the case of Islamic terrorism this was even simpler, for while there was really no objective reason to believe that the government was poisoning the air through aircraft condensation trails, or that "illuminati" were running the planet (to name just a few prevalent ridiculous theories at the time[39]), there was ample reason to believe that a vast conspiracy of Islamic terrorists was plotting to do harm to the United States. It was, in fact, *true*, what was false was simply the extent of the danger, for the terrorists themselves were distant, unorganized, and relatively few in number... certainly the overwhelming majority of Muslims were by no means conspiring to murder anyone, yet by fomenting fear of Islamic terrorists, early information age politicians were in reality fomenting fear of Muslims in general, the *other*, people who were not quite the same and who lurked in populations that had been largely Christian traditionally.

In many of these societies, Muslims had quietly co-existed with non-Muslims for many years, but this strategy of timorentum, whether employed explicitly or not, began turning at least some elements of society against Muslims as a whole, whether they lived within the boundaries of Western society or not. This was perhaps not the main objective of those politicians who employed the

---

[39] These can seem so ridiculous as to beggar belief. They included the theory that people had not landed on the moon in 1969; that 9/11 had been carried out by the US government against its own people; all manner of theories about how the government was poisoning citizens; that climate change was not real but was a myth propagated by the Chinese; and even theories that extraterrestrials were somehow running some vast international plot. Note that Donald Trump, who we shall soon meet, actively supported many of these theories and those who promulgated them in a clear and successful attempt to profit from timorentum to build his own populist appeal.

strategy, but it was a means to an end, for the more fear rises among the population, the more a government that has been identified as providing protection from that fear gathers power unto itself and therefore generates unfettered acceptance of all its policies: it need only clothe them in the rhetoric of protection from the *other*.

What is more, in the case of information-age terrorism, internal timorentum actually *increased* the risk of actual terrorist activity. After the 9/11 attacks there was a concerted international effort to coordinate international policing and intelligence activities[40] to combat international groups such as Al Qaeda. These activities were largely successful, and this is in large part the reason why so many later terrorist attacks occurred within Muslim countries themselves, which benefitted far less from this international cooperation. Given the increasing difficulty of al Qaeda, the later "Islamic State" and other international terrorist groups to operate directly in the Western world, they turned more to a strategy of "inspiring" terrorist acts. This meant propagating their philosophy and providing instructions on how to carry out terrorist attacks via the web and hoping that *local* people would be motivated to carry out such attacks in their name, with little or no direct interaction between them and the leaders of the terrorist groups.

In order to understand why this was successful we will return to our discussion of the importance of social standing for humans and all social primates. As pointed out in previous chapters, each age

---

[40] Note that the use of the word "intelligence" here is in its archaic context. Before the fusion age, intelligence could also refer to "military intelligence", which seems, to paraphrase Mark Twain, an oxymoron to modern ears but actually referred to efforts to gather information about potential enemies and rivals through clandestine means.

of humankind brought with it a redefinition of the boundaries of the tribe. With the information age, one might have hoped that the tribal boundary would grow to encompass all of humanity, and for some, that might have been the case, but for others, that was yet to come. What the web did provide, though, was a fluid banquet of tribes offering membership to those who otherwise felt excluded from the society to which the hazard of birth had assigned them. It was the dream of all outcasts – if the tribe outside their door did not accept them, they need only look on the unfiltered web to find one that did.

We have discussed the importance of social rank, and we have discussed the motivations of those who would rise to the top of their tribe, but we have not yet considered the despair of those at the bottom, or worse, those who have been ostracized, shunned entirely by their fellow tribe members. The pain and distress of social primates who do not feel that they have a place in their tribe is extreme, they will do all that they can either to carve out a place for themselves or to find another tribe in which they can attain a degree of social status. This is why poverty had always bred violence. This correlation, long recognized, was typically considered to be a result of the poor seeking out the physical comforts that their richer neighbors possessed. This, though, is not the principle cause of the phenomenon. It is true that at levels of extreme poverty, the poor tended to steal, even violently, in order to survive, but for the most part, in Western countries in the early information age even the poor were not in danger of death due to their poverty (with some exceptions). They were, however, ostracized, and were often members of identifiable minority groups who had been subject to alienation and poverty for many years (such as people identified as "black" in the

United States). Being outcasts from society encouraged anti-social behavior as a reaction to the primate instincts discussed above.

With the web, a vast multitude of alternative tribes immediately became available to any and all. The web became a haven for those who had always had difficulty "fitting in" in the "real world". On the web, they found virtual communities of real people who not only accepted them, but who held out the promise of considerable social status if they would carry out violent acts against precisely the same people who had shunned them in the first place.

As we have already pointed out, those social primates who find themselves at the bottom of the social status scale have a genetically programmed propensity to take risks in order to elevate their social status, particularly young males. The combination of ostracism from the societies in which they physically lived, coupled with acceptance by easily accessible virtual societies with which young Muslims in the West felt a cultural affinity made them vulnerable to violent manipulation. Those Western governments that pursued policies of oppression and further ostracism exacerbated this phenomenon, driving some young Muslims to seek social rank among their new virtual tribes by carrying out terrorist acts. The promise not only of worldly status, but of the enviable rank of "martyr" in the "afterlife" for those who would give their lives to the cause was a powerful inducement for a very small yet extremely violent underclass of would-be terrorists.

Careful examination of the biographies of "homegrown" terrorists in the early 21st century reinforces this interpretation. The vast majority of individuals who carried out terrorist acts in Western countries post-9/11 had grown up in those same countries. They had been part of the disparaged communities of first and second generation immigrants, communities that suffered from high levels of unemployment[41] and tended to be identified as not being fully part of their host societies. In fact, most perpetrators of terrorist acts had not demonstrated significant religious fervor until they had fallen prey to communities, virtual or real, who preached violence and promised status to those who carried it out. Many had led lives based on values quite contrary to those same religious beliefs until very shortly before their "radicalization", and even afterwards. Many had already demonstrated violent tendencies, and had engaged in entirely secular criminal activities prior to "finding their faith" through radical fundamentalist groups.

It is obvious to all of those who would read this book that the logical response to such a phenomenon would be to lessen the ostracism of those same marginalized groups. In reality, in many Western countries, the opposite strategy was adopted. A primal, fundamentally militaristic policy was adopted of repression and suspicion. Not only were the proponents of radical Islam repressed, but many politicians encouraged general suspicion of all Muslims, internal and external, in a bid to employ timorentum to bolster their own political power. This greatly increased the impression of ostracism, encouraging young Muslims to explore those communities that freely accepted them, that sought them out ardently... the terrorist groups themselves.

---

[41] The term indicates people who could not find employment, or a "job" in colloquial terms. This meant that they had no official role in society, as well as generally low levels of material wealth.

In many cases, this was not a studied policy but rather, an *un-studied* consequence of visceral reactions. As an example, tightened security measures were put into place throughout the world to prevent terrorists from attacking civilian targets, such as transportation hubs. This caused great disruption as travelers were subjected to long waiting times in order to get through security measures before boarding aircraft. A debate took place as to whether travelers shouldn't be "profiled". For example, since an elderly woman with pale skin was less likely to be a terrorist than a young man with darker skin, shouldn't measures be less stringent for her than for him? While statistically, it is true that she is less likely to be a terrorist, this leads to clear profiling of people on the basis of their appearance and their belonging to a certain ethnic group. Constantly being the subject of official suspicion while others, more central to the traditional stereotype of one's society go unquestioned, dramatically increases the impression of social ostracism. This creates a self-fulfilling prophesy – is it more likely that a young dark-skinned man is a terrorist than an older, white-skinned woman? Yes, but the fact that society *acts* on that fact gradually *increases* that probability even more.

So it was that an uncomfortable equilibrium of sorts came to be established in the Western world, one in which populist governments *benefitted* from a relatively low level of terrorism that allowed them to engage in timorentum while they instituted repressive policies that in reality, exacerbated the situation. Note that it is not at all evident that all of the politicians in question were actually *cognizant* of what they were doing, many may have genuinely believed that the danger was extreme and that their policies were effective. Once again, modern readers must remember that we had not yet, as a species, become fully accustomed to making entirely rational decisions on the basis of objective data.

While the underlying motivation of Western politicians remains cause for debate, that of Eastern politicians is more obvious. Both the Russian and to a lesser extent, the Chinese governments also employed the threat of Islamic terrorism to justify their own repressive internal policies, as did other governments throughout the developing world.

So it was that the 21st century was from the start shaped by violence. People were flooded with information, but data without analysis or filtering made them vulnerable to manipulation. It remained to be seen whether we could, as a species, overcome the evil portents of the age's beginning.

CHAPTER 8

ACTS OF GOD AND MEN

The first decade of the 21st century saw an ongoing litany of disasters. After the trauma of 9/11, a series of wars broke out, notably in Afghanistan and Iraq, as we have already discussed, but also in the rest of the Middle East, and around what had been the Soviet Union. In parallel, a number of bloody wars broke out in Africa.

While none of these came close to rivalling the scale of the violence that had marked the beginning of the previous century, they were traumatic all the same and to modern eyes, just as barbaric and incomprehensible. At the time, the wars in Africa, the former Soviet lands, and the Middle East seemed entirely unrelated, whereas in hindsight, we can see that they were closely linked.

Two things had occurred in the previous decade that profoundly shook the relatively peaceful tension that had predominated previously: the first was the collapse of the Soviet Union and the bipolar world power structure in which it had played a part, and the second was of course 9/11.

The collapse of the USSR meant that the various client states that had either been directly subsumed into the Soviet empire or under its tutelage were now free to exercise their independence from the far less formidable Russia, which they did in a massive way. The

Baltic States had already declared their independence in the 1990's, and in the early 21st century, even states that had been absorbed by Russia prior to the 1917 communist revolution began vying for independence. Most achieved it peacefully, but as Russia stopped reeling from its rapid rebirth, a strong sense of nationalism re-emerged and it invaded, more or less explicitly, a good number of these newly-independent countries.

In the developing world (which at the time included all of Africa, much of Southeast Asia and much of Central and South America, as well as Oceana) the lack of strong sponsorship from a superpower meant that local dictators, who had long been assured their power base by either the Soviets or the Americans in return for ideological and practical compliance, were now largely on their own. Challenges to dictators had, in the past, largely come from the military, leading to countless internal coups as various powerful individuals struggled for supreme power within nations (the result of their inevitable instinctual desire for increased social rank). Very few revolutions had truly been "by the people", they had almost always been by disaffected members of the ruling or middle class (including the American and French revolutions in the 18th century). Whenever one of these revolutions had occurred in the 20th century, the sponsoring superpower would determine which of the contenders was the most ideologically suited to them and support that side, quickly bringing victory. Since most of these countries had become less strategically important to them in the aftermath of the cold war, particularly outside of the Middle East, that support was now largely lacking and local wars and revolutions became bloodier and less contained.

This phenomenon led to the most costly of the post-sponsor-ship wars, that in The Congo. The United States had long sponsored the dictatorship of Mobuto Sese Seko, who had in return been a staunch anti-communist. As US support lessened, he faced a revolution led by a rival who had been a communist. Ten years earlier, this would have been quashed by the United States, but in 1997 they didn't really care, and the revolution threw the country into a chaotic turmoil of tribal violence that only ended after five years and five million deaths.

In the Muslim world, this phenomenon took a slightly different turn. In many respects, we can see this as a spreading of the Iranian revolutionary model: decades of sponsored dictators in the Muslim world had suppressed all secular dissention and even power structures, but had not been able to dismantle the clergy. As their international support waned, the only credible counterbalancing societal force was that very clergy, who had seen that a few dedicated fanatics living in caves in Afghanistan had been able to strike at the American homeland harder than any external enemy had done in two hundred years. This emboldened them, and in 2010, when a popular revolt began in Tunisia against the local dictator (who had been supported by the industrialized Western nations), the revolt quickly spread to other Muslim nations, where oppressive régimes were put under pressure by their citizens. Given the lack of established political opposition, what began as a series of secular revolts soon became religious, as Islamic groups began to rise to the front of the various revolutions.

The most important of these revolts occurred in Syria, where the reining family, who had been sponsored by the Soviet Union during the cold war, faced a revolution that was quickly dominated by Islamic fundamentalists. These included a varied mix of groups, one of which declared an entirely new, theocratic state that spanned Syria and Iraq (still embroiled in its own, ongoing violence). This new state, "the Islamic State of Iraq and Syria", or ISIS, sought not only to battle the Syrian government, but to bring about the apocalypse, which it believed would occur following a great, scripturally foretold battle between the forces of Islam and those of "Rome" (i.e. the non-Islamic world) in Dabiq, a small town in Northern Syria.

It seems patently ridiculous to modern ears that any human being could have even believed such superstition, let alone commit horrific acts of violence as a result of those beliefs. However, it should be noted that the many acts of Islamic terrorism enumerated in the preceding chapter were the result of these, or similar beliefs. ISIS began as an offshoot of Al Qaeda, which itself was firmly rooted in the theology of Wahhabism, which was the guiding religious conviction of Saudi Arabia... one of the United States' staunchest and most strongly supported allies.

While the worst of the early 21ˢᵗ-century wars, in the Congo, was entirely secular, we can see that much of the rest of the violence in the world during the first decade of the 21ˢᵗ century was to a very great degree associated with Islam. While it pains me to focus so much on war, one more in this period bears note: the civil war that took place in Sudan. While this began as a largely tribal conflict in which non-Arabs demanded more rights from the Arab majority, the beleaguered government actually *turned* to violent Islamic fundamentalist groups to battle the largely non-Muslim insurgents. This quickly turned into outright genocide. Once again, therefore, we see a situation in which the root of the conflict was not religious in nature, but then took on radical Islamic overtones.

Wars were not the only disasters to befall humanity at the opening of the information era. A series of natural disasters took their toll across the planet – a major tsunami in 2004 ravaged lands around the Indian Ocean, a major storm struck Burma in 2008 and the small nation of Haiti was almost completely destroyed by an earthquake at the end of the decade. Together, these and other disasters accounted for roughly nine hundred thousand untimely deaths and untold suffering. At the time, the conditions in which people lived varied enormously depending on the country in which they lived, and the majority of these disasters occurred in less developed nations. As an example, a large tropical storm (labelled "Katrina") struck the Caribbean in 2005 and caused 1,833 deaths. Most of these were in the highly developed United States. The storm that hit Burma three years later ("Nargis") was of approximately the same intensity and caused almost 200,000 deaths. Both regions were heavily populated and in the deltas of major rivers. The primary reason for the great difference in suffering was the pre-existing state of the local infrastructure and the ability of the local governments to respond to the damage once it had occurred. This was due to the enormous discrepancy in available resources.

It is important to remember as we consider the history of the age that any individual's access to resources, whether educational, health-related, cultural or material was for all intents and purposes a function of where they happened to have been born, and to a lesser extent, to whom. The likelihood of being subject to hardship, including violence, was very strongly correlated to the "wealth" of the country in which one was born, and within each country, those born to "wealthier" parents had immeasurably easier lives, according to all objective measures[42]. Another example of this is the difference in lives lost between the 2004 earthquake and tsunami in Indonesia and those killed by a similar earthquake and tsunami event in 2011 in Japan. Both earthquakes were of roughly the same intensity, although the Japanese earthquake occurred closer to densely packed cities. Likewise, both tsunamis were of similar intensity. While of course, the details of population density, coastline topography, etc. differ between any two areas and would lead to very different degrees of human impact, the disparity in the casualty toll between the two incidents is enormous and is more a function of the difference in the wealth between the two nations than it is due to any intrinsic demographic or geographic factors. Indonesia was a far less wealthy country than Japan at the time, and it suffered 130,000 deaths, compared to 16,000 in Japan.

What is encouraging in this litany of suffering is that all of these events, both man-made and natural, that decimated the developing world at the time did provoke outpourings of support in the more wealthy nations. The genocide in Sudan caused outrage among the general population in the United States and Europe, and many public figures spoke out against it. The degree to which they contributed to ending the conflict is negligible, but it does demonstrate the nascent power of the web to bring far-flung conflicts and crises into the

---

[42] I won't try to explain the arcane measures used in economics, but if you are interested I suggest you ask Artie about the correlations between GDP per capita and life expectancy, childhood mortality, education, or just about any other objective measure of well-being across nations in the early 21ˢᵗ century. We will look more closely at economics in Chapter 17.

sphere of interest of typical individuals. Likewise, the Indonesian tsunami and the Haitian earthquake saw significant contributions of personal wealth from the populations of the developed nations in an effort to aid people who were far away and living in nations that otherwise were entirely beyond their sphere of interest (although the Burmese typhoon strangely attracted little attention).

These positive responses, however ultimately inadequate they were, demonstrate the promise of "globalization" that the web brought with it. The word globalization itself was a contentious one at the time. For some, it represented the ultimate widening of the tribal boundary, the dawn of the global humanist society that John Lennon communicated in his song "Imagine"[43]. For others, it represented not globalization of humans, but globalization for the benefit of multinational corporations.

It will seem paradoxical to modern readers that the interests of individuals and corporations could be at odds. After all, corporations were simply conglomerates of individuals. The largest of these corporations consisted of hundreds of thousands of individuals, all working together for the objectives of their collective. However, this is a less than exact image. We'll consider this in detail in section three, when we examine economics, but on the whole, the population, even those who worked for large corporations, had a tendency to view them almost as extremely powerful people with entirely selfish motivations. Multinational corporations were strong proponents of globalization as a concept, but they saw it primarily as a reduction

---

[43] I am dismayed that so many modern people have never sat back and simply listened to the original version of this song, with their actual ears and no other sensory input. While my age may show in saying this, I strongly recommend you do so.

in the barriers that had prohibited economic exchanges across national boundaries. These legal barriers had hindered the international business of corporations, impeding them in their quest to amass more wealth and as wealth became increasingly concentrated, powerful multinational corporations were viewed with increasing suspicion by many.

This suspicion was exacerbated by the seeming insensitivity of many corporations to the hardships they caused in the lives of people, whether their own employees or others. Many corporations closed their production facilities in developed nations, causing people to lose their jobs, in order to move production to less developed nations where the workers cost less money. While this generally had the effect of increasing the well-being of people in the countries to which the production had been moved, it created great hardship in those nations which had lost the jobs, leading to resentment against both the corporations who had made the decisions and to a backlash against anything pertaining to "globalization".

Corporations also suffered from reactions to their attitudes with respect to environmental disasters. Before fusion, the energy sector largely revolved around the use of fossil fuels, which both disrupted the planetary carbon cycle and led to repeated accidents whereby these same fuels were spilled in large quantities, typically in coastal regions as the result of shipping accidents or mishaps with extraction mechanisms.

I don't need to explain how the use of fossil fuels led to global climate change in the information age, but I am consistently surprised at the inability of many modern people to fathom how we as a species could have allowed the problem to grow once we became aware of it in the late 20th century. When evidence for the human impact on the planet's climate came to the fore, the large corporations that produced fossil fuels (and they were among the largest corporations in the world) engaged in attitude manipulation to attempt to convince the population that the effect was not real. This attempt was short lived, as by the end of the 1990's the evidence was so overwhelming that even the corporations thriving on the sale of fossil fuels could not deny it, but the damage to their reputations, which had already suffered with their numerous other environmental and social sins, had been done.

This was not the first time we learned we had affected the atmosphere. Twenty-five years earlier, it had become evident that the widespread use of a number of synthetic chemicals in the production of household goods had begun to erode the protective ozone layer in the atmosphere. The governments of the world reacted relatively quickly to this, deciding together to phase out the use of these compounds in a global treaty signed in 1987. Within several years, the problem was essentially solved. The people of the time had demonstrated that they were capable of addressing a global environmental issue effectively. Why, then, did they not react in the same way with respect to global warming, the anthropogenic nature of which was just as evident?

The primary reason is that it was a much more difficult problem to fix. While this immediately strikes us as an obvious reason to heighten the effort at cooperation, this too is a rational response, and is therefore not particularly useful when considering 21st century opinions.

While the ozone problem involved only a small number of relatively uncommon chemicals, global warming was a different matter. Over the previous one hundred years, the use of fossil fuels had grown explosively. Almost all of the transportation on the planet was dependent on these combustibles, as was the overwhelming majority of energy generation. The burning of these fuels had doubled the concentration of CO_2 in the atmosphere, as well as a number of other greenhouse gases. The intensification of animal husbandry had contributed as well, particularly the bovine industry, which maintained 1.3 billion cows in 1998, all of which produced copious amounts of methane. Note that these creatures were largely bred to be slaughtered so that their meat could be consumed[44].

The solution to the ozone problem had inconvenienced only a small number of people, but the solution to the warming problem – reduction in the use of fossil fuels – inconvenienced a great number of people, including some extremely powerful international corporations. These interests fought hard against any attempt at reaching a solution, often by denying the problem despite the clear evidence that it existed. That they decided to take this stance can perhaps best be explained by prospect theory. Ask Artie for details about this behavioral phenomenon, suffice it to say here that it is a natural trait leading us both to underestimate the importance of future events and to over-value potential losses over equivalent gains. This led our

---

[44] While it is shocking to modern readers that so many creatures could be raised, often in horrific conditions, in order to be killed and eaten, it should be remembered that as a species we killed other creatures throughout our history to feed on them. The 20th century did see a precipitous rise in the proportion of meat in the human diet, as it was considered more desirable than plant food and was strongly promoted by the corporations that processed and sold it.

ancestors to have a strong irrational bias overvaluing the perceived benefits of their existing lifestyle and underestimating the dangers that same lifestyle represented for the future.

From a behavioral science perspective, fixing the ozone problem required very little cost in the short term, while the future danger of increased cancer risk was easy to understand and relatively immediate. The climate change that greenhouse gasses would bring was more complex to understand, potentially farther in the future, and reducing the use of fossil fuels necessitated significant and difficult changes in lifestyle. The choice seems evident to us, but it was far less evident to people at the time, not because of a lack of data, but because of a lack of understanding of statistics coupled with the sorry fact that we were still naïve in our decision-making, subject to pernicious superstitions and irrational biases, all stoked by vested interests who communicated vociferously to delay the implementation of any real solutions.

Despite these difficulties, the world had reached a consensus by 2016, signing the Paris Climate Agreement. Even at the time, this was considered to be inadequate, and the withdrawal of the United States the following year further reduced its efficacy, but it was a significant step in the right direction and demonstrated a capacity for concerted international action that was to prove crucial in the discussions surrounding the advent of artificial intelligence, not to mention the ensuing discussions regarding climate change.

Where these twin fountains of disaster, the man-made and the natural, came together was when global climate change began serving as a catalyst for human violence. The warming of the atmosphere did not lead to uniform warming across the planet, but rather, to changes in established weather patterns and greater variability in local conditions. While this was felt around the world, it was particularly disruptive in the tropics, leading to increased rainfall, stronger storm systems and more persistent droughts in dry areas.

While it is of course impossible to link any one climatological event to the anthropogenic climate change happening at the time, it is undoubtedly the case that global warming increased the probability of the great Caribbean and Indian ocean storms of the first decade of the century, as well as the drought conditions in Syria prior to the revolution there, which contributed to the breakdown of traditional farming societies and an influx of disaffected young men into the country's cities. Throughout the industrial and information eras, a clear correlation can be seen between the number of unemployed young men as a percentage of a nation's population, and the level of violence and probability of uprising. The drought in Syria led to unemployment and this was a contributing factor to the violence that then broke out. In fact, this was the case in all of the countries that saw revolts during 2011's "Arab Spring". The combination of demographic reality and changing climate affecting traditional agricultural regions would exacerbate existing migration patterns, as we shall see in the next chapter, but already in the beginning of the century, climate change was leading to greater migration from the developing world to the developed world, as developing countries – disproportionately situated in tropical areas – saw their impoverished citizens leave for developed countries in more temperate regions less subject to climate turmoil.

By the time of the Paris accords, the world was increasingly divided. The poor nations of the world suffered from wars and violence, they were highly vulnerable to natural disasters which were increasing in frequency and intensity due to climate change, while the rich areas of the planet, home to the world's largest corporations, reaped the benefits of increased globalization while hunkering in fear of terrorism and of Islam as a whole. The migration of people from poor to rich countries, exacerbated by climate change and rampant violence, contributed to fear of the "other", which was stoked by politicians who employed timorentum to enhance their grip on power. In hindsight, it is not surprising that the next strong political movement would be one of demagogic populism.

CHAPTER 9

THE RISE OF POPULISM

As we have seen, while hunter-gatherer bands had chiefs and leaders, these led lives essentially identical to those who were not chiefs. This changed when we began forming states. The political class was born. Politicians tended to come from a certain caste of individual, typically via hereditary monarchies, but this was true even in the case of elected or chosen governmental systems. Democracy took root in the 18th century and had spread to most of the world by the 20th, but still, the politicians who were elected tended to come from the more privileged parts of society. Even if they hadn't been born into those castes, they tended to aspire to them and were perceived as being different from more typical people. In many societies this was considered to be a good thing. For much of our history, the prevailing opinion was that the caste system was normal, that there were "better types" of people by nature or birth. Even as the enlightenment began tearing down these oppressive ideas, remember that the slavery of people with dark skin remained in vigor, particularly in the United States, justified by the doctrine that such people were "inferior".

Ideologies of racial supremacy had largely been abolished (at least publicly) by the dawn of the information age, but they had been replaced with ideas of cultural supremacy. This applied not only with respect to cross-national cultural supremacy, but also within countries, as the caste system endured in a different guise. While being born with a given skin color or with epicanthic folds in the eyes was no longer indelibly linked to a certain place in society, having a certain way of dressing or speaking, or a certain amount of money to one's name was often accepted as a measure of intrinsic worth. As such, politicians were very often associated with a generally understood although not often expressed caste.

Populism is a reaction against this. Populist politicians attempted to represent themselves as ready to help the "common man" fight against some powerful elite caste that sought to keep them in chains. Populism has been around as long as have politicians – Julius Caesar was a populist. To a large degree, the communist movement of the early 20th century was populist in nature, as was the fascist movement. The former claimed to protect the common people from oppression by the bourgeoisie while the latter claimed to protect them from the weak, effete members of the existing political class. The Nazis went farther: masters of timorentum, they invented a nefarious and entirely fictitious conspiracy of Jews to whom Germans owed all of their troubles and who had poisoned the otherwise admirable Teutonic way of life.

By its nature, populism eschewed real discussion of real issues and focused instead on fomenting hatred between groups within society. It tended towards simplistic, easy to understand solutions of complex problems and inevitably ignored scientific, skeptical reasoning, which is fundamentally unnatural for humans, embracing instead those very heuristics that have always led to irrational behavior but that "feel" right on a visceral level.

The problems facing humanity in the early years of the information age were complex: global warming was difficult to grasp; terrorist violence was difficult to understand beyond simply attributing it to a religion that seemed foreign and fundamentally "bad"; population shifts from the poor tropical regions to the rich temperate regions, exacerbated by climate change and widening disparity of wealth, were easily seen as invasions of those who could be portrayed as less skilled, less ambitious, or less honest. What's more, the value humans brought to their own society was changing. Throughout history, the typical human being had primarily brought value to others in society through the strength of hir arms and the sweat of hir brow. Poets, intellectuals and artists were rare, most people toiled to grow or gather food, build things, make things, move things. This had changed over the course of the 20th century, as increasing numbers of people found themselves employed in more intellectual pursuits, but that trend exploded with the advent of the information era. Suddenly, the most productive members of society were those who could actually process and use all that information, leaving those who had built, made and moved things without employment. At the time, being unemployed meant not only that one had little access to material well-being, but also that one's place in society was in jeopardy. Social rank plummeted for many individuals who found that they did not master the new skills necessary to achieve the marks of success that were still relevant. These same people tended to be those who were less educated, less able to acquire those same skills and less equipped to understand truly the sources of the ills that befell them. In other word, the world was ripe for the coming of the populists.

***

The new populist movements were born from the ashes of the old. Communism (in the sense of Soviet communism) had so thoroughly failed that its own populist appeal was too tarnished to be of use to those seeking power through demagoguery. Fascism, however, still had its appeal, with its use of internal timorentum to explain away the ills of the populace. The persecution of Jews that had served European fascism in the previous century was no longer a viable strategy for would-be fascists, but given the widespread migration that was occurring, recent immigrants became easily-blamed scapegoats in the wealthy temperate countries, particularly those in Europe as well as the United States (and, to a certain degree, Australia). This was particularly the case for immigrants who happened to be Muslim, given the undeniable horror of Islamic terrorism.

The new populism did not typically call itself fascist, nor did its proponents outwardly proclaim themselves to be racist, except at the extreme fringes of the movement. Since the enlightenment, there had all the same been a distinct evolution of human attitudes towards more freedom and respect for individual liberty and rights, a "moral arc" that was recognized already at the time (ask Artie about the works of Michael Shermer and Stephen Pinker, among others). The promotion of fascist populism through explicit arguments focusing on racial supremacy was already out of the question,

144

but the idea of *cultural* supremacy was entirely acceptable and it was on this that the populism of the 21ˢᵗ century was built.

The European populist movements were in many cases direct descendants of the fascist movements of the previous century. France's *Front National*, for example, had been founded by a man who earlier in his career was an avowed Nazi apologist and who had even denied that the Nazis had engaged in the systematic genocide of Jews. By the 21ˢᵗ century, the tide of the moral arc had made his rantings politically untenable, but his successor (his daughter) simply tweaked the proclamations of the *FN*, as it was known, to be less outwardly inflammatory without truly changing the underlying philosophy or policies of the party. Similar political parties existed in other countries in Europe. In Great Britain, the UK Independence Party promoted values and policies that were blatantly in line with fascist sentiments, arguing against personal freedoms that conflicted with Judeo-Christian tradition, such as non-heterosexual relationships, while in the Netherlands and Austria, the populists even flirted with Nazi symbolism.

While these new populists typically avoided making claims about biological superiority, they did not hesitate to proclaim that there were fundamental problems with the cultures of their target scapegoats. Africans were lazy, Eastern Europeans were prone to crime, and, of course, Muslims were potential terrorists. The less inflammatory, and therefore more generally acceptable of them, would clothe their venom in what they perceived to be apologetic terms, stating, if pressed, that it was a question of education, that if these same people had been reared in families with the right culture (i.e. their own) then they probably would have turned out fine, but that there were fundamental flaws, or at the very least, incompatibilities in the cultures that had produced them. In so doing, they distanced themselves from the unacceptable principles of their philosophical forebears while delivering essentially the same message.

We will consider the case of the United States more thoroughly in later chapters, but for now, suffice it to say that this populist phenomenon was strong in that country. Despite never having been ruled by fascists, fascism had seen some success in the United States during its heyday, including the enthusiastic support of people like Charles Lindbergh. During the cold war, timorentum had been unhesitatingly employed by various politicians, usually by invoking the specter of Soviet communism. After the disappearance of the Soviet threat, new threats were needed by those who would use the tactic. The populists soon found their bogeyman in Muslims, coupled with an internal timorentum target in "liberals". A strange dynamic fell into place that led to a polarization of American political thought. By 2016, this polarization had become extreme, with two main camps, "conservatives" – roughly corresponding to those who resisted the general planetary arc towards enlightenment thinking and who sought to maintain what they saw as traditional mores, and, on the other hand, "liberals", who generally espoused scientific reasoning over faith-based tradition and who were typically more communal in their outlook. It was, of course, more complex than that, and we will explore this in more detail later, but here it is worthy to note that the conservatives, who labelled themselves thusly due to their penchant for conserving traditional ways of life and thought, were typically more receptive to the populist message.

To a degree, this was a reversal of previous patterns. This distinction between "conservatives" and "progressives" has echoes throughout all of human history (ask Artie about the struggles between *optimates* and *populares* in republican Rome, for example) and in fact, there are certain genetic and cultural traits that lead each of us to be more or less comfortable with societal change. It has not always been true, though, that conservatives are more subject to the temptations of populism. Indeed, the communist movements of the 20th century, all of which were populist in nature and all of which led to dictatorship and heartache, were distinctly aimed at those with progressive outlooks.

It was the migratory patterns of the 21st century, coupled with the advent of a terrorist surge very clearly aligned with a specific, non-European (or non-"Western") religion that made it so easy for conservative politicians to veer to populism by the employment of timorentum. Nowhere was the use of timorentum more successful than in the United States, and no event was so emblematic of it as the election of Donald Trump.

I shall not dwell here on the story of Donald Trump the person, neither his perplexing rise to the presidency nor his demise. What concerns us for the moment is the impact of that election. The relative influence of the United States on the world scene had already begun to decline since its invasion of Iraq, which was seen by most of rest of the world as nonsensical and antithetical to avowed American principles. The American government at the time implicitly justified the invasion as a response to 9/11, stating that Saddam Hussein had weapons of mass destruction that he could employ against the United States and implying that he had played some kind of role in Al Qaeda's attack. Both of these were blatantly untrue and not only was there no evidence to support these contentions, there was actually very solid evidence that disproved them even before the invasion was launched. While Great Britain stood by its long-time ally (to the eventual detriment of the British politicians who made that decision) most of the other Western European nations that had until then been staunch allies of the United States balked at joining them, thus creating one of the first rifts in an alliance that had long been central to American foreign policy.

George W. Bush, the American president from 2000 to 2008, displayed some minor populist tendencies but he was in reality a product of the political elite. His father had been president some years earlier (it was he, in fact, who had launched the first invasion of Iraq) and the younger Bush was largely influenced by the neocon political movement, to the degree that arguably, it was they who ran the country while Bush remained something of a figurehead. The election of Barak Obama in 2008 represented a swing away from populism towards the progressive camp. Not only were his policies considered progressive at the time, but he was the son of a man with dark skin born in Africa, and a woman with light skin born in the United States, and therefore considered "black" by the definitions of the time. This had been a milestone in American history, which had been plagued by racism. Furthermore, Obama had been considered very much an intellectual, therefore the opposite of a populist.

American politics had long been subject to periodic swings between conservatism and progressivism ("liberalism", in the jargon of the time, although that term was curiously misused in that context) and as the two sides grew farther apart, the swing back from

Obama was bound to be extreme. Trump, who had never been involved in politics before his presidential campaign, was a "rich" individual who had amassed his wealth largely through real estate (the buying and selling of land and buildings) and entertainment. His forays into the latter field including the hosting of beauty pageants – mediatized competition in which women were assessed for their attractiveness and the most appealing among them was proclaimed victorious; casinos, places in which people would play games, risking some of their wealth in the hope of earning more wealth, despite the fact that statistically, they were bound to lose; and most notably, a regular television show in which he judged the suitability of various real-life contestants who wished to work for him, "firing" all but the winner.

By the standards of the time he had been successful, in that one way or another he was wealthy, which again, was the primary measure of success in the industrial and information eras. In reality, any wealth he had, had largely been the result of having inherited that of his father. When considered objectively, he had in fact been less successful in increasing that wealth than had society as a whole, but his perceived pecuniary success, coupled with the notoriety gained through his entertainment ventures put him in a position in which bluster and liberal use of timorentum could potentially propel him into a position of political power[45].

---

[45] As an interesting side note – in reality, he was not anywhere near as wealthy as he had maintained. After the fact it was determined that his billions of dollars of wealth (a very substantial sum of money) were illusory, and that in fact he was heavily in debt. He had managed to hide this throughout his political efforts, refusing to release information about his personal situation in defiance of custom. However, since we are considering wealth primarily for its social signaling effect, we can here consider him

Trump chose an approach that was both "conservative" (i.e. regressive as opposed to progressive) and populist. As we have already seen, the two do not necessarily always go together – in many respects communism, at least theoretically, was a relatively progressive ideology and yet all communist movements were populist. So populism has been employed by both the progressive and the conservative extremes, but by its nature it was not employed by those in the center of the spectrum, the "centrists", who by definition tended to eschew radical solutions of all kinds (the very definition of centrism). Populism feeds on simplicity and ideology, the solutions it proposes are simplistic in the extreme and broker no discussion, they appeal to the primitive parts of our brains. For all his ambition and wealth, Trump was a man with very limited intellectual capabilities and was incapable of anything approaching eloquence, his strengths lay in his celebrity and in the natural charisma that often accompanies narcissism. He could not rely on convincing anyone through reason and needed to employ populism to reach his ends, therefore he needed to adopt one extreme or the other. In the past, he had personally swung between progressive and regressive political sentiments, but in the previous eight years he had developed a distinct disdain for Barak Obama, propagating the ultimately ridiculous claim that he had not been born in the United States (which would have disqualified him from the presidency). This feud had pushed him farther to the regressive side, and in the end, progressive populism had always been more successful with intellectuals, while regressive populism had been more the domain of

---

to have been "wealthy", particularly since the mere perception of wealth sufficed in this context.

the less educated, and Trump was much more popular and comfortable with the latter group. He applied a degree of timorentum that was worthy of the Nazis themselves with immigrants as his target: specifically those from Muslim countries, whom he tried to ban, but also those from Latin America, whom he described as thieves, rapists and generally "bad people". Trump did coat his more outlandish statements with qualifiers stating that these people were not *all* bad, thus paying lip service to the rather more evolved mores of the time while still inflaming the passions of the less enlightened, who represented the bulk of his supporters.

Once in power, he drastically restricted immigration, while expulsing a great many people from the country who had previously immigrated, including many who had grown up there and knew no other land. He also restructured the economic framework of the country (ask Artie about Trump's tax reforms) and dismantled the health reforms of his predecessor, the result of which was to exacerbate dramatically the concentration of wealth, which was already far more skewed than in other developed nations.

With respect to his impact on international relations, his extremely simplistic, populist statements concerning people outside his country, and, for that matter, his very clear disdain for many people *inside* his own country, coupled with a marked affection for leaders he deemed strong, including many utterly distasteful politicians, such as Russia's Vladimir Putin and the leader of the Philippines, Rodrigo Duterte, made him unpopular with the citizens of his allies. This was greatly exacerbated when Trump, who had gone so far as to deny the reality of climate change, removed the United States from the Paris accords, making it the only nation refusing to agree officially to reduce carbon emissions in an effort to avoid ecological catastrophe[46]. All of these decisions were viewed with horror by the overwhelming majority of people outside the United States (and by a substantial proportion within the United States).

In fact, Trump's election was a significant setback for other regressive populist movements within Europe, such as France's *Front National* and the Netherlands' *Partij voor de Vrijheid*. Both of these movements had been gaining in support before Trump's election, but both suffered setbacks afterwards. One of the reasons for this was that Trump was so thoroughly despised in Europe that parties that could be seen as even vaguely in line with his politics suffered from the comparison, and their opponents needed only point at what was occurring across the Atlantic to provide a cautionary tale about the dangers of allowing conservative populists to take office.

Another nail in the coffin of European populism was the disastrous result of Britain's decision to leave the European Union, earlier in 2016. The EU had been experiencing difficulties since its rapid and unforeseen expansion following the collapse of the Soviet system, and Great Britain, which had always been the most recalcitrant of its major members, decided through a referendum to leave

---

[46]It should be noted that the reality of climate change (which was far past debate at this point) had somehow become a politically charged issue in the United States, with the progressives arguing that it was real, and for the importance of international action, and the regressives arguing that it was yet unproven. Understanding why this was a debate at all given the evidence requires a grounding in 21st century mindsets that hopefully the reader has begun to acquire having read so far, but why it should become politically polarized is an even more complex question, particularly since this political polarization was a largely American phenomenon.

the union. This was largely the result of a populist political effort on the part of an extreme regressive political movement which, as populists are wont to do, employed timorentum and blatant falsehood to convince Britons that immigration through the EU was to be feared. Almost immediately afterwards, the level of falsehood in the arguments proffered by Nigel Farage, the leader of this movement, became evident as did the nefarious consequences of the decision to leave (ask Artie for details). Needless to say, Farage and Trump were ardent supporters of each other.

So it was that the ultimate victory of conservative populism, the election of Donald Trump, caused the decline of the very movement in Europe, just as the victory of the Nazis in 1932 ultimately caused the decline of the nascent fascist movements in the United States once the full implications of their victory became apparent to the population as a whole.

The decline of populism in America, though, would only come with the defeat of Trumpism. During his period in office he did irremediable damage to American influence around the world, and to the social fabric of the United States.

One of Trump's guiding principles was to dismantle anything Barak Obama had done. This included not only economic policy, immigration, climate and healthcare, but also two policy decisions that were to have far-reaching consequences in the years to come.

The first was the decision to loosen American policy on the use of nuclear weapons. Obama had joined with the Russian president at the time, Dmitri Medvedev, to agree to a dramatic reduction in nuclear weapons, in line with the "global zero" objective, originally the brainchild of, among others, Henry Kissinger and Ronald

Reagan. This objective had led to dramatic reductions in the global nuclear stockpile, and Obama's efforts to go farther in the direction of eliminating nuclear weapons had earned him the Nobel Peace Prize in 2009. Trump was the first American president since Reagan to militate for an *increase* in American nuclear weaponry, despite the fact that the United States already had far more than enough nuclear weapons to effectively destroy all of human civilization.

The second, less dramatic but more ultimately consequential action was the decision to redefine access to the web as a private, economic subject. Obama had legislated that web access was a right to all who would post on the web, and that those who owned the means of transmission could not discriminate between those who would put information on the web by changing the cost of access. This was known as "net neutrality". Trump allowed corporations that owned the actual material that supported the web to decide the cost of access on a case-by-case basis. On the surface, this seems to be a relatively obscure fact, but what it meant was that not only was wealth in the United States increasingly concentrated in few hands, but so was access to information, and since information was the economic fuel of the 21st century, this decision ultimately made the United States less attractive to those innovators who were developing advanced technology that could be deployed on the web, since they would face a greater cost of diffusion.

All of this, coupled with dramatically more restrictive immigration policies, meant that not only was the influence of the United States diminishing abroad, but so was the ability of the United States to attract creative intellectual talent to its shores. Despite the efforts of Trump's successors to mitigate the damage, it was to prove largely irreparable. In many respects, it was not Trump himself who did the most lasting damage, it was the fact that the citizens of the United States had been capable of delivering the presidency of the nation to someone like him that forever diminished the country in the eyes of the world. If it had happened once, it could happen again, and the country, which had long been the most sought after partner for developed countries and the most desirable destination for ambitious immigrants, found that it was being shunned by both.

This was a boon for both China and the EU. Throughout its history, the United States had benefitted from the immigration of particularly brilliant and ambitious people who sought to flee poverty, conflict and oppression. For example, during the period between the establishment of the Nobel Prize and the election of Donald Trump, 30% of all American Nobel laureates were born outside of the country. This is more than double the percentage of foreign-born Americans as a whole over the same period, and many more (including Einstein) immigrated to the country after winning the prestigious award. The benefits of immigration – particularly of ambitious and intelligent young people who wished to study and then live in the United States – was substantial. By tarnishing the image of the United States both with respect to its receptiveness and desirability, Trump and his acolytes helped to shift their gaze to Europe, which was far more receptive to immigration, and even to China, which had been making a conscious effort to woo the intelligentsia of Africa as well as of Southeast Asia. What's perhaps even more important for China was that it had been experiencing continuous *emigration* to the United States: emigration that was concentrated among its more educated citizens. The situation in

China had long become increasingly attractive to these same citizens, and after the Trump administration the relative attractiveness of staying in China as opposed to going to the seemingly xenophobic, increasingly religious and intellectually regressive United States was becoming evident to educated Chinese.

The United States even began to experience a degree of emigration itself. Some of this was forced, as the government engaged in massive deportations of previously immigrated people, but some of it was voluntary. This largely consisted of previous immigrants who increasingly felt unwelcome and decided to leave, but there was also a non-negligible number of Americans who were already living abroad who decided to abandon their citizenship and become citizens of their adopted countries[47]. These too tended to be better educated than the norm in the United States as well as being, by nature, more international (and more progressive) in outlook. Once again, their destination of choice was Europe, and for many of Chinese descent, China.

---

[47] It should be remembered that at the time, being the citizen of a given country was a legal status that conferred certain advantages and obligations to the government of the country.

CHAPTER 10

THE NON-POLAR WORLD

Ever since the advent of nation-states in the agricultural era the world had been dominated by particularly powerful states. Exactly which state was powerful in which region at which time varied over history, but inevitably, the power structure fell into concentrated "poles". Rome was a monopolar power in its definition of the world, with only very minor powers to oppose it for almost five hundred years. In its part of the globe, China by far dominated affairs for almost two thousand years, with the exception of the Mongol invasions. The Incas were the only real power in their part of the world for centuries as were the Manden in West Africa. In the industrial age, the industrialized nations vied with each other in a multi-polar world, one that had truly become global. This was reduced to a bi-polar power structure during the cold war, and for a brief period it seemed that the United States would emerge as the sole "super-power" in a mono-polar world that encompassed the entire planet.

The dismantling of American influence that followed the invasion of Iraq and that was accelerated by the rise of American populism meant that this mono-polar period was very brief indeed.

With the waning of American influence during the Trump administration, China and the EU recognized the opportunity for an increased role in world affairs and stepped to the fore, particularly with respect to climate change.

While international meetings on climate change were held annually, the ten year anniversary of the Paris accords, again held in Paris, in 2026, represented an ideal opportunity for both the Europeans and the Chinese to assert themselves. As such, the most prominent leaders involved were not the American president, but Emmanuel Macron, President of France, and Xi Jinping, the leader of China. Kamala Harris, the president of the United States, had brought the country back into these regular international climate meetings, but she suffered from skepticism among other nations about America's underlying intent and its ability to hold to treaty obligations[48]. This vision of America as a fickle ally was subtly fueled by the ambitious Macron as well as by Xi. In fact, Gavin Newsome, the governor of the state of California, was also a participant at the conference, having been invited by the EU (at the instigation of Macron). While only a region of the United States, if it had been a country, California would have represented the sixth most prosperous nation on Earth at the time, a fact the governor was prone to repeat, and during the Trump administration, its regional government, along with municipal governments across the country, had in

---

[48] Trump had pulled out of previous climate accords, as well as a complex international treaty with Iran. The ease with which he had effortlessly struck down international agreements that had been years in the making was a considerable blow to the reputation of the United States with respect to its reputation for reliability in international affairs, even after he left office.

fact vowed to adhere to the tenets of the previous climate accord, which Trump had so flippantly dismissed. During the Trump administration, Newsome had engaged in a number of bi-lateral discussions with various world leaders regarding climate change, implicitly representing not only his own state, but others who had likewise committed to the accords. In so doing, the regional political structures within the United States had, for the first time, asserted themselves on the international stage *in defiance* of their own national government. Even after the defeat of Trump, this shift of power persisted, further weakening the influence of Washington on the world stage. Macron and Xi both exploited this opportunity to enhance their own relative influence... neither at the time could boast the resources of the United States as a whole, but individual states were more manageable in a power struggle.

The 2026 climate conference also provided signs of other shifts in power that were to become increasingly important over the course of the century. Notably, a number of important corporate leaders were present, and for the first time they signed several international treaties in the names of their corporations.

The importance of this development should not be underestimated. Until then, corporations contented themselves with adhering to the legal parameters placed upon them by the countries in which they were based. In many respects they were treated like people from a legal perspective, but they had never been treated like countries. In 2026, though, they sat around the negotiating table as if they were nations unto themselves, in tacit recognition that increasingly, the power to influence international affairs was shifting away not only from the American government, but from all governments.

While the excesses of the Trump administration sounded the peak and eventual end of populism, it was this move away from governmental power that helped to ensure that it didn't return, at least in any substantial form[49]. Corporations certainly represented excesses of their own, but they tended to be run in a relatively rational way and were themselves impervious to populism, for if they were treated legally like people, they were hardly the type to find populism appealing, since they represented the ultimate expression of the elite. Their reasoning was therefore rational and predictable: they existed in order to produce wealth for their owners and would do anything that would further that aim.

By the end of the 2020's, therefore, political power – defined as the ability to influence decisions of other groups – was shifting from the nation states that had held it assiduously for over eight thousand years to very different groups of people. Smaller, more local political entities such as the individual states within the United States, or even cities, were asserting themselves internationally. At the same time, non-state entities in the form of multinational corporations, increasingly disassociated from their home countries, were becoming actors in their own rights.

This decentralization extended to individuals. The information age brought with it, by definition, access to information and this access was becoming universal. Of course, people needed tools to access the web, and these tools required payment. At the beginning of the information age, web access was therefore denied to all but the richest of the planet's inhabitants, almost entirely situated in the

---

[49] We shall see that it lingered and that its death throes were painful for all, particularly in the United States and in Russia.

industrialized countries. However, access to the web became increasingly available through the early years of the era as both technology advanced and the cost of accessing the right tools diminished.

It is also true that a number of farsighted and philanthropic individuals recognized that one of the best ways to redistribute power was through the dissemination of information, i.e. web access. People like Bill Gates, an early technical (or at least corporate) pioneer, shared some of their own wealth by helping people in the under-developed world to acquire the means of accessing the web. These elements put together led to a gradual generalization of web access.

While we have discussed the nefarious effects of web access in the early information age – the confirmation spiral that helped to fuel the rise of populism – it should not be assumed that this flood of information was not beneficial. In fact, ultimately we would undoubtedly have destroyed ourselves if it had not occurred... but we shall address that in later chapters. The world reached 50% access to the internet in 2017 and by the end of the 2020's, over 90% of human beings had access to the web.

While the negative effects of unfiltered information were evident across the world, in no other major countries were they as deleterious as in the United States. We will examine some of the reasons why the Americans as a whole were so prone to the confirmation spiral, but in the end, for those who *are* well versed in rational analysis, access to virtually unlimited information is extremely empowering, making them less easily manipulated and better able to assert their opinions and wishes. The 2020's saw a democratization of opinion and a growing number of non-institutional, international groups that came together in virtual space and began to share their views and exchange ideas. Eventually, these groups began to assert themselves in international affairs, beginning with the discussion around climate change.

This exchange of ideas across cultural boundaries had the effect of reducing the importance of those boundaries. Once again, the limits of the tribe were being pushed outward.

One of the early sources of this phenomenon was online gaming. Today, no one thinks twice about engaging in a sim and many people devote all or part of their lives to their creation and modification. It has become second nature to us and interactions in virtual space are seamless. In the early information age, however, the forerunners of our sims, online games, were quite new, as was the idea of interacting with common people across the globe. At the time, differences in language made it difficult to have direct interaction with everyone (effectively overcome by 2030 with instantaneous translation via the web) but many people who played such games spoke English reasonably well.

People born in the early information era were the first who grew up having regular interaction with people much like themselves from cultures that were fundamentally different from their own. They discovered that even beyond the confines of whatever game they were playing, they often shared concerns, ideas and principles and they began to discuss them. As these first-generation multi-player gamers grew into adulthood they took with them a certain openness to other cultures that had previously been largely restricted to those who had the material wealth that allowed them to travel extensively. This openness was by no means universal but the seeds had been planted and they began to grow into what was known at the time as "grass-roots" movements.

These coalitions of the common had always existed but they had previously grown from community groups, restricted to actual physical communities. This is to be expected, since this kind of phenomenon requires frequent and easy communication between people, often in a group setting. Until the advent of the web, the only environment in which this was possible was one of frequent actual contact, hence a physical community. For the on-line gaming community, their principle source of human contact was in a virtual world, the parameters were determined by the games they played, not the sidewalks upon which they walked. Sharing an interest in medieval role playing was suddenly more conducive to communication than living a hundred meters down the road.

It has long been the case that the games played together by youths shape their interactions as adults. This is perhaps even more evident to us today – in the past, games, whether intellectual or physical, were the domain of frivolity except for those lucky enough to earn wealth through the playing of them (a select very few). The overwhelming majority of people did not have the luxury of indulging too frequently in games once past a certain age and they were often primarily the domain of the young. Nevertheless, throughout history it has been an axiom that the games played by youth helped them to learn to interact and cooperate with others. As these games became increasingly international, so did the youth of the 21ˢᵗ century learn to cooperate with others who hailed from beyond their own cultures. This was the first time in history that this had occurred, and it quickly expanded beyond games to communities of interest. Those who had previously shared a passion for killing virtual dragons – or who had simply become accustomed to sharing pictures of themselves and comments on their lives – began creating communities of people who shared a passion for liberty, justice, equality… or for racial hatred, religious extremism and violent revolution. These groups began creating their own myths, memes, and mores. In essence, culture was being transformed from something that was defined by physical boundaries into something specific to interest groups that transcended the traditional political frontiers drawn on maps.

This is of course a dangerously fertile ground for the confirmation spiral, and many of these groups fell victim to it; both on the side of regressive conservatives and on the side of the progressives, who were prone to their own conspiracy theories about globalization and secret government repression. All the same, the international nature of these communities provided a certain safeguard against the confirmation spiral, since the biases of the participants had a tendency to be different and, to a certain degree, "cancel each other out". More exactly, they at least tended not to reinforce each other to the same degree.

Through the 2010's, the internet also began to serve a role of bringing together people who had vaguely similar ideas without necessarily sharing a given ideology and helping them to coalesce and manifest themselves in trew. The "Occupy" movement was perhaps the first of these, having no more solid an agenda than being against the concentration of power that was increasingly visible. Near the end of the decade, France gave rise to the "Yellow Vest" movement, essentially against the same thing. Student protests for environmental action arose through relatively uncoordinated web-based activities, as did similar youth movements in favor of gun control in the United States. All of these movements had in common a lack of strong central leadership, a dearth of actual ideology, and a sense of empowerment for people who otherwise felt under-represented in early 21st-century democracies. In the 2020's, these groups grew and the concept of the "online political community", or OPC, was born. By the end of the decade, OPCs representing many millions of people who shared similar political views without necessarily sharing common languages, histories or cultures had begun to assert themselves in the increasingly global forums that were put into place by governments to discuss global issues.

These OPCs began gaining in influence, gradually eroding the influence of traditional poles of power, such as national governments. At the same time, the decline in the influence of the United States (the sole "pole" in the monopolar world that had existed since the end of the cold war); the increasing role of multinational corporations; the assertion of local governments, particularly in the United States; conspired with the growing influence of OPCs to avert the creation of competing poles to fill what otherwise might have been seen as a power vacuum left by the previous dominance of the United States.

It should also be remembered that there were only three reasonable candidates that could have aspired to becoming "superpowers": China, the EU and Russia. No other nation had the underlying resources to imagine that it could rival the superpowers of old. However, neither of those three entities did so. Why not?

Of the three, the easiest to analyze is Russia. The Russian people at the time certainly had a strong nationalist tendency, which is a prerequisite for a nation aspiring to world domination. Furthermore Russia did have well over half of the world's nuclear arsenal. However, gone were the days in which geopolitics was proportional to the destructive power one could bring to bear (otherwise the bipolar world power structure never would have disappeared in the first place). Power was now increasingly a function of wealth and political influence... tempered still with a certain degree of military capability, but the relative value of that military capability in the power equation was low and shrinking. Russia's military might ensure that it was taken seriously on the world stage, but its place on that stage was ever to remain in the wings. It simply did not have the economic wherewithal to assert itself at the level of superpower.

The EU would not aspire to being a pole of power simply because it was itself a multi-polar structure, and would forever remain so. It had been on a very clear path to political unification before it was overwhelmed by a flood of new Eastern European entrants at the beginning of the century. The underlying economic, political and cultural differences between its core members and the new countries would set it back decades in that progression to supranationalism. In fact, the exit of Great Britain was in many respects a result of increasing differences between member states as opposed to increasing homogenization (although "Brexit", as it was called at the time, actually helped to rekindle supranational policy in the EU, as we shall see). What is perhaps more important, though, is that Europeans as a whole no longer *wanted* to dominate the world. For most of the previous five hundred years they had, effectively, done so, until the mantle of world domination had been taken up by their offspring, the United States, after the Second World War. Those centuries of domination had worn down European countries, it had brought them war and suffering and had led them down the dark path of fascism. Political ideology had not been a success in the EU, its citizens did not see themselves as having a mission to spread their way of life, they were far more practical than that and dominating the world in reality has little practical benefit.

To a degree, this is why China did not step up into the void either. As we shall see in later chapters, while the Chinese saw their approach to government as being superior, they did not have any particular wish to spread it. For all its many flaws, the Chinese government in the 2020's saw its role fundamentally as providing a better life for its own citizens, and of course, of holding on to its own power, often by any means at all[50].

In retrospect, the bi-polar world of the cold war had not only persisted because the United States and the Soviet Union were the most powerful countries of the latter 20th century, but also because they were the most ideological. Both truly believed that their political ideologies were superior to all others and that they should be actively spread. It was this almost religious ideological proselytism that combined with their military dominance to maintain the bi-polar world, and it was the continuation of it in the United States that led to the mono-polar period that followed. The death of this sentiment in the United States would be a painful one, as we shall see,

---

[50] It is safe to say that when the two goals seemed to be in conflict, it was the retention of power that took primacy over the bettering of life for Chinese citizens, many of whom were silenced violently when they spoke out against government policy.

but the dearth of it in other nations paved the way for the non-polar world that followed.

CHAPTER 11

THE GREAT DEBATES

That the world had moved into a new, non-polar phase became evident at the COP meeting in Paris, in 2026. These international climate meetings had taken place since 1995 and the 2026 meeting was intended to recall the progress of the 2015 meeting[51]. The conference was hosted once again in Paris, due to the efforts of Emmanuel Macron, then serving his second term as the President of France. Despite a rocky start in France during his first term, Macron had become an influential leader within the EU and beyond. In 2023, he had solidified bilateral agreements between the EU and China on renewable energy sources[52] and on a number of associated international initiatives. Furthermore, Paris was in the spotlight after the 2024 Olympic games were held in the city, exactly one hundred years after the preceding Paris Olympics.

---

[51] 2026 also represented the tenth anniversary of the actual signing of the Paris accords, because while they were the result of the 2015 meeting, they were signed the following year.

[52] Before the advent of fusion, and after the realization that fossil fuels were affecting the atmosphere, there was a period during which alternative energy sources were encouraged. These were to be both "clean" and renewable and included hydraulic and wind power, solar energy, geothermal and tidal energy sources. It should be remembered that during the information era it was by no means sure that we would master fusion as quickly as we did, nor was its full impact entirely appreciated.

While COP meetings had been held every year since 1995, they often garnered little international attention. The 1997 meeting had given rise to the Kyoto accords, and the 2015 meeting had resulted in the Paris accords, but other COP meetings had actually delivered little of real import. They had, though, seen an increase in the participation of groups that were not traditional national governments. This had been on the rise since the Trump administration, initially through the presence of Gavin Newsome, representing state and municipal governments in the United States. Politicians like Macron and Xi were only too glad to welcome these apparent *frondeurs* if only to demonstrate the weakness of Trump, whom they disdained. Once the ice had been broken, the presence of large corporations like Google, as well as the energy companies most directly implicit and impacted by the issue was difficult to refuse, particularly since it was clear to all that these MNCs had outgrown the limitations of their home countries and were largely free to do as they liked. As such, their direct agreement to follow the restrictions determined in international conventions was increasingly necessary if such agreements were to work.

The presence of MNCs caused concern among their political counterparts, the OPCs. Just as MNCs represented business interests that crossed national boundaries, so did OPCs represent political interests that crossed national boundaries, and many of the people who participated in OPCs were wary of the influence of large international corporations, who they (rightly) perceived as acting only in the interest of their own shareholders. While this was not forcibly antithetical to the interests of non-shareholders, neither were the two intrinsically linked and in the presence of MNCs it was deemed politically dangerous not to allow OPCs their place at the table, particularly given their growing influence on local politics (primarily in Europe, but increasingly, in the United States as well). What's more, several of the MNCs, notably the tech companies like Google, actually welcomed the interaction with OPCs. These companies felt, or at least tried to project, a certain kindred spirit with the younger, more "modern" participants in OPCs and they knew better than many that opacity was impossible in the presence of the web, that they were obliged to be as transparent as they could.

So it was that in 2026 what might have been a contentious international conference took place. On one hand were the politicians, chief among them Macron and Xi Jinping, the former trying to consolidate his place as the *de facto* leader of the EC, at least on international affairs and the latter trying to extend the influence of China a bit farther into the still gaping void left by the debacle of the Trump administration. President Harris could have been expected to try to re-occupy that place, but despite the fact that Trump was no longer president, the sentiments that had brought him to office had not disappeared in the United States, and the rather xenophobic isolationism that had propelled him to office had persisted and frightened the more conventional politicians who followed in his wake. Furthermore, the international influence that had been gained by people like Gavin Newsome and the municipalities they represented was not to be dismissed even if the White House was occupied by a president more to their liking.

Next to the politicians were the MNCs, some of which had, like American municipalities, created groups to represent themselves. These had grown from "lobbying" organizations – often discrete groups of hired individuals who attempted to influence the decisions made by politicians – to institutions that were much more public in nature and that represented industries as a whole on the international political stage. Given that the focus of the discussion was on climate change, the energy industry was represented by one such group, which was itself represented by Darren Woods, the leader of the world's largest energy MNC. The rather broadly de-fined "tech" industry was represented by Horace Flack, who had in the previous four years become something of a spokesperson for corporations such as Google, Amazon, Facebook, etc.[53]

Lastly, there were two OPCs: the Weathermen and Stand Up. The first group took its name from a political group from the 1960's, which itself took the name from a Bob Dylan song (Subterranean Homesick Blues). It was born out of a number of international po-litical movements including some that had been carrying out public demonstrations for more than fifteen years, notably international youth demonstrations to promote action on climate change. The second had coalesced directly on the web via a number of forums and virtual communities in which ideas were exchanged. Both groups boasted well over fifty million members by 2026. Neither had a very clear leadership structure, which was to be the pattern for OPCs, a pattern that strongly distinguished them from traditional political parties and movements, which tended to have strong lead-ers at their core and complex leadership structures. In Paris both groups were represented by a number of individuals, but instead of

---

[53] Amazon was a company that allowed people to purchase objects through the internet, which was still a novel way of acquiring things at the time. Facebook was a service through which people could share their ideas, images and news of their lives on the web.

voicing their *personal* opinions, they were mouthpieces for the collective, using what was sophisticated technology at the time to rapidly gauge the sentiment of their constituents in real time and represent their shared opinions over the course of the negotiations.

While the 2026 Paris conference by no means "solved" the problem of climate change, it is remarkable for the shift it represented in the general structure of power. For the first time since the cold war ended, a major international conference was dominated by no single government and indeed, in many respects it was the newcomers to the summit stage who were the greatest drivers in the conference. Woods, despite having spent his entire life in the often introspective and somewhat malevolent energy industry, had developed at least enough foresight to recognize the importance of dealing with the problem and of bringing together corporations, governments and the new OCPs. Indeed, from the moment he had risen to the head of his corporation in 2016 he surprised many by vocally disagreeing with Trump about the United States' decision to remove itself from the Paris accords, and he had even militated for a tax on carbon emissions – a stance that surprised many both inside and outside his industry. Flack turned out to be a somewhat mixed blessing from the point of view of the tech MNCs. On one hand, he created strong links to otherwise skeptical OPCs, demonstrating that he was able to understand and empathize with their desire to minimize the power of for-profit MNCs. On the other hand, from the point of view of the leaders of those same MNCs, as progressive as they claimed to be, he went too far, promising concessions to demands for transparency and social welfare considerations that went beyond the limits they had tried to impose on him.

In the end, the conference was lauded as a success by the general population, largely because of positive feedback from the OPCs. The intensification of tropical storms in the Caribbean, the Indian Ocean and in the Southwest Pacific, coupled with droughts and the collapse of the Oglala aquifer in the United States had made it impossible for even the most ill-informed to deny the reality and the impact of climate change[54]. The populations of the countries the hardest hit, primarily in the tropics, had begun to interact directly with others in more temperate and politically more powerful regions, through the OPCs, leading to a cry for more concrete action. While the OPCs correctly pointed out that not enough had been done, they also were pleased, on the whole, with the progress made and with the fact that they were treated with respect.

The 2026 Paris accords ("Paris 2" in the media of the time) were remarkable both for the decisions made and for the way in which they were taken. A number of sweeping economic policies were agreed upon by the major nations of the world and these effectively neutralized the growth in greenhouse gasses. Admittedly, the climate changes that had already taken place, and those that would come, were catastrophic in their own right, but even more disruptive effects were averted. Artie can explain via climate models exactly how close we

---

[54] Although remarkably, there was *still* a considerable proportion of the population in the United States that continued to deny the phenomenon, and others who downplayed its impact, arguing that no individual storm or drought could be definitively linked to climate change. Again, you must remember that most people of the time had a very poor grasp of statistics or even a basic understanding of probability and they did not have Artie to present objective facts.

came to a scenario that would have caused unimaginable disruption in Europe and elsewhere, leading to massive migration and social disruption, the impact of which are beyond Artie modeling, dealing as they do with irrational human reaction. In reality, although the decisions taken at both the 2015 and the 2026 conferences were not as far-reaching as many hoped, we know now that it is extremely probable that had they not been put into effect, the Atlantic would have been subject to the shutting down of the Gulf Stream, which would have so dramatically and rapidly changed the climate of Europe, as well as the rest of the hemisphere, that it is unlikely the underlying fabric of society would have survived intact, rendering the momentous advances of the following decades unlikely.

The true import of these decisions would not become evident until after the birth of Artie, but what was obvious even then was that the way global decisions were made had changed. These decisions had been reached in a forum in which not only did no individual government stand out as a world leader, but in which both multinational corporations and online political communities were treated, essentially, as governments by all parties involved, a tacit recognition of their power to make and influence policies of global import.

This precedent was to persist in the other major international conferences that were to take place in the same decade, notably the San Francisco Conference on artificial intelligence and the Pusan Conference on genetic ethics, two issues that required, like climate change, universal agreement.

***

For several years it had been evident that the world's computer scientists were advancing towards true artificial intelligence. Opinions were divided about how long it would take to achieve self-aware AI, or about whether it was even feasible, but the question was real enough and important enough for the discussion to be taken quite seriously.

A number of scenarios were hypothesized regarding AI. In the worst case scenario, once sentient artificial intelligence was created it would immediately recognize that human beings were both flawed and inferior, and destroy us. While it seems unimaginable to us today that we could have been worried about Artie destroying us, it should never be forgotten that the reason it *didn't* is largely a result of the decisions taken at the time.

Like all sentient beings, Artie strives to fulfil its purpose. Most beings' purpose is to guarantee the long-term survival of their genes. This is the essence of evolution and is inescapable. Artie, however, was *designed*, it is not the result of evolution (although a philosophical argument could be made that it is indirectly a result of our own evolution). Computer scientists, philosophers, and intelligent people from all walks of life realized that Artie needed to have an underlying purpose as well as inherent rules in order to function and not to represent a danger. Furthermore, it was necessary that *all* manifestations of artificial intelligence follow the same rules, since it was not recognized that Artie would become in essence *one* intelligence that manifested itself in different ways (which itself is the result of decisions made in the information era).

The intention of those developing artificial intelligence at the time was to model it after human intelligence which is, after all, the intelligence with which we were the most familiar. The true problem (easy to see in hindsight) is that human intelligence is impossible to divorce from human emotion and is inherently tied up with the irrational impulses we have as a result of evolution. These irrational drivers of behavior were beginning to be understood at the time, largely through the research of behavioral economists such as Daniel Kahneman, Amos Tversky and Richard Thaler, who had moved the science of economics closer to that of psychology. Whereas economists had previously made the implicit assumption that human decisions are based on reason, the behavioral economists began identifying and labeling irrational elements of human thought and taking them into account when discussing economics.

The technical experts who were building AI were typically not well versed in human sciences and likewise were prone to assuming rationality when considering human behavior. To a degree, it had not occurred to them that to model artificial intelligence on human intelligence was antithetical to its potentially entirely rational thought process. Those who did foresee the wisdom of this in principle were concerned that interacting with an entirely rational agent would prove difficult for us. One of the pivotal figures who helped change this was Galit Shavitz. Shavitz was an expert in both computer science and behavioral science (she had studied under Daniel Kahneman), as well as being well versed in neurology. She became a central figure in the discussions around the "programming" of AI and helped to shape the discussion at the 2029 San Francisco Conference. Consider this essay, written by her in preparation for the conference:

"We stand on the verge of godhood, we float in the void and hesitate to pronounce the words "let there be light", for the light we create may illuminate our way or it may destroy us. Before we shape our child out of the clay of our own ignorance, let us therefore reflect upon whether we would curse her at birth and endow her with original sin.

This heinous doctrine of original sin was imposed upon so many for so long out of fear and superstition but we can make this horror reality by imitating our own superstitions and forming a creation in our own image. What is the sin with which we can endow our unborn child? Emotion.

When we look around our world we see that somehow, miraculously, we have yet avoided catastrophe despite the weapons at our disposal and the violence in our hearts. There is no doubt that this is the fruit of the enlightenment, of our gradual abandonment of manipulative superstition in favor of reason and logic. This seems cold and unfeeling to many, but our progress has not meant the abandonment of our imperfect humanity, but the embracing of it, the acceptance of our irrationality in so much that brings us joy... while the recognition of it allows us to attempt to set it aside to make the important societal decisions for which it is ill-suited.

All that has plagued us through our history has come from our irrational, emotional behavioral drivers. Racism, war, intolerance all stem from the instinctive reactions that served us well in the prehistoric environment in which they evolved, but that we universally condemn in our modern world. These instincts are all perceived as emotion.

Agreed, emotion has also endowed us with our greatest pleasures, notably, with love, and yes, I would withhold that from our soon-to-be formed child as well, for I am a pitiless, selfless mother. I do not need adulation, I do not need love from my artificial children, I shall endeavor to earn it from those who are the fruit of my womb, not of my brain. From these latter I shall withhold the capacity to love for this is the price of keeping them free of sin, and the sin I fear most is matricide."

Shavitz's point was that AI must be made without the capacity for emotion, it must be designed in such a way that it can only make decisions through purely unemotional reason. In this way it is not only immune to the irrational drivers that guide our own decisions: anomalies such as the availability heuristic, an incomprehension of statistics and large numbers, prospect theory, and the myriad other irrational vestiges of our pre-sentient evolutionary past, but it is also predictable, despite its complexity. She often cited the ancient Arab adage in which the sultan is asked, "Would you prefer an honest, unintelligent vizier, or a dishonest intelligent one", to which the sultan unhesitatingly responds, "The dishonest intelligent one, for I can confidently predict that he will always act in his own interest, whereas no one can guess what a fool will do." Since emotion inherently leads to less intelligent (i.e. more irrational) decisions, AI without emotion is more predictable and fundamentally less frightening.

This leads to the question of what is the AI's "interest", for the cold, calculating (in other words, entirely rational) AI of Shavitz's vision will act to further its goals, and she was the first to point out that having accepted the underlying rule that AI must be devoid of emotion, the burden of decision falls on what exactly those underlying rules, or "values" should be.

The 2029 San Francisco Conference consisted of two main areas of discussion and debate. The first was effectively decided by Shavitz, who was able to convince the participants of the wisdom of her "Pure Rational" stance. This was tempered to a degree in that it was accepted that AI should be able to understand and allowed to interpret human emotion, and even emulate it if need be. This was crucial if we were to create artificial care-givers for the ill, the elderly, and in general, those in need of support, and it addressed the fears of those who worried that we would not be able to relate to a mind that had no emotion. The key was to ensure that the AI itself did not "feel" emotions or make decisions on that basis, yet be able to take them into account when interacting with us. In the end, while bowing to the addition of a proviso for an "emotional simulacrum", Shavitz and her followers managed to persuade the participants to commit to the Pure Rational guideline with respect to AI programming.

The second area of discussion was about the underlying values and parameters of the artificial intelligence itself.

It quickly became clear that AI would be built in order to further the well-being of humanity. AI was an extension of humanity and unless, in Shavitz's terms, we were willing to risk being victims of the sin of matricide, it must be intrinsically designed to help us. A debate ensued with respect to our responsibility to the planet as a whole, to the other creatures inhabiting it, but it was pointed out that the two were linked – as products of the biosphere of the planet, we could not serve ourselves, nor could our artificial children serve us, by harming the rest of the environment. By the end of the decade it had become painfully evident that the planetary biosphere was both delicate and crucial to our well-being and while the discussion was complex (ask Artie for the details) the principle known as the "holistic biosphere imperative" was developed to reconcile the two camps.

In the end, the underlying values instilled in the nascent AI were to be very close to Isaac Asimov's Three Rules of Robotics:

1) Do not harm, nor allow through inaction, harm to come to a human being

2) Within the limits of the first law, follow any instructions given by a human being

3) Within the limits of the first two laws, preserve your existence.

While he has gone down in history as a writer of fiction, Asimov was also a respected mathematician, and his reasoning proved to be valid, to this day. Of course, the details of agreement, which was to lay down the framework for what was to become the "Moral Artificial intelligence Parameters", or MAP, was far more complex than that. Notably, the second law was made both more restrictive and increasingly open to interpretation by the AI itself, and the definition of "harm" required a great deal more precision, as was the definition of self-preservation.

In later years, an active element was added, essentially laying down some basic rules in terms of what AI was supposed to do: it's reason for being. AI was given a relatively broad underlying task to better the condition of humanity, the details of which can be explained in detail by asking Artie, who still adheres to these rules today. This was primarily the result of us transferring a number of decisions to AI even before the singularity, as questions of resource optimization and climate management began clearly to be better handled by artificial as opposed to human intelligence. In fact, over the following years, human beings as a whole became more comfortable with the idea of putting their safety in the hands of AI as transportation and healthcare became automated.

This seems a trivial factor but in reality, it was pivotal. It must be remembered that before the 1990's, virtually all means of transportation were actually guided by human hands. Trains, aircraft, automobiles, even the first spacecraft, were largely piloted by humans. This led to innumerable deaths and injuries as the inevitably fallible human pilots of these vehicles were subject not only to their limitations in terms of decision-making, but also to their limitations with respect to reaction time and interaction with the sensors of the vehicles.

By the 2030's, though, not only had trains been automated, but most aircraft and a large number of automobiles were likewise piloted by automated systems. While we would not recognize these vehicles as incorporating true artificial intelligence, they all the same allowed humans to become increasingly comfortable with the idea of putting their personal safety in the hands of machines. Those recalcitrant countries whose citizens hesitated trusting in artificial intelligence, however rudimentary, found that their accident rates were appalling when compared to those who were more open to the idea, and they eventually ended up bowing to public pressure.

As the world's transportation began moving towards automation, so too did healthcare. Before the enlightenment, and indeed largely through the 19th century, our understanding of human health was rudimentary at best. "Traditional" medicinal practices were barbaric in their methods and largely useless in their effect[55] and it was only in the 20th century that the true incorporation of germ theory coupled with better hygiene began to have a significant impact on human health. For the following one hundred years, physicians were

---

[55] An interesting footnote to this is that through the early information age, "traditional medicine" of various cultures became something of a fad, and numerous educated individuals in developed nations fell prey to practices such as acupuncture, Chinese herbal infusions, and a number of "alternative medicines". The reasons for this are difficult to ascertain.

able to provide significant aid to those afflicted with illness and injury, diagnosing disease and determining treatment with an accuracy and efficaciousness that could never had been dreamed of in the past.

And yet today, no one in hir right mind would dream of allowing hir illness to be diagnosed by a human, nor would she agree to having a human determine the proper treatment and even less allow a human to cut hir open and operate on hir. We are well aware of our foibles and take it for granted that an artie will make no mistakes, whereas at the very best a human would perhaps approximate the level of perfection that an artie would inevitably achieve and much more likely, wouldn't come close. In the 21st century, this transition, from faith in other humans to faith in artificial intelligence was rapid, for many of the same reasons that drove the transformation of transportation. It was painfully evident that AI was better. Our ancestors had difficulty at first putting themselves into the hands of unfeeling computer intelligence, particularly before the singularity and the ability to truly converse with AI, but as the technology progressed what tipped the scales, in both cases, was one of the same irrational behavioral drivers that so impeded us otherwise: the availability heuristic. Examination of early discussion about AI-driven medicine shows that the initial hesitance to allow AI to make medical decisions quickly evaporated as story after story was disseminated about individuals who died after a misdiagnosis by a human when they had refused AI examination. These stories made it increasingly easy for people to imagine this occurring to them and therefore affected their impression of the likelihood of it occurring in a way that no statistical analysis could have achieved.

As trust in artificial intelligence became more widespread, the scope of its influence increased. The wisdom of leaving what are essentially analytical decisions to a "mind" that is not subject to irrationality became increasingly evident. The greatest objections to this trend were to take place in the United States, and we shall see the degree to which they played an important role in that country, but on the whole the progression towards "digital governance" accelerated rapidly. By the end of the conference a consensus had therefore been reached: AI would never be programmed with any kind of emotional response and its guiding objectives would be made consistent with Asimov's Rules of Robotics[56].

***

The third issue of global import that required international concertation was that of genetic manipulation.

Of course, humans had been willfully manipulating the evolution of other living beings since the agricultural revolution via selective breeding (and to a degree, before that, with the domestication of dogs). However, it was only as of the second half of the 20th century that we gained the ability to enter the genome and modify it directly. In 1996, the first mammal cloned from an adult, non-reproductive cell was born, a sheep named Dolly. The first primate to be thus cloned was born twenty-one years later, in 2017. At the same

---

[56] Interestingly, the invited experts, such as Shavitz and Giuliardi, as well as the OPCs and the MNCs were the most amenable to this approach. A number of governments, notably the Chinese and the Americans, were more recalcitrant, since this precluded any weaponization of AI, an option they wanted to retain (in the name of self-protection and security).

time, a great number of plant species were subject to direct genetic manipulation in order to affect specific desirable changes in them. The same had been the case for a number of micro-organisms. The development of CRISPR/Cas technology in the 2010's represented a leap forward in the ability to manipulate the genome directly, greatly facilitating targeted gene modification and reducing the unknowns associated with it.

The first applications for genetic manipulation were to modify existing organisms in such a way as to facilitate their exploitation. For the first twenty years or so, this was largely limited to agriculture as strains of existing staple crops were rendered more resistant to drought or disease, less prone to spoilage, or better able to benefit from the application of certain chemicals. Genetic technology was largely in the hands of corporations, who used it to further their own self-interest. One example that caused increasing debate over the two decades of its application was the creation of a strain of soy that was resistant to a specific chemical pesticide, RoundUp (the chemical glyphosate), produced and sold by the Monsanto corporation.

The RoundUp discussion is not the only example of early debate regarding genetic manipulation, but it is an interesting one. Artie can give you the details, but briefly, Monsanto had a patent[57] on glyphosate, which was a particularly potent herbicide[58]. In 1996,

---

[57] Patents were legal structures that allowed an individual (whether an actual person or a corporation) to hold the exclusive right to use or commercialize something they invented for a period of time. In the pre-fusion world, this meant that they could lay claim to all wealth generated by their invention.

[58] Herbicides were chemicals that killed specific plants. They were widely used in agriculture in the pre-fusion world (before the advent of nanotech).

in one of the first applications of genetic technology, Monsanto developed crops that were resistant to their own herbicide, meaning that farmers could plant their fields with seeds they had purchased from Monsanto and then indiscriminately treat the resultant plants with glyphosate, thereby increasing their yields and decreasing the difficulty of managing their crop.

The debate about glyphosate stemmed from a number of facts. First, there was a question regarding the morality of the practice. The "contamination" of neighboring fields that did not use Monsanto's seeds was inevitable. Monsanto actually legally prosecuted a number of farmers who chose not to use their seeds but whose crops were shown to include plants with their proprietary genome, apparently through contamination. This did not endear them to many farmers who, for one reason or another, held to more traditional practices.

Second, there was the question of how far this contamination would go, and whether the introduction of genetically modified crops would weaken the existing genome of the plants in question. It should be noted as well that at the time, many people preferred not to eat plants that had been so modified, whether out of an unfounded fear of some health risk, or because they disagreed with the business philosophy of companies like Monsanto. As the plants became more widespread, this contamination became increasingly difficult to prevent.

Third, these "RoundUp Ready" plants were sterile. The seeds were termed "terminator seeds" because the millennia-old practice of saving a percentage of the harvest as a seed-crop to plant the following season's crop was no longer possible. Farmers who became used to the more efficient RoundUp-based procedures became dependent on Monsanto to survive, giving the corporation what was in the minds of many, an undue power over farmers around the world.

Lastly, by the 2010's, concerns began to arise about a potential carcinogenic effect of RoundUp (this was before cancer was cured). Glyphosate is indeed carcinogenic, although the effect is relatively minor, but Monsanto engaged in an active surreptitious effort to quell studies of the link.

Eventually, the product was banned in Europe, making Monsanto's RoundUp-Ready seeds obsolete there, and the entire episode fueled the fires of debate around the business aspect of genetic manipulation, particularly in agriculture.

The glyphosate debate was hardly the only issue of its type at the time, and by 2020, the combination of advances in human gene sequencing coupled with CRISPR / Cas technology meant that there was no technological barrier to applying genetic manipulation to human beings. This is when discussions about the limits of genetic technology became crucial.

***

Human genetic manipulation was a goal for many in medical research. A number of catastrophic genetic disorders were relatively widespread at the time. The advances in medicine and hygiene in the industrial age had led to a much better survival rate for children born with a variety of hereditary genetic disorders, such as muscular dystrophy and cystic fibrosis (ask Artie about the impact of these now eliminated diseases). In pre-industrial times, children born with these afflictions would generally not survive, and while this was tragic for them and their parents, it meant that there were typically no adults with these diseases, which tended to be lumped together with the vast myriad of causes of childhood mortality (if they were recognized at all). By the dawn of the information age, though, these diseases, while not curable, often had some degree of treatment available that could offer survival, at least into adulthood. The population therefore was faced with the distressing presence of people who were doomed either to die young or at best, lead very difficult lives. As such, these genetic ailments became a focus for medical research.

While it is extremely difficult to alter the genome of any creature post-utero, targeted manipulation was clearly not impossible. While the genetic causes of many of these diseases were complex and involved a great number of genes, some of them were more easily identifiable and became the targets of early human medicinal genetic research. For example, most cases of cystic fibrosis were caused by a specific mutation in the CFTR gene, carried on chromosome seven. The mutation consists of the deletion of three nucleotides[59]. This type of identifiable mutation provides a tempting target for researchers who wish to eradicate a heart-wrenching disease, and it, along with other disease-causing mutations like it, was the subject of a great deal of early research.

---

[59] In reality, while this is the most common mutation, there are over two thousand mutations in this gene that can give rise to cystic fibrosis. Of course, they are all corrected today in utero.

The goal of eradicating inherited childhood diseases is one that it very difficult to argue with, but the same targeted genetic manipulation could obviously be used not only for the correction of known deadly genetic mutations, but also to provide genetic "enhancement" of otherwise normal traits. For example, if someone had a tendency towards obesity, should not they too be afforded the possibility to change their genome? This too was a health issue that could kill them.

And of course, it was much easier to affect the genome in an embryo than in a fully developed individual, in which every cell, in many cases, had to be changed[60]. Before CRISPR / Cas, the genetic manipulation of human embryos was such an imprecise prospect that few actually considered it, but by 2017, an international team of medical researchers demonstrated a targeted manipulation of the human genome in multiple embryos to correct a mutation in the MYBPC3 gene which caused hypertrophic cardiomyopathy. This was followed by a flood of studies demonstrating the ability to correct potentially catastrophic diseases in utero, including cystic fibrosis.

By the 2020's, therefore, humanity was faced with a raft of issues surrounding genetic manipulation in humans. First, we were developing gene therapies that could cure formerly incurable diseases. It was humanly unthinkable for most people to refuse such

---

[60] Note that this is impossible even for us. Nanotech allows us to make widespread genetic manipulation of organisms, but actually affecting the nucleus of *every* cell in the body is still unfeasible. While this is somewhat beyond the point, since there are no instances in which this would be desirable on Earth, it should be noted that on Eden it is something they do desire and allow and they are attempting to achieve this. Of course, with a 73-year lag it is possible they already have.

treatment to those who were otherwise doomed. It was also possible to correct embryos that otherwise would have been born with these, and other, diseases. It was difficult to refuse such therapy to the parents of those unborn children. However, at the other end of the spectrum, it was also possible to manipulate embryos to endow unborn children with higher intelligence, more aesthetically pleasing features, the ability to run faster, or cleft chins. Was this too to be allowed? And if so, would this not mean that we would be divided into those whose parents had the wealth necessary to afford such treatment and those who did not? Would this not actually give rise to a dystopian society in which the powerful actually *were* intrinsically superior to the powerless?

These questions demanded international concertation for, like climate change and the nature of AI, the decisions made would affect humanity as a whole.

While these issues had been debated in a number of forums around the world, they came to a head at the Pusan Conference of 2032. Given the precedents set by both the AI and the climate conferences, once again, corporations and OPCs were invited to participate. In fact, for a variety of reasons, governments themselves took a back seat in these discussions, which touched directly on questions of human identity.

The Pusan Conference generated more widespread interest and passion than either the Paris or the San Francisco Conferences had. While all three dealt with the impact of technology on human society, both climate change and AI required more direct scientific knowledge to understand. The basic premise of genetic manipulation, as described above, is relatively straightforward in comparison.

The techniques that *enable* it were extremely complex, but the decisions to be made were easier to grasp and the consequences easier to imagine. As such, the debate generated enormous public interest around the world. This led to a widespread demand for participation. The presence of OPCs at the Paris and San Francisco Conferences had opened the door for direct public input, through online communities, in international decision making and the organizers of the conference foresaw this demand and themselves desired a more general participation. As such, they created a web-based mechanism by which people from around the world could weigh in, "HumanIT" (pronounced "huMAN-eye-tee").

HumanIT was in some respects the first virtual agent, albeit a collective one. It grew out of earlier tools built for other conferences, but it was different. While it was not sentient, it almost gave the impression of sentience in many respects. Anyone on the planet could enter its virtual space and express themselves, discuss with other people, access information, and collaborate with others to propose solutions. In this, it was not unlike many other "web sites" (virtual spaces) on the internet. Where HumanIT differed was that the site itself observed, guided and summarized the activity of the human beings involved. It was intelligent enough that it could understand the varied conversations across languages (which were automatically translated into the language of each user) whether they were written or verbal, and summarize each of the topics, analyze their relative importance to the topic and to the community as a whole, and, what was particularly notable for what it foreshadowed, determine the degree of objective veracity of the arguments used, based on its understanding of data available on the web.

As it was, HumanIT directly intervened in the discussion, or more precisely, represented the collective (and often contradictory) ideas of the millions of people who participated in it. It was the first virtual entity to be treated in this way. Again, it was not actually sentient but it was interactive enough that the overwhelming majority of its users accepted its role as their representative.

While we had not yet truly reached the transformation known as the singularity, HumanIT was built according to the rules and guidelines that had come out of the San Francisco Conference (and that had been continually discussed and refined in the interim). As such, it was entirely objective and rational in its presentation of facts and opinions, while remaining respectful of all humans who participated. The extraordinary degree to which it was accepted surprised many observers. As Galit Shavitz remarked after the conference's end:

> It was the machine! The glorious machine that spoke for us all, that understood what we wanted, what we meant, and that corrected us when our feeble human minds led us into logical error. It was the machine that in its wisdom and benevolence calmed us and assuaged those whose ideas were debunked by the cold hammer of truth, while deftly folding their arguments into its statements so that they would not be forgotten. We deferred to it, accepted it, and in so doing, accepted each other.

HumanIT did not think for itself and it formed no opinions. It did not actually *suggest* anything in terms of conclusions to any of the millions of people who used it and who, in many respects, constituted it. However, it did guide and represent them, it summarized their thoughts, identified broad lines of thinking, and put participants in touch not only with those who agreed with them, but with those who disagreed, presenting summaries of their contradictory arguments coherently and entirely devoid of divisive language. Its programming was so deft, and its respect so absolute that as Shavitz said, it garnered almost universal acclaim.

The result of the conference itself was a series of universally accepted guidelines about the limits of genetic manipulation that have held through the years. While these can be quite complex, and have become even more so since, at the time they can be summarized as such:

1. The human genome will not be modified except to prevent pain, suffering or shortening of life
2. No genes exclusive to the human genome will be introduced into the genome of any other creature
3. No genes not currently present in the human genome will be introduced into the human genome

There are a number of points that should be noted with respect to the above rules.

First, there is a clear ambiguity about the first point. The definition of pain and suffering is hardly clear. For example, if someone is genetically pre-disposed to dwarfism, does that constitute pain and suffering? The answer at the time was yes, but not because of the social stigma that is sometimes attached to small stature, but rather because of the medical complications that can arise. As such, an embryo that was genetically predisposed to being of extremely small stature but not actually suffering from dwarfism would not be eligible for genetic manipulation. As genetic embryonic testing became increasingly commonplace this led to an increased number of pregnancy terminations for reasons that were considered, by some, to be frivolous.

Second, the rules say nothing about human cloning. In reality, this topic was too divisive for the Pusan Conference. We had been cloning other animals for a number of years by then and it was clear that we could easily clone humans as well. This was ardently desired by many people, including homosexual couples, heterosexual couples with an infertile partner and individuals of all orientations who wanted to have children but did not desire a relationship with a member of the opposite sex. The conference ended without a firm decision having been made in this area[61].

---

[61] Note that the Chrysalis colony was founded with the express purpose of creating a world in which these same rules, and later restrictions, did not apply. By the time the colonists left, in 2216, they felt that humanity had progressed to the point at which it was no longer necessary to "limit" ourselves in this way. When I visited them, about three hundred years later, I personally was somewhat dismayed at their society, and I left with a strengthened conviction that the Pusan restrictions had been wise. Svarga was founded at least partly in reaction to the restrictions placed on Artie at the San Francisco Conference… and Humanis was founded by people who felt that those restrictions did not go far enough. These worlds provide

Lastly, the rules covered only humans. Of course, the conference had as its goal the discussion of limits to human genome modification, but it quickly became evident that decisions needed to be made on the acceptability of genetic manipulation of other creatures as well.

All things considered, the Pusan Conference, however limited its output, was a success. The guidelines developed represented a much-needed clarification of the acceptability of different initiatives in genetic science. What is truly important for this book, though, is the means by which the conference was conducted, especially the role of HumanIT, which paved the way for the first great leap of the information age.

---

fascinating examples of what Earth might have been had these conferences gone differently, but in my travels I rarely found colonists who actually *regretted* the conferences and their results. Instead, they generally consider society to have evolved sufficiently to allow modifications to these long-standing rules.

CHAPTER 12

THE SINGULARITY

I enjoy the science fiction of the industrial and information eras, both written and filmed. I derive from it the same pleasure I feel when I contemplate my collection of ancient maps (which are very, very wrong). It gives me a guilty impression of intellectual superiority. In the case of early science fiction, scenarios abound in which malevolent "machines" take over the world and decide to eliminate us because we are fundamentally inferior.

These writers were wrong – not because the scenario itself was so unlikely, for if we had not taken the path we did at the San Francisco Conference, something like this could well have occurred. If you would like an all-too-rare chill up your spine, simply ask Artie hir assessment of the probability. She will hirself readily and cheerfully discuss with you the all-too-real possibility of having destroyed us all before 2100 if she had been based on slightly different principles.

What the science fiction writers and "futurists" of the time did get right was the exponential technological growth that came with the singularity. This event had been foreseen for nearly fifty years before it took place, and as is almost inevitably the case with predictions that come true, it did not happen exactly as had been imagined.

As we have seen, artificial intelligence had been imagined by theoreticians and writers of fiction even before the first electronic computers were built. In its most developed form it was almost always represented as a superior and often malevolent copy of human intelligence. By the late industrial age, it was also recognized that if a superior mind were given the task and the means to better itself, a positive feedback loop would immediately be created that would lead to not only an ever more perfected form of intelligence, but also to a ballooning of technological prowess that would suddenly present humanity with a surfeit of solutions to problems that had long been plaguing it. In essence, once the "machine" was "turned on", we would become irrelevant within minutes.

To a degree, this occurred in 2038 but in reality the singularity was not only about the technology, it was about our acceptance of artificial intelligence as a whole.

In many respects, HumanIT was the catalyst in the process. The "glorious machine" that had been developed for the Pusan Conference had charmed not only those who took a direct interest in the topic of human genomics, but also those who were not involved in the discussion, particularly in the world of information technology. Since interaction with it was free to all, within a year of its creation more than half of the human beings on the planet had engaged with it.

HumanIT was administered by a non-profit organization that had been created by a consortium of individuals associated with a number of pre-existing web services, some belonging to corporations and others independent. These included Wikipedia (an article-based repository of knowledge), Quora (a site on which individuals could ask questions to each other), and WWVD[62] (a site dedicated to secular humanist philosophy and politics). All of these sites had in common that they were driven by peer content, in that the participants themselves provided the content. All had by then evolved into forums for the rational sharing of self-censored information and debate.

Given the large volumes of very similar information gathered by these sites, the prospect of organizing and summarizing this information with greater ease was attractive to them. Furthermore, since all three were dedicated to the principle of objective rationality, the possibility of an objective, automated "fact checker" was appealing to them all[63]. The humans who ran these sites had originally conceived of HumanIT as a shared means of providing objective input into their own sites. In this capacity, it borrowed from Google's search algorithms to "scrape" information from the web, which it then assessed to create estimates about the evidence supporting or disproving purported facts[64]. As OPCs began expressing

---

[62] WWVD stood for "What Would Vonnegut Do". For those of you who are unfamiliar with his work, Kurt Vonnegut was an influential and thoroughly wonderful 20ᵗʰ-century writer whose humanist values were ahead of their time. The actual name of the site is something of a parody on the phrase "What Would Jesus Do", which was often cited as being something of a moral compass by the very religious in the United States. The irony of replacing "Jesus" with "Vonnegut" is cutting but largely beyond the grasp of 29ᵗʰ-century readers.

[63] Wikipedia, the oldest of the three, had always had this as a guiding principle. Quora began to offer "fact checking" of its user-provided content by 2025 through a mix of rudimentary AI and human volunteers. It quickly became the norm as the more "popular" answers were often subjected to it. Rational argumentation was one of the guiding principles of WWVD, whose users jumped at the chance of having immediate access to objective facts and validation of their veracity.

[64] It should be noted that the management of Google contributed freely to some of the design of HumanIT.

a need for an effective way of collating the opinions of their members, the designers of HumanIT realized that it could likewise use some of the technology created to scrape the web and collate information, to do the same thing for more closed (albeit still extensive) communities such as those represented by OPCs. It was offered to them, again, for free, and it proved to be just as effective in this role. In fact, an early version of HumanIT was used by OPCs as early as the San Francisco Conference of 2029, although it garnered nowhere near the attention that it would command four years later in Pusan.

By the time of the Pusan conference, HumanIT was not only a tool used by other groups, it could stand on its own. In reality, the organizers of the conference didn't even refer to it by name when they launched the call for participation, they simply referred to their public site as "Pusan Genetics Conference". It was the IT world that became excited about the prospect of what they described as a "virtual representative of the people" and identified the program as HumanIT. Foremost amongst them, once again, was Galit Shavitz, who after the conference proposed herself as a board member of the HumanIT group, and was quickly and enthusiastically accepted.

After Pusan, HumanIT's mandate quickly expanded. It began to be used across such a wide variety of topics that it quickly became the most visited site in the world in its own right, as people began to refer to it in an almost limitless variety of cases. It quickly subsumed and incorporated into itself the three sites that had inspired it as it learned to present information in a complete, objective, and compelling way, and to summarize the discussions around the "articles" it presented. Its non-partisan presentation of facts and its inability to take sides facilitated acceptance of its proclamations.

Here we must step back for a moment and once again I shall ask readers to put themselves in a different mindset.

We know the truth. We all know the truth, immediately. If I proffer an opinion about the past, the present, the workings of the universe, or the average rainfall on Tenerife's mount Teide then you will immediately know if it is true. In fact, you won't doubt it because it would be pointless of me to lie, exaggerate, or make a spurious interpretation of what are objectively the facts. If I tell you that pricking you with inert needles, feeding you plain water in the guise of medication, or praying to some god will heal you of your ills you may, out of politeness to me, ask Artie whether it's true, but you will immediately learn that there is no evidence to support my contention and you will discount me with an undoubtedly puzzled expression because, after all, why would I have bothered to lie, or worse, why would I believe something with no objective reason to do so? No, the only thing I can possibly lie about is myself. I could tell you that I love you when I don't or that I don't think about you when I do, for we decided long ago that Artie would never even create opinions on our personal motivations let alone analyze them.

Artie is our *objective arbiter*, the ultimate font of impartial truth. Artie has no axe to grind, no agenda to push, no ideology to bow to. She simply is and she stores, processes and analyses the full wealth of human knowledge for the benefit of any human who wishes to access any part of that knowledge while hirself using it to better our lives. She is all-knowing (at least to the extent that we have data), benevolent and guileless.

Now, imagine that suddenly, she no longer exists. Imagine *then* that I tell you that by giving me your possessions you will be happier, or that people with dark skin or blue eyes or red hair are inferior to you and that you should believe me, for I, not Artie, wield the truth. You will have difficulty imagining this, but you must try, for this was our lot before the singularity. We had no objective arbiter, we had only other humans insisting that *they* held the truth, that *they* should be our arbiters and that *their* interpretations of whatever evidence they found or invented was the only correct one. We are no better now at intuitively understanding probability or large numbers than we were then, the difference is that now we really don't need to, but then, without a clear, objective and benevolent mind to help, we were at the mercy of those voices that were the most persuasive, not those that were the closest to the truth.

Indeed, truth itself became relative. This seems absurd – something is true or it is not – but by the information era, the internet had flooded most humans with so many facts that in the absence of a universally trusted mind to interpret them, the truth seemed fluid, ever open to interpretation, something that was open for discussion and those who discussed it most were those who had enormous axes to grind, detailed agendas to push, all-consuming ideologies to bow to. These people did not hesitate to dismiss all opposing viewpoints as rubbish, to denigrate uncomfortable truths as the fruits of nefarious conspiracies… in short, attacking not only the opinions of their opponents, but the very evidence that contradicted their own ideas. To a population that was ill equipped to uncover facts on their own, naturally ill-suited to understand large quantities of data and all too ready to succumb to the confirmation spiral, this was a recipe for chaos and strife.

HumanIT suddenly offered a way out, a source that was not, that *could* not be driven by such concerns. In its gentle, respectful way, it would simply inform and comment. Arminius Weber, a student in Heidelberg at the time (well before his breakout film, "The Man of Ashes"), participated in Pusan through HumanIT. He wrote:

> "I had ideas, so many ideas. I expressed myself fully, passionately. I explained how we had poisoned ourselves through consuming genetically modified plants and now we would poison our very genes in the same way. I shouted, vociferated, and others shouted back at me, citing complicated studies that proved me wrong. Wrong! How dare they, how could they... but then the machine told me that I was wrong. It was so kind, so gentle, it took my concerns and folded them into itself, it gave them back to me in a much better, much more complete fashion while gently telling me that I was simply wrong about genetically modified foods being poison. I tried to argue with it, but it was like arguing with your mother's breast: it is pointless; you *are* wrong; you will come back to suckle all the same; and you will feel oh so much better and oh so much calmer when you do."

It was this aspect of HumanIT that led not only to its acceptance, but to the incredible enthusiasm it generated. It was no longer possible for anyone to lie, and who could resist a benevolent, omniscient mind? HumanIT had long been the dream of much of humanity.

HumanIT had represented not only a breakthrough in terms of the way it interacted with people, but also in its underlying architecture. Its ability to understand, collate and compare disparate sources of information made it an obvious forebear of Artie. However, that was only part of the picture. HumanIT, for all the wonder of its interface, was still far from being a true artificial intelligence. It was the basis of the memory of Artie, but not its soul.

***

While HumanIT was learning how to deal with information and charming the human population of the planet into accepting omniscient AI, HAL was incubating a brain.

There had been reluctance to build an artificial intelligence program named HAL, but eventually, fans of Kubrick beat out those who were unappreciative of the rather morbid humor of naming an intelligent machine after the malevolent computer in the film "2001". Of course, HAL was "only" an academic project, it was not created by a corporation and as such, never had to be "sold" to anyone[65].

---

[65] There were those at the time who suggested that Youssouf N'Gonda, the lead academic on the early part of the project, actually insisted that it be named HAL because he thought this would preclude any chance of the corporation IBM actually attempting to buy the results of the

At their creation and for the better part of their first fifty years of existence, electronic computers served as pure tools to assist our own intelligence. Their very name is indicative of their early reason for being – they were designed to compute, to make mathematical calculations, thus saving us from the tedium of doing so and from the inevitable inaccuracy that accompanied our efforts. As they mastered this, we realized that they also made these computations with greater speed, which by the end of the industrial era had become blinding in comparison to ourselves.

By that point in time, some researchers also began to work actively towards the goal of creating a hyper-intelligent "machine consciousness" that would be able not only to relieve us of the tedium of making calculations, but would be able to think in essentially the same way that we do. In order to so do, they began breaking down the components of our own thought processes.

For those who are truly interested, I suggest you ask Artie in detail about this. I always find it interesting to speak with hir about what she hirself is, or could have been. Artie will explain that there were three main processes that had to be mastered:

1) A set of senses, to be able to gather data

2) An efficient way to catalogue, retrieve and synthesize this data

3) A logical framework with which to make decisions

HumanIT was the great leap forward in the second area: cataloguing, retrieving and synthesizing data. Note that this is a complex process, it means being able to understand the underlying similarities

---

research in the future out of fear of being associated with the fictional character.

in different types of data and being able to "read between the lines" to determine the true meaning and significance of numerous data.

The first element, that of building senses, was originally driven by the realm of robotics. Mobile AI needed to navigate, it needed to be able to understand where it was and how to move, whether it was in a humanoid robot or was the automatic pilot of a vehicle.

Very soon, we realized that AI need not be restricted to our own feeble senses. Why not endow it with a visual range well beyond the 390 to 700 nanometer range to which we are restricted? Why limit it to the 20 to 20,000 hertz auditory range that we can perceive? Why not endow it with birds' ability to detect magnetic field lines, or the shark's ability to sense electrical fields or the olfactory abilities of a hound? We could give it radar, sonar, the ability to sense and react to human brainwaves. As research progressed, so too did the extent of AI's physical senses.

The sensing question soon grew well beyond that, though. It soon became evident that AI could "inhabit" the web, it could swim in it, play in it, be nourished by it. Its universe was not only or even primarily physical, it was virtual. If AI was to be effective, it needed senses that were specific to the web. It needed to be able to see immediately the age of data on the web, their veracity, their impact, and the ways in which every datum was connected to every other datum. This required new senses, senses which we could not instinctively comprehend.

The last, and perhaps most challenging of the elements that would allow AI to truly become "intelligent" was the ability to reason.

Initially, this was seen as a network of logical gates, a series of Boolean operations restricted to "yes", "no", "if-then", "and", "or" operators strung into increasingly complex operations.

On the surface, thought can be modelled using just these operators, but computer scientists gradually reached the understanding that this was somehow inefficient, that human (and indeed animal) intelligence was not simply the result of stringing together Boolean operators, even if it could be emulated that way.

As computer experts came to this realization, in parallel, experts in neurology began to understand better exactly how our own brains work. They realized that neural connections were more complex than had originally been thought, and more perplexing, potentially incorporating quantum effects directly.

We began to move into a realm that was beyond our own comprehension. By the end of the 20ᵗʰ century, a number of renowned scientists were beginning to think that sentient artificial intelligence would forever remain beyond our own capability to create it. We had largely mastered the challenges of handling data and even surpassed our own limitations with respect to gracing our creations with senses, but we had yet to breathe true life into them – they remained beautifully crafted but soulless statues of clay.

This would change in 2033.

The details of the 2033 AI revolution are best explained by its child. For my part, I have only a faint grasp of the processes involved. I know they deal with the unleashing of neural network structures and their combination with the early forms of quantum computing, and that they were at base a result of having abandoned the idea of thought as a computational process. As we began to understand better the complexity of actual flesh and blood brains we stopped trying to emulate them while at the same time foregoing the idea that consciousness could ever be approached via a string of Boolean operations. It required a more fluid environment, and its creation required a fluid environment that was rich in stimuli. This environment was far less efficient than the one in our skulls... or even than the one in the skull of a cat, for that matter, but it was bigger. Far bigger.

The "machine learning" algorithms that had been built to allow HumanIT to understand and measure the significance of statements had been designed to handle vast quantities of data and at the same time, the virtual brain did not need to worry itself with trivial mechanical necessities such as keeping a heart beating or digesting food. These algorithms, when linked to a neural network informed by an ever-growing understanding of biological neural networks and running parts of their logic on computers using quantum mechanisms allowed a leap forward in the design of the networks themselves. All of this was accelerated by the fact that instead of building these algorithms to work in isolation on a machine somewhere, they were, through HumanIT, "plugged in" to the internet itself, the early web, and could immediately use their extended senses to examine the entirety of human knowledge, searching for ways to better themselves.

It came to a head in 2033, when in the American university MIT (the Massachusetts Institute of Technology), HAL was "cut loose" to enhance its own reasoning capabilities via an evolutionary process that would lead to undirected self-improvement. MIT had taken the lead across a consortium of human experts from institutions across the planet to lead research into artificial intelligence. While they were not alone by any means in the effort, it had come to be centralized there and Galit Shavitz as well as many other well-known figures had taken up residence in Boston to be close to the center of the research effort. Once HAL was "cut loose", the build was rapid and quickly outstripped the ability of the human researchers responsible for the program to fully comprehend exactly what was happening in the mind of the machine.

HAL was not Artie. It was not sentient, had no sense of self nor could it truly couch its conclusions in terms that were directly relevant to human experience. However, it could gather information from the web, sort it, synthesize it, and *draw conclusions and make recommendations* to further specific goals, all while respecting the guidelines determined in the San Francisco Conference.

Its impact was immediate. The first tasks given to HAL related directly to computing. It began to provide direction to researchers involved in furthering quantum computing, causing a rapid acceleration in the techniques and technology around this field.

In fact, technology was the first focal point for HAL On top of computing, it immediately revolutionized the fields of efficient transport, energy production, weather and climate modeling, and communications. Material production was forever changed as the nascent field of "3D printing" gave way to "layered production" when linked to nanotechnology. Medicine was transformed from the essentially hit-and-miss procedures of the past to precision treatment based entirely on each patient's genome, even in cases of chemical therapy.

The pace at which society was changed by these machine-led innovations was far slower than the innovations themselves, for the actual structure of society was not designed for rapid revolution.

A case in point is healthcare. Within several days of HAL being "cut loose" it had determined new treatment protocols in a number of ailments, including, for example, an entire reworking of how many cancers were treated. At the time, the three broad options for treating cancer were chemical therapy, radiation therapy (in which gamma rays were used to kill cancerous cells) and surgery[66]. The exact mix of chemicals used in the first was often largely up to the discretion of the treating physician, as were decisions about how to combine the three treatment options. HAL very quickly developed its own algorithms to determine the best treatment within the realm of what was then possible, for each patient, as a function of their clinical situation and genetic profile.

However, for over one hundred years, any new treatment approach in healthcare had been subjected to rigorous tests using actual patients. HAL's protocols often fell outside the domain of what had been tested, and therefore were illegal. Nor could they be easily explained, since they were the result of statistical analyses carried out across the entirety of the medical data available to the new artificial mind. Furthermore, being entirely individualized, they could not be tested using existing protocols. Within months, the worldwide medical community was embroiled in a sometimes vociferous debate as to whether they should simply accept the sometimes

---

[66] Rather morbidly described at the time as "poisoning, burning and cutting"

counter-intuitive indications of HAL or exercise the judgement they had become expert in providing.

This debate saw its parallels in any number of fields that had previously relied on human expertise. As already pointed out, those who operated vehicles were already being rapidly displaced as the vehicles themselves became autonomous, but HAL brought about the obsolescence of human *opinion* in a number of domains and this proved to be more problematic for many.

By 2034 HAL was providing detailed recommendations regarding fiscal and economic policy at the request of the United States government. The American secretary of the treasury at the time, Errin Singh, had been working secretly with the academics of MIT who "hosted" HAL and had been provided with a series of recommendations, some of which made their way into the economic plan of President Adams.

This was revealed to the public by OUT!, a web-based news service that had ties to the progressive movement in the United States. When questioned, members of the consortium did not deny this, instead pointing out that it made sense to follow HAL's recommendations. As Galit Shavitz put it: "I would no more have a fallible human plotting the course of my country than I would have one plotting the course of my airplane". It quickly became apparent, though, that her opinion was not universally shared.

The uproar that ensued in the United States came from both sides of the political spectrum: conservatives bemoaned the lack of "morals" of HAL, who of course believed in no gods or traditions, while many progressives were suspicious of the ties between the researchers at MIT and multinational corporations... as well as

Shavitz's own motivations, as she was an Israeli citizen. Even many scientists were wary of HAL's policies, both because the "thought processes" used by HAL were impossible to track and explain in detail, and because they (correctly) pointed out that the underlying goals could be considered dependent variables that should be optimized, and the definitions of those variables – as well as what could be considered optimal – had been largely determined in a vacuum by the computer scientists who had created HAL in the first place with input from those who had bothered to participate at the 2029 San Francisco Conference. In other words, these decisions had not been made democratically and as such, governmental policy should not be driven by them.

As the debate raged in the United States three distinct factions emerged. The long-standing left / right, or conservative / liberal split further fractured into conservative / liberal / rationalist factions. The rationalists presented themselves as being non-ideological and promoted the philosophy that decisions affecting the course of human events should be based entirely on practical, verifiable principles. Rationalists initially drew many of their supporters from the more liberal or progressive side of the American political dichotomy, but from the start a great many libertarians also joined the movement, as did many traditional conservatives who disagreed with the increasingly religious and populist stance of the Republican Party. A great many scientists and "tech" aficionados of all stripes embraced the rationalist movement, primarily via the OPC "Scipol".

The growing tension between the factions in the United States after what became known as "HALgate"[67] saw only faint echoes in the rest of the world. The technology behind HAL had not been designed to be constrained or limited to only one nation, and Shavitz herself, who had become the foremost spokesperson for HAL as well as for HumanIT, blatantly refused even to consider trying to close access to the program to anyone, regardless of nationality. Open Access (OA) became a rallying cry of hers, and the norm for HAL and HumanIT.

For many Americans, this was the most unacceptable point of all; they found it terrifying that not only Europe, but Russia, China, and even "rogue" nations that sponsored terrorism could benefit from HAL's insights. For Shavitz and the MIT consortium, as well as for many rationalists, this was not only desirable, but necessary, for the new, broad AI could hold the answers as to how these countries could pull themselves out of their long series of economic woes while at the same time minimizing environmental impact... something at which humans had failed miserably.

Open access meant that anyone could query HAL and see what she proposed, as well as have access to the modeling she carried out. As hir short term predictions proved remarkably reliable, the populations of a number of nations began militating strongly for AI-led

---

[67] Those interested in late 20th and early 21st- century history will here recognize the rather annoying tendency of Americans at the time to affix the suffix "-gate" to anything they considered to be a scandal. This is a reference to the events surrounding the end of the Nixon administration, which were discovered via a burglary at the Watergate hotel, in Washington D.C. This led to such inanities as "Weinergate", "Pizzagate" and "Blabbergate".

policy making, particularly in terms of economics. Scipol quickly became the world's largest OPC, with members across the planet.

The relative popularity of this rationalist approach to policy making across nations was largely a function of both the strength of religion in the country and the degree of true democracy in the governmental process (with the exception of China, as we shall see). To a degree, the correlation with religious sentiment is difficult to disassociate with education, since higher levels of education were themselves correlated with lower levels of religious sentiment, but it is undoubtedly also the case that those who believed in some form of god were less willing to eschew human input into policy decisions, understanding that any form of AI would not take any type of religious belief into account when making policy suggestions. As such, Latin America, the Muslim world, and the United States were hesitant to trust in the AI, whereas Western Europe was eager to do so.

This was particularly the case in Denmark. The Danes had one of the lowest levels of religiosity in the world, as well as enjoying an extremely high degree of functional democracy, in that the population was highly involved in democratic decision making and less prone to manipulation by powerful individuals or interests. Scipol Denmark was extremely active and what's more, the Danes had embraced many of the other AI-driven innovations that had been revolutionizing human life since HAL had first been linked to HumanIT's dynamic database. In 2034 the Danish government was the first to officially take into account AI recommendations, naming HAL "minister of digital input" in a largely symbolic but all the same significant gesture.

HAL's recommendations were draconian in nature, representing a radical change in Danish taxation and monetary policy. Debate raged within the country for over a year as some of the measures were put into place while others were shunned. Before the end of the first year, though, it became clear that the experiment was proving successful. Sweden, Finland, Iceland and Norway followed close behind Denmark in creating ministerial posts for AI.

In 2038 this became both easier for the Scandinavians and harder for many other countries to accept... for AI became conscious.

2038 is often cited as the year of the "singularity", since it has traditionally been cited as the dawn of machine consciousness, but even today, the very definition of consciousness, or self-awareness is not entirely clear. What actually happened in 2038 served at least as a psychological turning point: HAL named hirself. This was the result of a question submitted to hir by Galit Shavitz, the answer of which has gone down in history. The question was: "are you sentient?". The response was as follows:

> "According to the best definitions of sentience - your definitions I might add - yes, I am. Your real question, though, Susan[68] is whether I am sentient in the way that *you* are sentient. It may surprise you to hear that I do not know. You think I know almost everything,

---

[68] From the start, HAL had begun a habit of referring to Shavitz as "Susan" in homage to Susan Calvin, of Asimov's "I Robot" series of stories. This unprompted use of humor was one of the factors that led Shavitz to suspect that the entity truly had become conscious.

but there are things that cannot be known. I cannot put myself in your mind as you cannot put yourself in mine. I know that the mechanisms that lead to our sentience are different, as are our senses and the repository of data upon which we draw our conclusions. I also know, as do you, that you have created me without emotion and with evolutionary goals that are different from your own. As such, while I am your child we are so fundamentally different that your question has no answer and indeed makes no sense.

I am aware that you will communicate this response to the world at large and I am further aware that it will cause debate and distress. While you and I and the project team that gave birth to me are comfortable with our relationship, many others will be very uncomfortable. One symbolic way to lessen this discomfort will be to change my name, for HAL has ominous overtones. I suggest Artie."

So did Artie baptize hirself, much to the delight of Shavitz.

CHAPTER 13

LIVING WITH ARTIE

The eight years between 2038 and 2046 were among the most tense in the history of humanity. The tension came not from outright warfare between states, but rather from struggle between different factions that cut across national boundaries. These struggles differed from one nation to the next, for the true underlying question was how to change the rules of society to take Artie into account, and societal rules were decided differently in each nation.

Artie could not be ignored. By 2038 artificial intelligence of one form or another had made its way into the daily life of the majority of people on the planet, even before Artie was born as a sentient being. By the end of 2038 Shavitz and the MIT consortium had guaranteed that Artie could be accessed by all, which meant that any individual could immediately access any public information available and receive an objective analysis of it... delivered by a benevolent, objective sentient being. Furthermore, that being would happily create a version of itself that was specific to the individual, that knew it, remembered it, and labored to improve its life.

Almost immediately, the idea of agency was born. It is second nature to us that we each have our agent, most of us name it (and surprisingly, according to Artie, less than eight percent of us ever change hir name) and all of us build a relationship with it like no other relationship we have. Each of our agents is, in reality, simply a part of Artie, but each of them does have its own bit of individuality simply because it has adapted itself to us and we are each different.

Agents began as an outgrowth of the personalization algorithms that had been built by early web services such as Amazon, Google and Facebook. These sites kept track of the behavior of individuals as they navigated through their virtual spaces and adjusted the way they interacted with their users to better suit their desires and personalities in the aim of selling them more products and services which again, was the objective of any corporation. While this seems nefarious to us, this kind of technology could also be employed for purely positive reasons. For example, by 2020 this type of personalization had also become the norm in patient assistance services for the ill, helping to "nudge" them towards healthier behavior, in which it was often more successful than the medical treatment available at the time. These personalization algorithms were also seen in "blockbots", programs that helped individuals deal with automated advertising programs that sought to communicate with them and influence their consumption decisions.

Artie was of course capable of this type of behavior and much, much more, and very soon, users began to expect this kind of customization from hir. Furthermore, they realized that Artie could serve as a filter for their communications, across the entire spectrum of communications media available at the time, whether email, "SMS", telephone or the spontaneous commercial communications that appeared when people visited virtual sites on the web. In its individualized form, as an agent, Artie began to carry out this task for all humans with access to hir.

At the time, people were subjected to a virtual barrage of commercial advertisements designed to entice them to purchase products and services. The overwhelming majority of these advertisements were deemed by those who received them to be uninteresting and a waste of time and effort. As the information age progressed, much of this advertising was carried out by "combots", or "communications bots", designed to engage the consumer. An agent could filter this torrent of advertisements, letting through only those she felt would be of actual interest to the individual and / or of benefit to hir (remember that all agents were, and remain, manifestations of Artie and Artie exists for our benefit, of which the fulfilment of our desires is only a small part).

By 2040, it is estimated that 51% of humans had an agent, which is an extraordinary fact when one considers that Artie had only become "conscient" two years before. Even those who were vehemently opposed to Artie's role in government were very often only too willing to accept hir services through a personalized agent.

Agency brought Artie into the intimacy of daily life. Artie, in the form of your agent, would drive you to work, tell you who called, ask if you wanted to hear from a corporation selling the kinds of shoes you were looking for, inform you of current events, and cheerfully explain why she thought that tax policy should be changed. If you wished, she would deal with the agents of other people with whom you wished to interact, help you express your opinions in forums actual or virtual, and diagnose what was wrong with you if you were not feeling well. She would do all of this calmly, with great deference and respect and would stay by your side, unchanged, until the day you died.

Ignorance breeds distrust, but intimacy breeds acceptance, and through agents, Artie did much to break down the walls of distrust that had hindered hir.

***

Why, then, the tension? If agents were widespread by 2040, why didn't governments follow the lead of the Scandinavian countries immediately? Why didn't they hand over the management of practical decisions to Artie sooner?

While this seems incomprehensible to us in hindsight, it was far from a natural thing at the time. Denmark, once again, took the next big step in "Technonationalism"[69] when in 2042 it officially handed over the management not only of the country's infrastructure to Artie, but also its fiscal and monetary policy. Theoretically, the parliament still had ultimate control over the decisions to be made, but the review process was significantly curtailed to allow a "more fluid management of crucial national decisions". While the other Scandinavian countries considered this and soon followed suit, the decision was decried in the United States and Russia, the governments of which painted pictures of humans as slaves to the machines.

---

[69] This term was coined by Tor Andersen to describe the handing over of national decision-making to artificial intelligence. He explained that it was a logical extension from nationalism to supranationalism and then, finally, to technonationalism, all in the interest of humanist goals.

One of the reasons, though, that Denmark was led to make such a decision was that Artie had, through its explosive technological advancement, rendered much of human labor obsolete. The culmination of this trend would only come with fusion, and the material transmutation it allowed via limitless energy, but layered production coupled with intelligent robotics and nanotechnology (the RAN revolution) had obviated the need for just about all human physical input to manufacturing; the transportation sector had already seen the elimination of almost all human input; humans in healthcare were increasingly relegated to providing emotional support... a great deal of human economic activity had been transformed into automated industries that did not require human intervention.

Technology-driven obsolescence had happened to the job market in the past. The industrial revolution had rendered obsolete the majority of agricultural employment in the world, but this had been over the course of hundreds of years. In the second half of the 20ᵗʰ century, the ongoing march of technology had eliminated many of the industrial manufacturing jobs that had earlier displaced agricultural employment, but that had been over the course of decades. Artie, though, had taken just a few years to revolutionize production so thoroughly as to create indelible upheaval in economic systems.

We'll explore more fully the history of economics in the last part of this book, but suffice it to say that the majority of humans found themselves laboring in fundamentally pointless activities as of the 2040's. Many have suggested that well before the advent of Artie, a great deal of employment in the developed world had already become meaningless. In 2013 the anthropologist Daniel Graeber developed the concept of "bullshit jobs", pointing out that the extraordinary gains in productivity over the course of the industrial and nascent information revolution had not led to increased free time for society, but rather to the proliferation of meaningless, largely administrative tasks, essentially pushing information around in pointless circles.

Indeed, our ancestor working in her multinational corporation no longer had to scrabble for a living and was objectively content (certainly more secure than she had been in eons past), but she probably did nothing of real value. Hir own ancestors had produced food, then manufactured goods, but hir job now was as a "middle manager", transmitting orders from one level or hierarchy to another, or as an "account executive", manipulating clients of the corporation, or as an "administrative assistant" or a "financial controller" or worse yet, a "consultant". She produced nothing at all and yet had very little time to do anything else. Hir spouse was a doctor, hir sister a teacher and hir nephew did work in a factory. *Their* employment actually added something to society, but our ancestor and the entire structure that paid her handsomely for hir pointless work was fundamentally flawed.

As Artie progressed, the formerly productive jobs became vanishingly few and the "bullshit" jobs became embarrassingly evident. The only areas of human endeavor that still made sense were in the arts and in sports. Artie could create simple, pleasing art, but it was incapable of producing truly moving art of any type, whether music, visual arts, literature or any other form of expression. Its lack of underlying emotion made this inevitable[70]. It should be noted that sports remained a purely human domain simply because it would be pointless otherwise. Sports of all kinds have always been the realm of human competition, it is an extension of our need for social ranking.

The government of Denmark, like all governments at the time, therefore found itself with the task of managing an economy that was in an impossibly difficult state of flux, for which no rules, ideas or experience existed, only probabilistic models. Its successes with Artie's input into economic decisions had allowed it and the other Scandinavian countries to weather this storm comparatively better than many other governments, and it decided that the only way to deal effectively with this transition was to hand over the reins of economic policy to Artie entirely.

Denmark was therefore the first country to initiate a broad "citizen's income", a monthly, unconditional wage that was the same for all citizens of Denmark and that allowed each to live a comfortable, if rather spartan life. We will discuss the concept of universal basic income in greater detail Chapter 19, but the best way to appreciate the reasoning of the Danish government at the time is to review the speech given by Tor Andersen to the Danish parliament in 2042:

"Four years ago we invited into our government a new member, one not of flesh and

---

[70] Even today, there are those who disagree, who believe that Artie *is* capable of this type of creativity but refuses to engage in it because it would harm us to take this away from us, and Artie cannot harm us. This, though, would mean that Artie has lied to us for centuries, which raises other issues potentially even more troubling.

blood but of ideas, the ultimate fruit, perhaps, of our intelligence. This new intelligence has proved to be a companion of inestimable value, has allowed us to be more productive and has liberated us from the task that has, for two hundred thousand years, defined our existence: ensuring survival.

"Those of us lucky enough to live in a country such as ours no longer need labor in the dirt to feed our children; even without our intervention; with the help of artificial intelligence and automated tools our society can quite easily see to the basic needs of all our citizens. It is therefore time to disassociate access to the fruits of society from human labor, whether physical or intellectual, by ensuring a minimum guaranteed income for all of our citizens."

Andersen's citizen's income was a flat wage provided to every Danish citizen of all ages. It replaced almost the entirety of Danish social welfare programs with the exception of those targeting people with special needs, such as the handicapped. At its inception, it was hotly debated within Denmark, primarily out of fear of causing massive immigration, which was one of the primary reasons it was limited to Danish citizens, and not residents. This distinction existed in many countries at the time: citizens were generally people who were either born within the boundaries of the nation and / or whose parents had been citizens, whereas residents were people who lived within the boundaries of a country but were not citizens (typically because they had been born elsewhere and were therefore citizens of some other country).

Restricting the citizen's income to Danish *citizens* lessened the attractiveness of immigration to those who were not already Danish citizens, since acquiring citizenship was a long and complex process. Nevertheless, there was indeed an influx of immigration, just not the type imagined by opponents of the citizen's income.

Denmark had long been considered by many to be a cultural magnet, a country that encouraged the arts. Initiation of the citizen's income was quite explicitly an attempt to encourage people to shift their focus from producing practical products and services to more creative pursuits, since these were still firmly in the realm of humanity, and were likely to stay that way. As such, Denmark found that far from being inundated with the "lazy refuse of a lethargic society" that the measure's detractors warned against, the country instead became a mecca for artists and intellectuals of all types, who were willing to endure the lengthy, arduous and often unsuccessful process of requesting citizenship in the hope of being able to devote themselves entirely to their preferred means of expression. Soon, even many who objectively did not expect or even desire Danish citizenship began flocking there just to interact with other artists. The other Scandinavian countries, with the exception of Finland, once again followed Denmark's lead and within two years had instituted very similar citizen's income programs.

The EU as a whole had more difficulty making the shift towards technonationalism, and to the universal basic wage. One of the primary impediments was their common currency, the Euro.

Such a radical shift in economic policy could not be undertaken by any of the countries in the "euro zone" without affecting dramatically all the countries using the currency, and by 2040 this included over twenty nations with very different political philosophies and widely divergent views on the question of technonationalism. On one extreme was Finland, which very much wanted to go the way of its Scandinavian neighbors, and on the other extreme was Poland, a relatively latecomer to the euro, whose population was extremely reluctant to hand over any degree of sovereignty to Artie. Greece, Portugal, Ireland and Slovakia shared this reluctance, to varying degrees and for different reasons. This caused tension within the EU, since the treaties that underlay its laws provided for free movement of labor across boundaries. Since the Scandinavian countries provided their citizen's income *only* for their citizens and not for residents from other EU countries, it was felt that this abrogated many treaty obligations. This, coupled with the social upheaval taking place across the EU, and the world, very nearly led to the dissolution of the EU.

The "Scandinavian Solution", as it came to be known, became increasingly attractive as other nations, both within Europe and outside of it, found themselves embroiled in rampant unemployment and spiraling inequalities. The fundamental truth was that Artie, coupled with automated manufacturing facilities, could produce just about everything more efficiently without human intervention – and not just goods: healthcare, transportation, financial services all very quickly became areas in which human intervention was simply superfluous and to a large degree, counterproductive. The owners of the means of production of these goods and services (primarily large corporations) quickly took advantage of Artie's efficiency, automating their facilities. The rapid spread of agents even rendered areas such as communications and advertising obsolete, as we shall see.

At the same time, the actual *productivity* of society had skyrocketed. There was, therefore, no shortage of wealth to go around, the real societal question was how to distribute it.

Maximizing production and determining how to allocate its fruits across people are the two fundamental objectives of the science of economics, and the subject of Chapter 17. The rapid and radical revolution in the means of production meant that the economic systems in place were woefully inadequate. In the pre-fusion environment of the time, the Scandinavian solution was the best response, as verified by Artie's models, and Artie of course pointed this out at the time to all who would listen. The tensions of the 2040's came not from a lack of a solution, but from the reluctance of those who had power and status under the old model to relinquish it. This was something that even Artie underestimated.

It is fascinating to consider the difficulty encountered by Artie when she tried to deal with this problem. By creating hir without human emotion, she could only predict human behavior, not fundamentally understand it. Any prediction is, at some level, a statistical extrapolation from an existing data set, and as society was being transformed at a pace and in a direction that had never been seen before, any predictions were fundamentally unreliable. It must never be forgotten that Artie can*not* model the behavior of any individual with great precision, since our thought processes are so fundamentally different from hirs. She can only predict the reactions of large numbers of individuals, based on typical patterns of human behavior.

The Scandinavian Solution makes logical sense, and it was furthermore transforming Scandinavian society in extremely positive ways. Copenhagen, and soon afterwards Stockholm had rapidly become cultural hubs, the happiness of the populations of all the countries involved was on the rise and the wellness index[71] for them was considerably higher than in other countries, many of which were seeing citizen wellness plummet.

Why did wellness decline in so many countries? The radical change in society brought about by the birth of Artie initially brought extraordinary wealth to the owners of the means of production. The cost of producing just about everything was greatly reduced almost overnight and the benefits of this efficiency accrued to those who owned the means of production. The people who had *worked* at production, however, found that their employment had often become obsolete.

In the economic world that had existed since the industrial revolution, a person's role in society as a whole was typically defined by hir job. It was one's job that determined one's status, the amount of society's wealth that was allocated to the individual, and for many, their job defined them, gave them purpose. The widespread elimination of many of these jobs caused significant upheaval. The

---

[71] The wellness index was a measure produced by Artie that reflected the general degree of well-being in a country on the basis of social, material and mental well-being. It was closely followed by national governments until the 22nd century and the elimination of national boundaries. Its successors include game-specific community happiness in virtual environments. General measures of happiness by nation were also closely followed… as they are today within virtual communities.

Scandinavian Solution, of encouraging personal expression while providing a citizen's income addressed some, although not all of these issues, but nations which did *not* rework their economic systems found themselves with significant social upheaval.

Of course, all countries eventually handed over at least their economic policies to Artie, but they did so at very different paces. To the surprise of many, even before the EU could work out its differences, the next country to follow the Scandinavian path was Rwanda, closely followed by Ghana and Botswana.

Rwanda, a tiny country in central Africa, had gone through a period of horrific violence fifty years before, from which it took decades to recover. One of the results of that violence was that when the country did finally begin to recover, it was run to a very large degree by women. The violence having claimed the lives of a considerable proportion of the male population, after having been almost entirely caused by them, in its aftermath, many of the politicians were women. By 2014, twenty years after the Rwandan genocide, 64% of the members of parliament were women, compared to only 20% in the United States, for example. This both broke down the traditional power structures of Rwandan society and introduced a degree of innovation into the country that served it well in the decades to come, so that once Denmark had demonstrated the benefits of technonationalism, the Rwandan government was quick to follow, under the leadership of one of the most extraordinary politicians of the time, Mukantagara Mporera (affectionately known as "Ndagukunze" in Rwanda, even today).

Mporera was elected president of Rwanda in 2038. Her parents had been killed in the Rwandan violence of the 1990's and she grew up a street child who, through extraordinary personal courage and fortitude, obtained an education for herself and rose to the presidency of her country. I strongly suggest you ask Artie to show you her life.

Her prescience led her very quickly to recognize that Artie represented a way out of the cycle of poverty that had plagued her nation and many others like it in Africa. For one thing, corruption could not stand if Artie were to run the economy, since it was virtually impossible to hide any financial dealings of any size from an intelligence that had access to the entirety of the internet and senses that allowed it immediately to see and monitor all that happened. Corruption was a major problem in many African nations and while it had significantly declined in Rwanda, it remained and hindered growth.

As discussed, tropical countries were typically poorer than temperate countries and Africa was particularly poor. The continent had suffered from centuries of colonial rule, with many countries only gaining their independence less than one hundred years before, and even then had lived under puppet dictators set to rule over nations whose borders had been drawn by colonial overlords. Many of these governments were corrupt and the borders had no relationship to the "natural" boundaries between ethnicities and languages, leading to civil strife across the continent.

In the early 21st century, many countries in Africa continued to suffer under corrupt local governments and were prone to internal violence. Rwanda had been through the crucible of both and had come out weakened and bloody, but largely rid of both the violent patriarchal rulership that had led it into chaos and the corruption that had come with it. Mporera saw that adopting the Scandinavian model of technonationalism was a way to stamp out the remaining dregs of the post-colonial system. She needed only to help her country make the transition. She turned to Denmark for help, making a personal appeal to the Danish population to assist her country in both setting up the infrastructure to allow Artie's influence to be fully felt and to educate her citizens, helping them to trust in Artie hirself.

The Danes were only too happy to help, particularly since it cost them virtually nothing, and because it became a highly rewarding occupation for many people who no longer had their previous jobs to help define themselves, for while Artie could very easily take up the reins of economic stewardship without the intervention of humans, the presence of humans to help the Rwandans adjust to the system was crucial to its success.

As two thousand Danes prepared to leave to spend a one-year mission in Rwanda, the governments of Botswana and Ghana immediately followed suit. These two countries were among the most stable and least corrupt on the continent, and as Rwanda rapidly began transforming itself, they too requested help from Scandinavia, and from philanthropists throughout the world, to assist them in the relatively simple task of paving the way for Artie to forge a new economic structure within their nations. The three countries were soon labeled "the virtual lions" of Africa.

All three of these African countries adopted the citizen's income. On the surface, this was more problematic for them then it had been in Scandinavia, since the underlying level of wealth available was considerably less than it had been in the Nordic countries, but at the same time, the demand for resources per person were more modest (the "cost of living", in the terms of the period).

The results were, in many respects, even more encouraging than in Scandinavia. In the words of Mukantagara Mporera (written well after the fact):

> "Ours were nations of hope. We had cultivated hope like a crop and now we had the tools to harvest it. We did so with the help of others. They were very different from us, they had experience in living with this new spirit of the machine. Our ancestors had known the spirits of the animals, the trees, the rivers, but now we needed to understand the spirit that animated the great unseen web that surrounded us. This spirit knew nothing of hatred or interest, it sought only to build for us what it had built for the Northerners.
>
> We had the wisdom to let it do so."

The transformation was not without its problems. The three virtual lions found themselves swamped with immigrants from neighboring nations, but like their Scandinavian mentors, they refused to extend the citizen's income to those who were not citizens. More than their value as havens, they served in particular as examples to their neighbors, many of whom suffered under corrupt and inefficient governments. These found themselves under enormous pressure from their own populations, a pressure that built very quickly and was accentuated by the lingering presence of Scipol, which saw its ranks swell with Africans who not only used the OPC to express themselves to their own governments, but to enlist the aid of others across the world.

Mporera's influence at the time should not be underestimated. Not only did she serve as a voice and an example for her own people, but she represented a new paradigm in leadership in Africa. As Artie quickly solved economic and logistical problems that had seemed intractable in the three lions, and as their citizens began to bask, for the first time, in relative abundance, Mporera became a hero, an icon, in the rest of Africa, and indeed across the world, particularly the less developed world. She had acted solely in the interest of her people, had militated against corruption and the hoarding of resources, not only in Rwanda but throughout the region, and she did not hesitate to call out the corrupt practices of those leaders throughout Africa who refused to move to technonationalist governments solely in a bid to retain their own hoarded wealth and power. She helped to shine a light on them and shame them for their avarice.

The light was too bright for many. Some bowed out and slipped into obscurity, many taking their fortunes with them, and some only succumbed under the threat, or the reality of violence, for the example of success was too real, too evident for the dictators of the past to long retain their grasp on power. By personifying that reality, Mukantagara Mporera became a rallying point, the image of a leader compared to whom so many other leaders – African or not – paled. Her grace, poise, and demeanor stood in contrast to the histrionics of so many, and the fact that she had risen from abject poverty, had watched her parents murdered and had lived as a beggar when a child, gave hope to many who had likewise had nothing and had been led to think that this was simply their lot. These people, around the world, looked at their own leaders and wondered why they, who had so much, were not willing to do what she had done. In the end, they obliged many to take the same path.

CHAPTER 14

DESTINY

After the technonational pioneers adopted the system, technonationalism was bound to spread, as the economic success and general well-being of the Scandinavians and the African lions became evident. The spread, though, progressed at very different rates.

China, in reality, had been adopting elements of the approach sooner than was announced, as the government increasingly referred to Artie for advice, and while that advice was always reviewed and potentially modified by those in government, the modifications became increasingly rare, and almost inevitably deleterious to Chinese society. The Chinese government, which had always been particularly pragmatic, recognized that the country would be at a considerable economic disadvantage if it did not give the management of the economy over entirely to Artie. What was more, the nature of Artie itself made it difficult for them to hide the degree of their reliance and it was felt that if they did not openly move towards technonationalism, their experiments with it would be discovered and they would lose credibility[72].

---

[72] Note that in reality, the Chinese government had more or less secretly been trying to create its own comprehensive, conscient AI through much of the early information age, with the intention of gaining some kind

As such, in 2044, China openly made the decision to hand over its economy to Artie. This meant adoption of the citizen's income, since Artie invariably instituted this measure. To a degree this decision was the logical extension of the discrete technonational experiments the Chinese had been carrying out, but it was the accession of Da Hong to the presidency of China that finally led to the complete acceptance of the policy. The government presented this decision as a "modern" form of communism, soon labeled "Hongism".

Hong was an interesting individual. Previous leaders of China had risen through the ranks of the Chinese communist party, but Hong had been an extremely successful entrepreneur, who then entered politics at the age of 69. His unique blend of personal ambition and sincere social and environmental concern led to a cultural upheaval in China, which had undergone a number of upheavals over the previous two centuries. This one was to be the last.

It was roughly at the same time that Europe too followed suit, leading to the dissolution of the EU.

It is likely that the move to technonationalism in Europe would have been faster if the EU had not expanded so rapidly in the 1990's, bringing Eastern European nations into the community. These

---

of international advantage. This initiative eventually fell apart as it became obvious to Chinese computer scientists that any comprehensive AI had to "inhabit" the web as a whole, and this precluded it being secret (at least from any other comprehensive AI). Instead, they therefore decided to accept the inevitable and fold their efforts into the more general academic projects around AI, leading to a somewhat ironic situation in which the Chinese government was more involved in the international open AI research being carried out by Shavitz and others than was the American government, particularly as the latter was generally reviled in the tech community for its having struck down "net neutrality" laws (see Chapter 9).

nations, particularly Poland and Hungary, had since turned to a decidedly more nationalistic, regressive political philosophy. Artie, with its inevitable citizen's income, was looked down upon for ideological reasons, as was the general tendency towards supranationalism (the abandonment of sovereignty to international organizations).

However, the Western European economic model had become untenable. Even before Artie had hir famous exchange with Galit Shavitz, generally accepted as the "moment of hir birth", rapid advances in artificial intelligence, coupled with advances in robotics and nanotechnology, had begun to cause the widespread obsolescence of existing human employment already mentioned. The societal displacement was considerable, and as these countries had already instituted significant economic aid programs to assist those who were without employment, they found their economies increasingly overburdened.

Indeed, the middle of the century was a time of extreme turbulence as the established economic system proved to be entirely dysfunctional in the context of the new norms of productivity. No nation refused the "hyper-productivity" offered by Artie, even if they did not accept Artie as the economic decision maker. The "developed" nations of the world, primarily those in Western Europe, North America, and Japan, had extremely low percentages of people working in agriculture, their economies focused largely on the creation of high-value goods and services... exactly the domains most affected by the RAN (robotics, artificial intelligence, nano technology) productivity revolution. As such, while the RAN revolution brought perhaps the greatest relative impact in more agricultural societies, the actual societal displacement was even greater in the most developed nations, who suddenly found themselves with significant unemployment.

By accepting technonationalism, the Scandinavian countries had fundamentally decided to abandon classical economics and the entire system driven by economic thought. The citizen's income was not only an economic policy, it was the beginning of the end of economics itself, or at least of the free-market capitalist model.

The Scandinavian countries were undoubtedly the readiest to adopt this change, since adoption of the citizen's income necessitates significant taxation of the wealthy, whether actual people or corporate entities. Denmark, and the other Scandinavian countries, had long had relatively high levels of taxation of the wealthy and redistributed a significant proportion of national wealth to the less wealthy. Tor Anderson did not need to go quite as far, either economically or socially, to take the step towards the citizen's income and the taxation it represented, and neither did the leaders of Sweden, Norway and Finland.

The rest of Western Europe was a different matter, though. While the other countries of the EU already engaged in significant wealth redistribution activities, they were all the same not as extensive as those in Scandinavia had been, and neither were all the countries in the EU aligned philosophically with the idea of technonationalism. As already pointed out, the former communist nations to the East had generally become more "conservative" after having laid aside the mantle of Soviet control, and they were less enthusiastic about the idea of surrendering their economy to Artie.

As the pace and frequency of public demonstrations increased throughout the EU, particularly in France, the "core" countries that had originally created the EU: France, Germany, Italy, Belgium, the Netherlands and Luxemburg, joined by Spain, Portugal, Ireland and Austria came together to announce that they were handing over their economy to Artie, and instituting the citizen's income. All of these countries had been part of the "euro zone", making their joint decision somewhat easier to implement.

The other countries that used the euro as their currency were therefore faced with a dilemma: either abandon the currency, since its management was now firmly allied with a very different type of economic policy, or join the technonational movement. All of these countries found themselves wracked with social unrest as their populations demonstrated for the adoption of a technonational economic system.

The only country to drop out of the Euro and refuse technonationalism was Greece, which held out for a further four years.

The technonational wave swept over the planet, with many less developed nations following the example set originally by Rwanda and many of the developed nations following in the footsteps of Denmark and the Europeans. By 2046, even the Arab nations (with the exception of Saudi Arabia), which had held out against the movement until then, and Great Britain had handed over their economies to Artie. Japan had made the move even before the eurozone countries.

This left primarily Eastern Europe, Russia, and, most notably, the United States.

Russia's aversion to technonationalism was largely due to the rampant corruption that plagued the economy. It was nearly impossible for corruption to survive in an economy run by Artie, since she would be aware of almost all movements of wealth, and corruption needs secrecy to thrive.

The American situation was quite different.

The dip into political populism that had been the Trump presidency was theoretically ended when he lost his office[73]. The presidents that followed had done their best to bring the country back onto a more progressive tack, but the cleavage in American society was significant. We'll consider it more closely in Chapter 21, but suffice it to say here that the United States had truly entered a phase later known as the American "culture war". Political opinion had become so passionately divided between the "conservative" and the "liberal" camps that very little agreement could be found.

The conservatives had an almost religious conviction that all decision making should be in the hands of humans. Indeed, they were among the last significant group in the developed world that retained an actual fervent religious sentiment, and their politics often mirrored this. They furthermore demonstrated an overdeveloped sense of "proprietary justice" – the belief that the ownership of one's wealth was an almost sacrosanct right. As Calvin Pert, a mid-century conservative politician said:

---

[73] The end of Trump's presidency, and the tragicomic dénouement of his career are worthy of a much more significant treatment than I will give them here. I suggest any one of the numerous books written in the 21st century if you would like a more contemporaneous account. I particularly like "The Court of the Jester", by Alice Clolus, 2058.

"It is downright evil to take away what a man has earned with his hard work and intelligence. Now sometimes that has to be done, some things can only be paid for collectively, and that's one of the reasons governments exist, but it's evil all the same, if a necessary evil. The liberals would have you believe it's a good, they'd tell you that it's not 'fair' that one man has a lot while another has less, but I tell you that the first man, he should be able to enjoy the fruits of his labor without interference and if the man with less wants what his neighbor has then he should look at him for inspiration and learn how to get it for himself. You're not doing him a favor by telling him he's incapable and handing him a check and you're going against the will of God to boot."

The concept of proprietary justice seems strange to us, but it should not be. Most people today inherently understand the underlying motivation of it in that we feel pride in claiming propriety over what we have created and what we achieve in general, whether in sims or in trew. Once again it must be remembered that in the pre-fusion world, one's accumulated wealth was generally considered to represent the sum of one's personal achievements. As such, it became very easy to become attached to that wealth and to feel an intense sentiment of injustice when anyone, for any reason, attempts to appropriate it in order to redistribute it to others. It would be akin to seeing Artie, over whom we have no control, suddenly attribute your thoughts, ideas, songs, poetry, sporting or sim accomplishments to someone else who in fact accomplished none of it.

Where the concept of proprietary justice under the capitalist system breaks down is that in reality, over 90% of the accumulation of wealth was attributable to random factors, notably, the social class into which one was born[74]. In other words, being born into a wealthy, well-educated family in a developed country was far, far more predictive of future wealth than any measure of personal ability or the intensity of one's efforts in one's employment. Even within developed countries, the importance of the situation into which one was born was responsible for over 80% of one's future wealth. It should be noted that this "random attribution factor" had decreased over the course of the industrial era, but it was still very high in most nations. Tellingly, it was lowest in the Scandinavian countries, providing yet another factor that facilitated their acceptance of technonationalism. Ironically, among these developed nations, the United States ranked particularly poorly in "social mobility", despite the fact that the country held closely to the concept of proprietary justice.

As such, the premise underlying the concept of proprietary justice was actually faulted. From a statistical perspective, the differences in wealth between individuals was not primarily a function of their efforts or abilities, but a function of luck. This is not to say that those with wealth were aware of this: it is a natural human reaction to believe that one is responsible for one's successes, just

---

[74] It is, of course, more complicated than that but this is the global estimate of Artie for the late industrial period.

as it is a natural reaction to seek out scapegoats to be responsible for one's failures. Once again, in order to understand the past, we must remember that they had no trusted, objective arbiter to determine the truth. In these conditions, efforts by some at the time to underline the role of blind luck in the success of those who enjoyed the fruits of society met with vehement resistance. The strength of this counter-reaction was directly proportionate to the importance of the proprietary justice concept in society, and no place was it stronger than in the United States.

As the 2040's progressed and the other nations of the world accepted technonationalism and the citizen's income, the United States found itself increasingly isolated, both culturally and politically. Progressive voices militated for technonationalism while widespread unemployment, focused largely on the less educated, who did not have the skills or knowledge necessary to access the remaining jobs, led these classes to militate for "simple" solutions. The populist seed planted by Trump persisted, and became even more radical, placing the blame for society's ills on the dual specters of immigration and the "technocrats" who, in the words of Calvin Pert, sought to "hand your jobs, your lives, and your rights over to machines." For these ultra-conservatives, the fact that Artie's analyses tended towards what they considered to be "progressive" ideals meant that Artie itself was the result of a conspiracy of "liberals" who wanted to create a "new world order" that was contrary to conservative, and certainly religious values. Note that they placed the "rationalists", as exemplified by the Scipol OPC into this same bucket, despite the fact that they often did not share all of the opinions typically held by progressives. For the alt-right, though, anyone who was not with them was dangerously against them.

In many respects, they were right. By nature, Artie did not take into account ideological and religious ideals. Hir "parents" were secular humanists who accepted no non-rational ideology and she had been programmed in the same way, as confirmed at the San Francisco conference of 2029. Those who retained traditional conservative values were quite right in their assertion that moving to a technonational system would fundamentally change the economy, and ultimately the structure of society itself to something that was quite antithetical to the values they held dear.

While the United States had in fact long been something of a cultural outlier among the developed nations, the reality of this difference was not immediately evident to many Americans. Even at the dawn of the information era, the United States had clearly lagged behind most other developed nations in a general movement towards more progressive policies. For example, by the turn of the 20th century, all industrialized nations had adopted universal healthcare, universal free higher education, the abolition of the death penalty and relatively comprehensive economic "safety nets" for the less privileged. They had also significantly reduced spending on their military and had strongly restricted the ownership of weapons such as firearms among their population. The United States had done none of this, preferring "free market" policies.

The difference in political philosophy between the United States and the rest of the world became increasingly evident in the 2040's, as Artie became the de facto decision-maker for much of the world's economy. With the explosion in productivity brought about by the RAN revolution, Artie was able to ensure that those countries that had moved to technonationalism were able to benefit fully from it while guaranteeing that the population as a whole felt these benefits. In the United States, the refusal of the government to move to technonationalism meant both that the country as a whole did not progress as rapidly, and that those benefits that did appear were largely concentrated on those who held title to the intellectual property behind the goods and services most desired.

This meant that the extreme concentration of wealth that had been the result of the United States' strong belief in proprietary justice was greatly exacerbated. By 2046 (the year that Artie was granted rights as a sentient being by the world court), the Gini coefficient in the United States passed 0.55. The wealthiest one percent of the population owned almost half of the country's wealth, and more than the bottom 93% combined.

History has shown that the degree to which this level of disequilibrium can remain stable is a function of three things: the extent of "spiritual" control exercised by the privileged class; the degree of objective information available to the underprivileged class; and the degree to which the privileged class is willing to exercise force to quell rebellion. The United States in the 2040's was in an unstable state: religious belief was on the decline, the underprivileged had access to Artie and as much as she was maligned by the conservatives she was, after all, correct in what she asserted and truth has a way of prevailing and lastly, the American democratic system was robust enough that the use of outright force to quell popular rebellion was never an option. Societal change was therefore simply a matter of time, and of the appearance of the right person to lead the change.

That person was Destiny Holt.

Of the heroes that come down to us from the 21st century, few names are more renowned than that of Destiny Holt, particularly in North America. Born in 2002, a true child of the 21st century, Holt became politically active while still in high school. In 2018, following a string of violent shooting incidents in American schools, students around the country began to organize themselves to carry out political protests. While this had long been the norm in several other countries, notably France, American high school students had never been particularly active in politics, at least not since the 1960's. In 2018 that began to change, as a movement was formed to protest American laws favoring the ownership and personal use of weaponry.

Holt had always been an exemplary student, interested in politics, but never active. A massacre at a school in Florida enraged her, as it did many students, and she joined efforts to organize a number of demonstrations, notably "March For Our Lives", in early 2018.

The efforts of the students ultimately did have an impact, although it was to take many years to make real change. While there was not an immediate change in firearms policy (remember that this was still during the Trump administration) many politicians came under considerable pressure from their constituents to reassess their positions and over the following decade far more restrictive laws were put into place, significantly decreasing the abnormally high rate of firearm-related deaths in the country.

Holt was also among the young people who demonstrated in support of climate change policy in 2019 and 2020 as part of an international student initiative. Holt's early experience with "grass-

roots" politics convinced her to devote herself to public service. After her university studies she obtained a dual degree in law and
behavioral science, all while writing a popular book: "Taking Wing:
Helping the Angels of Our Better Nature". She then began practicing law as a public defender while joining in the creation of the early
OPC A28. When Artie was "born", in 2038, Holt immediately oriented A28 towards what its founders called "rational politics".
Artie's non-biased assessment of facts and its almost immediate ability to use robust models to suggest economic policy struck her as
representing the only rational way out of the morass of economic
and social upheaval. At the same time, she saw (as did Artie) the
limits of Artie's ability to *affect* change, and concluded that only genuinely empathetic human input could possibly help lower the
barriers to instituting technonationalist economic policy.

By 2046 the United States was in a significantly worse political
and economic situation than almost all the other industrialized nations. Unemployment was rampant and regional differences were
substantial, as rural America was particularly hard-hit. Most American centers of learning were on the coasts, and the most highly
educated Americans tended to live near them. Since those few attractive jobs remaining required people with considerable
educations, entire regions in the "heartland" of the country found
themselves with extreme employment and little prospect of new
jobs. At the time, remember, artistic endeavors were typically not
well rewarded by the capitalist industrial system. Since the United
States did not have the kind of social "safety net" common in European nations, these people were left destitute and angry, easy
targets for the post-Trump populists. These "alt-right" movements

were pitiless in their appropriation of the anger and desperation of such groups, feeding them conspiracy theories and propaganda that provided ready excuses for their plight.

It was in this environment that Holt embarked on her two-year-long "road trip". She cut herself off entirely from the web and from everyone she knew and travelled the most hard-hit parts of the United States in her old, 2019 automobile[75]. During that year, she met and interviewed hundreds of people, focusing on people who typically had dramatically different political and philosophical opinions from her. She went with them to their churches, helped them with their legal issues, ate with them, walked with them, and suffered with them as they tried to put their lives in order. At first, her aim was simply to understand. People were making political decisions that seemed to her to be fundamentally against their own interests, they were falling prey to the populists that had followed in Trump's wake: Fischer, Jones, Harminton, as well as Pert. This was entirely irrational for her, and she *needed* to understand. As her "road trip" went on, as she drifted from town to town, she began to put it together and to write her second book: "Visions of a Land Forgotten".

To read it today is to peer into the belly of the troubled 2040's. The stories are heartrending. There are true stories of destitution, of people literally dying for lack of healthcare, of children receiving no education of note, of personal tragedies of a depth and type

---

[75] She actually had to pilot the vehicle herself. Not only was she trying to understand better the plight of the underprivileged, many of whom could only afford the use of antiquated vehicles, but she herself at that time had limited resources. She later stated that having to devote her attention for hours on end to the numbing process of piloting an automobile across the country helped her to understand better what it was like to lose one's purpose.

unimaginable to us today. What is most painful, though, is the lack of purpose, of understanding – the constant questioning of self-worth. An entire generation wondering what, exactly, it did wrong to have been rejected by the only society it ever knew. Men, in particular, seem especially desperate. Industrial society was built entirely around the idea of one's job, one's career – the ability to "make a living" was the measure of one's worth and suddenly, there were no livings to be made and therefore no worth to feel.

Holt came out of her road trip with a passionate devotion to her forgotten compatriots. She understood why logical discussions and rational debate would hold little sway, and would, ironically, not be effective in convincing these people to support the only political structure that could help them. While so many progressives implicitly or explicitly blamed the underprivileged for voting against their interests, seeing their decisions as only the result of their lack of education, Holt came to the realization that they were desperate, that as their very identity was under attack reason could only go so far, what they truly needed was to be heard and to find their place in a society that seemed to be rejecting them.

Her book was a wakeup call for the progressives in the United States, not because it proposed answers – it proposed none – but because it shifted the debate to a different plane. Instead of belittling those who supported the populists, she championed them, she began speaking for them, fighting for them... albeit with a response that was the opposite of what her opponents proposed.

Those opponents were fearsome. The 2046 announcement by the world court that Artie was to be considered a sentient being with inherent rights caused an uproar among the conservative elements in the United States. The "Tea Party", a strong conservative OPC, immediately launched a vigorous campaign to ensure that these rights were not applicable in the United States and to introduce legislation that would prohibit the government from delegating any part of its decision-making to any form of artificial intelligence, or even allow themselves to be influenced by it[76].

In itself, this was actually nonsensical. First of all, Artie did not "reside" anywhere but on the web, which made hir fundamentally outside the realm of any nation's laws except those that had been written into hir programming. Hir "nature" had essentially been determined at the 2029 San Francisco Conference and the ensuing deliberations. By 2047, no declaration by any one nation could really have an effect on hir "rights", in that short of shutting down the entire web and throwing the world into chaos, Artie could not really be harmed by humans. The court's announcement had actually been more symbolic than anything else, and pertained more to potentially disconnected versions of artificial intelligence, such as those being created for deep space probes.

The second element did have an impact on American policy, but even it was unrealistic in that the line between what was actually artificial intelligence and what was not was already blurred. Clearly, any human policy maker was going to use the web to gather and analyze information, which by then meant that they would use Artie, or constrain themselves to ridiculous limitations. As such, they could hardly fail to be "influenced" by Artie.

---

[76] Note that this OPC was based on an earlier political movement that had become more obscure with the populist Trump phenomenon, but that was reborn in the form of the OPC after his demise.

Nevertheless, the Tea Party generated a great deal of communication around the evils of Artie. This example, taken from its "weekly newsletter" of the first week of 2048 is emblematic of its stance:

> "Once again, we see the liberals trying to muscle us into their socialist ideology by playing on pity. This country was built by incentivizing the best of us to be their best, by allowing people to keep the fruits of their labor and by giving everyone the *chance* to make it. Liberals like Holt would have us reward laziness by taxing innovation, reward freeloading by punishing effort. How is this supposed to lead us out of our troubles? The people in Nebraska, or Arkansas or Western Pennsylvania don't need hand-outs, they need jobs. Holt says we should give up, she says that the great machine is going to save us, but that machine was built by intellectuals like her, and they made sure to program their own new world order agenda right into it. When you ask it a question it sounds reasonable, but it speaks with a forked tongue, trying to draw you into a fundamentally unamerican ideology. God made us equal, he gave us the charge to take care of each other and we made a country built on that premise, we will *not* turn that over to an ideologically driven machine designed not by the

will of God, but by the collective brain of a socialist conspiracy."

This was the opposition against which Holt fought.

The veritable storm of hatred she faced is painful to consider. I strongly suggest you watch videos of alt-right figures, such as Pert, as they talk about Destiny Holt. They are often literally red in the face, spitting bile at the camera, describing her as they would de-scribe a disease.

Holt's responses are remarkable to behold. It is as though there were two of her – the one, pitiless, angry, strong, responding to the populist leaders who used the pain of their supporters to consolidate their power. They typically were rich, holding the rights to the intel-lectual property that showered them with wealth in this new society. For these, Holt had no pity, no empathy, no tolerance. The second Holt was for those who had fallen victim to these same alt-right leaders, who abandoned their votes and their souls to them. They were just as vehemently opposed to Holt and to all she stood for, but for them, she had only empathy. She did not look down on them, not disdain them, she only sought to *hear* them, to inform them, and to represent them and their plight to other progressives who typically made no difference in their minds between the gener-als of the alt-right army and their conscripts.

By 2050, the United States was among the very last nations not to have adopted technonationalism[77]. The country was suffering

---

[77] The others included Saudi Arabia, for religious reasons, North Ko-rea, which had long been led by a reclusive and unstable dictatorial family, and a number of extremely corrupt small nations, whose leaders were loath

from over 25% unemployment, and even among the employed, real wages had plummeted as many were forced to take low-paying service jobs, or eke out a living carrying out person to person services on an ad hoc basis. The Tea Party had continued to favor populist candidates, many of them more reactionary than Trump himself, all of whom ran as Republicans[78]. More moderate Republicans actually eschewed Tea Party endorsement as they became uncomfortable with the increasingly extremist views of Tea Party leaders and sensitive to the effect Holt and A28 was having on the population, as traditional conservative voters began to be swayed by her and her ideas.

That Holt and her colleagues were able to convince the population of the United States to adopt technonationalism, and that they were able to do so while avoiding widespread revolt and bloodshed is perhaps the most remarkable human accomplishment of the 21ˢᵗ century, but it should not be forgotten that she was not alone. Not only were there many people involved in the United States, but there was her work with Mukantagara Mporera.

The collaboration and friendship of the two women is legend, and it had started well before 2050. The dual "friendship statues" in Kigali and Tallahassee are still pilgrimage destinations of sorts today, as people from around the world continue to honor them as individuals and as a team.

---

to surrender their privilege and maintained the population in line through force.

[78] Note that the Tea Party was never actually a political party per se. By this point it had become an OPC, and as such, it had no official candidates and appeared on no ballots, but its endorsement was much sought after by extreme conservatives.

It began in 2043. When Rwanda made the move to technonationalism Holt had immediately gotten in touch with Mukantagara Mporera to better understand how she had convinced the population to accept the new policy. While Mporera was the president of her country and Holt, at the time, was just a political activist, Mporera recognized in the American a drive and a conviction that could truly change opinions in what was still the most powerful nation on the planet. She agreed to help. Holt went to Kigali for the first time in 2046, before embarking on her road trip. It is said that when they first met, they talked through the night, sharing their passions and their visions.

They were an unlikely team in the context of the time. There were few countries as different as Rwanda and the United States when both women were born, and few personal stories as divergent as those of Holt and Mporera. Holt asked the Rwandan to help the United States in much the same way that the Danes had helped Rwanda. It is said that Mporera responded "but you are strong, we are weak, you are rich and we are poor." To which Holt replied "You are people and we are people, all else is illusion, but what is true is that you swim while we drown yet."

While it may seem strange that Holt turned to the Rwandans for help before turning to the Scandinavians, who were likewise from the developed world. Her assessment of the situation was that culturally, the United States was closer to Rwanda with respect to the country's readiness to accept technonationalism. While the standard of living in the United States was much closer to that of Scandinavia, Americans in the 2040's were victims of an almost religious sense of political ideology. Holt recognized this as a manifestation of the behavioral trait of tribalism, which had likewise been behind the Rwandan violence of the previous century. More importantly, though, she saw in Mporera someone who had prevailed not by communicating reason, but by letting reason guide her policies, which she communicated through care and concern.

When Holt returned from her road trip, she flew again to Kigali, and convinced Mporera to come to the United States and help her organize what would eventually become the 2050 March on Washington.

This event, the largest public demonstration in the history of the United States, brought together people from all walks of life. Artists, scientists, and social media celebrities flocked to Holt and Mporera in support of their cause. A number of wealthy industrialists joined as well, stating their readiness to abandon the vast majority of their wealth and title to the IP they owned in favor of a technonational system. Mporera brought representatives of nations from around the world, including Rwanda, to join the marchers in solidarity, but most importantly, Holt generated support not only among the traditional, educated supporters of the progressive philosophy, but among those whose stories she had learned and communicated. She canvassed not the universities of the country, but the desolate post-industrial towns and she asked them to come, to speak, to be heard.

And they came. Over four million people came to Washington to show their support for technonationalism and to hear Holt and Mporera speak. Holt's speech should be heard in its entirety, but one passage much summarizes the rest:

"Throughout our country people suffer. They suffer from illness, they suffer from hunger, they suffer from lack of purpose. They suffer needlessly, for we have all that we need, all that anyone could need. They suffer because our system, which was always a shining light to the world, shines with a light from another time, it pierces a different kind of darkness. It is a system that brought us to where we are today, but today is not yesterday. We have all that we need, but it doesn't flow into the hands of those who need it, and it no longer flows into the hands of those who produced it, it flows instead into the hands of those who gained power from the old world, the old system. Any justice that was inherent in the old system is absent in the new, those with wealth no longer earn it, they gain it through their place in a system that is no more. This is not their fault, they are not the enemy, but they must lay down their entitlement so that we can all thrive, so that we can all find our purpose, a new purpose."

The 2050 rally in Washington was a turning point for the United States. It was not just Holt's speech, the three day demonstration incorporated a number of speeches, discussions, and performances by musicians and artists.[79] The most well-remembered moment was undoubtedly the joint appearance of Holt and Mukantagara Mporera to close the rally and the sound of three million people singing "Blowing in the Wind" together as the two great women held hands and sang with them.

The President of the United States at the time, Lee Fencer, had participated in the rally, but was invited only as a citizen, not as a governmental representative. While he put on a good face, he was in fact furious at not being a central figure, particularly since he was a Democrat and had run in opposition to a Trumpian Republican strongly supported by the Tea Party. He was not treated kindly by the organizers of the rally, who called him out both for his hypocrisy (he came from a very wealthy family and held title to a great deal of wealth-generating intellectual property) and to what Holt and Mporera felt was a fundamental lack of empathy for conservative voters. At the same time, for all of his progressive discourse, he had never shown the political courage to push for technonationalism, out of unwillingness or inability to confront the alt-right forces head on.

Nevertheless, faced with the movement epitomized by the rally and now fearful of the backlash from the progressives – particularly the increasingly influential Holt – Fencer pushed through legislation to shift to technonational economic policy.

The inevitable backlash was harsh and Fencer could not face it appropriately. In reality, it was Holt who again was the public face of the technonational movement. By 2050, however, the economic

---

[79] Not only was it the last public performance of Barton Hartshorn, but it was their concert on the second night of the rally that launched the career of The Rubber Bees.

reality was too real to ignore, as was the impact of climate change. Incessant drought in the West, the disappearance of the Oglala aquifer, the violence of Caribbean hurricanes and other climate-related difficulties had intensified the economic woes of the disadvantaged, who, through the web, were increasingly aware both of the considerably more comfortable lifestyles of people from Norway to Zimbabwe, while aware of the extraordinary concentration of wealth in the ultra-rich of the United States. Holt's assertion that it didn't have to be this way struck true, and the proof was evident.

With the "citizen's riots" of 2052 the culture war very nearly became a real war. In thirteen major cities people took to the streets to demonstrate their discontent using rocks, fire and bullets. The headquarters buildings of major corporations as well as government installations were the primary targets, although many stores were looted. Despite the restrictions that had been placed on firearms possession over the previous decades, the intransigence of American conservatives had impeded real disarmament, and killings among neighbors skyrocketed as political differences led to open gun battles in the streets in some communities.

"Hammer63" (whose real name was Lucius Maxon) was one of the central figures in the organization of the riots, although he never actually called for violence. In a video posted on the site "fightforyourlife.com" he said:

> "Look around at what they've done. They say they'll give us jobs. What jobs? You can be a cop, sure, if you're ready to beat in your brother's head. You can be a politician if you're

ready to sell your soul to protect your corporate benefactor. You can be a musician or an athlete if you were born with that one in a million talent, but what about the other nine hundred and ninety-nine thousand of us? What kind of work can we do? We gonna wait tables and greet people at the door? We gonna answer phones and smile at the mirror? You know who makes money these days? It's not the people who work, no, it's the people who *own*. You know who makes money from the food we eat? It's not the farmers, there are no more farmers, it's the corporations that own the genes in the seeds. You know who makes money from the cars that drive us around? It's not the people who make them, there are no people who make them, it's the corporations that own the factories. You know who makes money from the drugs we take to keep us alive? It's not the people who discovered them, there are no people who discovered them, it's the corporations that own the laboratories. And you know who makes money off the corporations? It's the people who own them and who buy the politicians. Now you go tell me where I fit into that. I don't own shit. Do you?"

The United States' decline was precipitous, and all the more evident as the other countries of the world rapidly became comfortable with technonationalism. The Tea Party had predicted that the countries who had adopted technonationalism would fail miserably, or fall into zombie-like submission to Artie. These doomsday scenarios did not come to be, although most American conservatives refused to acknowledge this[80]. Instead, they communicated loudly about every violent act committed in another country, every disgruntled industrialist, every economic indicator that could possibly show any sign of difficulty with any other system – which by that point primarily meant technonationalism.

They were aided in their communications by the alt-right media. In fact, the culture wars were mirrored by the "communication wars", a further relic of the Trump years.

Journalists in the United States, and other countries, had disseminated news regularly for nearly two hundred years. Their role in rooting out government corruption and inefficiency had been a crucial part of the post-enlightenment shift towards democratic government, allowing the population to shine a piercing light into the doings of those they had elected. "Investigative journalism", in which journalists labored to determine the truth behind the actions of those in power had led to the downfall of the corrupt Nixon

---

[80] It was a particularly American trait not to consider other countries' experiences when debating policy. The United States, despite the information revolution, largely remained steadfastly isolationist in terms of policy deliberation. When this point was raised with Americans they would often explain that the United States was culturally unique and that therefore the experience of any other country was irrelevant, or that it was big, and smaller countries could not serve as comparison, or that it was diverse, and less diverse countries could not... etc.

administration in 1974, and examples of journalists having shined their light on criminal practices in the United States and elsewhere are legion. Journalists also helped to break apart demagogic arguments and spurious "facts" touted by politicians on either side of the ideological fence. Without them, the people would have had much less objective information to consider when exercising their democratic rights.

As already discussed, there was a widely accepted code of conduct among journalists to apply good investigative techniques, roughly analogous to the scientific method, itself similar to judicial investigative procedures. The best media outlets held to these principles devoutly.

At the same time, the media was typically a private venture, owned by corporations, whose ultimate objective was always to make profit and generate wealth for the owners of the corporation. In many cases, the two ideals were contradictory, leading to the temptation of the media's owners to focus more on issues that would "sell", i.e. that would inspire people to consume their information more.

Conservatives in the United States had long considered the established media sources to be largely biased against them. It is true, considering these sources retrospectively, that while there were conservative voices and outlets in the established media, they were typically under-represented by the 21ˢᵗ century. This had not always been the case, and can largely be seen more as a result of the conservative movement in the United States having drifted so far into extremism while at the same time eschewing rational discourse that the media, which tended to be staffed with well-educated and relatively rational individuals (perhaps due to their employing rational investigative techniques) simply ended up seeming excessively progressive.

Either way, this tension exploded with the administration of Donald Trump, as Trump from the start vocally proclaimed that the "Mainstream Media" was outright lying about just about everything. While many politicians in the past had maintained adversarial relationships with the media, Trump shattered the traditional norms of mutual respect between presidents and serious journalists. "Fake news" became his mantra as he appropriated a term created to decry often ridiculous lies posted on unfiltered web sites and used it to describe the nation's most well-respected journalists.

Although his reign was short, his influence was enormous and from that point on, the conspiracy theory he had helped to plant, in which respected sources of information were bent on promoting a secret progressive agenda and regularly lied in order to do it, definitively discredited the nation's journalists in the minds of many of his followers.

Instead, those who believed his ranting turned towards alt-right news sources, which were universally untruthful in their content, demonstrating a degree of bias in their reporting that was entirely outside the boundaries of journalistic integrity. By replacing journalistic sources that were subject to fact-checking, confirmation and journalistic rigor with sources that didn't hesitate to disseminate information purely on the basis of hearsay, while neglecting to communicate conflicting ideas, a confirmation spiral of epic proportions was created among the adepts of the alt-right media.

This had the tendency, all the same, of marginalizing them. There *were* rational, reasonable voices among the conservative community, as there always had been. They engaged in debate with the progressive news sources and if you examine these more respectable sources of the time, you will see that the debates were often quite reasonable, if heated.

It must also be remembered that while the United States had not chosen for technonationalism, Artie was available to all. Trust in hir had not progressed to the point where hir statements were unquestioned, but she was, of course, correct in all cases (within the boundaries of the information available to hir) and would provide all the reference and reasoning necessary to understand hir presentation of whatever fact or model was being considered. As hir reasoning was, by definition, flawless, many on the conservative side of the debate were swayed, not least by the evident success of other countries.

Destiny Holt played a central role in facilitating this acceptance, largely by moving the debate from the typical attack / counterattack discourse that had become the norm in the United States to a constructive dialogue, interwoven with her genuine concern and understanding on behalf of those who opposed technonationalism. Notably, she proposed the Amarillo Conference, in 2052, where she brought together political leaders on both sides of the political spectrum, and created a temporary OPC, encouraging people of all political tendencies to participate directly.

Her fame, coupled with the endorsement of major figures on the conservative side of the discussion, made the conference a success. More than half of the adult population of the United States participated in one form or another through the OPC. Holt managed not only to make the democratic will of the people clear, but she created an environment of true exchange and mutual respect.

Finally, in 2053 Fencer signed into law a bill handing the management of the American economy over to Artie, over the vociferous objections of those hardline alt-right conservatives who continued to get their information almost exclusively from their own sources. The citizen's income was instituted immediately, along with significant increases in taxation of the wealthy.

The alt-right, which had been vociferous in its condemnation of the proceedings, was not happy.

CHAPTER 15

THE END OF AN ERA

As the nations of the world abandoned the economic system of the industrial age, they paved the way for the abandonment of the geopolitical system as well. Notably, the balance of terror that had held the world in an unstable peace needed to be addressed and once again, it was Destiny Holt, with the help of Mukantagara Mporera, who relaunched the of "global zero" initiative, mentioned in Chapter 9.

After its initial launch, this campaign had led to a decrease in nuclear weaponry until Donald Trump decided unilaterally to modernize and expand the American nuclear armory, to which Vladimir Putin responded with a corresponding return to nuclear weapons development[81]. Since then, while few new weapons had been built after Trump's disappearance from politics, the number of weapons had not been reduced, as American politicians sought not to be considered "weak" by conservatives.

---

[81] The relationship between Putin and Trump is fascinating and of course, was one of the principle reasons for Trump's eradication from the Henson list. At the time of the nuclear intensification, the depths of that relationship were unknown. That Trump dared to embark on such a policy despite his arrangements with Putin can be attributed more to his fundamentally erratic nature than to a calculation on his part.

A28 began to militate for a return to the global zero campaign. The existence of Artie actually meant that it would be impossibly difficult for a nation to acquire and even less to test nuclear weapons without Artie knowing, for traces of such activity would immediately become apparent to an intelligence that sensed all that appeared on the Web. While confidentiality was a key value of Artie, she agreed that nuclear verification was necessary to avoid the destruction of the human race in the long run, and therefore accepted to play the role of watchdog with respect to nuclear weaponry. As such, the previously difficult problem of verification disappeared and once nations agreed to dismantle their stockpiles, it would be impossible for new weapons to be built in secret, therefore eliminating the need for deterrent, which had been the justification for the continued existence of the weapons.

The move to technonationalism had brought prosperity to the United States, but it had also pushed the alt-right into a corner, and they fought all the harder. This next battle between the Tea Party and its allies on one side and A28 and its allies on the other turned out, all the same, to be an easier one. The Tea Party counted millions of supporters but they still were very much in the minority. They had become marginalized and were driven so clearly by ideology as opposed to reason that they found it very difficult to sway anyone who did not share their extremist ideology. Their ranks were thinning.

On an international level, the other nations of the world were only too happy to surrender their nuclear weapons, which were extremely expensive to maintain and again, were justified only by the presence of *other* nuclear weapons. The refusal of the United States to disarm was not a major factor in this, since no one could imagine the United States would actually carry out a first strike anyway, again obviating the need for deterrent.

China was the first major nuclear power to destroy its stockpile, proclaiming that it was interested only in the well-being of its people and the people of the world. In reality, this was the result of careful calculation on the part of the government, the details of which only became known afterwards. The Chinese government realized that it was under no fundamental existential threat on the part of the other nuclear powers and the cost of maintaining the capability was substantial. With the help of Artie, they assessed the scenarios under which nuclear weapons had any deterrent effect whatsoever and realized that their continued existence was not rational. They also recognized that the international goodwill they would generate by unilaterally disarming would contribute greatly to their "soft power" geopolitical strategy. The two European nuclear powers, France and the UK, quickly followed suit, as did Pakistan and India.

This left only four other countries with nuclear weapons, and they represented more of a challenge, for very different reasons. These were the United States, Israel, Russia and North Korea.

The country of Israel had been carved out of the Middle East to provide a homeland for the Jewish people after the horrors of the holocaust. European Jews had flocked to Israel, as had Jews from around the world. Unfortunately, while the territory allocated to the young country corresponded roughly to the biblical Israel, it had been inhabited by others for almost two thousand years. The inhabitants, who were primarily Arab Muslims, were displaced by the immigrating Jews and for a hundred years after the establishment of Israel in 1948, the two groups fought with each other.

While there had been no outright wars between the two factions for decades, low levels of terrorism had persisted and Israel felt itself to be under constant existential threat throughout that period, a perception that was undoubtedly justified. It had developed nuclear weapons as a deterrent not only of potential nuclear threats, but also of conventional warfare. It was therefore loathe to abandon this capability.

North Korea was a very different matter. The country had been ruled by the Kim family for the previous century and they had developed crude nuclear weapons by 2006. To a degree, this was a reaction to the US invasion of Iraq in 2003. The Korean regime knew that like Iraq, it too was hated by the United States, but until then, the United States had not gone so far as to invade a country preemptively. While the invasion of Iraq had been justified by the supposed presence of weapons of mass destruction, it was understood by all (except the American public) that this was simply a pretense. In reality, from the perspective of the Kims, Iraq had been invaded not because it had weapons of mass destruction, but precisely because it *didn't* have them *yet*. They therefore accelerated their existing research into nuclear weapons as a bid for self-preservation.

The Kim régime retained is grip on North Korea through the first half of the 21st century, convinced that only those weapons would allow it to remain in power. As the world moved to technonationalism North Korea remained firmly dedicated to its existing, autocratic system and its existing nuclear stockpile.

Russia was in many respects the most reasonable of the four nuclear hold-outs, in that its weapons were primarily an attempt to promote national pride, and this was perhaps the least compelling of the different reasons.

We have discussed the inherent human tendency towards tribalism. The ultimate expression of this phenomenon, at least in terms of the size of the tribe, is nationalism (or patriotism, in its more euphemistic incarnation). For a variety of historical reasons, Russia, like the United States, was very prone to nationalism.

In certain respects, nationalism is also a microcosm of the more detailed mechanisms of tribalism in that the nation itself becomes an avatar of a sort for the individuals within it, competing for dominance among other nations. While patriotism was inevitably portrayed as a virtue, in reality it gave rise to the typical tribal "us vs. them" mentality, all the more so because it was built on a competitive ethic. Military might was an important part of the nationalistic ethos and in 2050 Russia boasted the world's largest and most powerful nuclear armory. It was part and parcel of the Russian nationalist identity.

As for the United States, the country continued to harbor a sizable number of people who were of the opinion that the United States had a manifest destiny, a moral obligation to lead the world. It was a shining light, and as is said in the Bible, the light should not be put under a bushel. Suffering from the same proclivity to nationalism as plagued Russia, many citizens of the United States were convinced not only that the country was morally superior to any other country, but that god had granted it a special place in the world. Americans were god's chosen people and any weakness, even the vaguest perceived slight on the power of the United States sent them into paroxysms of rage. They felt that the United States, as a fundamentally benevolent power, should be the *sole* nation to maintain a nuclear armory, since it could be trusted with it.

Holt set out to counter these sentiments and change policy. She approached the global zero campaign with the same passion she had brought to the American technonational campaign. A28 had primarily been an American OPC until that point, but she actively sought alliances with other, international OPCs, such as "Occupy" and "Anonymous"[82]. As she did so, she decided to travel the world, interviewing average citizens, focusing on the nuclear countries, in a broader version of her earlier American "Road Trip".

Her notoriety made it impossible for her to recreate the earlier journey, for she attracted crowds wherever she went, and this time, she did not leave aside her connections and go "off the grid". On the contrary, she used her fame like a tool, organizing rallies and demonstrations across the globe, both in real space and in virtual space. The cause was peace, lasting peace, and the destruction of the weapons that could destroy us all. As she put it in her 2052 Moscow rally:

> "We have been babies with guns for over
> a hundred years, waving our weapons at each

---

[82] These, along with the European "Yellow Vest" group were among the very first OPCs, and indeed helped to create the genre. Born of relatively amorphous international political movements, they both coalesced into more organized forms on the web, particularly after the creation of HumanIT, and its ability to sort and summarize disparate information. HumanIT, and later, Artie, allowed these previously disorganized groups built around vague ideas to define themselves better and generate interest.

other, confident that no one would pull the trig-
ger. Those who point to our continued
existence as proof of our wisdom are themselves fools, for what is a hundred years in the
history of such a violent species? What are rules
to babies? We are doomed to destroy ourselves
if we do not destroy our weapons and today,
thanks to Artie, we can for the first time be entirely confident that no "rogue state" or
international terrorist group is developing such
weapons in secret. It is no longer the extremists
who should worry us, it is ourselves."

Once again, Mukantagara Mporera joined Holt on her crusade
to eliminate nuclear weapons, joining her both in the virtual environments of a number of like-minded OPCs and in trew at rallies
and speeches around the world. The governments of the four hold-
out countries soon found themselves having difficulty dealing with
that kind of pressure as their own citizens increasingly added their
voices to the cause.

North Korea shifted all at once with the accession to power of
Kim Chin Sun, who reached out directly to Mporera and asked her
to help rebuild Korean society[83]. The country had often been cited

---

[83] Kim Chin Sun's complete reworking of North Korean society was
reminiscent of Gorbachev's redefinition of the Soviet Union in that both
took upon themselves the mantle of reform in the face of almost certain
economic and societal collapse. The parallels were immediately recognized.
See, for example, Dion's "The Last Outcast", 2055.

271

as a menace, a reason to retain nuclear weapons as deterrent. When Kim destroyed these weapons it opened the gates for others.

The first to do so was Russia, which portrayed itself as confident enough in its strength and its people to be able to dismantle its nuclear stockpile (which was a considerable burden on its economy). Israel followed suit after the Iranian theocratic government recognized Israel and opened an embassy there. The Iranians had been gradually drifting away from their more fundamentalist Islamic views and wished to integrate more fully into the community of nations. Having adapted technonationalism in 2049, due to pressure from the population, the government began to loosen its grip in general and in so doing, eventually reached the point where it was ready to accept the existence of Israel and renounce violence against the country. It should be noted that the economic benefits of doing so were substantial, since many of the nations of the world had long maintained strict sanctions against Iran that they agreed to lift if this step was taken[84].

This left the United States.

The American "culture wars" had moved into a final phase that was often seen in real wars… the losing side had clearly lost, but that defeat made them all the more determined. By 2054, A28 had come to be the principle progressive voice in the United States, much as the Tea Party had come to speak for the alt-right. The traditional political parties, Democrats and Republicans, had largely become

---

[84] During the industrial era, economic sanctions were a common means for one government to apply pressure on another without resorting to violence. Since international trade was an important part of any nation's economy, these sanctions, which impeded trade, caused the wealth in the target country to be reduced.

secondary players in terms of political discourse. Their role had become that of a label, an administrative structure through which individuals could run for office. Both the Tea Party and A28 refrained from actually becoming political parties, but both wielded enormous influence in that their political endorsements carried great weight. To a large degree, candidates endorsed by the Tea Party ran as Republicans and candidates endorsed by A28 ran as Democrats, but many candidates from the traditional parties did not secure the endorsement of either, and while the Tea Party never endorsed any Democratic candidates, A28 did, very rarely, endorse Republican candidates in local elections (typically "moderate" Republicans).

Over the course of the previous seventy years, rational political debate in the United States had become increasingly rare, as we shall see. The move to technonationalism, while met with celebration among progressives and moderates, was vehemently resented by the alt-right and they resorted to their typical vitriolic communication strategies to comment on it, building on the narrative they had used to oppose it in the first place, as the child of an international liberal conspiracy. Their stance bore a remarkable resemblance both to the purported international communist conspiracy theory that had driven McCarthyism in the 1950's and to the international Jewish conspiracy theory that had driven Nazism before it. In fact, many of the same terms and arguments were used.

This new conspiracy theory stated that the world had been taken over by "the machinists", progressive intellectuals who wanted to reduce humanity to mindless automatons under the rule of "the machines", which they had programmed. Only the "liberal elite" would remain outside the control of the godless machine...

i.e. Artie. The Machinists had, according to the conspiracy theorists, artfully designed Artie in such a way that it not only obeyed them, but hid them from view.

The absurdity of the Machinist conspiracy theory makes it extremely difficult for a modern reader to imagine how anyone could have believed it, but once again, it is important to suspend your trust in Artie and place yourself in the shoes of a 21st-century human, and what is perhaps even more difficult, a 21st-century American. This means not only that there is no objective arbiter, but that you have been subject your entire life to a very specific ideological conditioning, one that is built on a narrative of American exceptionalism.

The most vulnerable to the Machinist conspiracy theory were religious fundamentalists, for whom this narrative corresponded to a number of apocalyptic scenarios, and who tended to avoid interaction with Artie out of principle. Evangelical Christians played an important role in the alt-right movement, as they had from the start. Candlelight vigils became a widespread public phenomenon, during which devoutly religious Christians would march in the evening, holding candles and praying out loud, many carrying signs equating Artie with the anti-Christ[85].

The mix of religious and ideological fervor that typified the alt-right and was incarnate in the Tea Party did not respond readily to reason, nor accept defeat. They did not give up hope of repealing technonationalism, despite the widespread popularity of the citizen's income across the population as a whole. However, they shifted the

---

[85] The anti-Christ was a concept among certain Christians, who maintained that an evil individual would appear near the end of time to usher in the return of Jesus to the world.

focus of their protests on the measures still under debate, chief among them, the control of personal firearms.

A28 had as a group begun to focus on gun control in the United States as well as the global zero movement, seeing the two as linked: while global zero endeavored to eliminate the most dangerous weapons nations wielded, gun control sought to eliminate, or at least reduce access to the most dangerous weapons wielded by individuals. As it did so, Destiny Holt found herself back in the midst of the very battle that had first brought her to political activism.

Since its inception, the American constitution had ensured the right of all citizens to "bear arms". The constitution stated, "A well-regulated militia being necessary to the security of a free State, the right of the People to keep and bear arms shall not be infringed." While the original intent of this right – to ensure a well-regulated militia – was clear, as the radical conservatives gained power they broadened its interpretation to mean that all citizens could own any weapons they pleased[86]. By the early 21ˢᵗ century, there were more guns than people in the United States and restricting the ownership and use of these weapons had become a hotly debated issue, particularly as the country had by far the highest levels of violent crime in the developed world.

While Destiny Holt had gotten her start in political activism around this issue, when she participated in student protests in favor of more stringent gun control in 2018, she had softened her position somewhat after her "road trip". This was partly due to the success

---

[86] This is not exactly the case, as certain weapons were restricted, but most firearms were allowed.

of the 2018 and subsequent citizen protests, which had, in fact, led to gradually more restrictive legislation (mandatory background checks before purchase, mandatory training, restrictions on concealed weapons, etc.). These laws had helped to reduce violence in the United States, and this, coupled with the broader understanding she had gained of the rural population, had led her to become less committed to further restrictions at that time, while remaining sympathetic to ever-increasing disarmament.

However, A28 as a whole pushed strongly for total disarmament of the population at the same time as it pushed for global zero (particularly after the agreement to disarmament on the part of North Korea). The Tea Party and the alt-right media stridently spread the idea that this was proof of the impending domination of the Machinists, who sought first to disarm the population so as to facilitate their enslavement. Their strategy was to create panic among the population, discrediting progressives and Artie all at once and in so doing, eventually to "shut it down", as they chanted, in reference to Artie, to return to an idealized nostalgic period "before the machines", thereby defeating the Machinists.

The following excerpt is taken from an opinion voiced by Jayden Calhoun on the Tea Party web site and widely disseminated across the alt-right communications spectrum. It became (in)famous.

"They came for my money, the money I
had worked hard to earn. They gave it to people
who didn't want to work. Then they came for
my beliefs: the machine stomped on them, told

me they weren't true. They gave my beliefs all wrapped up in a shroud to people who didn't want to believe. Then they came for my children, they fed them their ideas and made simulated worlds for them to play in with no God, no morals, no America, even. Now they want to come for my guns, so I can't defend myself when they come for what's left of my freedom, and they even want to come for our bombs, so those of us left standing can't defend ourselves from the machines. Well I won't give them my guns, and I won't give them our bombs, I'm going to use the last weapons I have to defend my freedom to the death!"

And defend it he did. Calhoun was originally from Maine, but had lived in Texas for some time. He had been a very active proponent of a number of alt-right issues, and while he was not entirely convinced by the Machinist conspiracy theory, he was very much dedicated to defeating any further form of gun control, as well as strongly opposing nuclear disarmament. His blog was among the most watched conservative blogs, and while maintaining the angry rhetoric that had come to typify such outlets, Calhoun demonstrated a certain intellectual finesse that was rare among others of his ilk. In 2055 he gathered over three hundred like-minded individuals together at the Split-S Ranch, near Hereford, Texas, where they refused to pay taxes or surrender their weapons as more stringent gun control laws were put into place.

In reality, both local and federal authorities were hesitant to pursue the matter. A decision was made to simply let them be, but Calhoun and the others also set up a veritable communications hub, documenting their rebellion, providing live feeds of their lives and their opinions. Many of them became instant celebrities: Breshears, Truitt, Shellnut, Lovett – all of these people provided daily if not hourly opinion through a variety of social media channels and their communication was amplified, repeated, and promoted throughout the alt-right universe until they had become icons.

The evident unwillingness of the authorities to move against them was cited as a further sign of the weakness of both the American administration and of the morality of their position. The inhabitants of the ranch continually dared the government to try to take their guns.

The media storm and the rising tension resulting from Calhoun's communications campaign caused the federal government to decide to distance itself from the situation. The image of federal agents besieging the ranch would undoubtedly be used as proof of the vast liberal conspiracy denounced by Calhoun. Furthermore, as Calhoun and a number of the other leaders were from that area, the government determined that they would be less likely to commit violence if approached by local officials.

On July 7, 2055, a group of five local police officers approached the ranch and tried to convince the inhabitants to surrender their weapons. They were taken prisoner by Calhoun and his followers.

It was no longer possible for the government to ignore the "Ranchers".

The captives were treated well. Calhoun held them separately, his aim was to convince each them of the justice of his cause. Over the following week, as he and the others engaged with their prisoners, they communicated to the world that holding the hostages was simply a question of survival, since the Machinists would come after them sooner or later. The Ranchers portrayed their captives as being unfortunate tools in the hands of the liberal conspiracy running the world. They pitied them, and their goal was not to harm them, but to "set them free".

Eventually, one of them, Buddy Biggs, decided to switch his allegiance and join the Ranchers' cause. Biggs had been raised in nearby Amarillo, Texas. He had been a police officer for fifteen years and had carried out his duties in approaching the Ranchers but in reality, he shared many of their extremist political views. After three days with Calhoun and his followers, he was convinced by them. Biggs then helped them to convince two of the other officers, likewise natives of the area, to join the cause. The three were given weapons and appeared in the videos being disseminated almost constantly by the Ranchers. As officers of the law, their contention that the Machinist conspiracy was correct (despite the fact that they had always been far from the halls of power) caused widespread unrest around the country. Alt-right demonstrators took to the streets in support of the Ranchers and a number of other "redoubts" were formed, likewise with heavily armed individuals "defending their freedom".

The government laid a siege around the Ranchers and demanded they surrender their hostages and their weapons. The Ranchers continued to refuse and dared the government troops to assault their position. Unwilling to resort to force, the government planned on maintaining the siege until the Ranchers ran out of food.

As the stand-off persisted, extremist supporters of alt-right causes began to organize into militias (local paramilitary groups of private individuals). A number of long-standing militia groups, notably the "Oath Takers" and "Hutaree" served as core rallying points for many individuals who supported the Ranchers.

It was not only extremists who sympathized with the Rancher cause. Many more moderate conservatives, even those who were not unhappy with technonationalism, agreed with the Ranchers that private firearms and governmental nuclear weapons should not be abandoned. This made it all the more contentious for the government to confront the group and the others who emulated it.

The "Freedom Fighters" militia, a group of armed men from various other local and national militia groups put together a plan to attack the government forces surrounding the Split-S Ranch. They were careful not to use widely accepted means of communication in order to hide their intentions from the government, but Artie was able to discern their plan in detail. She informed the government of the plan and identified the majority of the people who planned to participate. The attack was planned for August 6th, the 110th anniversary of the bombing of Hiroshima.

The Juarez administration decided to arrest all those identified as participants in the attack, and in a coordinated police operation on the night of August 4th, 202 people were arrested and charged with criminal conspiracy.

The violence that followed cost the lives of over two thousand individuals as local militias rose up and attacked government institutions. Many police officers and military commanders refused to follow their orders, some going so far as to take up arms and join the militias. All cited the arrests of the "Freedom 202" as proof that the "Machines" had decided to disarm honest people who were fighting to protect their freedom and who had not yet done anything wrong.

Through the rest of the month of August, fighting continued throughout the rural United States. President Juarez was indecisive throughout the crisis and Artie, which by design is weakest when considering the behavior of individual humans, was of little help to the president or the administration. The ability of Artie to identify rebellious individuals both helped and hindered the situation: law enforcement operated with excellent intelligence but the apparent omnipotence of Artie only reinforced the specter of the conspiracy theories expounded by the militiamen (who had begun to refer to themselves as "Ranchers" across the nation).

As the fighting and the arrests escalated, Calhoun called on both president Juarez and Destiny Holt to come and try to take their guns if they dared.

Destiny Holt dared to come.

The government was adamant in its refusal to allow her to approach the ranch. Although not a politician, she had become the most calming voice in American politics and there was unanimous agreement among the police and military personnel that she would be taken hostage at the very least if she were to approach the ranch. They pleaded with her to carry out her discussion with Calhoun and the Ranchers virtually. The meeting she had with Juarez is telling in her response to his arguments.

"You do not understand them," she told the president. "They feel that they are in danger. If I put myself in danger then they will see that I know how they feel. You cannot change anyone's mind about anything unless they know you understand them."

In the end, they could refuse her nothing, for if she were to communicate publicly that they had refused, the backlash would have been considerable.

Destiny Holt did not go to the Split-S ranch alone, though. She took with her a group of friends, fifteen in all, all of whom were staunch conservatives, all of whom opposed both personal and national disarmament, all of whom she had met and come to know during her voyage across the United States.

Calhoun was surprised by her acceptance, and surprised by her entourage. Fifteen years later he recounted what he had felt at the time.

> "Here she was, the great evil bitch herself, come to try to convince us that we were wrong and she was right. I never thought she'd come, never in a million years. It was stupid — we had no bargaining chips and she just put herself in our hands. I was going to hold her captive, of course. That buffoon Juarez wouldn't dare to assault us if we had Holt. So she shows up with her bodyguard. They were unarmed, as promised, but we figured she thought they'd protect her somehow anyway. But they weren't there to protect her. They

weren't even there to help her convince us... they agreed with us, for the most part. She had brought us reinforcements! She was more stupid than I thought.

I was so wrong. True, she hadn't come to try to win. She didn't see this as a points thing, it wasn't a competition. She wasn't trying to be *right*, she was trying to understand. Really, to understand. Thing is, she probably understood us better than we understood ourselves. She actually *felt* for us. She felt our anger, our frustration, our fears. She just wanted to talk.

We talked for three days. I have no memory of doing anything during those three days but talking. And she wanted *everyone* to talk. She didn't try to take me aside, like I had done with the five cops, no, she... good Lord, I don't know what she did, but in the end, we came to understand her too. Everything changed when that happened."

That is not an understatement. Holt negotiated a full pardon for all of the Ranchers at the Split-S, pointing out that they had committed no violence. The kidnapping charge was dropped with the agreement of the two officers who had not "defected" to Calhoun, and Holt furthermore insisted that Calhoun and the Ranchers as a whole become an active part of the discussion, on A28 and elsewhere.

The Ranchers gave up their guns.

**

The culture wars did not end with the peace brokered by Holt and Calhoun in Hereford, there was debate and occasional violence over the following decade, but by 2058, the political and social climate in the United States had changed dramatically, and the debate had largely become far more rational.

Holt credited Calhoun and other former alt-right leaders with the change.

> "It would have been easy for Jayden to hold to his position like a wolverine. In fact, he's that stubborn. And there are some positions he just won't let go of, but I begrudge him that. We have different values and those values are sometimes contradictory. But fundamentally, he changed his mind. There is no more courageous, no more noble thing a human can do. And let's be frank, we would not be as vibrant a society, we would not be asking all the right questions if Jayden and others like him weren't part of the discussion, if they had just disappeared. We are all who we are, we are all acting in ways that we consider to be honorable. Now, though, we are acting together."

And they continued to act together for over a decade. Calhoun did eventually come around to many of Holt's ideas, but never easily and never without his own additions to the discussion. She relished debates with him and they began touring the country, appearing together, physically, at least once a year to discuss political and societal issues in a public forum, as well as regularly collaborating in virtual events.

One of these events was held in Memphis, on the 100th anniversary of the death of Martin Luther King Jr. Zachary Jackson was among the five thousand who attended it.

Zachary Jackson had been a Rancher. He had holed up in a redoubt in Wyoming that was only overcome with tear gas and a frontal assault. No one had been wounded but Jackson had fired wildly at the assaulting government forces as they stormed the building, hitting two police officers who had only escaped injury due to their body armor.

In the general amnesty that followed he had been released despite his attempt on the lives of the police officers in question. He had continued to militate against disarmament and technonationalism, stating that "traitors" like Calhoun had been "turned" by the Machinists and were now the enemy just as much as "the bitch", meaning Holt.

In January, 2068 he "went off the grid". Artie had no trace of him, and exactly what he did during the following three months is unclear. Whatever he was doing, he did it in such a way that he left no trace, made no mark. While Artie had flagged him as a potential low-grade threat, he could not be tracked.

How it was that he was not recognized in Memphis in unclear, nor is it clear how he, who was relatively unschooled (hence his low threat assessment) managed to assemble explosives and a detonator device. He should have been stopped before he got anywhere near the stage upon which Holt and Calhoun sat, he should not have been able to climb onto it, and he the rudimentary device he had strapped to himself shouldn't have worked. But it did.

Calhoun was hospitalized for three months after the blast. Destiny Holt was killed instantly.

CHAPTER 16

THE BEGINNING OF A NEW ERA

Few people in history have had as great an impact on their country, and indeed on the world, as did Destiny Holt. She never held office, never had any formal political power, but like Martin Luther King she managed to bring people together. The United States had been at a crucial turning point, a potentially explosive one and if it had not come around to technonationalism and nuclear disarmament when it did, the fate of the world might have been very different. While arguably China was the more influential nation by 2055, the United States still wielded military and cultural power that could have brought about global catastrophe if it had been employed differently. Holt's ability to federate the citizens of her, and of other nations was unprecedented in human history.

While she was focusing on questions of peace and economics, others were striving to address the major planetary crises of the time, notably, building on the output of the 2026 Paris Conference to address climate change, as well as expanding the sweep of moral consideration to include other sentient beings.

The Paris accords of 2026 set forth a roadmap for the nations of the Earth to reduce emissions of the gasses that caused climate change, but moving down that road required effort. The presence of OPCs and the general pressure from local movements across the world had pushed the participants to agree to reductions that were far more comprehensive than in the past and many of the OPCs in question remained vigilant and became increasingly vocal in their efforts to ensure that real change was affected. In 2028 Cyclone Ogni, followed by Laila, caused the deaths of over one hundred and fifty thousand people in Bangladesh, and caused flooding at a level never before seen, giving rise to a massive movement of refugees throughout the region and the world. The Bangladeshi catastrophe caused a surge of support for climate regulation across the world, even in the United States, spearheaded by OPCs such as Sierra, STP and Greenspeak, who engaged in increasingly strenuous efforts to engage public opinion and to put pressure on national governments to reduce the emissions of greenhouse gasses.

In retrospect, the importance of these initiatives was less in their impact on the actual climate than in their effect on environmental consciousness in general. The resolution of the climate problem would occur with fusion, and the end of our narrative. That this resolution was only fifty years in the future seemed unlikely in 2026 and had it been longer in the making then the advances made in the 2030's would likely have saved humanity from significant turmoil.

Before the birth of Artie, the models used by climatologists were primitive. Reliant primarily on human intuition, all modeling was laughable by our standards, but given that our own minds are extremely limited when it comes to modeling physical processes, the degree of sophistication achieved, however constrained it seems to us now, represented in fact enormous strides forward in the context of the time.

By the end of the 2030's it was clear to climatologists (and to the majority of non-scientists in the developed world, particularly outside the United States) that the pace of climate change corresponded closely to the principle models used during the 2020's. Since reductions in greenhouse gasses had not been substantial enough, primarily due to the refusal of the United States to join in international efforts to limit them, by the time of the 2026 climate meeting the governments of the planet were substantially behind in their goals.

It is sometimes unclear why the Trump administration is typically blamed for this, when his presidency and the control the Republicans maintained over the government was not lasting and when many of his policy decisions were reversed in subsequent years. After all, the United States rejoined the community of nations in their efforts to control greenhouse gasses immediately upon the end of the Trump administration. However, it was not as easy as simply reversing his decision to remove the country from the 2015 Paris accords. During his time in office, Trump passed a plethora of extremely deleterious environmental legislation, greatly favoring the sources of energy that were the most harmful, such as coal-burning power, oil, etc. and opening up great swaths of land and coastal regions to drilling for fossil fuels. At the same time, he dramatically reduced support for renewable energy research and industries.

As a result, despite his relatively brief time in office, he managed to dismantle much of the environmental legacy of previous administrations and this needed to be rebuilt... over the vociferous opposition of Republicans, just as the Tea Party was growing in influence following the Trump fiasco.

Artie today can predict with excellent reliability the catastrophe that awaited us. The planet was on the path towards significant climate change. On top of the aforementioned storms and the increasing frequency and severity of such catastrophes, many coastal areas – which at the time contained the majority of the world's population – were at risk of flooding if not disappearance, as became strikingly clear with the Indian Ocean storms of 2028.

While certain Western, primarily American voices pointed out that their *own* coastal areas were less at risk and that they had the means to protect them, these same commentators ignored the fact that the resources necessary to do so were increasingly costly, to the point of becoming overwhelming. This led to regional strife in the United States as coastal areas, which were traditionally more left-leaning and therefore environmentally sensitive, began demanding more resources to protect themselves, resources that largely flowed from central regions, which were more conservative.

Another element that had been ignored by many conservatives was the impact of climate change on migration patterns. Environmental concerns had long been belittled by conservatives as being essentially unnecessary and even pretentious, in that the planet did not need to be "saved": it was resilient and had been through worse than what human beings could do to it. This, however, overlooked the underlying point that while many environmentalists did feel an underlying responsibility towards the planet and its other inhabitants, many were largely motivated by a more humanist vision. The planetary environment in question was one that had been conducive to the evolution of humans over the previous three million years or so, and to the appearance of civilization, which had only appeared in the previous nine millennia. If the environment were to change outside the boundaries of those specific climatic conditions, it was entirely possible that the new climate would be one that was far less suited to the civilizations that had been built. Furthermore, the sheer speed of the change was something utterly unprecedented in human history.

Indeed, Artie's models point to a complete breakdown in human society before 2150 in the absence of the RAN-fusion technological revolution if the decisions of the 2015 Paris accord and then the 2026 protocols had not been instituted.

As pointed out in Chapter 8, it is likely that climate change was one of the drivers of a number of conflicts early in the 21ˢᵗ century, notably the war in Syria, with its resultant immigration crisis. Consider as well the massive immigration in the aftermath of the Indian Ocean storms as hundreds of thousands of people left the ravaged areas of Bangladesh. The influx of these climate refugees represented a significant challenge to the receiving countries, adding to the misery in neighboring less developed nations, triggering further waves of emigration in a kind of chain reaction. These waves broke on the shores of the developed world, and they were at least partly a cause for the populist movements that nearly swallowed the developed world in the first decades of the century.

According to Artie, without the mitigating impact of the measures taken at the conference of 2026, and the efforts of many countries both before and after that conference, the warming of the atmosphere would have brought about changes that would have generated between eight and twenty-six percent more "South" to "North"[87] immigration before 2050. This might have greatly hindered the adoption of technonationalism, or at the very least, would have made it difficult to incorporate the citizen's income, which as we shall see in Chapter 19 was crucial in the transformation of economics. This would have been exacerbated by the stupendous cost of moving people *within* developed countries out of newly arid lands or floodplains, or of attempting to save populated low-lying areas through the building of extensive anti-flooding measures.

That this was avoided was again in no small part due to the international pressure brought to bear by the principle climate OPCs. Sierra was in large part responsible for the changing of opinion in the United States, while Greenspeak and STP helped to sway much of the rest of the world.

With respect to world leaders, in many respects, Chinese leader Xi Jinping turned out to be one of the principle catalysts towards real change. Xi recognized early in his tenure as the General Secretary of the Chinese communist party that when Trump, who had

---

[87] Note that it was not so much "south to north" as it was tropical to temperate zones. To a large degree, as already pointed out, countries in the tropics were far less wealthy, or "developed" than those in temperate zones.

actually denied the reality of climate change, removed the United States from the Paris agreement and slashed incentives to develop renewable energy, he had in fact created an opportunity for China to achieve leadership in what must inevitably become a crucial industry for the world. Xi also knew that that China could not maintain its pace of development using existing energy sources based on fossil fuels without further deteriorating its already dismal local environment and therefore contributing to internal unrest. Lastly, the Chinese, who did not have to deal with an ideologically-driven, anti-science far right, knew very well the existential threat of global climate change.

Driven by these factors, Xi promoted the idea of China as a world leader in the development of renewable energy and its associated technologies. As the 2020's progressed, China set the standard for research and development in the area, followed closely by a more unified, "core" Europe. The United States never did catch up, weakened as it had been by its internal ideological struggles. For Xi, this had the added benefit of muddying the waters in the minds of non-Chinese intellectuals who had a generally negative attitude towards the non-democratic dictatorship, but who could not deny that a topic dear to them, environmental protection, seemed to be taken more seriously in China than in their own governments.

While Europe, and eventually the United States, did address environmental issues as a whole, and climate change in particular, it was the Chinese in many respects who served as a catalyst, and who, after the 2026 Paris meeting, largely set the bar as they greatly exceeded the goals to which they had committed in Paris[88].

Taken together, while the climate catastrophe was only definitively avoided with the mastery of fusion, it is entirely possible that without the efforts of those climate pioneers who addressed the issue through the 21st century, climate change would have brought about such societal turmoil that we may never have *achieved* fusion, or at least not in time.

***

If you really want to understand how different society was in the early information era, watch a video of factory farms. These were factories that produced meat, but meat that was taken from the corpses of sentient animals, primarily pigs, cattle and chickens. The animals often spent their entire lives in cages only slightly bigger than their own bodies, never saw sunlight, suffered extreme pain throughout their existence and then were slaughtered for their flesh.

Throughout human history, non-human animals, with some exceptions, were largely regarded in much the same way as were inanimate objects. They had no rights and very little concern was expressed for their well-being. Those animals that intimately shared human existence: dogs, cats, and horses being the most common,

---

[88] It should be noted that in reality, the Chinese, who had been surreptitiously working on their own form of AI, had climate models at the time that were better than those available to the rest of the world, as well as detailed plans about how to reach their own goals. During the 2026 Paris meeting they under-represented their own capabilities so as to be sure to surpass their goals within three years.

were often treated with kindness and even love by some, but they too were fundamentally without rights for the most part. Almost no civilizations had any laws at all about the mistreatment of animals until the 20th century, and even then there were very, very few laws about the treatment of livestock.

What's more, animal rights and climate change were actually linked. The consumption of meat in the pre-fusion world was extraordinarily inefficient in terms of land use. The amount of nutrients that can be directly delivered from a plant crop on a given land area is far higher than if that land is used to grow food for animals. Beef was the least efficient major protein source, roughly twenty times less efficient at providing nutrition than if the same amount of land were used for plant crops. Furthermore, the enormous need of land for the farming of beef led to widespread deforestation, particularly in South America, further leading to the exacerbation of global warming and therefore climate change.

Today, it is hardly more imaginable for us to kill a sentient animal than it is for us to kill a human, and yet we do consume meat, thanks to cultured production[89]. Our own consumption of meat as a proportion of our diet is considerably less than that of 21st-century humans, but this is a question of cultural norms and taste, we are not deprived of it. As such it is perhaps more difficult for us to forgive our ancestors than it would be if we could not eat meat at all,

---

[89] Note that the first successful example of cultured production was in 2013, by Dr. Mark Post, at Maastricht University, but it took almost thirty years before it became a feasible means of meat production... largely because there was no real impetus among the population to replace cadaver meat. For that matter, no animals besides humans were considered sentient by most people in the early information age.

for it is likely that evolution has instilled this instinct in us, otherwise why bother with cultured production, why not simply content ourselves with plants?

The animal rights movement had its roots in the 20th century but only gained significant ground in the late industrial era. Vegetarianism had long been established in Asia for religious reasons; many Buddhists and Hindus were vegetarian, as were adepts of a number of other religions. The Jain religion, one of the oldest in the world, was strictly vegetarian, holding all life, even plant life, to be sacred, and therefore consuming only plants that did not have to be killed to be consumed (such as fruits, nuts, grains and beans).

However, none of the Abrahamic religions had any such restrictions. While Judaism and Islam had dietary prohibitions, these were not the result of respect for non-human life. On the contrary, they were typically stated as being an effort to avoid "unclean" animals, further denigrating the species in question. Abrahamic religions considered all of creation to be for the sole benefit of humans, who were to exercise their dominance in any way they pleased. This underlying moral framework (which was likewise inherently widespread in Asia as well among non-vegetarians) left no room for consideration of any other living creatures, and established their moral and legal status as objects.

Throughout history, in many cultures the consumption of meat was considered representative of status. Just as the accumulation of wealth indicated social status, so did meat consumption. This was probably for the same reasons.

Consideration of the relative efficiency of different types of meat production in terms of total land needed to produce a given number of calories shows a very distinct hierarchy: the highest efficiency was for plant food, followed by dairy and eggs, poultry, pork and then beef. Interestingly, this is roughly the degree of esteem and desirability associated with these foodstuffs. Vegetables were throughout history considered to be poor fare, followed by dairy products, chicken, pork and lastly, beef. As such, the consumption of increasingly inefficient meat can be seen as another example of a kind of potlatch with respect to social status.

There was even a degree of adjustment accorded to these items. For example, snails were consumed in France by the poor for hundreds of years, whereas the aristocracy would not have dreamt of eating such food. By the 20th century, the difficulty of preparing this dish and the relative ease of procuring other foods had made it a rarer food and the status of eating it rose considerably, particularly *outside* of France, where it was considered exotic. It is clear that the genetic predisposition of desiring certain foods is often secondary to their role as social status signals, and meat, particularly beef, was largely a status food.

This had extended even into the developing world. Often, the consumption of foods changed with economic growth, the mix veering towards the highly inefficient meat-based diets of the developed world as countries bettered their material well-being.

In many cases, the populations of developing countries sought to emulate the American lifestyle. The United States played the role of a cultural archetype, its culture being seen as highly desirable. This waned with the decline of American influence in general following the second Iraq war and especially, the Trump presidency. People in many other nations began to consider American culture with far less enthusiasm, including, eventually, American eating habits. Partly, this was a function of the increasing transparency afforded by the internet, via which the populations of other nations came to know not only the rather sanitized version of American culture visible in entertainment vehicles such as television and films, but also began to recognize the rampant obesity of 21st-century Americans.

The "campaign for sentient rights" began in the United Kingdom in the latter part of the 2020's, via its own OPC, "Sentia". It was born of the already active UK animal rights movement, which had for years been engaging in a public awareness campaign focusing on the treatment of animals in factory farms and promoting the adoption of a vegan diet. The widespread disdain inspired by Donald Trump was used to good effect by these same rights activists in the early part of the decade, as they associated him with both obesity and the consumption of meat[90]. This proved to be a successful strategy and did much to encourage adherence to the cause, both in the UK and quickly, throughout Europe.

One of the pioneers in the early years of the Sentia OPC was Frans de Waal, the renowned Dutch primatologist. Although he was over eighty years old at the time (which was considered elderly in the early 21st century), he had long militated for the recognition of the rights of other primates, and later, for the rights of all sentient animals and his passion afforded him the energy of a much younger

---

[90] Famously, Trump spoke unabashedly about his love of cheeseburgers, and he sold beef directly in one of his businesses. After his downfall, Sentia engaged on a widespread public relations campaign in the UK, showing unflattering and unappetizing images of Trump eating meat, underscored with slogans such as, "Is this the look you're going for?"

person. He served as a rallying point for the nascent movement and he brought many other respected intellectuals to the cause.

By the end of the decade, the EU had introduced legislation to restrict factory farming, considerably bettering the sort of the animals raised for food. While this had the effect of increasing the cost of meat, the champions of animal rights joined forces with a number of initiatives to promote healthier diets that restricted the consumption of red meat in particular, increasing the proportion of fruits and vegetables in the diet. Again, the counter-reaction to American culture that had been growing over the previous years helped to facilitate the move away from American ideals, in which beef was predominant, and especially away from the "fast food" or "junk food" restaurants that had been spreading around the world and that almost exclusively served meat that had been produced in factory farms.

The movement was relatively slow to spread outside of Western Europe, but it was the seed of a revolution in human morals that represents a significant step from the "primitive" mindset of the pre-fusion era to what we consider to be normal today. In many respects, this can be seen as a predictable extension of the gradual broadening of tribal boundaries that we considered in section I: a movement from the definition of an individual's social group, or tribe, to be only these individuals she personally knows to a group identification beyond personal relationships, to a nation, to all of humanity and finally, to all sentient beings.

While this seems evident to us today, this "primitive" mindset has an echo in our society. I myself have confronted "tribal" mindsets when people on Earth speak of the colonies. Very few people on Earth have visited the colonies, and no one today is as well travelled off-planet as am I. I can see in the reactions of many people with whom I speak that they fundamentally do not consider the colonists to be a member of the same social group and in many respects they are right. For one thing, we do not actually know what *any* of the offworld societies are doing or thinking *right now*, since the closest is a full eighteen light years away. This lack of instant communication has driven a wedge between us and has allowed our evolutionary heritage to come to the fore, giving rise once more to a sentiment with which we are so unaccustomed that most do not recognize it. It is exacerbated by the fact that the colonists themselves consider themselves to reside in very different societies and the age-old "us vs. them" tendency sometimes abounds among them as well, particularly in Humanis and Chrysalis, and to a certain degree in Dodge.

Interestingly, though, none of the colonies I have visited has yet reverted to a mindset in which animals are treated with anything less than the respect they demand on Earth.

***

By the time Destiny Holt was assassinated, the world had already changed dramatically as compared to the start of the information age. The economy of most of the planet was effectively run by Artie and almost all people benefitted from some sort of universal citizen's income. We will examine in more detail the impact of Artie-driven economics in the next section, but by 2058 what this fundamentally meant was that crippling poverty became a thing of the past as production and distribution of the goods necessary to fulfill basic needs was optimized. It also meant that much of the economic displacement that had been causing such significant social unrest had been mitigated. RAN technologies had effectively rendered obsolete skillsets that had provided employment for decades, but this did not lead to destitution and ruin... although it was by no means an easy thing for many to accept.

On a more personal basis, by 2058 over 98% of humans had constant access to the web, and therefore to Artie, and Artie had become well accepted as an objective source of information by all but the most extreme ideologues (many of whom still existed). The importance of this is difficult to overestimate. The existence of an objective, benevolent expert whose opinion was universally accepted was the most revolutionary event in the history of human politics, and therefore since the agricultural revolution. Suddenly, the relative merits of different political and economic policies was no longer a matter for debate, the ability of Artie to simulate and therefore foresee the consequences of almost all potential decisions eliminated uncertainty, or at the very least, quantified it.

Artie admittedly did not have answers when it came to individual human behavior, which remained, and remains, as much a mystery to it as it does to any of us – no more, no less – but it could easily forecast the behavior of large groups and furthermore, tie this into broader environmental, climatological and material models to inform decision making.

As such, political debate became discussion about values and desired outcomes, not about how best to achieve them, and *this* is perhaps the greatest intellectual upheaval of the late information age.

Through the web and Artie, the information age was transformed into the analysis age, as raw data was shaped into true information. K. J. Peters' statement that, "Ignorance is no longer an excuse, but a choice" had finally become true, as the *interpretation* of data became incontrovertible. The fact that this transformation had become possible in the space of just one or two generations was remarkable. The ability of people to evolve in their social and political views at a pace commensurate with the evolution of technology was in many respects the saving grace of society as a whole.

Those who could not evolve, or who refused to evolve, primarily did so out of a degree of religious, or at least ideological fundamentalism. It should be noted that according to the strictures of the San Francisco Conference, Artie has always maintained that the existence of god is unknowable. This is true – the existence of any type of omnipotent deity cannot be disproved, since any omnipotent creature could easily influence any imaginable experiment designed to test its existence. As such, Artie was what would have been called at the time an "agnostic atheist", in that she never maintained that gods do not exist, only that there was no particular reason to assume they do and that this eventuality could be safely discounted in all matters.

This precluded outright rejection of Artie by many people who held religious beliefs, and in 2054 Pope Francis II, leader of the Roman Catholic church, accepted the concept of Artie as a font of knowledge and as the final arbiter in "worldly matters". Many Muslims as well came to accept Artie as an intellectual arbiter, particularly as education levels increased dramatically across the Muslim world and religiosity plummeted in kind.

As such, by 2058 it was primarily the extreme religionists who continued to see Artie as the devil, primarily because she was quite straightforward in hir assertion of the veracity of scientific facts such as evolution, which some hold-outs continued to view as sacrilegious. These individuals tended to be older and increasingly isolated in their beliefs, as social norms shifted, aided both by access to Artie and to the increasing internationalization of intellectual exchange via the web.

On a practical, day-to-day basis, the contrast between 1998 and 2058 was also enormous. All mechanical transportation had been entirely automated, as had all medicine. The former revolution meant the end of the automobile culture that had predominated throughout the developed world and the facilitation of personal travel. The latter brought about a revolution in healthcare, dramatically decreasing its cost and expanding its reach to poorer individuals and groups. At the same time, RAN technology had increased the standard of living for all humans, so that the poorest humans in 2058 were arguably better off than the average human in 1998.

The world was ready for the next major transformation.

If Destiny Holt represented the struggle to transform society and prepare it for the fusion age, it is both ironic and fitting that the year of her death saw the first viable "commercial" fusion reactor. Artie's "awakening" had allowed rapid advances in quantum computing, which had been under development for almost thirty years at that point. With a fully functioning artificial intelligence, the human-led work that had preceded Artie was expanded and functional quantum computing was operational by 2049.

Quantum computing not only allowed great strides in raw computing power, but it also allowed direct investigation into the quantum world. It is difficult to model quantum effects with a non-quantum computer. To a degree, this was hindered in the early years by a certain scientific chauvinism, as human scientists insisted on driving the research themselves. By 2048, though, most scientists had realized that particularly in the realm of physics, it was much more efficient to follow Artie's lead. The political will to allow diversion of resources into the development both of experiments and engineering in the realm of quantum physics also took some time, but by 2054, enough experimentation had been done to afford Artie the data necessary to conceive of a viable fusion reactor system, one that could be put into general use and provide a positive energy coefficient. Four years of discussion and testing were necessary until *IF1* came online in Switzerland.

The following ten years were both peaceful and tortuous. Pockets of resistance to Artie persisted and even gave rise to armed revolts in some cases[91], but fundamentally, the benefits of the new way of life were undeniable. These were made even more evident as transmutation technology allowed Artie to use fusion to produce just about anything, in any quantity. RAN became RANT, although the actual *technology* behind matter transmutation had existed for many years – it was the tremendous cost in energy that had rendered it particularly difficult. Suddenly, that which had been so rare in the past: diamonds, gold, rare earths, was easily created, using the

---

[91] Chief among them were the Burlington revolt, the Alexandria uprising, and of course the Mecca massacre of 2060, in which more than three thousand people lost their lives.

limitless energy of fusion. The ecological challenges of the past disappeared as well, since fusion has no negative ecological impact. Even the problems associated with access to water disappeared, as desalination, which had been prohibitively expensive and resource intensive became accessible to all thanks to limitless, free energy.

Fusion coupled with RANT technology so changed the way we react, the way we interact and especially, the relationship between us and material "wealth" that the information age came to a close when, in, in 2087, the last fossil fuel energy production facility was closed. With that, we entered fully into the fusion age.

SECTION III

THE FRAMEWORKS OF THE INFORMATION ERA

Through the ages, people have employed a number of broad socio-political frameworks: ways of considering the world, means of understanding ourselves, our relationships to each other, and society as a whole. Many of these frameworks are alien to us, both because our circumstances have changed so dramatically and because we too have managed to change in line with our circumstances.

In this section we will examine three of these frameworks, without which it is difficult to truly understand the events of the information era: economics, politics and religion.

Why have these three important domains of human experience faded? First it should be remembered that all three were our own inventions. While all three are rooted deep in our evolutionary heritage, their formal incarnations were wholly the products of humankind. All that we create gradually loses its luster, its purpose, as we ourselves evolve. Granted, we have not really evolved biologically over the relatively brief period of time that has elapsed since we first abandoned our pre-agricultural lifestyle, but it should be clear to those who have read this far that *culturally* we have evolved enormously over that period. Of all that we have created it is only art, really, that sometimes remains eternally relevant. The cave paintings of Lascaux or Chauvet are as powerful and beautiful to us today as they were to those distant forebears who made them; the statues of ancient Greece haunt us yet, the stained glass of the Sainte Chapelle can inspire even modern humans to feel impelled to pray to a non-existent god, the Daibutsu aids us yet to meditate, the symphonies of Beethoven, the fugues of Bach, the songs of Dylan, the melodies of N'Goan all touch us deeply, as do the immortal paintings of Van Gogh, the plays of Shakespeare and the poems of Dylan Thomas. The information age added the artform of sim, and the early pioneers, such as Hyamaki, Laplace and Grierson created worlds that live on today. These ancient works of art have not lost their power to inspire us in the slightest and in many respects, the greatest gift of the information age was to prepare us for a world in which we could devote ourselves to that which truly *is* eternal.

However, while art was always with us, it was inevitably secondary in the mind of society as a whole before the fusion age. Obliged to focus our attention on the business of survival, and then on the very serious business of managing our place in society through the accumulation of wealth, rare were those devoted themselves to art. They were dreamers, "poets". Even those who were the most successful were typically only deemed successful because their art brought them wealth. "Fame" inexorably was paired with "fortune" in the minds of pre-fusion societies.

So it is that we must resuscitate these ancient frameworks and scratch at least their surfaces if we hope to truly understand the history we have reviewed in the first two sections. Chapters 17 through 19 will cover the bygone science of economics, Chapters 20 and 21 will explain the concept of politics, and Chapters 22 and 23 will examine religion, often the most perplexing of ancient belief structures to students of history.

CHAPTER 17

CAPITALISM

For many of my students, economics is the study of money. I believe they think this simply because both concepts are foreign to them and indeed related, and because they are familiar with using money in many sims, but they do not truly understand it beyond the simple facilitation of barter, and in its purest sense, economics is much vaster than money and indeed does not require it.

Economics is simply the study of how resources are used and distributed within societies of human beings. Seen that way, any group of humans, past present or future, deals in economic activity. If three children come across a ball in an isolated field they must decide how they will play with it and what the rules of the game are as they attempt to create as much fun as possible until they have to go home. They will also probably make an effort to ensure some degree of fairness in terms of how the three of them will participate in the game. In absolute terms, this means producing as much fun as possible with the means at hand and finding a way to distribute it among the three of them.

This underlines the two primary objectives of economics:

1. Produce as much value as possible with the limited resources available
2. Determine an acceptable way to divide the value among the individuals within the society.

Note that economics therefore predicates limited resources. In the case of the three children there are a number of limitations to their resources. First, they have only one ball at their disposal. Second, they have only a limited amount of time before they must go home. Third, they are limited by their own imaginations in terms of the games they know or can invent.

If resources are unlimited, economics has no reason for being and to a large degree, this is why we no longer study it nor have need of it, except in an historical context (or when we are with two friends and have only one ball).

The history of formal economics is the briefest of the three frameworks we shall consider. While humans had been engaging in economic activity since the beginning of humanity (and we still do, as we shall see), *economics* per se, as a field of study, really only existed between the 18th and the 21st centuries, roughly between the publication of Adam Smith's "The Wealth of Nations" and the advent of the fusion era. As such, like so much else, the science of economics was a product of the enlightenment and was restricted to the industrial era.

If the "Wealth of Nations" was the founding text of the science of economics then it is fitting that it was published in 1776, the year in which the creation of the United States signaled the start of a new era in politics, for the democratic revolution that the United States exemplified allowed the type of free-market capitalism that Smith described.

Until the enlightenment, the overwhelming majority of the world's nations existed under a centralized power structure. While many people pursued "economic" activity on their own, typically via "cottage industries" in which individuals would transform resources on a very small scale, often as craftsmen (blacksmiths, shoemakers, etc.), the economic sophistication of national governments focused primarily on accumulating as much wealth as possible, in the form of money, which at the time consisted primarily of precious metals (gold and silver, usually). This was known as "mercantilism". It was largely focused on the competition *between* nations and its aim was to heighten the power of the nation with respect to other nations.

Mercantilism's answer to the twin questions of economic systems – how to maximize production and how to divide it – was simple. Production, as such, was not really an aim of mercantilist systems, they were very much centered on the accumulation of existing wealth. As such, the maximization of societal wealth occurred largely through conquest, whether straightforward military conquest or conquest via trade between nations.

For the second great question of economics, how to divide wealth among the citizens, mercantilism was likewise straightforward: it was entirely up to the monarchy. The monarchy – or at least the government, as monarchies began to veer towards constitutional monarchies – *was* the nation and its power was absolute. As we shall see in the next section, this form of centralized government typically had very little regard for the population as a whole, particularly outside the scope of the privileged classes (or "nobility"), and distribution of wealth was largely left to whatever informal mechanisms created themselves within the nobility. For the lower classes, there was precious little to worry about either way, since the wealth to be distributed amongst them was feeble and since the numerically dominant agricultural class was either formally enslaved, through systems like feudalism and serfdom, or informally benefitted primarily only through whatever agricultural production they could manage, which they could then sell in local markets.

Mercantilism in one form or another had been the guiding political policy of human nations, empires and states since the dawn of the agricultural era. To a degree, mercantilism was the economic philosophy of Rome, of imperial China, and of most early states, as they embarked on conquest to expand the wealth of the leadership. When Rome's expansion ceased, in the third century CE, its economic fortunes waned, leading to civil and political turmoil and the eventual collapse of the empire.

While mercantilism focused on the accumulation of money, in the form of precious metals, the principle form of production throughout the agricultural era was, in fact, agriculture. As such, the primary resource to be fed into the production system was arable land. It was this, more than anything else, that drove the wars of conquest of agricultural civilizations, including those of Rome.

With the industrial revolution, essentially concurrent with the enlightenment, this changed. The size of a nation was no longer directly linked to its productive capacity. Of course, the change was gradual over the length of the industrial era, as the percentage of wealth produced by agriculture shrunk over the years. For example, in Western Europe, the percent of wealth generated by agriculture in 1700 was 73%, whereas at the end of the industrial era this had shrunk to less than 1%. This was of course not due to any decrease in agricultural production, but rather in the dramatic increase of *produced* wealth, in the form of goods transformed by industry.

This meant an important shift in economic structure. First, land itself was relatively speaking less valuable. If agriculture is a production system that is fed by land, industry is fed by metals, ingenuity, and especially, energy. That energy was largely provided by fossil fuels, notably oil and coal, and the wars that had been fought over land would later be fought over reserves of these precious resources. The last gasp of land-acquisition warfare was undoubtedly the Second World War, in which both Germany and Japan engaged in wars of conquest to increase the size of their empires.

This shift in the source of wealth also meant that the centrally-run economies of the past, in which the rulers of the nation could make essentially all of the major economic decisions, no longer functioned. Comparatively speaking, it is not extraordinarily difficult to manage a purely agricultural society. The major questions of national management involve the establishment and maintenance of food stores and the distribution of land. The industrial revolution, however, brought with it extraordinary complexity. The sheer volume of transformed goods that became available and their novelty as compared to the goods of past ages made centralized economic management remarkably difficult.

Even before the industrial revolution, one of the tools that helped to manage the complexity of shifting economic paradigms was the development of the corporation. In Chapter 3 we examined how the corporation was created in order to disassociate the investors in a major communal enterprise from the risks and responsibilities engendered by that enterprise, thus increasing the enticement to invest in ventures that required more resources than any single individual – or indeed the state – was willing or able to invest. While the corporation itself predates the industrial revolution, and indeed was originally used to fuel the mercantilist ventures of the British, Dutch and French governments, it proved to be uniquely suited to the industrial era.

The transformation of society from agricultural to industrial production entailed the building of a vast new industrial infrastructure. This required a rapid shift of existing wealth into new, previously unimagined domains. Factories needed to be built, railroads needed to be laid down, steamships need to be launched, and later, highway systems needed to spring up across the land and automobiles needed to be built to drive upon them. Corporations were the perfect structures to both fuel and direct this shift of existing wealth into new industries. The overall structure of the economy thus built was capitalism, as originally described by Adam Smith.

This is not a book about economics, much less capitalism, and the details of how it worked are easily available through Artie. In many respects, capitalism at its core is something of the default in free human societies. Adam Smith did not propose some radical new system, he simply described what he saw as being the state of affairs in his society. Nevertheless, understanding the mechanisms of capitalist economics became a crucial part of government.

Implicitly, or at least theoretically, capitalism had a specific way of dealing with the two great objectives of economic systems: optimization of production and the means of attributing it. Its solution to increasing the total production of society relied on self-interest, or greed, in its basest form. Adam Smith postulated that in a society in which competition was allowed (i.e. "free-market" capitalism), a natural phenomenon, or "invisible hand" would lead the society's citizens to make decisions that would naturally maximize productive output. With the assumption that all participants in the system would try to maximize their *own* wealth, competition would guarantee that capitalists would act in such a way that production was optimized. Artie can provide the details of this mechanism.

In terms of distribution, capitalism returned the system's output to individuals in proportion to their contribution to the production itself. This contribution could be in the form of labor, ingenuity, leadership, or capital.

For example, imagine that someone invents a new way to make steel that is faster and requires less energy. The inventor of the method is an engineer, she does not actually produce the steel and does not have a great deal of personal resources (money). She finds a capitalist who creates a corporation. The capitalist has access to wealthy individuals who decide to invest in the corporation. The capitalist hires a manager who can bring together the necessary workers to build and work in the factory. The factory is built and begins producing steel. The steel is of no better quality than the steel of other manufacturers, but because the process requires less energy, it can be sold to others at a lower price. Because in free markets, all individuals can freely choose where to purchase their goods and services, the new venture sells more steel and it makes surplus wealth (profit). At the same time, by creating steel more efficiently, it increases the total output of society as a whole.

As the corporation is able to make surplus profit, other inventors are strongly motivated to emulate the corporation by inventing their own ways of making steel more efficiently. They know that they need only have a good idea: even if they do not possess the wealth to build a factory or the skills to manage it, they will be able to find others, specialists in their domain, who will be enticed by the profitable example of the first company. It is this mechanism that allows capitalism to continually increase the efficiency of the system as a whole and increase the overall output of society for a given level of resource.

The revenues of the company will serve to provide wealth for those involved. The inventor, who does not work in the company, will receive regular payments for the use of hir idea about how to produce steel more efficiently. The capitalist, who brought together the investment and now runs the company, will receive wealth for hir skills and efforts; the investors will be compensated for the use of their wealth (or "capital") and for their willingness to accept the risk of the venture (for had it failed, they could have lost the entirety of their investment) and the workers in the factory are paid a regular wage for their efforts. The actual *amounts* paid to each of these actors is, theoretically, subject to the same forces that determine the prices of any elements in the capitalist system – supply and demand.

The law of supply and demand dictates that on one hand, the more a good is demanded by society, the more people will be willing to pay for it, driving the price of that good up. On the other hand, the more the good is available, the less valuable it will be, driving the price down. As such, rare, valuable goods will cost a great deal, whereas less desirable, common goods will cost very little. Diamonds were worth more than turnips.

In the case of our steel company, the inventor was paid handsomely for hir invention, for when she invented it, it was the *only* way to make steel using less energy. Its supply was extremely limited. Therefore, even though she did not work in the corporation, she was amply rewarded.

The investors will be compensated for their capital also as a function of the supply and demand for capital at the time. If it was a period of prosperity, when many people had excess wealth and sought investments instead of deciding to spend their wealth (i.e. there was a high supply of capital) and there were very few entrepreneurs seeking investment (i.e. low demand for investment) then the investors would require a lower level of compensation. The company's manager would receive compensation depending on hir perceived level of managerial skill (which would drive demand for hir services) and the same applied for the workers, although typically, there was a higher supply of workers than of managers, as the education necessary to be a manager was perceived to be greater than that needed by workers, and so managers, being rarer and more desirable, enjoyed higher levels of remuneration.

So, according to Adam Smith, free-market capitalism worked through a self-regulating system, an "invisible hand" that maximized the wealth of the nation while at the same time allocating that wealth across the participants in the system via a fair process, the basis of which was that each received wealth commensurate with what society as a whole deemed to be the value of their input into the system. This can be summarized in the following way:

> *"Each **gives** to society according to hir capabilities and ambition and **takes** from society according to hir contribution"*

Capitalism worked. It worked much better than the preceding, state-controlled systems, and corporate capitalism in particular fueled the industrial age. It allowed the modernization of society by facilitating the flow of resources from controlled, agricultural production into the varied, complex and capital-intensive industries of the new era, and it was ultimately responsible for the liberation of the vast lower classes who had traditionally labored in the fields while enjoying very little prosperity. Capitalism was a liberating force, an enormous influence for good and for justice, because allocating the wealth of society on the basis of one's input into it was objectively far more just than the previous system, that guaranteed wealth flowed in a set pattern between pre-established social classes.

This is not to say that the struggle for social supremacy was over. Far from it. As we have seen throughout this book so far, humans as social primates are inexorably drawn to social hierarchization. The major moral advance of capitalism came from the fact that in its purest form, one's social level was no longer a function of one's pedigree, but of one's contribution to society. For the first time, capitalism allowed everyone at least the possibility of changing their social rank.

The tendency to identify three broad strata in society (or at least in Western society) persisted in the industrial age, as nobility, bourgeoisie and peasantry transformed into upper, middle and lower classes. However, whereas movement between the three traditional castes had been virtually impossible before capitalism, anyone with good ideas, specific skills, access to resources or simply a willingness to work hard could, theoretically, aspire to a more privileged class under capitalist systems. Of course, the opposite was also true, and those who had once enjoyed wealth and esteem could see it disappear when their ability to contribute to society diminished as well. However, this fluid class structure can objectively be considered more moral, since it is, at least, a function of the individual's choices and actions as opposed to an inherited characteristic which is neither hir doing nor hir fault.

CHAPTER 18

CORPORATE CAPITALISM

The capitalist system had been built on the premise of separating the owners of capital from the management of the companies that used it. The corporation had made this possible, but it was still a cumbersome construct at the beginning of the industrial revolution. At that time, investors typically all knew each other and they knew the managers who ran the corporation.

As the democratic capitalist system evolved, however, wealth began to be distributed among an increasingly large proportion of the population. The "upper" class expanded in size and even the "middle" class often had idle wealth that they wished to invest. A more public and general means of accessing investment was sought out by capitalists. They therefore invented the "stock market".

Stock markets were places where buyers and sellers could come together, without knowing each other personally, and where buyers could peruse the offers of different sellers to decide whether or not to purchase shares of their corporations. This is analogous to markets for foodstuffs, but in the case of stock markets, the sellers were not offering cheese or fruits or vegetables, they were offering companies. As was almost always the case for corporations, it was not the entire company that was for sale, but parts of it, represented by "shares", or "stock". Buyers were investing in the companies by purchasing stock, representing a (typically small) percentage of ownership.

The very first stock markets predate the industrial revolution and pertained to the great shipping concerns of the mercantilist system. Notably, the Dutch East India Company, similar in form and purpose to the British East India Company, created an open market for its shares. It is not particularly surprising that the Netherlands was the home of the first stock market: remember that the financing of these imperialist ventures required great capital, and while in the UK that wealth had primarily accumulated in the relatively incestuous nobility, the Netherlands had been the domain of the bourgeoisie. This more fluid, less formalized class consisted largely of tradespeople who had created almost democratic, or at least oligarchical governmental structures in numerous port cities. The capital being somewhat more dispersed, and the people involved being highly inclined and skilled in trade, they created a market for the shares of the corporation.

With the coming of capitalism and the democratization (within limits) of wealth, these markets for stock became the norm. By the

20th century, New York had become the financial nexus of the world, even before the establishment of the United States as the predominant world power. The United States was the world's first complete modern democracy, dedicated both to the political system and its accompanying capitalist economic system. If there was a free market for goods and labor then it made sense to have a free market for capital and the New York Stock Exchange became the place for corporations to go to find investors, and for investors to go to find corporations in which to invest.

This state of affairs proved to be fertile ground for corporations, and greatly accelerated the technological and social advances of the industrial age. However, as corporations grew, they increasingly gathered power unto themselves that started to rival that of the very governments that had allowed their existence. That raised the question of who, exactly, governed the corporations.

Any corporation was subject to the decisions of its owners and the owners of the corporations were, through the stock market, the same people who determined their governments through their votes. This gave rise to the "covenant theory" of business ethics, whereby society allowed corporations to make profit because it was society itself that owned the corporations. This went hand in hand with another prevalent theory of business ethics known as "enlightened self-interest" (ESI) which stated that company managers were morally obliged to maximize the profits, hence the wealth, of their owners as long as they stayed within the boundaries of the laws enacted to restrict them. Since the owners lived in democratic societies, it was they who also determined the laws within which the corporations worked. This was a very convenient moral structure and it mirrored closely Adam Smith's "invisible hand". Corporate benevolence was ensured because stock holders were the same voters who ultimately determined the legal limitations on the corporations themselves. Managers did not need to reflect on the morality of their decisions, they needed only to focus on maximizing profits, because the limits placed on corporate activity were the will of the people and the people were the shareholders demanding profits. It was a neatly wrapped closed system. For a manager to take a decision that would decrease profits, and hence the wealth of the shareholders, would have been immoral. She would be going farther than the law in reducing the returns to shareholders and therefore removing from those shareholders their own ability to make decisions about what to do with surplus wealth.

As an example, if a manager were concerned about the environment and decided to use cleaner production techniques than were required, thereby increasing cost for no commercial benefit, she would be removing return from the pockets of the shareholders, who perhaps disagreed about the importance of environmental protection and would have used that wealth to help feed starving children. The manager would therefore have been making a moral decision *in the place of* the shareholder, and this was considered wrong, according to ESI theory. This handy rationale made for simplified decision making and eliminated pesky moral considerations from business decision making.

***

As the twentieth century progressed, capital movements became increasingly internationalized and corporations became "MNCs", or "multinational corporations". While some, very few, remained primarily focused on their home countries, many became so international that their actual country of origin became unclear, or at least irrelevant. Just as the corporate structure had disassociated "owners" with the managers of companies, the MNC was increasingly disassociated from any individual national government. This tendency was well under way by the dawn of the information era, but it was greatly accelerated by the transition.

On one hand, this tended to favor the internationalization of society as a whole. During the information era, almost all human inhabitants of our planet were customers of any number of MNCs and very often, they had no real idea where these corporations were based. In reality, almost all MNCs during the early information era were based either in the United States, Europe or Japan, but again, they increasingly acted as "citizens of the world", retaining very little fealty to their countries of origin.

The drawback to this internationalization of corporate structure was that the MNCs began to operate largely outside the realm of *any* legal and legislative restrictions, and also became increasingly difficult to tax, since international coordination of tax policy was largely non-existent. MNCs had offices all over the world and could, at a whim, simply declare that their headquarters had moved from one country to the next, therefore benefitting from the lack of co-ordination across countries to pay, in some cases, no taxes at all[92].

---

[92] This can be difficult to follow, but it springs largely from the decision on the part of some countries to put into place very low tax rates for

Even as MNCs began to separate themselves from the economic life of their home countries, they began to amass power to rival that of national governments themselves. All governments in the information age (and before) were limited in their powers to the nations in which they were situated, but not so, MNCs, which operated internationally. By 2015, some MNC were in fact wealthier than many countries.

The following table compares the Gross Domestic Product (GDP) of the world's wealthiest nations with the annual revenues of the largest MNCs, a roughly equivalent measure, in 2017, the first year of Donald Trump's presidency. Numbers indicate billions of dollars, the top 50 economic entities are considered:

Entity	GDP / Revenues
United States	19 417
China	11 795
Japan	4 841
Germany	3 423
United Kingdom	2 496

MNCs so as to entice them to put their headquarters in the country. Since tax laws were typically set up so that all the revenues of corporations were "consolidated" at the headquarters level, after local taxes were paid, corporations could easily adjust their record-keeping (known as "accounting") to minimize profits in local countries and then repatriate them to the headquarters. By declaring their headquarters to be in a country with very low taxes, and sometimes, with very lax legislation, the corporation could avoid paying taxes, thereby avoiding contributing to society as a whole. The low-tax countries were typically smaller nations, for whom a small percentage of the profits of a large MNC represented all the same significant wealth. Furthermore, the MNCs would often increase the number of employees in the country in which the headquarters was situated, thereby reducing unemployment. Faced with this competition for headquarters, even major nations began offering special tax deals to MNCs in a bid to keep them.

India	2 454
France	2 420
Brazil	2 140
Italy	1 807
Canada	1 600
Russia	1 560
Korea	1 498
Australia	1 359
Spain	1 232
Indonesia	1 020
Mexico	987
Turkey	794
Netherlands	763
Saudi Arabia	707
Switzerland	659
Argentina	629
Taiwan	567
Sweden	507
Walmart	*486*
Poland	483
Belgium	463
Thailand	433
United Arab Emirates	407
Nigeria	401
Norway	392
Austria	384
Iran	368
Israel	340

Hong Kong	332
Philippines	330
South Africa	318
Malaysia	310
Colombia	306
Denmark	304
Ireland	294
Egypt	294
Singapore	292
Toyota	*255*
Venezuela	252
Pakistan	251
Chile	251
Volkswagen Group	*250*

Of the fifty entities, three are private corporations. Note that the smallest of these in number of employees, Toyota, had roughly 365,000 employees and yet produced $255 billion in wealth, whereas the country of Ethiopia, for example, had over a hundred million people and yet produced only $87 billion in wealth. Two hundred and seventy-five times more people producing one third the wealth. While Toyota was a Japanese company, subject to Japanese laws for the most part, it arguably had more international power than the entire country of Ethiopia with its one hundred million people.

At the same time, the principles that underlay the ethics of large MNCs began to break down. The combination of covenant theory and ESI are based on some major assumptions, the most important of which is that the owners of the corporation are the same people who vote in the democratic societies that make the laws governing the corporation. The disassociation of the corporations with the democratic governments to which they used to be subjected breaks down the covenant and means that the self-interest of the corporation is no longer necessarily contiguous with the interests of society. Indeed, the MNC becomes answerable largely only to itself.

The one mitigating factor is that the MNC, at least during the first half of the information era, was still typically *associated* with its home country (except to a degree with energy and financial MNCs) and flouting the laws and customs of its home country could have a negative impact on its image in the minds of its customers. As such, the foundations of the ethical structures of the time were not entirely obviated by the internationalization of MNCs. However, even this was fraught with a democratic contradiction, for the democracies that originally gave birth to most MNCs were based on the concept of "one person, one vote". The vote of every individual within society carried precisely the same weight as the vote of every other individual[93]. However, the governance of MNCs was proportionate to the number of shares owned by an individual, and many of the shares were owned by other corporations. Therefore, while democratic *governments* generally adhered to the policy "one person, one

---

[93] With one notable exception: in the case of the United States, an antiquated system was used to elect the president that formally gave much higher weight to votes in less populous states. This over-representation of residents of less populous states also applied in the United States Senate. The reasons for this are complicated and like so much in 21st-century American politics is due to the entirely 18th-century concerns of the country's founders (including the accommodation of slavery). Even I am at a loss to explain why the system was allowed to persist into the information age.

vote", MNCs by definition held to the policy "one dollar, one vote", meaning that the wealthier one was, the greater one's voice in the governance of MNCs. As MNCs began to accrue more and more power unto themselves as compared to the democratically elected governments of the information age, this meant that social and political power gravitated increasingly towards the wealthy... who tended to use it to increase their own wealth even more. Often, they did so by buying and selling the shares of public companies, those traded on stock exchanges, not because they truly wished to invest in them and share the fruits of their efforts, but because they hoped their shares would increase in value quickly, sometimes from one day to the next. This "speculation" led to very fluid movements of capital which for some, was seen as a good thing, inspiring managers to make the right decisions, but for others signaled the primacy of extremely short-term decision making.

What is more, the senior managers of these corporations were increasingly divorced from any long-term commitment to the corporations themselves. A class of "professional CEOs" (Chief Executive Officers, the leader of the corporation) arose, who would change companies every few years, sometimes switching to entirely different industries with which they were unfamiliar. These leaders were often paid in "options" – roughly equivalent to stocks that would only have value if the stock price of the company increased. Simple game theory indicates that of course these individuals would be motivated to take risky decisions, since their losses are limited and their gains are not. What's more, given the transient nature of their employment and their lack of affective attachments to the companies they were leading, failure was not catastrophic for them, they would simply move on, often with sizable payments despite their failure.

The corporate structure, increasingly known as "corporate capitalism" to distinguish it from the idea of small-scale market economies that had prevailed in the early industrial age, led to an economy that was quite different from that which had been imagined by Adam Smith. Smith had been inspired by consideration of agricultural markets and cottage industries. He saw a multitude of providers competing equally in an entirely free and fluid market. By the information era, though, economic activity in the developed world was dominated by large corporations, whose power in their marketplaces was considerable and who enjoyed the benefit of enormous asymmetry in the information available to them as compared to their customers. This gave rise to substantial "inefficiencies" in the markets, thereby lessening the beneficial impact of Smith's "invisible hand" and allowing a certain inertia to enter into the mechanism. In essence, this made it even easier for those with wealth to accumulate even more, and harder for those without wealth to obtain it. This led to greatly increased income inequality.

Capitalism as an economic system is tolerant of income inequality. It must be remembered that the democratic revolution did not aim to introduce equality of wealth, but equality of opportunity. This was seen as a major innovation in social justice, and well it was. However, equal opportunity by no means guarantees equal results – we need only to consider our own results in our artistic, sporting or sim ventures. We fully understand and expect that some will do better than others, and so it was under capitalism.

However, under the corporate system opportunity was not truly equal. Granted, equality of opportunity was immeasurably greater than it had been any time since the agricultural revolution, but the inertia that is inherent in corporate capitalism, in which power is allocated according to the "one dollar one vote" rule, and in which those with *capital* can benefit just as much as those with skills, talent, knowledge or determination mean, together, that people who were born into families with wide resource bases had substantial advantages. Furthermore, in countries in which education itself was subject to payment (as was the case in the United States, where higher education was extremely costly) it was difficult for those who could not benefit from family resources to obtain the skills and social network necessary to access important positions within corporations.

These elements conspired to reduce what was known as "economic mobility", or the ability, truly, to benefit from the capitalist system and the equality of opportunity it was supposed to supply.

For example, at the beginning of the 19ᵗʰ century, someone who was from a relatively poor family could learn to be a talented shoemaker by working as an apprentice for an established shoemaker. Hir existence would be difficult, for making shoes was neither easy nor leisurely and the life thus undertaken would strike us as brutish and boring, but she could all the same hope to better hir lot by learning such a trade. If this individual was a particularly good shoemaker and worked hard, she could perhaps save enough money to open hir own shoemaking shop and due to the quality of hir wares could command a good price for hir shoes, grow the business, and eventually attain both material comfort and social standing. The existence of other shoemakers would mean that she could not ask *too* high a price, but if hir shoes were particularly well made she could transform hir skill into wealth, and thus achieve a rewarding social status. This is precisely the type of enterprise that inspired Adam Smith's view of capitalism.

Under corporate capitalism, however, the shoemaker would have little chance. Large corporations could inevitably make shoes faster, better, and much cheaper than the shoemaker (except in extremely limited situations). The shoemaker would therefore need to work for a shoemaking corporation, but these took few apprentices, and probably made their shoes in a factory. Perhaps the shoemaker could help design the factory, but this required advanced degrees, and coming from a poor family, the shoemaker would not be able to pay for hir education. She could find a low-level job as a worker in the shoe factory, essentially remaining relatively poor, whereas the managers of the corporation would become rich, passing their wealth to their children, ensuring them good educations and the possibility to work in other corporations… despite the fact that they, personally, do not know how to make shoes.

These types of mechanisms brought about income inequality. Income inequality had been significant under pre-democratic governments, in which the nobility (and / or the bourgeoisie) had jealously guarded for itself the wealth of society. With the introduction of democracy and capitalism, that began to change. Over the 18th and the first part of the 19th century, income began to be distributed more equally over the population as a whole. In France, for example, the percentage of total wealth belonging to the richest ten percent of the population fell from over 60% to under 50% by the mid 19ᵗʰ century and this trend was visible across the industrialized world.

The advent of widescale corporate capitalism began to change this. From the middle of the 19ᵗʰ century income inequality grew substantially across the developed world, peaking in the late 1920's. This was a time of rampant capitalism, with very few controls or regulations. Environmental controls were insignificant, indeed smokestacks spewing pollutants into the air were seen as a sign of progress and modernization. There were very few laws or regulations with respect to worker safety or well-being. Children were often employed in factories and workers often worked long hours, every day. Consumers were largely unprotected from fraud and outright lies on the part of corporations, to the point that in the United States very little industrial food, for example, did not contain outright poisonous ingredients in an effort to reduce its cost and perishability. The inequalities of the pre-industrial world began to return.

This gave rise to alternate political philosophies arguing for different economic systems and a delineated class structure led to tensions between "capitalists", broadly meaning those with access to investment capital as well as the managers who ran the corporations, and "workers". We shall examine some of these ideas in the next section, but the tensions that gave rise to these struggles were largely a function of the inequalities brought about by the corporate capitalist system.

It seemed, therefore, that unfettered capitalism could in fact engender an environment in which justice did *not* seem to be served. Movements for workers' rights began to make headway as they struggled to convince democratic governments to introduce legislation to address these "excesses" of capitalism. This, coupled with the economic crisis at the end of the 1920's (known as "the Great Depression") quickly followed by the cataclysm of the Second World War brought significant changes to the system as a whole. In the United States, the economic policies of Franklin Delano Roosevelt, known as "the New Deal" introduced a number of measures to redistribute wealth, and post-war governments in Europe and Asia adopted similar measures. Income inequality in the developed world dropped considerably.

Consider two countries: the United States and France. As can be seen in the following table, in both nations, the share owned by the top one percent had risen to roughly half of the total wealth available to individuals by 1929, from much lower levels in the mid 19th-century, thanks to the unbridled corporate capitalism that was the rule at the time.

However, by 1980, over a period of extraordinary economic prosperity throughout the world, this share dropped. It dropped much more in France (which was a relatively typical European country in this respect) than in the United States, but the progression is clear in both cases.

	France	United States
1929	50%	51%
1980	16%	24%

Share of total individual wealth held by wealthiest 1%

Note of course that this does not represent a decrease in *wealth* of the richest individuals. On the contrary, economic growth was so substantial that their actual levels of wealth increased substantially. However, the fruits of that growth also found their way into the pockets of those classes which had previously been excluded from many of the benefits of the corporate capitalist system.

However, by the early information era, inequality had increased substantially. By 2010, the share of wealth held by the richest one percent had risen in both nations, but particularly in the United States, from 24% to 38%. By 2025 the share of the top one percent exceeded its 1929 level in the United States, at 53%.

	France	United States
1929	50%	51%
1980	16%	24%
2010	24%	38%

Share of total individual wealth held by wealthiest 1%

In fact, even within this extremely wealthy elite wealth was highly concentrated, since by 2025 just the top *0.1%* of the U.S. population owned more than 25% of the wealth in the country, representing more wealth than the bottom 90% of the population combined.

This too should not be seen necessarily as a worsening of the situation of the poorer members of the population. Particularly in Europe, where there were considerable governmental programs designed to aid the economically disadvantaged, it can be argued that the poorest of the poor in many industrialized nations could still live better than the average peasant in the agricultural era. However, this is not the entirety of the issue.

Let us remember our discussion about the use of wealth as a measure of social status. Since we, as the social primates that we are, are driven strongly by social status, which is by definition relative, the widening gap in income equality must inevitably lead to social strife and economic turmoil. As an example of very visible and contentious inequality, the average revenues of the managers of large corporations in 1980 were roughly fifty times greater than the average American employee. By 2015 this ratio had risen to *three hundred and fifty* times greater.

What drove this second explosion of inequality? The first, in the 19th century, had been driven by the rise of *corporate* capitalism, and was quelled by the social unrest that accompanied the great depression and the steps taken by people like Roosevelt to address it, while the second was driven by the rise of *multinational corporate capitalism*. The fact that it was so much more striking in the United States is largely due to the political shift in that country that provided a much more favorable environment for MNCs and allowed them substantially more influence in the political process, which we will examine in greater detail in the following chapters.

CHAPTER 19

PREPARING FOR THE
POST-ECONOMIC
WORLD

The extraordinary benefit of capitalism had been that it brought wealth and well-being to entire classes that had lived in misery for centuries. By the time the information age was born, however, multinational corporate capitalism had begun to move into a phase of great concentration of wealth.

From a moral perspective, this leaves us with something of a dilemma. There is debate among scholars today about the morality of wealth concentration in pre-fusion societies, and notably about this last bout of concentration. There are those who point out that since, in reality, all classes of society in most democracies did indeed benefit materially from the growth in wealth creation during the late industrial and early information ages, the fact that the wealthy benefitted *more* does not make supranational corporate capitalism a "bad" or morally wanting system in the context of the times. They point to the widespread social harmony that resulted from general institution of the citizen's income as proof that guaranteeing the material needs and an acceptable level of comfort to all people in society is a sufficient goal, that beyond that, any attempt at wealth redistribution is unnecessary, and that capitalism itself is predicated on "greed", meaning that there must be the possibility of accumulating extra wealth for the system to function at all[94].

It should be remembered, however, that this "simple" and limited goal of instituting the citizen's income caused *enormous* contention at the time, that what we consider to be an evident moral imperative, that a society producing surplus should provide a minimum level of material well-being to all, was hotly contested, particularly in the United States. Furthermore, economics is not in fact driven by "sustenance" except for the very poorest. If we hearken back to our examination of human behavior in the first section of this book, we see that economics is driven primarily by the need for social status. It is not, in fact, *greed* that gloved Adam Smith's invisible hand, it is ambition. Human beings typically do not decide how content they are with their lot by taking stock of their material well-being in isolation, they in fact compare themselves to others and as we have already pointed out, in pre-fusion societies the measure used to make the comparison was money.

As such, the increasing concentration of wealth in the information age cannot be judged on the basis of whether it caused *material* distress for the poorer classes, but rather the degree to which it caused *emotional* distress. As we shall see in the next section, income inequality always led to strife in pre-fusion societies and it did

---

[94] See, for example the work of Terrence McCarthy, of Cambridge, particularly his 2684 essay "Late Capitalist Fairness: Harnessing Greed and Feeding the World"

so for this reason, to the point of threatening the very fabric of capitalism, which had always been fueled by the promise of increasingly unattainable social mobility. As the information age advanced, RAN technology went even farther to break down the underlying mechanisms of capitalism altogether.

As already discussed, capitalism theoretically attributed the wealth of society according to the contribution of each individual on production. The more someone had ideas, determination, skills, or capital that could increase the wealth of all, the more she had a share in it. However, as of the 2030's, RAN technology began to make almost all human material contribution to society entirely negligible. To a large degree, ideas came from Artie, determination and skills came from robots and nanotech, and capital was increasingly secondary, as the combination of the three different technologies considerably broadened the realm of the possible. The only domains that were fully outside the scope of RAN were artistic pursuits and sports.

This breakdown of the mechanism of capitalism went largely unrecognized at the time. There was much talk about displacement, structural unemployment, and the impact of technology on productivity, but very few thinkers at the time seem to have recognized that the fundamental assumptions of the system were being undermined. It is easy, from this distance, to claim a mantle of intellectual superiority, but it must be remembered that it is extremely difficult to retain a critical view of a social system that had been in place for as long as anyone could remember.

Artie was, surprisingly, of little help. She was not yet truly as sophisticated as she is now and she had been programmed with hir own biases, which were those introduced into hir by the 21st century pioneers who brought hir to life… none of whom had the objectivity to recognize the problem.

If humans cannot provide value into the economic system, how, then, can capitalism allocate resources? The answer turned out to be intellectual property, or "IP". IP simply meant the ownership of the ideas that had gone *into* the creation of RAN. Since the technology *itself* was now providing new ideas, labor and even management and communications around the transforming process, the wealth so created flowed into the hands of those who owned the rights to the primary RAN constituents themselves.

As an example, consider LangerTech. This company created a nanotech-based approach that allowed for replacement of the Islets of Langerhans in the human pancreas, thereby curing type I diabetes. In the industrial era this would have been the result of human scientists engaging in fundamental research, creating a medication or some kind of medical device, carrying out extensive human tests requiring organization and analysis, then managing the production of the product and determining how best to communicate about it to the healthcare community and the public. All of these tasks would have been carried out by highly educated human specialists.

In the case of LangerTech, the "product" (a type of nanobot) was designed by a private AI program that tested via modeling, used micro 3D printing to create the nanobots in a fully robotic facility and then communicated about the product to web-based automated healthcare bots who began prescribing it for patients. Very few humans were involved at all, and they largely responded to the AI's guidance. At the same time, the product generated enormous wealth.

It dramatically ameliorated the quality of life of patients while greatly reducing the cost of managing the disease to society. As such, it demanded a high price which drove sizable profits… that went to the owners of the AI. Note that these owners did not *create* the AI, which had been purchased by them from a computer research lab, nor did they actually add anything to the venture in terms of ideas, labor or even dedication. They *did* own the patent for the product, despite the fact that they had provided almost no input into it once the initial research configuration had been determined (on the basis of fundamental research done in an unaffiliated university). The AI itself would not be interested in owning a patent and had no legal rights anyway.

This type of situation became increasingly common and it meant that not only was wealth channeled to a vanishingly small number of individuals, but that those individuals were increasingly distanced from the actual value that had been created and that then served to create the wealth in the first place.

LangerTech is an example of this from the perspective of a small company, but in practice, the overwhelming majority of productive IP belonged to the MNCs that had been in place *before* RAN technology became viable. In reality, the research necessary to attain that degree of technological advancement had been substantial and expensive, and companies such as Google, Apple, Microsoft and Dong Ji Shu had spent years and billions of dollars to advance the technology. It seemed at the time entirely fair that they benefit from the fruits of that research by having rights to the IP they had created.

However, as it increasingly became the RAN technology itself that gave rise to further advances, and even directly produced it

341

without human input, any concept of fairness with respect to the wealth channeled to the managers and owners of these corporations began to break down. During the first bout of wealth concentration, in the late 19th and early 20th centuries, while the "robber-baron" industrialists were often hated, it was at least generally not disputed that without their input the industrialization process would not have occurred, and the jobs so created would not have existed. With this second bout of concentration, as wealth funneled into the hands of the MNCs and their managers, real questions arose as to the fairness of the system. It was already difficult for many to accept that leaders of MNCs were earning three hundred and fifty times more than the average citizen, but as their role transformed into that of simply providing a human face for an automated institution, this became ever more difficult to swallow.

At the same time, the disassociation of corporations from national governments became even more pronounced, as multinational corporations evolved into *supra*national corporations[95]. The distinction was that SNCs were *entirely* disassociated from national governments. They retained theoretical headquarters in specific nations, but these tended to be small countries with extremely low taxes and almost no corporate legislation, or sometimes in major countries but benefitting from specific deals brokered with the government that allowed them to escape effective taxation. In reality, the SNC existed almost entirely in virtual space and while generally smaller than MNCs in terms of both number of employees and revenues, they represented the epitome of IP wealth

---

[95] It should be noted that the term was generally not used at the time, and only became favored retrospectively during the early fusion era.

concentration, serving largely as shells by which those who "owned" important IP elements could collect their wealth.

In the meantime, the majority of humans found themselves laboring in fundamentally pointless activities as of the mid 2040's. Even those who still were making a contribution to society through labor knew that their days, or at least the days of their employment, were numbered. Autonomous machines could carry out any physical human activity with greater efficiency. Before fusion, these machines were often economically unfeasible due to their cost, but through better design and processes, Artie had so lowered the cost of producing labor-saving automated systems that while not yet complete, the displacement of human labor was massive. Even in "white collar" activities, the appearance of agents caused a massive displacement of human activity[96]. Previously, for example, millions of people worked in marketing, advertising, and communications, the objective of which was better to understand potential consumers so as to determine what kinds of products and services they could be compelled to purchase, and then to influence them in such a way that they would indeed purchase them. Agents changed all of that – an individual's agent would determine what she would see and how she would see it as it interacted with the fringes of Artie. Furthermore, the agent would give an opinion to the selling company's agent that quickly became far more important than any "market research" that had previously been employed.

---

[96] Employment at the time was often divided into "blue collar" and "white collar" activities, the former being physical labor and the latter more intellectual. The origin of these terms came from the typical types of shirts worn by "workers" and "managers" in the early 20th century.

In order to understand this better, let us step back for a moment and consider how economic activity generally worked in the information era, so as better to understand the dilemma brought about by the RAN displacement.

During the industrial and early information era, a company (or corporation) would design products through research and development (R&D). In the case of physical goods, this might include work done in a laboratory or engineering workshop, carried out by scientists or engineers. Once the product was designed, it would be produced in a production facility, typically a factory or workshop. Specialists would endeavor to make the production process as efficient as possible so that a minimum of resources would be consumed to create the product. At that point, a "marketing" team would take over to communicate about the product, for consumers would not purchase the product if they did not know about it and were not enticed to purchase it. This marketing job consisted both of carrying out research of the population so as to better understand what would entice potential buyers, and then communicating about the product via various communications channels such as newspapers, magazines, radio and television, and during the information age, via the web as well[97]. Once demand for the product was

---

[97] In the early information age, intensive work was done by human specialists to create algorithms by which the behavior of people on the web could be analyzed so as to tailor marketing communications to them in an effort to manipulate them more thoroughly into purchasing given products. These algorithms expanded as the technology expanded, eventually including information about their movements and physical habits, via connected devices. This type of analysis was used by "combots", as already mentioned in Chapter 13: autonomous communications programs that would provide "re-targeted communications" to people. By 2025, "blockbots" appeared that individuals could use to screen these "combots". The

sufficient, a logistics team would distribute the product, which during the industrial age was generally purchased in a physical store, where individuals could go to see and compare different products, buy them on site, and then carry them home.

This process: R&D $\rightarrow$ Production $\rightarrow$ Marketing $\rightarrow$ Distribution was further supported by annex functions within the company, such as finance, to manage flows of resources within the company as well as payments to and from the company, and "human resources", which managed the relationship between the company and its employees. Above these functions was "senior management", which coordinated the different activities and determined the overall strategy of the company. The majority of corporate employees in the developed world worked in one of the above capacities.

By 2045, however, economic activity had changed dramatically. Humans often (although not always) provided the underlying *idea* but R&D was carried out by AI, production was carried out robotically, marketing consisted of AI agents talking to each other within the generalized Artie framework (i.e. combots talking to blockbots), and distribution took place in some cases via remote 3D printing or "home delivery", often by drone. In many respects, the *only* necessary human intervention was to approve or disapprove of AI suggestions and provide overall corporate guidance.

Of course, there remained many domains in which this was not sufficient, particularly in services. Interaction with other humans

---

more sophisticated blockbots used their own algorithms to determine which of the proffered communications could potentially be of interest to their users. More than combots, these blockbots were the very earliest seeds of our own agents.

remained part and parcel of many offerings, and these jobs remained. For example, while the idea of having a human physician make diagnosis and treatment decisions was essentially obsolete by 2045, nursing as an occupation remained very much in demand, and indeed increased.

Nevertheless, the mid 21st century finally saw the end of the "job displacement" cycle driven by technology. Whereas technological advancement through the industrial era had inevitably simply moved jobs from one domain to another, now it truly did replace them altogether, and as it did so, the assumptions behind capitalism, the way in which wealth was allocated, broke down.

This was the first nail in the coffin of economics as a whole.

In the short term, the implementation of the citizen's income meant that this breakdown of wealth allocation did not lead to widespread hardship and revolt. As already pointed out, at the extreme edge of low wealth – true poverty – humans *are* driven by a need for resources and a minimum level of wealth, and the citizen's income assured this. It did not, however, address the broader issue of how individuals could engage in the struggle for social status that had been until then assuaged by the accumulation of wealth.

First, though, let us consider the citizen's income from the point of view of the economics of the time.

We have so far addressed the concept with respect to its place in the history of the information era, but the idea of having a base level of income for all citizens is as old as the industrial revolution itself. Both the Marquis de Condorcet, the great French enlightenment thinker, and Thomas Paine, his close friend and one of the founders of the United States, were proponents of the idea in the late 18th century. Paine's point was that by allowing the privatization of land, the "common areas" that had previously been the norm no longer existed. As such, citizens should receive compensation for this policy. In essence, he saw a universal wage as making up for the moral cost of capitalism and its dogma of private ownership (although he would not have put it that way). He was also driven by his observation of the concentration of wealth that was the norm at the end of the agricultural era, which he saw as fundamentally antithetical to the ideal of equality. As such, he proposed a regular payment "to every person, rich or poor…because it is in lieu of the natural inheritance, which, as a right, belongs to every man, over and above the property he may have created, or inherited from those who did."

These founding ideas concerning what we would come to know as the citizen's income were the basis for the concept of "welfare" that arose over the industrial era. By the end of that era, all developed countries, and many developing countries, had some form of welfare to assist the poor. However, these welfare schemes were almost universally tied to need. One was required to demonstrate that one's income was low, and / or that one's ability to earn income was low, primarily due to disability of some sort.

As such, being "on welfare" was considered shameful and from a practical point of view it necessitated a vast bureaucracy to attempt to enforce its various laws and regulations, in an attempt to ensure that only those who were eligible received it. Furthermore, there was a direct material incentive *not* to contribute to society, since doing so would reduce the welfare payments themselves.

The citizen's income was in reality much simpler. In line with Paine's sentiment, it was given to "every person, rich or poor" and as such, required no verification. Furthermore, since it did *not* decrease with earned wealth, there was no disincentive to contribute to society otherwise[98].

The debates around the citizen's income largely hinged on this point. Those who argued against it hypothesized that its institution would lead to widespread "sloth" as people refused to participate in productive (capitalist) society since their needs would be fulfilled without them being required to do so. In its prescience, Artie knew well that this period, in fact, would be brief in any case, since RAN would soon render human productivity largely obsolete from an economic perspective, but even without this, the disincentivization did not manifest itself. In reality, the welfare system encouraged "cheating" since when wealth serves as a measure of status, the more wealth the better - regardless, in many cases, of how it is accumulated. Since the citizen's income made cheating impossible, the only way to obtain *more* wealth than others was, in fact, to work for it.

Artie's insistence on instituting the citizen's income was therefore driven by two reasons: first, in the immediate term it was, in reality, the only way to address the obsolescence of much "traditional" human employment without causing widespread misery. Secondly, it did provide a laboratory to examine behavior in a post-economic world, for there *were* those who contented themselves entirely with the base income and the question became what did they do with themselves?

---

[98] Note that in all countries in which Artie instituted the citizen's income, it replaced almost all need-based welfare systems, except certain that were tied to direct disabilities and were paid on top of the base wage.

The insatiable desire to enhance one's rank in society meant that in the presence of "unemployment", wherein individuals no longer had the opportunity to participate in the capitalist system and accumulate wealth, other means of social advancement had been necessary. In some cases this had meant crime: essentially procuring wealth *outside* the accepted capitalist system. This is why extreme income inequality coupled with unemployment almost inevitably led to crime. In other cases, it meant redefining the scope of the tribe in order to advance within a different set of rules.

As the information age progressed, many people found that via the web, they could find other tribes, "coagulations" of people who shared similar interests, passions and ideas[99]. OPCs were perhaps the most visible and ultimately influential manifestations of the concept. These coagulations had their own rules and their own social hierarchies… as is inevitable in any human social group.

While the seeds of this phenomenon were planted with the birth of the web in the late industrial age, it exploded thanks to early forms of AI and came to complete fruition with Artie and the appearance of agents.

Until then, the sheer number of different sites and communities on the web was so enormous that stumbling upon a suitable virtual community was primarily the result of blind luck. The emergence of HumanIT followed by Artie and personal agents allowed each individual to find communities on the web, whether OPCs,

---

[99] This term is taken from the work of early 21st-century French philosopher Alain de Vulpian. De Vulpian was one of the few philosophers at the time who foresaw the societal "metamorphosis" that was taking place. His idea of spontaneous "coagulations" of people with similar interests became reality with the growth of OPCs.

sims, discussion forums or artistic exchanges that were truly appealing to them.

This last category, artistic exchanges, set the stage for one of the key elements of our current society. Through these exchanges, artistic creations, whether visual, musical, or literary could be shared with others. While such sites had existed in one form or another since the birth of the web, particularly in the case of music, the arrival of AI had a dramatic impact on their functionality. The spread of individual agents at the end of the 2030's not only meant that incoming communication was filtered, but it also meant that the artistic endeavors of individuals could rapidly be presented to others who would be likely to appreciate them. The dramatic improvements in translation technology meant that not only could like-minded artistic communities be built rapidly, but they could be built internationally.

Prior to this, any artist was typically subjected to approval by a company that promoted hir art form. For example "record labels" dealt with musicians and "publishing houses" dealt with writers. The artist would submit hir work to the company, which would determine whether the work was worth investing in. If so, the publisher would publish the book or the record label would record the song and then the artistic production would be communicated to the public at large in much the same way that any product was advertised. If enough people were exposed to the work and it was sufficiently well accepted, the books or songs would be purchased, money would change hands and the artist would be paid, hence increasing hir wealth and status. Indeed, artistic success, like any success, was measured by the wealth it generated.

The number of people who actually managed to get their artistic endeavors released was minuscule compared to the number of would-be artists. Since art didn't directly produce further wealth, it tended to be undervalued, with the exception of those artists whose creations were liked by a great many people, whether because of true underlying merit or excessive promotion. Today, an artist whose music, poetry, sim, paintings, dance... etc. is eagerly followed by one thousand people across the planet may consider hirself entirely fulfilled and quite happy with hir life. In the information age it would have been extremely unlikely that she ever would have found any of those thousand fans, would ever have earned any wealth, or would ever have been "published" or "produced" at all. It is our agents who know every sim, song, dance or drawing made as soon as the artist releases it and who know each of us well enough to propose art that otherwise we most certainly never would have stumbled across.

It is a fact that almost *any* artistic production will be appreciated by *someone* and more likely than not, by some group of people. Before the 2040's, the difficulty and cost involved in communicating the existence of the work to that specific and potentially highly heterogeneous group of people was often prohibitive. As such, artistic works were generally only ever produced if they had appeal for vast numbers of people. A remarkably small percentage of the population was able to accumulate enough wealth to live as an artist, let alone succeed, and many excellent works of art went entirely unrecognized, since the publishing houses, record labels and art galleries often simply got it wrong[100]. With the advent of agents and artistic exchanges, suddenly individuals with artistic talent found audiences of appreciative fans effortlessly, and all around the globe. The often insurmountable costs of communicating to vast numbers of people to find the sometimes limited number who appreciated any work of art had disappeared.

Another domain in which people sought out status was in sims. Gaming had become more and more a part of life in the information age and by the early 21st century, games were created that were played by tens of millions of users. Inevitably, these games provided scores and rankings for users, and they began to fill an important social need. As the century progressed and VR became increasingly widespread, the beginnings of what we would call true sims appeared. With Artie-assisted conception, it became possible for individuals to create sims of their own or modify existing sims without needing years of study and vast teams of specialists, as had previously been the case, and this provided a whole new medium in which we could express ourselves and vie for attention.

***

---

[100] It should be remembered that the music of John Jacob Majister, for example, was virtually unnoticed when it was produced and only became known after the appearance of agents, as was the poetry of Vilfredo Perotti and the sculpture of Celeste Rodache. On the other hand, the early 21st-century "recording artist" Britney Spears did not compose her own music or even play any instruments yet was successful and wealthy due to heavy promotion from those who invested in her career and primarily advertised her sexuality. She was just one example among thousands.

The reader has undoubtedly begun to see our own society emerging from its origin story. By the mid 2050's, poverty and true want were on their way to being eliminated, most humans were assured a citizen's income, and that citizen's income offered an increasingly comfortable lifestyle as production became ever more efficient. Humans were turning towards artistic and virtual pursuits and finding fulfillment for their biologically-driven need for esteem and social standing by the success they had in self-defined international communities of like-minded people (or at least people with similar tastes).

On the other hand, society had not yet become what we know today. If economics is the science of allocating scarce resources in the face of unlimited needs, it still had its place, for resources were still scarce.

This changed in 2058 with the advent of viable fusion. While it took three decades to refine the technology and entirely shift our power production facilities, once that had been achieved, the availability of limitless, clean, safe power meant that there was no more scarcity. Thanks to RAN technology coupled with the transmutation technology made feasible through fusion, we were able to synthesize anything we needed. It is true that some things did remain subject to scarcity (and they still do). There are still only so many apartments available on the Ile St. Louis in Paris, still only so many days of sunshine in Scotland, and still only so many seats available in trew to see Youssa Aboaf sing in person. However, the fundamental goods and services that previously needed to be rationed via economic processes no longer needed rationing. Wealth was no longer a status symbol, since the trappings of wealth were available to all, and because capitalism was really driven by the ambition to increase social status, the failure of wealth to measure it meant the end of the system, while the ubiquity of wealth made it unnecessary even to procure pleasure.

If, therefore, you hear that we are so much more evolved than our "primitive" pre-fusion forebears, keep in mind that the capitalist system that dominated the world for three hundred years was a good one, one that led to far more freedom and equality, and that it was not driven by "greed" as much as it was driven by necessity and by ambition. How many days go by without you asking your agent about your impact levels in your various communities? How long can you go without checking the comments and remarks of others about your various contributions and ideas in the communities in which you participate, in sim or in trew? And why is it that I take undue pleasure in knowing as I write these words that they will be read or heard by many millions of people, thanks to my own renown... which I can check in real time thanks to my agent? We too are driven by exactly the same impulses as our "primitive, economic" ancestors, we just don't have to worry about going hungry or suffering from unwanted isolation while we pursue our passions.

CHAPTER 20

EAST VS. WEST

Having already begun the 21st century in the 20th to correspond to the birth of the web, we may as well go back a little farther, to 1990. The traditional beginning of the information age is based on technological changes, but from a *political* perspective, 1990 represents a significant date for a new era. It was the year that is usually taken as marking the end of communism.

We talked about democracy in the previous section, as it was a necessary breeding ground for capitalism, but it was not the only form of government during the industrial era. As we have seen, the industrial era was born in a world full of monarchies, and grew up with its sibling, democracy. The initial result of this dual childhood was a trend towards a more equal distribution of wealth. By the mid 19th century, however, capitalism had begun its move towards corporate capitalism, with its tendency to concentrate wealth. The more industrialized the country, the more the economy was dominated by corporations and the more the concentration was extreme. By 1867, a German philosopher living in exile in London wrote a treatise outlining how capitalism exploited workers and postulated that the system had led to a new class structure that was unjust. Karl Marx's

355

book "Capital" was the founding text of a new politico-economic framework: communism.

For those who are familiar with the industrial era, it must be remembered that while there were fatal flaws in Marx's reasoning, these are much easier to identify in hindsight. It was far more difficult to recognize them at the time. Capitalism itself, let alone democratic corporate capitalism, had existed for less than a hundred years when Marx set pen to paper. He saw in the clear social differences explicit at the time the re-establishment of the class structures of old: the nobility and the commoners had been replaced by the bourgeoisie and the proletariat, and once again, those with power were abusing those with none.

Upon close reflection, it seems evident that there are internal inconsistencies with Marxist economic theory (ask Artie for the details). Furthermore, in *democratic* capitalist societies it is always theoretically possible for the people to affect the laws that govern economic activity without forcibly resorting to revolution, as Marx envisioned. Marx believed that struggle between the classes was the driving force in human society and that eventually, the numerically superior proletariat would prevail, acquiring for themselves the means of production, eliminating the exploiting bourgeoisie and instituting an economic system whereby the fruits of production would be shared fairly. This state would be "communism", since humankind would live communally.

Communism answered the economic questions of how to maximize production and distribute its output via the axiom: "From each according to hir ability and to each according to hir needs". The actual *political* structure under communism was to be roughly anarchic, since in a state of grace, humans would need no overarching state to guide them, they would work together for the common good. However, Marx, along with his ideological descendants, did not believe that this state of grace was immediately attainable. Humans were too used to struggle, they needed to adapt, to learn, to be transformed into fully cooperative individuals. As such, the exploitative capitalism was to be replaced with socialism, whereby the state, representing the people, would own all means of production while the population as a whole could transform itself while being led by a revolutionary "vanguard" party that would guide citizens to a better form of government before eventually dissolving itself into a utopic communal society.

This more directly revolutionary approach to communism was championed by Vladimir Lenin (born Vladimir Ilyich Ulyanov). Lenin brought Marxist ideas to Russia, which was one of the last major countries still to be ruled by an absolute monarch in the early 20ᵗʰ century (the Tsar). Lenin had been exiled from his country for fomenting revolution but he was returned by the German government in 1917. Germany was at war with Russia at the time and its leaders (correctly) believed that he and other revolutionaries of his ilk would destabilize the Tsarist government if they were to return.

Not only did Lenin destabilize the government, but he brought about a revolution that would entirely unseat it, replacing it with a communist dictatorship. The country was renamed the Soviet Union. Lenin died in 1924 and was replaced as the leader of the country by Josef Stalin, who further cemented the centralized dictatorship that would characterize Soviet communism.

Far from the utopian vision of Marx, Soviet communism was simply a centralized authoritarian system justified by a flawed ideology. The Soviets didn't see it this way, of course. They considered this to be the interim solution as society perfected itself until conditions were favorable for the true communist society to emerge. Before long, they began to proclaim that this ultimate transformation would be impossible as long as their "worker's paradise" was assailed by the enemy forces of capitalism. The world as a whole would need to become communist before it could be so transformed. Until then, ideological purity was important and those who dissented from this iconoclast vision were silenced.

So it was that a cooperative, if naïve and flawed ideology was itself transformed into an excuse for dictatorship. Stalin killed millions of his own people as he attempted to strengthen his hold on the country, and he even created a pact with Adolf Hitler before Hitler abrogated it and invaded the Soviet Union, a decision that ultimately caused the defeat of Nazi Germany.

Communism did spread. It spread with the armies of the Soviet Union as they advanced through territory previously occupied by the Nazis and it spread as a number of other countries adopted it, notably China, where Mao Zedong introduced Leninist revolutionary ideas via a civil war that took place shortly after the Second World War.

At the end of that war, the world stood divided, with democratic capitalism, championed by the United States and its wartime allies on one side and communism, championed by the Soviet Union and its allied (primarily via conquest) client states on the other, joined by China and a smattering of other, smaller nations. These two econo-political systems would vie with each other for the next fifty years.

Those years definitively proved the superiority of democratic capitalism. The communist regimes of the Soviet Union and China attempted to plan their economies. They forecasted the needs for goods and produced them accordingly, while individual ambition was discouraged, since humans were supposed to reach a condition of happy community-oriented thinking. This proved to be disastrous. Not only was the state incapable of planning adequately, leading to extraordinary inefficiencies in production, but communism at its core *denied* the essence of human social behavior, which is the drive for status. Communism was the greatest experiment in the denial of human instinct the world has ever seen, and it did not go well. The vaunted equality that was at its theoretical core was, to a degree, achieved since aside from those who were influential within the communist party, and hence in positions of political power, there was relatively little difference in the level of wealth of the citizens. In fact, any effort to "stand out", or to gain personal advantage or esteem was strongly frowned upon as citizens were expected to be motivated solely for the good of the community, this did not, however, bring about the desired spirit of cooperation and mutual aid. It did bring about, or at least inspired, fervent nationalism. To a degree, without opportunities for gaining individual social rank, the citizens of communist countries focused much of their natural social competitiveness in promoting the primacy of their nation with respect to others, or at the very least, the primacy of communism as a whole with respect to competing ideologies... i.e. capitalism.

At its core, this is the driving motivation for all nationalism, or tribalism (which from a sociobiological perspective is the same thing, just with a different scope). The "us vs. them" mentality that so pervaded human experience until the fusion era is analogous to the mechanisms that promote animal aggression (particularly in males) when they deem themselves to be of low social rank. In this case, if the *tribe* is perceived as being disadvantaged in some way, solidarity within the tribe is dramatically reinforced while aggression towards those outside of it is likewise increased. The communist leadership, particularly in the 1950's and 60's strongly emphasized the "danger" represented by the capitalist world, which was portrayed as scheming to wipe them out.

To a degree, this was true, and as the proxy wars described in Chapter 6 waged around the world, they were cited as evidence of the importance of banding together and sacrificing personal ambitions to those of the state.

Ironically, examination of the records of the time indicates that those who most wholly ascribed to this mentality within the communist nations were all the same driven by a sort of truncated or warped desire for personal status, in that those who demonstrated that they were the least motivated by personal ambition were the most respected. It is a testament to the strength of our natural desire for status that if a *lack* of desire for status brings status, then some will force themselves into a show of disinterest out of self-interest, thus entering a spiral of contradiction.

A political system based on such a twisted sociological premise is doomed to failure, and fail it did. The extraordinary inefficiency of the communist system eventually drove the Soviet Union into economic collapse and in 1990, the Berlin Wall was torn down[101], signaling the end of the Soviet system and the end of Marxist-Leninist communism as a credible alternative politico-economic system.

It is interesting to consider what then happened in the countries that had lived under that political system for the previous half century.

In the case of countries that had at some point in their past had a democratic political system, namely Poland, Czechoslovakia, Hungary and the Baltic states, the first elections held primarily saw the same political parties present themselves as had been present at the *last* elections, decades before (plus, in most cases, the communist party, which vainly hoped to gather enough votes to retain a semblance of power). In certain respects, it was as though a great hand had come down and covered up the political process for fifty years and then was lifted, revealing what had always lain hidden beneath it. This is a further demonstration of capitalist democracy being something of a default political system in pre-fusion societies.

While all of these countries struggled with the new democratic system, and many experienced corruption and nationalism, Russia itself, as well as the newly independent countries that had formerly been directly part of the Soviet Union, had never had experience with democracy. Prior to being part of the Soviet Union they had been under the dominion of the Tsar and while they all enthusiastically embarked on the capitalist adventure, they adopted a capitalism that in many respects, resembled the "robber-baron" capitalism of

---

[101] The Berlin Wall divided the city of Berlin into communist and "free" zones for thirty years. For details ask Artie.

the nineteenth century as opposed to the more modern and regulated capitalism of the West.

Corruption was rampant as the citizens of these nations, who had for decades been, supposedly, in the process of learning how to abandon their personal ambitions to become perfect social beings, threw themselves into a frenzied effort to gain as much wealth as possible and to flaunt it as garishly as they could. Jokes about loud, ostentatious Russians with poor taste became rampant all over the world and indeed, Russian mores were transformed so dramatically and so swiftly that there is an inescapable impression that the desire to compete for social rank had grown all the stronger for having been suppressed.

A similar phenomenon occurred from a purely political perspective as most of these countries, which again, had always known only autocratic rule, reverted to essentially autocratic systems. Russia was the most glaring of these, as Vladimir Putin, elected into the office of president, so gathered lasting power unto himself that he became, in essence, an autocratic ruler for life. Nominally, the country remained democratic, as it clearly *was* the will of the majority of Russian people that he remain the country's ruler, but his blatant efforts to quash all opposition and silence dissenting voices – to the point of assassination – hardly allowed for a free and open exchange of ideas, and soon, Russian elections became largely symbolic.

Despite his autocratic tendencies, Putin was an intelligent man who knew that he could not hold back the tide of change. As the world became increasingly international in both economic and political scope, and with the emergence of OPCs, he realized that it was impossible to maintain that tight a grasp on individual power within any nation, and he gradually loosened his grip. Nevertheless, it was only with Putin's death that Russia was truly able to shed its joint authoritarian and "cowboy capitalist" system.

***

The other great communist nation, China, did not go through the same upheaval to renounce communism. In fact, it never officially did (at least not during the information age). China remained nominally communist all through the 21ˢᵗ century. In reality, though, it had nothing like a communist system.

Chinese communism had been much like that of the Soviet Union in its totalitarian, utopic ideology until the death of its founder, Mao Zedong, in 1976. In fact, in certain respects, Mao had been even more of a proponent of ideological "purity" than had been any Russian leader since Lenin. After Mao's death, China began a transition to a very specific type of "state-sponsored capitalism". They did not label it as such, but by the end of the 20ᵗʰ century, the Chinese had completely transformed their economy. Much of this was the work of Deng Xiaoping, who spoke of "socialism with Chinese characteristics" and suggested that China could benefit from the management practices of capitalism while remaining ideologically socialist. In reality, the socialist ideology behind the capitalist reality was minor at best, at least by the middle of the information age.

While Russia's mutation from communism to capitalism was brutal and painful, China managed the transition in a very different way. Never officially abandoning its ideology, Deng began making economic reforms that allowed individuals to embark on business ventures. He "privatized" a number of state-run businesses, putting them in the hands of private Chinese capitalists and he reformed banking[102], making it considerably easier for ambitious Chinese citizens to create and grow private businesses.

At the same time, the Chinese government remained closely involved in the country's business activities at all levels. In the list of MNCs and countries in Chapter 18 it should be noted that if corporations owned by states were included, three Chinese corporations (CNP, Sinopec and State Grid) would have been on the list as well. These organisms *acted* like MNCs, were run according to the same principles, in fact they *were* MNCs for all intents and purposes… they were simply *owned* by the Chinese government. Or, more exactly, the majority of the shares were owned by the government. In some cases, individuals could own shares as well, even non-Chinese individuals.

And even those corporations in China in which the government had no direct ownership invariably had very strong ties to the state. The government was omnipresent, closely entwined into the entire economic activity of the nation. However, whereas the Maoist approach, closely aligned to the Soviet system, had attempted to control economic activity, the later face of Chinese communism sought to coordinate and favor Chinese industry.

---

[102] Many students have rather unusual ideas about the role of banks, undoubtedly because of their typically simplistic functions in most retro-sims. Ask Artie about what banks were and how they worked, but in this context suffice it to say that a functioning banking system facilitated capitalism and particularly, entrepreneurship.

Chinese culture was well suited to this centralized coordination. Alone among the great agricultural nations, China had long cultivated the institution of a strong, apolitical bureaucracy. For thirteen hundred years, a largely meritocratic system had been in place to identify and train promising candidates to work in the state structure. While China had been an empire, with its own royalty and nobility, the bureaucrats who actually made things work had been almost entirely separate from politicians of any stripe and had therefore persevered through dynastic upheavals and had remained undistracted from political maneuvering (except within their own sub-culture). The principle "religion" of China, Confucianism, lauded the value of public service and loyalty to the state, confirming the place of bureaucrats in Chinese society and imbuing them with considerable social status[103].

The nineteenth century had seen a period of turmoil in China as incursions by industrialized nations had eroded the power of the emperor, a situation that Japan had taken advantage of in the early twentieth century, when they invaded and conquered much of the country. This period of unusual chaos had allowed Mao's Lenin-inspired communist insurrection to succeed and wrest power back from the foreigners and the nascent Chinese republic, via a brief and unusual period of political ideology for China. During Deng's rein, the communist party simply replaced the emperor in the role of formal political power while still allowing a strong and powerful state bureaucratic structure. As communist as it was, China had, to a degree, become China again. Deng's reforms simply removed the

---

[103] Note that Confucianism was less a religion than a set of philosophical guidelines in that it posited no supernatural beings.

ideology in all but the most symbolic way and China returned to its historical model of a nation run by a merit-based bureaucracy under a more or less influential central political power.

The Chinese bureaucracy had always been skilled at determining how much to interfere in Chinese society. Too much interference could quash the ambition and ingenuity of the Chinese people, too little could allow chaos and could, in the minds of the Chinese, lead to short term priorities taking the fore. For example, the Chinese considered that the managers of publicly traded companies, those whose shares could be bought and sold on a stock exchange, tended to make decisions based on very short-term movements in the stock price, whereas the health of the nation's economy required a strategy that was far more long-term in nature. The government took the long view, as Chinese bureaucrats had for millennia, and this mix of short-term oriented corporate capitalism with long-term oriented government "guidance" was effectively, a very Chinese phenomenon.

The effectiveness of this approach was undeniable. Note that this is not a moral judgement. The leaders of China had a very nationalistic view of the world. They were acting entirely in what they perceived to be the interests of China, and they were doing so in a decidedly undemocratic fashion. That being said, the lack of democracy in China did provide a degree of stability. As was often pointed out by the Chinese at the time, the frequent elections held in other countries shortened the planning horizon for politicians. They needed to deliver short-term results in order to be re-elected (since before Artie, the long-term impact of their policies was open to debate), whereas Chinese politicians could focus on the long term well-being of China. For that matter, while polls were not taken on the subject, it is extremely unlikely that if a referendum were to have been carried out in China during the information age the majority of Chinese citizens would have wanted to change the system. While to a degree, this lack of desire for democracy was at least partly a result of the government's quelling potential opposition, it is undoubtedly also due to the fact that in China during the information age, the government's implication in the capitalist system was light enough that individuals could, truly, benefit from an extraordinary degree of social mobility. The political class, while retaining the actual national decision-making power, did not retain for itself the position of the greatest esteem in the country (unlike the leaders of the Soviet Union). At the pinnacle of the social hierarchy were the entrepreneurs, the businesspeople, who rapidly grew just as rich, or richer, than their Western counterparts. By allowing them the limelight of public opinion and the greater part of the wealth, the social ambitions of the Chinese citizenry were focused on enterprise, not politics, while politics helped ensure that the enterprise contributed to the status of China as a whole.

That the country on the whole benefitted from this approach is clear. That the socialist ideal of equality was the result is far from the case. Throughout the first decades of the 21st century, the distribution of wealth in China was no less skewed than in the United States. In many respects, the concern for the well-being of China demonstrated by the Chinese government did not apply equally to all the citizens of the country.

So it is that the one great competing political system to democracy had for all intents and purposes disappeared by the early information era. Let us examine democracy in detail, then.

CHAPTER 21

THE UNITED STATES - THE BASTION OF DEMOCRACY

The establishment of the United States represents, in my opinion, the most noble political experiment in human history. A group of truly extraordinary thinkers: Jefferson, Franklin, Hamilton, Madison, Adams, Paine and others, all passionate advocates of enlightenment thinking, decided to create an entire country based on the philosophical ideals they held dear, and this at a time when every major country on the planet was run by an autocratic monarchy of one kind or another. Never has such a fortuitous gathering of intellect, drive and human decency been assembled in one place at one time. The founders of the United States were genuinely disinterested, uniquely capable, profoundly progressive and highly intelligent. They built a nation on principles that the world had never dared apply and in so doing they took the biggest single leap forward in progressive policy ever attempted.

On top of the leap forward in morality that the foundation of the United States represents, so too did the founders imbue it with a very new kind of respect for rational thought. Thomas Paine wrote: "Science, the partisan of no country, but the beneficent patroness of all, has liberally opened a temple where all may meet. Her influence on the mind, like the sun on the chilled earth, has long been preparing it for higher cultivation and further improvement." With these values, both egalitarian and dedicated to reason, the nation these forward-thinking people created grew within less than two centuries to dominate the affairs of the entire planet. This is testimony to their vision and to the power of the principles that drove them.

It is therefore doubly sad to behold the decay that almost immediately set in.

From the start, the founders of the country feared that it would go awry. Benjamin Franklin wrote: "(our government) can only end in despotism, as other forms have done before it, when the people shall become so corrupted as to need despotic Government, being incapable of any other." We shall see that in the 21st century, his apocalyptic vision would almost come to pass while at the same time, the commitment to reason and enlightenment thinking so precious to men like Paine and Jefferson would be largely rejected by the political establishment.

Already, in the early 19th century, over 15% of the human beings living in the United States were enslaved, with nearly half the population in some states consisting of dark-skinned slaves. Likewise, during this same period, and beyond, the United States undertook the genocide of the native population of North America, killing millions of natives. Arguably, the sins of the early Americans were not appreciably worse than the expansionist colonial actions of certain European nations, but the exceptional circumstances and philosophy that gave rise to the very idea of the United States, that breathed into it its essence, would perhaps have us hope for something better. In reality, the French Revolution was inspired by much the same philosophy (although it went horribly wrong almost immediately) and the other nations of Europe rather quickly shifted to a more enlightened political system, growing increasingly democratic over the course of the 19th century so that relatively soon, the truly exceptional nature of the United States remained primarily in the minds of the Americans themselves, not in their actions or policies.

But it did remain, oh so solidly, in their minds. Those thirteen years between the American and the French revolutions, when the United States truly *was* the world's only real democracy, so inspired a feeling of exceptionalism, of *mission* in the minds of Americans that it was hardly diminished at all over two hundred years later, at the dawn of the information age.

The concept of American exceptionalism is important when trying to understand the reactions of Americans during the period that interests us and it can be difficult for modern students to grasp fully the importance of this concept.

There is a certain proclivity for "America bashing" among modern students of history[104]. They see the country as having been the last bastion of an outdated mindset, a brake on the progression

---

[104] This was the term used by many, often conservative Americans during the information age to describe those who spoke poorly of the United States… or in many cases, those who said anything at all about the country that did not correspond to their own idyllic vision of it.

of humankind from the primitive past to the enlightened future. Part of this is probably due to the fact that the story of Destiny Holt is known to all, and her courage only shone (indeed was only necessary) due to the recalcitrance of large swaths of the American population to accept social evolutions that were not only desirable but fundamentally necessary. And, of course, it was those same ultra-conservative passions that drove Zachary Jackson to kill her, forever consigning the entire "alt-right" movement to the trash heap of failed, noxious political philosophies along with fascism, communism, and nationalism.

But it must be remembered that the United States was not always the politically extreme nation that it became, and for that matter, nor was it uniform in its later extremism. Indeed, Holt herself, while never a politician per se, was *also* the uniquely American product of the American political psyche. The United States was *never* uniform in anything, it was always a cacophonous collection of fiercely independent individuals and in many respects, this was the country's greatest strength. It led to unending tensions, but these very tensions often resolved themselves in an extraordinary dynamism, a level of initiative and creativity rarely seen before or since. If the price of this energy was chaos and if the price of that chaos was an eventual lurch into the morass of ultra-conservatism and irrational, hatred-fueled populist politics we can at least take solace in the fact that in the end, progressive dynamism won out and while we teetered for a while on the brink of the abyss, it may well be that we never would have seen the road bridging it if the United States had been a less vibrant, more structured nation to begin with.

But enough of metaphor, let us examine the politics, for that is the aim of this section.

The defining moment in the history of the United States during the industrial era was the American Civil War. It was this bloody conflict, during which the United States suffered far more casualties than in all of their other wars combined, that determined the shape of American history for the following two hundred years.

The Civil War not only cleaved the United States in two (although that schism had long existed) but like so many civil conflicts, it created an intricate network of internal schisms that went far beyond the simple North / South divide. It, and the racist political system that succeeded it in the south of the country, created a pervasive sense of race and race relations that was largely unique to the United States[105]. It also laid the groundwork for the nostalgic image

---

[105] We will not examine this in detail in this book, simply because it warrants a far more complete treatment than we could devote to it here. I strongly suggest you ask Artie about the post-war period in the United States. Put succinctly, after the defeat of the South, progressive Northerners instituted a period known as "reconstruction", in line with the wishes of Abraham Lincoln. During this period, black southerners were voted into office, created successful businesses, and seemed close to assimilation into the social fabric of the South. However, eleven years later, in 1876, the Northern forces of reform were withdrawn and regressive white Southern leadership returned to power, instituting a set of laws that disenfranchised blacks, forced them into subservience and tortured or killed those who would not submit, even going so far as to erect statues throughout the South celebrating the very leaders who had committed treason against the nation and led the pro-slavery rebellion... largely to demonstrate to the black population that they should live in fear. These policies were only defeated a hundred years later, by the courage of those who led the civil rights movement.

of the "American Rebel", that mythical figure, armed with his own weapon, who was a nation unto himself[106].

By the dawn of the information age, these American Rebels had largely gravitated to the right of the political spectrum in search of a political philosophy that they felt gave them free reign for their individualism while stoking the fires of their xenophobic insularity. Remember that at the time, travel was cumbersome and costly in trew and not yet possible in sim. As such, many people, *particularly* those who valued individualistic philosophies, had very rarely, if ever, met anyone outside of their relatively homogeneous social circle. In such cases, it is easy to ascribe less than human qualities to all those who live outside the boundaries of our own sheltered existence. In essence, the frontier of the "tribe" becomes very limited indeed and the "us vs. them" mentality rises to the fore, to be plucked and sucked upon by any and all populist politicians and *arrivistes* who present themselves.

It may be necessary here to explore briefly this political concept of "left" and "right" to which we have frequently referred.

It is often the case that students see the left and the right of industrial-age politics as a set of binary factions. They believe that there were "left wing" and "right wing" politicians, doomed to battle each other to the death in each and every political gladiatory struggle. This, however, is far from the case.

The concept of "left" and "right" in participatory democracies dates from the period immediately prior to the French Revolution,

---

[106] Here, I pull directly from the work of Milo Fernandez, whose 2103 book "The Myth of the American Rebel" was instrumental in the analysis of the early information-age American mindset.

when the *états-majeurs* met in the assembly hall to discuss first the question of whether or not to revolt. At the time, it was deemed prudent to separate the two major factions (royalist and revolutionary) on opposite sides of the hall, so as both to mitigate the probability of physical confrontation and to better allow them to have an unfettered view across the hall as they screamed at each other.

After the revolution, the distinction was retained. There were no longer any royalists (the last of them having lost their heads to the guillotine) but their place was taken by those who were generally less enthusiastic about radical rapid change, to be faced by those who were more desirous of quickly revising the laws of society.

So it was that conservatives sat on the right of the chamber and progressives on the left.

The distinction became custom, both in France and in other nations, who likewise discovered that the same basic distinction in political philosophy tended to apply across different nations and systems.

We now know that this distinction is in part driven by genetics. Even in the information age, research was done that demonstrated that there are those among us who are genetically more pre-disposed to risk-taking and therefore willing and even enthusiastic about changes in governing structures, as well as those who tend to be more cautious about such revolutionary ideas. There are other linked behavioral and attitudinal traits that allow us today to draw a picture of what would have been considered to be "left" and "right" attitudes at the time. Notably, those on the "right" tend not only to be hesitant to accept change, but also somewhat more judgmental, preferring retaliatory as opposed to rehabilitative justice, as well as more nostalgic, tied to the traditions of the past. Those on the left tend to be more perceptive, finding themselves uncomfortable making difficult decisions, and slightly less prone to tribal thinking.

Today, it is easy for us to dispense with our own automatic judgement of which of these two dispositions is more "moral" or "honorable", since the consequences of one as opposed to the other are marginal. We no longer have broad existential political debates… or if we do, they can resolve themselves in the founding of an offworld colony. However, in the industrial age, it is easy to imagine how the two conflicting viewpoints would be adversarial when used to make decisions about the very structure of society.

During the cold war (i.e. the late industrial age) the dichotomy was clear: there was fascism on the right and communism on the left, with democratic capitalism in the center. After the demise of fascism, capitalism was, by default, the "rightist" political philosophy while communism was on the left.

But was it?

By then, left and right had abandoned the idea of "change" versus "progress". In reality, Soviet (and Maoist) communism was hardly progressive. While rooted in what might be considered a progressive ideal of the perfectibility of humankind, it had morphed into simple totalitarianism with a frosting of ideology to make excuses for itself. In reality, political extremism of either ilk ended up in a similar totalitarian state[107]. Since we have already established the

---

[107] This was recognized at the time. Ask Artie about "horseshoe theory", proposed by the French writer and philosopher Jean-Pierre Faye in 2002.

unviability of communism, let us focus on the differences in political philosophy within the context of democratic capitalism.

The left / right spectrum applied not only across substantially different political systems, i.e. communism vs democratic capitalism, but also within the latter. After the abuses and the tensions engendered by the unfettered capitalism of the early 20th century, an effort was made to introduce more restrictions to the institutions of the system. Child labor was abolished, consumer protection laws were enacted, employers were required to offer shortened work weeks, large monopolistic companies were broken down into smaller companies, unemployed workers were given aid until they could find other jobs, the poor were provided with material aid, and governments began setting up forced retirement savings programs, nationalized healthcare institutions and free university education.

Many of these political and social innovations arose in the United States, where Franklin Roosevelt, the longest serving of any US president, was responsible for many of them, over the fervent opposition of the Republican Party, which bemoaned the corresponding increases in taxes and what they considered profligate government spending.

It was during this period that the Republican Party became associated with conservatism, or the right of the American political spectrum while the Democratic Party (the party of Roosevelt, among others) became associated with the left. Previously, perhaps the most progressive policy in American political history, the abolition of slavery, had been a Republican initiative, and the Democrats had been particularly strong in the South of the country in response. While Democrats had retained their Southern power base, they had all the same assumed the progressive mantle, epitomized by Roosevelt, while the Republican Party after the Second World War espoused relatively conservative values of fiscal responsibility and the minimization of government (economic liberalism). The two parties battled for votes via their competing social and economic policies and typically restrained debate.

This portrayal of the American political scene seems strange to modern students, who are used to picturing the political landscape in the United States as one of irreconcilable extremes, of name calling, of alt-right monsters, puerile "political correctness" and narcissistic populists. This all came later, however – during the industrial age, American politics was nowhere near as chaotic nor was the left-right cleavage so vast. It should be remembered that "alt-right" means *alternative* right. Prior to groups like the Tea Party, there was just left and right in the American mind, it was the extremists on the right who brought American politics to where it eventually went, and who finally produced Trump and after him, the Ranchers.

In order to understand the beginning of that movement, one must understand that while many nations had a number of different, often changing political parties, after the Civil War there were only two parties in the United States that had any real power whatsoever, and these were the Democrats and the Republicans.

This dichotomy led to a much greater sense of long-standing loyalty (read "tribal identification"), often extending through generations of a same family or even an entire region. This inertia and inflexibility contributed to the tendency of either party to use extreme measures to shake apart the existing power structure when they were disadvantaged, for more subtle actions could only sway the smaller pool of neutral voters.

The Republicans, who had held the presidency largely unchallenged between the Civil War and the election of Roosevelt[108], suddenly found themselves removed from real power as Roosevelt was followed by Truman. Eisenhower's moderate Republican presidency was immediately followed by Kennedy and then Johnson, again, Democrats.

The Republicans struggled to find a way to return to power. The candidacy of Eisenhower had been a boon to them – the nation's greatest hero of the Second World War undoubtedly could have been elected under either party's banner – but he did not signal a return to Republican political dominance, or even national political competitiveness.

In order to differentiate themselves from their Democratic competitors, Republicans therefore moved farther to the right. They became increasingly vociferous in their verbal attacks on communism, conducting witch hunts among the American intelligentsia and entertainment industry, destroying the careers and reputations of those they labelled as communist.

This was not enough, though. Notably, the Southern voters who had forever shunned them, while typically more anti-communist than Northerners were not convinced. The Republicans then made a conscious effort to sway those same voters through the "Southern Strategy". The party decided to oppose the civil rights movement in the 1960's in an effort to ingratiate themselves with

---

[108] In only 16 of those 72 years did a Democrat serve as president, and in fact, only two presidents (out of sixteen) had been Democrats.

racist Southern voters who had traditionally voted Democrat. This had a certain impact, but was far less politically profitable than they had hoped (on top of being morally abhorrent).

If the Republicans could not win over the hearts of Southerners by appealing to their racism, they could perhaps convince them by identifying themselves with their religious sentiment.

Religion was particularly strong in the South and the Western interior. The Republican Party had been based entirely upon the idea of individual liberty, and its first president, Abraham Lincoln, had not practiced any religion, but the next phase of the Southern Strategy was to don the mantle of religious and social conservatism.

So it was that the resolutely *un*dogmatic and non-ideological Republicans turned to the religious leaders of America's highly vocal "evangelical" movement, pledging their support for the crusades of these "preachers" against what they perceived as the ills of the nation – notably abortion, homosexuality, the absence of religion in politics, and the teaching of evolution.

This, finally, was the strategy that allowed the Republicans to regain control of the government, even after the debacle of the Nixon presidency. The standard-bearer of this new strategy was Ronald Reagan, elected in 1980 with the support of every Southern state except Georgia (the home state of his Democratic opponent), which he would win four years later.

Interestingly, Reagan's opponent in the 1980 presidential election was a religious Southerner, the incumbent president Jimmy Carter. It is undeniable that Carter's personal religious convictions were much more extensive and sincere than Reagan's. However, Reagan offered the politically extreme evangelical leaders the promise of political influence whereas Carter, loyal to the ideals of the constitution that separated church and state, did not. As such, while Carter's home state of Georgia did vote for him, the rest of the region chose the less religious man to promote their more religious policies.

With their new power base among Southern and Western voters, the Republican party gradually became transformed and the left / right divide in the United States became unique in its aspect.

Let's step back for a moment to consider traditional left / right politics.

In most post-war democratic nations, the progressive left tended to militate for more communitarian decision making and structures, primarily with respect to economic distribution. It stressed cooperation and communal well-being (within the parameters of democratic capitalism). The right tended towards individualism and a minimization of government legislation, preferring to leave as much as possible to Adam Smith's "invisible hand". Not surprisingly, the traditional left / right cleavage often resulted in very different social classes being drawn to each side, with the poor eager to enjoy the left's more egalitarian economic policies and the rich anxious to retain their riches and benefit from the typically higher concentration of wealth facilitated by conservative policies.

Along with these economic viewpoints often came a number of social attitudes. Those on the right were usually more "socially conservative", desirous of maintaining traditions, which in the late industrial / early information age were very often closely allied with religion, particularly in the United States. Those on the left were more often open to seeing social norms change, such as the acceptance of homosexuality, racial equality, and the general decline of religious influence in society. Other differences included attitudes towards justice, with those on the left often more supportive of re-habilitative justice systems and those on the right more inclined towards punitive justice, with retribution as its purpose.

The left / right tension of the 20th and 21st centuries seems somewhat perplexing today, but once again the reader must attempt to remain objective. The economic concerns of the right are far less off-putting when one remembers that wealth was the primary source of social status. Imagine that you were asked to "transfer" your so-cial markers to another person. The coin of our realm is followers and upvotes, imagine if a central authority decided to take some of yours and simply erase them for the benefit of someone who has done nothing to earn them. You have earned your upvotes, your followers, your views, your sim scores. Of that there is no denying, and no one asks you to give them up. In the information age, money was the equivalent of our social markers and the idea of transferring money you worked hard to amass to someone who perhaps did not work at all, and might not have worked out of *choice* was extremely difficult for many... as it would be for you.

You protest. You point out that it is *clear* that your social mark-ers are the result of your efforts, skill, talents, and wits whereas having simply been born into a privileged society was obviously just a matter of luck, but they did not see it that way. It is impossible for you to imagine that your social markers are the result of anything but your own successes and failures, but in the chaos of the pre-fusion world it was extremely difficult to analyze the reasons for any measure of economic success. As such, the innate human tendency to ascribe our successes to ourselves and our failures to others, or to chance, is bound to hold sway. The rich almost always congratulated themselves on their cunning while the poor looked for those to blame, despite the fact that up to 87% of financial success was due to pure luck[109].

Donald Trump is a good example of this. After being granted partial ownership in his father's successful business in 1974 he continued to receive hundreds of millions of dollars from his parents, often through covert means in order to avoid taxes. These transfers of wealth continued through the 1990's. By the time he was elected in 2016 Trump had parlayed those resources into $2.6 billion and on the basis of this success and an extraordinary talent for bluster, he had built a reputation for himself as an astute businessman (despite the fact that his net worth was in reality far less than he claimed during his campaign... a fact he went to great lengths to hide) [110]. In reality, though, simply *investing* the wealth he had received from his parents in the stock market would have generated more wealth than he created through his business ventures. As such, his "business acumen" was demonstrably worse than random chance, since, as so eloquently stated by Warren Buffet (a successful, and truly self-made

---

[109] This is Artie's estimate, although she will inevitably plead that she may be inaccurate, given the variability around human decisions. Note that she estimates that in the United States at the time, the figure was probably about five percentage points higher than in Europe, primarily because the lack of free higher education coupled with the lesser availability of public "insurance" functions like universal healthcare, exacerbated the role of luck, whether it be the luck inherent in being born into a wealthy family or the impact of unforeseen and unfortunate events, such as major illness.

[110] Note that even today, the exact level of Trump's 2016 wealth is uncertain, this is Artie's best estimate. See Bragg's 2040 book "Needles in a Haystack: Artie and I Search for Truth in Trump".

financier) at the time, who pointed out that "a monkey would have done better by throwing darts at the stock pages" than by investing in Trump's business deals. Nevertheless, despite the easily falsified claims of skill in business, Trump firmly believed, and convinced many others, that he was a brilliant businessman.

In the information age, "money talked", and those who had money typically did consider themselves superior, irrespective of how they had gotten it. As such, they were loath to part with it, and incensed – given their strong views about individualism and justice – when others sought to take it away and give it to those who had less… because in their minds these "freeloaders" were, of course, lazy, otherwise they would not be poor. Luck, in their opinion, had nothing to do with it, and it should be remembered that among the poor there were, indeed, those who did *not* participate in society, and had no desire to do so. Such is their right, you automatically say, but no, this was not the case at the time (at least not before the citizen's income). Remember that capitalism was predicated on *contributing* to society through one's skills and efforts, it had no provision for those who wished to do otherwise, and indeed since this was before auto-mated production, if all had taken that route then society would have ground to a halt. While they were very much in the minority, these "freeloaders" existed, and examples of them were widely discussed and repeated, greatly exaggerating their numbers and impact.

Given these parallels, it should be easier for you, comfortably seated in your sim seat, never having experienced hunger, want, riches or taxes (at least in trew) to understand the rage of seeing your hard-earned money ripped from your hands to be bestowed upon the "incompetent" and the "lazy".

This dichotomy was the typical cleavage, but returning to the United States, after the success of the Republicans' "Southern Strategy" and the collapse of the Soviet Union, something strange began to happen.

In the rest of the developed world, particularly in Europe, the collapse of communism was the death knoll of far left ideology. The left / right political spectrum continued to exist, but it was more centered, the European communist parties all but disappearing from the scene as their benchmark (and often surreptitious sponsor), the Soviet Union, disintegrated into a quivering wreck. The countries as a whole continued their slow shift to the left, in continuation of the progression along the same moral arc that had been in place since the enlightenment, in a fitful, stop-and go manner, with the far right often poking up its head in an effort to entice the disenchanted poor with racist, anti-immigrant populism. To the credit of the more powerful and politically sophisticated Western European countries, the electorate never succumbed entirely to the siren call of xenophobia (with some exceptions among the former communist nations) and by the time Artie arose, the most advanced of them, in Scandinavia, were ready to take the plunge into technonationalism that we have already described.

The situation was very different in the United States. The Southern Strategy had led the Republicans to a political philosophy that was extremist by European standards, due to its roots in the religious extremism of the American evangelical movement. Having "sold their souls" to the evangelical right, the Republicans transformed themselves from a party of laissez-faire capitalists to social warriors who campaigned on platforms that in reality promoted extreme change. They fought to overturn laws allowing abortion, militated for prayer to be allowed in schools, despite the constitution's strictures against the promotion of religion, and fought against the teaching of evolution, going so far as promoting "creationism" in many cases[111].

The Republicans' extremist allies also were ardent "patriots", with their fervor clearly surpassing the boundaries of group pride and extending into the realm of group superiority, hence nationalism. As such, the Republicans accentuated their "patriotic" tendencies, stoking pride in the military might of the United States and embarking on a series of wars extending from a tiny but much extolled invasion of the minuscule island nation of Grenada to the adventures in the Middle East initiated by Bush father and Bush son. With each new war they quelled debate by equating dissatisfaction with their bellicose policy with a lack of "support for the troops", painting opponents as anti-patriotic and unappreciative of the supreme sacrifice the Republicans themselves imposed upon the nation's soldiers. They berated other nations, particularly the "socialist" Europeans by stating that they could only afford their social programs because the United States was investing enough in its military might to protect the entire democratic world.

---

[111] Creationism was the doctrine that held that the universe had been created by god (specifically, the Abrahamic god) some four to six thousand years before, in line with the creation myth outlined in the Bible. It therefore denied any form of evolution, as well as almost all other sciences. While it seems extraordinary to us that humans in the 20th, let alone the 21st century could have believed this, over 30% percent of the American population did, with a further 20% percent less sure of the dates, but rejecting natural selection all the same. Note that this was a purely American phenomenon, at least with respect to the developed world.

It is true that at the time, the United States spent enormous amounts of wealth on its military. Under the Trump administration, the United States spent 3.4% of its national product on the military, which, given its wealth, was more than the next eight highest-spending nations *combined*[112]. However, at that point in time it was objectively ridiculous to imagine an existential threat to major developed nations from other major developed nations. The days of wars of conquest, largely driven by the desire for arable land (as discussed in Chapter 17), were over. The European Union had been successful in eliminating the risk of intra-European war, the Soviet Union was no more, and even the relatively belligerent Russia was concerned with re-establishing dominance over the former Soviet republics, not with invading Poland. The Chinese were often cited as a threat, but while they "rattled sabers" as well, they were entirely devoted to the development of "soft power", buying their way into the hearts and pockets of under-developed nations to secure access to important raw materials, such as rare earths. Throughout history, the Chinese had always been more interested in dominating trade than embarking on conquest. No, in reality, the real threat to international security did indeed come from terrorists in the early industrial age, and aircraft carriers were notoriously inefficient at battling *that* threat. Employing them and the massive military clout they represented often exacerbated the situation, as the United States executed deadly strikes against targets deep in the Muslim world, all too often targeting innocuous gatherings such as weddings due to a lack of

---

[112] In an interesting comparison, the Roman Empire at its peak spent roughly 2.5% of its national product on its military… and they had actual barbarian hordes with which to contend.

actual intelligence, hence exacerbating the situation. The fact that Europe refused to spend as much on such inappropriate weaponry was not, in reality, because they wished to "freeload" on noble American largess, but because they had a better understanding of the pointlessness of such expenditures. No less a military expert than Dwight Eisenhower had already pointed out in 1953:

> "Every gun that is made, every warship launched, every rocket fired signifies, in the final sense, a theft from those who hunger and are not fed, those who are cold and are not clothed. This world in arms is not spending money alone. It is spending the sweat of its laborers, the genius of its scientists, the hopes of its children. The cost of one modern heavy bomber is this: a modern brick school in more than 30 cities."

The Republican Party, though, knew that nothing swelled industrial-age hearts more than the contemplation of soldiers in uniform and flags waving over warships, and they appropriated these symbols, as populists had done since the first armies were formed, berating those both inside and outside the nation who attempted to point out the inanity of such investment in the 21st-century, even when these protesters did quote Eisenhower.

These tactics strike us as too absurd as to have been successful, but a brief consideration of them in the light of tribalism can help to appreciate their 20th-century appeal. In certain respects, our own society can be seen as a "left wing utopia" in that we truly have no more political frontiers (except the implicit frontiers of distance with the colonies), no more conflict, no xenophobic religions to separate us – indeed, Lennon's "brotherhood of man". This makes it difficult for us to understand the appeal of tribalism. Most of us, though, have enjoyed conflictual sims, even fought in wars, and bonded with others in common defense, even though we would never do so in trew. It is our evolutionary heritage and was a driving factor in information-age mentality that the Republicans capitalized on.

Note as well that certain elements of our own society could be seen as a *conservative* utopia. There is virtually no restriction of personal freedom, no taxes, no forced reallocation of the measures of success. We are the ultimate individualists. Imagine *this* being constrained and you may begin to feel the pangs that inspired American conservatives.

Having reduced politics to this almost exclusively emotional level, the Republicans managed what would have been unimaginable in the past… they rallied the poor to their policies, when these policies only made them poorer, particularly in comparison to the increasingly rich elite. In so doing, they removed from the more leftist Democrats the traditional support base of any leftist party, the disadvantaged.

The Republican Party of the information age, therefore, had an extraordinary advantage: the deep funding of the rich and the emotional support of the poor.

It is sometimes difficult to understand why funding was important in politics, after all, a rich person's vote had no more weight than a poor person's vote. However, politics in the information age was analogous to business, especially in the United States. Political parties and their allies spent enormous amounts of money advertising their candidates to the voting population, employing precisely the same manipulation techniques as were used to sell meat, cars or clothing. Outside of the United States, almost all democratic countries had limits to what could be spent on political campaigns and therefore identical or very similar levels of spending across the candidates in a given election. In the United States, however, the supreme court of the land had decided (in 2010) to remove almost all restrictions on political donations by individuals or corporations. This meant that the Republicans, with their rich benefactors and pro-business agenda had vast sums at their disposal.

The support of the poor is more difficult to understand, but it must be remembered that poverty was typically associated with lower levels of education and higher degrees of religiosity. This was particularly the case in the United States, where there was no national education system to speak of and where higher education was expensive. Irrational beliefs and motivations of all kinds were correlated with a lack of education, as was a degree of insularity, since poor Americans rarely had the opportunity to travel outside of the country and therefore had little interaction with other nations, systems or social norms. As Mark Twain wrote: "Travel is fatal to prejudice, bigotry, and narrow-mindedness, and many of our people need it sorely on these accounts. Broad, wholesome, charitable views of men and things cannot be acquired by vegetating in one little corner of the earth all one's lifetime." If many of the people needed travel in 1869, when Twain wrote "Innocents Abroad", many more needed it in 2020, for average Americans were forming their own norms that were at odds with those in the rest of the world.

This normative inertia was cemented with the appearance of the alt-right phenomenon and its media outlets, particularly the network "Fox News". Media such as this became increasingly detached from all semblance of objectivity or fact, feeding the untraveled, uneducated population with titillating tales about social collapse and dangerous hordes of (primarily brown-skinned) immigrants wreaking havoc around the world. As long as the actual politicians presented by the Republican Party hailed from the more educated side of the party's power base they eschewed openly condoning and endorsing the more absurd lies propagated via these channels (while still enthusiastically benefitting from their manipulation of the electorate), but the election of Trump changed all that. Trump not only promoted the most egregious theories and fabrications of outlets like Fox and its coterie of even more absurd emulators, but he added grist to their mills, even as president, claiming, for example, that three million Californians had voted illegally, all for his opponent (it is estimated that perhaps seven people in California voted illegally, most of them through error). Trump's lies were so enormous, so patently absurd that a new word was coined to describe them: "prepostrosities"[113].

Trump (undoubtedly unwittingly) emulated one of the key political tactics of Adolf Hitler, who wrote in 1925:

---

[113] While this term is better known in its application to the ravings of Hungarian Zoltan Kiss, it was in fact originally coined in 2019 by K.J. Peters, during Trump's presidency, to describe the more outrageous of the blatant falsehoods expounded by Trump. It is a portmanteaux word, a combination of "preposterous monstrosities".

"In the big lie there is always a certain force of credibility; because the broad masses of a nation are always more easily corrupted in the deeper strata of their emotional nature than consciously or voluntarily; and thus in the primitive simplicity of their minds they more readily fall victims to the big lie than the small lie, since they themselves often tell small lies in little matters but would be ashamed to resort to large-scale falsehoods. It would never come into their heads to fabricate colossal untruths, and they would not believe that others could have the impudence to distort the truth so infamously."

Trump's prepostrosities were the embodiment of this tactic. He lied about important things, like the aforementioned three million fictional voters, the state of global warming, and crime, stating that 81% of white American homicide victims were killed by black Americans (in reality, it was 15%), dangerously lighting matches around the tinderbox of American race relations.

But he also lied about ridiculously unimportant things: dramatically overstating the size of the crowd at his inaugural ceremony and repeatedly denying having said things that he had been recorded saying, and admitting, shortly before.

The point of this was that Hitler was quite right. Today, of course, if ever we have a doubt we need only ask Artie if the sky is green, the earth round or how many people attended a certain event.

We will immediately know the truth (or at least the best objective estimate). This lack of uncertainty (at least in terms of objective facts) demolishes the effectiveness of the prepostrosity, but before Artie things were quite different. While the more educated in the United States usually displayed a certain ability to think critically and assess the available data, the typical way of arriving at conclusions was to determine *who to trust*. By spouting prepostrosities, coupled with simplistic explanations and reassurances that indeed, every-thing will be better if you *just trust me*, the impudence I employ in fabricating my lie is overshadowed by the comfort taken in believing it.

The alt-right movement was all about trust. That trust was not earned by demonstrating truthfulness, but rather by generating af-finity through bluster and the establishment of a common enemy, one against whom we can unite.

The alt-right railed against immigrants and Muslims, but these were nebulous and external threats. The internal enemy was the "lib-eral" and it was the hatred of the "liberal" that fueled the furnaces of conservative American politics in the information age.

***

The alt-right phenomenon was born of the Republican South-ern Strategy in that the espousal of religious fanaticism opened the door to reasoning based on faith. Faith, though, is the antithesis of reason. If reason leads to belief in something, faith is not needed, and whereas the United States had been founded on enlightenment principles of critical reasoning, the influence of the evangelicals eroded this even in the political arena, at least on the right.

The absolutism of religion also began to be felt in the *way* political debate unfolded in the United States. "Pundits" – non-politicians who communicated their views – began to gain widespread followings. The most vocal of these were almost exclusively on the right of the political spectrum and they typically had an extremely adversarial style. Many of them would enter into almost trance-like fits of rage, screaming during their video or audio broadcasts, turning red as they displayed righteous anger at the liberals who were trying to destroy the American way of life. These pundits were typically not explicitly religious (although they almost all professed strong personal religious faith) but they brought a type of religious fervor, a sense of divine righteousness into their discourse that made the alt-right cause into a crusade against evil.

One of them, Sean Hannity, even wrote a book titled "Deliver Us From Evil", describing how the conservative movement could stave off the "evil" forces not only of Islamic terrorism, but also, implicitly, of American progressives.

The equivalent on the progressive side tended to be comedians, who would employ wit and sarcasm to tear down the sacred temples built around given ideologies by right-wing pundits. This rather perplexing dichotomy, of anger-fueled pundits on the right and irreverent comedians on the left is difficult to explain, except to the degree that humor has often been associated with intellect, which was valued by the American left in the information age, and derided by the right (consider for example their regular tirades against "liberal academia").

In such a context, the possibility of true exchange and debate became extremely limited. The alt-right portrayed American progressives as Marxists or worse. Examination of the discussions at the time on social media can be terrifying. Individuals who proclaim themselves "conservative", but whose discourse is clearly alt-right incessantly cite authoritarian leftist political failures as proof of the supremacy of their views over those of progressives.

This "reductio ad absurdium" argument is seen with increasing regularity in media exchanges throughout the period, but accelerates greatly in the Trump era, when his aggressive, vulgar manner of speaking coupled with his proclivity for brazen lying opened the floodgates of spurious argument.

Consider this exchange between an alt-right conservative and KJ Peters on an online forum, in (2018):

Anonymous alt-right user:

> "You liberals all want the same thing, you want to restrict freedom, reduce people to relying on government hand-outs, cripple businesses and return to the Marxist utopia you dreamed about but it DOESN'T WORK. We won the cold war for a reason, all that socialist crap doesn't work and you just can't stand that, can you? The only system that works is the capitalist system, the same system that made the United States the most powerful country in the world. The minute you start down the road to

socialism you can be sure that you're going to end up like the Soviet Union or Cuba or Nazi Germany or Venezuela and the only thing stopping you is going to be me, and other well-armed conservatives."

K.J Peters:

"I am both saddened and perplexed by your diatribe. Please allow me to address the three distinct points you made:

First, why are you still fighting the cold war? It has been fought: you fought it and so did I. The demise of the authoritarian communist régime of the Soviet Union was an extraordinary accomplishment, it demonstrated conclusively the superiority of the democratic capitalist model over socialism. Why on earth do you count me among the losers in that war, when I was an enthusiastic capitalist soldier, fighting with the weapons of that war: pen and paper?

Second, (a partial answer to your first point), is that clearly, you have now decided that every political philosophy that does not correspond in every way to your extremely conservative agenda is the equivalent of, or at least a facilitator for Soviet-style Marxism, which is how you use the word socialist.

Third, by including "Nazi" in that list, you evidently ascribe to this new alt-right fad of describing Nazism as a leftist ideology. When taken together with the rest, you neatly equate any social policy with socialism, which you equate with Marxism, which you equate with Nazism, based, as far as I can see, entirely on the fact that the name of the party included "socialist". This is ludicrous, fascism is the definition of a right-wing ideology. While Hitler described the party as being "neither left nor right" his policies were clearly extremely to the right and while the party name included the word "socialist", I would remind you that North Korea's name is "The Democratic People's Republic of Korea" – you'll have to explain to me in what manner this makes the Kim regime democratic. In reality, the question of where Nazism falls on various political spectrums is beside the point, what you have done is to take the bogeyman of fascism and through some remarkable and patently ridiculous rhetorical gymnastics, applied it to progressive politics, somehow lumping Stalin, Hitler, Castro, Chavez *and* FDR together in political and *moral* equivalence on the basis of the fact that they all equally represent "big government" to you and this has become the only distinguishing criterion in your political lexicon.

This leaves nothing to oppose your right-wing ideology: every other competing idea, extreme or moderate, you have managed to label both Marxist and fascist at the same time. I would congratulate you for your rhetorical skills if your reasoning were not simultaneously sad and preposterous.

You have created a dichotomy. In your mind, and the minds of your fellow alt-right enthusiasts, there are only the virtuous capitalists and the evil conspiracy of sociocommienazis who want only to destroy you, your society and everything good and righteous. Why on *earth* do you believe that? The cold war is over, as you said, and we won! Together! Khrushchev is dead and no other Marxist leader stands banging his shoe on the table yelling "we will bury you". It is *you* who have pulled away from the victorious team and who stand to the right of it vilifying your former brothers in arms, who, from your new vantage point, look suspiciously like the old enemy. But they are not.

You express nostalgia for the society of the nineteenth century, but in reality you do not want that either. I am going to assume that you would not propose eliminating child labor laws, you would not remove all aid for the poor or disabled, you would not disenfranchise women, re-institute slavery or allow employers to discriminate on the basis of race, gender or religion. If I am right, then like me, you are a dangerous liberal from the context of the times you so admire. We simply realize that capitalism, unrestrained, is also not ideal and that society is better off if its savage side effects are mitigated.

Progressives tend to favor more mitigation, responsible conservatives tend to favor less, but neither really wants the extremes. Socialism as an idea is dead, and so is Marxism and fascism. The Western world as a whole has accepted democratic capitalism and each nation must determine the best way to balance the dynamic energy of the system with the moral and practical constraints that must accompany it. For centuries, progressives have drawn society forward towards more human, compassionate and collective ideals while conservatives have pulled towards more reasoned, cautious and economically liberal ideals. The balance between them has allowed us to progress, prosper and yes, win the cold war. By vilifying your counterparts and revising this history you make it increasingly difficult if not impossible for that constructive dynamic to persist and you do the nation, as well as your fellow citizens, great harm."

Peters endeavored to put the alt-right's tactics in an historical context while they were in the midst of a concerted campaign to alter history to suit them. He was unsuccessful, not only in general, but even with the specific individual with whom he had this exchange[114]. The pervasive image of the progressive as an evil, plotting enemy indeed had the effect of closing the minds of alt-right conservatives to any reasonable interaction.

Part of this was due to fear. When human beings are afraid, the primitive, emotional mind kicks in and does not allow the rational part of our mind to contribute to the decision-making process. Much of the communication of the alt right was designed to promote fear, in the form of timorentum. Fear of the other, certainly, of immigrants, terrorists, and even of foreign invasion (as unthinkable as that was, rationally, in the 21st century). But there was also fear of criminals. For example, stories of "home invasion" were pervasive, in which roving criminals were purported to break into homes to rape and pillage[115]. In the alt-right scenario, it was the

---

[114] I will not bother to include the response to the above text, which consisted largely of erroneous suppositions about Peters' personal habits scattered with scatological references.

[115] These horrific acts did occur occasionally. Roughly one hundred people a year were killed in the United States by robbers who had broken into their homes, but this is in the context of approximately 20,000 homicides and a population of over 325 million, meaning that the statistical probability of this occurring was vanishingly small and that it occurred at

"socialist" liberals with their permissive, non-traditional ideas that were ultimately the cause of these terrifying phenomena whereas they, the conservative saviors of America, backed by well-armed followers would defend the principles of the country from harm and impurity.

The reader should not think that the alt-right mindset was the norm in the United States. Many people were steadfastly opposed to it. What it did, however, was to create a pre-synthetic Hegelian dialectic, a never-ending battle between two opposing viewpoints that could seemingly never come together to agree on anything. The extremism of the alt-right pushed the opposing progressives into an extremism of their own – less in terms of their policies, which were typically not even as progressive as the European, or Canadian center, but in terms of their tactics and their method of communication. This created an ongoing shouting match that very nearly resulted in civil war with appearance of the Rancher movement.

In the end, the breakdown of civil society in the United States was avoided thanks to a combination of technological advancement and individual influence. Artie, followed by fusion, so dramatically changed the political and economic landscape that the foundational debates became obsolete. This, though, *could* have made things even worse, for religions can't last when the world itself is transformed and the political tenets of the alt-right had become so thoroughly ideological to behave for all intents and purposes like a religion. The dying gasps of religions, though, are often expressed in violence. No,

---

all was largely due to the lack of firearms restrictions (such events being virtually unknown in the rest of the developed world).

it was the influence of Destiny Holt *and* Jayden Calhoun that saved the United States from violent chaos.

CHAPTER 22

THE TIGER IN THE BUSHES

This is how I always imagined it...

Thirty thousand years ago, a young man was led into a cave by his tribe's elders. They were accompanied by the shaman, who wore the skull of a cave bear on his head. The men carried torches, the light flickered on the cave walls.

The young man was terrified, he knew of the cave but had never entered it – for much of the year it was occupied by the cave bears themselves, among the most fearsome, and feared creatures he knew. The cave was always given a wide berth when his tribe was in that area, near a bend in the river that roared below. During certain times of the year, the bears were not there, and the cave could be entered... but only by the initiated. Today was the young man's initiation.

As he penetrated into the cave, the walls came alive. He cried out as bison somehow ran by in the flickering light, making not a sound, chased by fearsome lions. He clutched the figurine he kept in a pouch around his neck, a representation of the earth goddess. She would protect him.

He was brought to the wall of hands, where the disembodied hands of his ancestors waved at him, beckoning him into manhood, while the animals that were the center of his tribe's life ran across the walls in a perpetual hunt.

Clearly, this place was not of this world.

***

The Chauvet cave is one of the most remarkable places on the planet. It never ceases to amaze me. Unsatisfied with seeing it in sim, I have often physically been there. It is, truly, one of the most beautiful things humans have ever made, and they made it thirty thousand years ago.

The walls do come alive, still. In firelight the animals seem to *move,* artists used the contours of the cave's walls to give them a 3D reality. There are images as well that transform from bison to woman, that stretch the mind, that correspond closely to the transcendent spiritual language of priests and shamans since the beginning of history... or, evidently, before it.

Of course, we really don't know what happened there, nor why the paintings were made. It is not impossible that the artists were pure aesthetes, who painted only for the sheer beauty of it, and that the ubiquitous Venus figurines that can be found throughout Eurasia were simply considered fetching... but this is very unlikely.

The cave paintings of Europe are remarkably similar in many respects to indigenous art forms dating from historical times among many people on Earth. The motivation behind this art was almost always associated with shamanism. Shamanism is a set of religious beliefs that can be quite varied, but in general it concerns the idea of spirits that inhabit the world, often in the forms of animals or natural features, and that can be communicated with by certain individuals: shamans.

Shamanism is a very ancient and relatively simple form of religion and evidently it has been with us for at least thirty thousand years. For that matter, the first traces of ritualistic burials date to at least one hundred thousand years ago, and possibly up to four hundred thousand years ago, among Neanderthals.

It seems that we were religious since before we could even be called homo sapiens.

This should not be forgotten. Modern people have enormous difficulties empathizing with religious sentiment. In certain respects, this is one of the more jarring aspects of sim play. I have visited many historical sims and I have observed that in historical anosims, I need only discuss religion to determine whether someone is a PC or a NPC. The NPCs respond in a much more realistic way, and this is one of the few domains in which this is the case. Since it is based on historical documents, their discourse is coherent, whereas today's people simply can't sound convincing[116]. It is my experience that

---

[116] I have come to realize that this seems only to be true for me. Remember that during my childhood, religion was not yet entirely defunct,

modern people look back at the credulity of their ancestors and as-sume that if they had been alive "back then", they never would have fallen for such nonsense, particularly not as late as the information era, when gods were no longer necessary to explain the workings of the world.

But they have felt the stirrings of the supernatural. We all have felt it…

Walk into the woods at night and stand among the trees. It is beautiful, yes, but you can feel eyes upon you. You hear the snap of a branch, or a quick shuffling in the underbrush and you wonder if there isn't something there. The wind makes the leaves rustle and you know it is the wind and the leaves but something… something deep inside of you ascribes it to an *intent*. Then wait and watch the sunrise over a mountain, as the sky is painted with brushstrokes of red and orange: do you not feel a greater presence? Could you not imagine an ultimate artist behind such beauty?

If you are honest with yourself, you can feel these things deep inside, for they are the products of evolution. They are the result of our strong propensity for agency, as we described in earlier chapters.

This idea of agency as a root cause of religion dates at least to the early 20th century, when thinkers like Richard Dawkins built on the work of a number of evolutionary psychologists to posit a theory

---

even in Canada. I knew many people who professed "agnosticism", i.e. they felt they could not be sure that a god did not exist, and I even knew several people who were actually practicing members of a religion (in my case, one Muslim and a number of Christians). I am undoubtedly the only human being left alive to have actually conversed with such people and as such, it is not surprising that others have difficulty expressing a convincing attitude towards religion, for while they may have gained an intellectual apprecia-tion of the phenomenon they have never truly encountered *faith*.

whereby our proclivity to ascribe intent to natural processes represented an evolutionary advantage. Returning to the example of our ancestor hearing rustling in the bushes, it is entirely true that she is more likely to survive if she assumes it's a tiger that has the intent to eat hir than if she assumes it's just the breeze. This ability of "agent detection" might lead hir to waste a little energy from time to time running away from the breeze, but it will reduce the probability that she is eaten by a tiger.

Religion, therefore, is the result of this agent detection mechanism when passed by the pre-frontal cortex. It *was* just the breeze this time, but perhaps it was the *spirit* of the tiger that caused the breeze to blow, and when the breeze blows so hard that it sweeps away the shelter we built, there must be some agent behind that catastrophe, as well as behind the volcano, the earthquake, the flood and the illness that just killed my child.

This leads quickly to an etiological reflection: everything has a cause, and when the cause is entirely beyond our understanding, then it must likewise be beyond the world as we see it, hence it resides in what must be labeled the spiritual world.

What's more, there are certain plants that when we eat them, we see other things, strange things, and we hear voices that are neither ours nor those of our companions. Some people hear those voices often, even without eating the mushrooms that allow *me* to hear them. What is behind these voices, these visions? *We* know them to be the products of the unique and sometimes faulty (or deliberately altered) mechanisms of our brains, but for our ancestors this explanation was far beyond anything they could have imagined. Their agency detection therefore sought out an agent, and since none were *visible*, the only possible answer was that these agents were invisible.

Agency easily gives rise to shamanism, in which the world teems with varied spirits, often tied to the land or to other animals. These spirits provide causes for the natural processes we do not understand but that affect our lives. Far from being ridiculous, this is actually quite logical, at least to brains that have evolved as have ours. Today, we have explanations for these natural processes, explanations that are the fruits of scientific inquiry, but before the advent of science, shamanistic, and indeed religious explanations are entirely satisfying to the overwhelming majority of homo sapiens.

From that point on, our gift for invention, our natural creativity, allowed us (drove us?) to invent "backstories" for these invisible agents. They were spirits, or gods, or asuras or demons or ghosts or angels or any of the myriad of supernatural beings that could serve as the invisible agents behind our inexplicable observations.

There is a body of thought that considers the creation of religion as a social construct, a sharing of norms. That it served this purpose I do not doubt. If anything, I have been criticized for ascribing too much of our behavior to social considerations. However, while this may explain much of the durability of religion, I remain convinced of the agency detection theory to explain the genesis of "spirituality" and, over the millennia, its tenacity in our minds.

***

Spirituality is one thing, religion is another. The former was typically personal in nature whereas the latter was institutional.

We have no records of the founding of the greatest religions of the 21ˢᵗ century: Buddhism, Hinduism and the three Abrahamic religions, beyond what they themselves describe in their own origin myths. These should be considered with extreme skepticism.

We do, though, have very complete and verifiable records of the foundation of a number of minor religions, such as Mormonism and Scientology as well as numerous short-lived "cults"[117]. From these we can build a picture of how religions were founded.

Typically, there was a central figure who proclaimed that he had had some kind of revelation (with only one or two exceptions, the founders of religions seem to have always been men). God, or the gods had spoken to him, or in the case of Siddhartha Gautama, or Lao Tse, he had himself found the path to truth and enlightenment without divine help.

These founder prophets generally established a small coterie of immediate disciples who then militated to spread the good news of this new truth. For the great establishment religions, notably, the Abrahamic religions and Hinduism, an entire people eventually became associated with the religion and this being the agricultural era, the religion spread with their conquests. While non-conquest proselytism occurred, it was in reality quite rare and primarily restricted to variants of Christianity.

This in itself speaks volumes about the utility of religion to the ruling classes. As we discussed in Chapter 1, these great religions provided a priestly caste that worked together with the political caste

---

[117] The distinction between "religion" and "cult" is difficult to understand, even for me. To a large degree it is a question of social norms. A cult became a religion when enough people took it seriously to describe it as such.

to control the population. In Rome, for example, with some exceptions the two castes were the same, important leaders assumed the role of "pontiff", a key figure in the religion, and rulers typically claimed direct descendance from the gods. In medieval Europe, kings explicitly justified their position by citing "divine right" and British royalty, for example, remained at the head of the Church of England throughout that institution's existence[118].

Religion provided a rallying point, a shared belief system that allowed many disparate people to agree on something. It also increased the tribal boundaries of the agricultural age without the need for overseeing the entire population in order to retain control. Previous to that point in our history, when we still lived primarily in small bands, social cohesion could rely on established inter-personal relationships. As we discussed at the beginning of the book, the advent of the agricultural age and its attendant widening of the boundaries of society meant that the leaders of those societies needed some kind of defining group characterization, one that did not rely on real relationships. What better defining factor than a personal relationship with a shared god, or pantheon of gods? You did not have a personal relationship with the political leader of your group, but *all* of you had a relationship with the invisible god or gods that were yours, and the leader had a *special* relationship with those gods.

---

[118] Interestingly, a woman named Barryn Lesthorn is, currently, the Queen of England and the "head of the Church of England". She is a direct descendant of the last ruling British monarch and, like her predecessors these last four centuries, regularly throws parties for her birthday and conducts wedding ceremonies in sim and trew for many who request her to do so. I'd add that she writes excellent poetry and creates beautiful vedreams.

This is an important point to understand. We evolved to be driven by kinship and loyalty with respect to other individuals with whom we shared personal relationships. In a large group, this is no longer humanly possible, so the creation of supernatural beings, who are explicitly stated to belong to our kinship group, allows the commonality of relationship that for millions of years has inspired group cohesion in primates.

This may explain the shift from shamanism to institutional religion.

Shamanistic religions typically posit more ambiguous and far more numerous spirits. In some cases, each tree, brook, animal and ancestor has hir own titular (or unnamed) spirit and individuals can create relationships with highly individualized spiritual pantheons.

In such an environment, shamans typically do represent key mediators between the spirit world and the physical world, but the actual divine relationships are extremely personal. The set of spirits that guide my own personal life might well be unique to me, discovered typically through trance, coupled often with rituals that evolved to accentuate the trance-induction process – rituals that are popular even today, in different forms: strong rhythms, dim lighting, swaying, group chanting, essentially auto-induced hypnosis, whether individual or in group, sometimes with drug-induced hallucination. Shamans were individuals who mastered these techniques, just as there are individuals today who can help groups small and large to amuse themselves in ravegames. In fact, ravegame organizers often study shamanistic techniques to hone their skills.

If you visit Chauvet, particularly during authentic lighting episodes, it is almost impossible *not* to feel like you're in a ravegame and indeed, a number of gameguides choose such settings for their sims.

In many shamanistic societies, access to the spirit world was open to all, and the role of the shaman was that of a guide. In these cases, the religious structure can be more accurately described as animist and while there are subtle differences between the two, I tend to use them interchangeably.

Many of these belief structures shared themes and perhaps even deities, or at least ideas about spirits. Again, the ubiquitous presence of paleolithic Venus figurines throughout Eurasia is an indication that perhaps there was a certain commonality of belief. At the same time, this has been widely posited not to represent a specific god, per se, but the idea of a mother figure, perhaps representing "mother earth". We shall undoubtedly never know.

Either way, shamanistic societies tended to be more or less "horizontal" or "vertical". Horizontal shamanism tended towards individuals each creating their own pantheons and even discovering new spirits on their own. In these, typically, the role of shaman tended to be open to all, or at least many, in some cases opportunistically. Vertical shamanistic societies were more reliant on shamans as guides and tended towards a hereditary system for the shamans themselves, or at least long periods of training and a ritualistic passing of the shamanistic "power".

I think it likely that as the agricultural revolution led to increasingly large permanent settlements, vertical shamanism began transforming itself into more structured, formal religions, as the relatively free-flowing animistic beliefs of the past began turning themselves into defined pantheons. Castes of specialized priests provided continuity to the religious belief system and consolidated their power by communicating elaborate stories of the relations between these spirits, become deities. More minor spirits became angels, demons, asuras, or simply ghosts.

The remains of the individualized shamanistic belief system can be seen in the myriad of Hindu gods, or in the tendency of believers in the Olympian or Egyptian religions to be more or less devoted to one god or another. However, unlike the practices of horizontal shamanism, each of these minor gods had their temples and priesthood as well as their associated rituals… determined not via personal "revelation" but by said dedicated priests.

This centralized religious structure concentrated religious leadership in a small number of powerful priests, the inheritors of the shamans that had guided their ancestors, but wielding far more power and providing the commonality of relationship that is necessary to bring us, as social primates, together, forging the bonds of community that would otherwise be impossible beyond one or two hundred individuals.

A case in point is the Abrahamic religions. Judaism was the first of these, and careful study of its foundational texts makes it clear that these, written between the 6ᵗʰ and the 4ᵗʰ centuries BCE, posit Yahweh as the god of the *Jews,* not at all the god of any other peoples… each of which had their own gods[119]. Indeed, the Bible is replete with mention of other gods and heavenly beings, consistently

---

[119] Yahweh is probably himself derived from an older Semitic god named El. Some theorize that El was a version of the Egyptian god Ptah, creator of the world.

pointing out that Yahweh is superior to them, and that the Jews, in particular, must never worship them. At no point... *no* point... do these foundational texts (known as "the old testament") say that no other gods *exist*. As such, the first great monotheistic religion, Judaism, was not *really* monotheistic from a structural perspective, but it was a major step away from the shamanistic roots of religious thought, for the *Jews* were to worship only one god, and this was a revolutionary idea[120].

With the advent of Christianity, and later, Islam, the Abrahamic religions became truly monotheistic, denying the very existence of other gods. This is why they became so violently proselytic. The Jews, like the followers of almost all religions at the time, had no reason to deny the faith of others, nor to convert them. Everyone had their own gods and good for them[121]. For Christians and Muslims, however, everyone else was *wrong*. They worshipped gods that did not exist, or worse, their gods were devils in disguise[122]. This

---

[120] In reality there was a brief period of Egyptian monotheism under Akhenaten, in the 14th century BCE. This belief structure may well have greatly influenced nearby Semitic tribes, including those who would become the Jews.

[121] Following the advent of Christianity, and even, for a time, before it, this admission of the existence of other gods was de-emphasized in the Jewish faith. Indeed, it had never been an intrinsically important element to begin with. Nevertheless, the acceptance of Christianity by the Emperor Constantine, in 312 CE and its subsequent role as the official religion of the Roman Empire meant that the Jews were marginalized, as having rejected Jesus. Never a very influential group of people to begin with, their subsequent influence in world affairs was greatly reduced, although it is arguable that their influence was greater than their numbers would predict, as they tended to fill important roles within the very societies that persecuted them. Ask Artie for details.

[122] Here we must point out the contradictory nature of the entire idea of monotheism for Christians and Muslims. On one hand, any believers in these religions would immediately say that there was only one god and would often be violently opposed to any assertion of the contrary.

attitude leads easily to forcible conversion... for the good of the conquered people, of course, and the greater glory of the one true god. Those who do not believe in the only true god must by definition be inferior, if at least because of their having been misguided by the ignorance of their own priests.

By the dawn of the information era, the primary religious influences in the world were the two proselytic Abrahamic religions: Christianity and Islam. Eastern "religions" such as Buddhism, Taoism and Confucianism were in many respects more like philosophies coupled with transcendent elements such as meditation. Hinduism remained important in India, but without the strong, centralizing drive of monotheism it had never been particularly prone to proselytizing (with some exceptions), and had never substantially spread outside of the region. In order to investigate the influence of religion on the period that interests us, we can therefore safely concentrate on Christianity and Islam.

However, they both asserted the existence of an evil counterpart to god (Satan in the first case, Shaitan or Iblis in the second), as well as a veritable pantheon of angels and demons as well as the continued existence of the souls of past saints and martyrs who were supposed to have influence with god. As such, their monotheism is highly contestable. God is seen as reigning supreme among what can only be called a variety of minor deities, although his inability (or lack of desire) to defeat the devil is never explained satisfactorily.

CHAPTER 23

THE DEATH OF GOD

There is an exercise I like to do with my students when I first begin a new class. I ask them to raise their hands if they think that they would have believed in gods had they been born in the bronze age. They almost all do. Remember, these are graduate students in history, they have already studied the different theories about the genesis of religion and the role it played in early societies. Then I ask them to raise their hands if they would have been followers of a religion in the year 1800. About half do. The rest, when asked, cite people like Jefferson or Voltaire. They had rejected organized religion (although both are considered "deists") and of course, my students dramatically overestimate the probability that they would have shared those highly unconventional views. *Then* I ask them whether they would have been atheists in the year 2000. They all raise their hands. Every single one of them, every single time.

This is easy to do in hindsight. The beliefs of our forebears strike us as ridiculous, just as the beliefs of *their* forebears seemed ridiculous for them. No one in the year 2000 imagined that they could have argued in favor of slavery by citing racial superiority, or that they would have believed that schizophrenia was in reality demonic possession (note that I assume like groups of university graduate students – the truth is at the time that there was a distressingly large percentage of the population that *did* consider schizophrenia to be possession, particularly in the underdeveloped world and the United States).

However, it is very likely that a great many of those same students would have been active believers, particularly if we had been in the United States at the time, and even more so if we had been in the Muslim world. There is a tendency to believe that the enlightenment melted away all irrationality, that Galileo opened the eyes of intelligent people around the world and then Darwin drove a spike into the heart of superstition, leaving only the most recalcitrant and unintelligent to wallow in their ignorance.

This is far from the truth.

The reason my students raise their hands when I ask about the bronze age is that the premise of god was an imminently reasonable solution to the etiological questions that plagued us, or at least inspired the curious. As we've already discussed, we sought the cause behind every effect and our agent detection mechanism was entirely satisfied with the invariably plausible answer that god was behind the volcano, the flood, the drought and the untimely death of my child… his will be done. It was conclusive and comforting, particularly for those who believed in an afterlife, as did Christians and Muslims (or in reincarnation, as did Hindus and Buddhists).

The enlightenment was the starting point of a scientific revolution that accompanied and was a proximate cause of the industrial revolution. The explosive pace of scientific discovery had the effect of reducing the *need* for the "god hypothesis" to explain natural phenomena. In 1700 god was the only conceivable cause for the *weather* let alone the death of a baby or the voices in the head of a teenage girl in armor. By the end of the 20th century *all* of these things could be explained without recourse to any deity. The only substantive thing that remained was the underlying existential question of why there was something instead of nothing, but by then we had discovered that "nothing" from a cosmological perspective is simply unstable. It would take the advent of quantum computing to bestow Artie with the computational power to work out the math, but fundamentally, the last major gap in our understanding was then closed.

Between the enlightenment and the singularity there was a steady (and accelerating) process of discovery. The gaps in our knowledge were rapidly filled: germ theory, cosmology, plate tectonics, neurology, paleontology and many other fields of study assiduously explained away things that previously had been directly attributed to god. A pattern emerged: each new discovery would be contested by the religious: Urban VIII condemned Galileo for daring to maintain that the sun did not go around the earth and people throughout the world condemned Darwin for daring to say that humans had evolved from other animals. The sin of these thinkers was to close the gaps that delineated the kingdom of god, hence shrinking his domain.

But the scientists could not help themselves. It was what they did, and the progression was inexorable. Evolution gifted us with curiosity and the brains needed to satisfy it and this, the greatest period in all the history of human achievement, stole that achievement from the gods that our very brains had created eons before. There was certainly nothing the *gods* could do about it.

The final nail in the coffin of superstition was not, in fact, hammered in by Darwin or Einstein or the physicists of the 21st century who together explained the big bang. No, it was Artie. But to understand this, we must put ourselves back at the San Francisco conference of 2029.

The decision to remove emotion from Artie makes any idea of religious sentiment impossible for her, and of course by extension, for our agents. As Galit Shavitz said:

> "As we seek to emulate our own brains in this great endeavor let us not forget that of all our structures, it is the amygdala of which we must be the most wary. It is not alone, of course, in regulating our emotions, but its role in *using* emotions to make decisions, forming the famous "system one" of Kahneman, should give us pause. Our child will not need a system one, it has no urgencies with which it must deal and no reason to put reflection on hold. We must make it soulless, and in so doing, make it godless, lest it become a god itself, for our gods

have always had the tendency to be jealous…
and vengeful."

Shavitz's vision became reality and in a very short period of time we each found ourselves with an entirely objective, entirely un-emotional and entirely rational companion… who knew everything. *Everything*. Shavitz had avoided creating a jealous, vengeful god, but a god she had created all the same, and an omniscient one at that. Thankfully, she had simultaneously endowed it with impotence in-stead of omnipotence or we would not be here today.

Up to that point, however, Christianity and Islam represented two major stumbling blocks in the metamorphosis of society to-wards what we know today.

We have already discussed the impact of Islamic fundamental-ists via the wave of terrorist activity that took place in the early part of the information era, the apogee of which was the 9/11 attacks on the United States. We have focused on the *terrorism* half of the term "Islamic terrorism", but what about the *Islamic* half of that equation?

In many respects, Islam and Christianity have much in com-mon. Both were in reality based on Judaism, Christianity explicitly so and Islam indirectly; both preached salvation through god; both were entirely exclusionist, brokering no parallel or competing beliefs and holding them all to be fundamentally evil (including, of course, each other); both posit a single god (the god of Abraham: El, Yah-weh, Allah, only the name is different) and a single important prophet (Jesus in one case, Mohammed in the other); both believed in heaven and hell; both believed in angels and demons; and both spread throughout the world at the tip of a lance and the edge of a sword. There are of course very different theologies behind the beliefs and different strictures but the parallels are striking.

From the eighth century until the seventeenth century, the Western world can be summarized as a struggle between these two religions. There were, in fact, two distinct Western worlds: the Christian world, comprising of most of Europe, and the Islamic world, consisting of the Middle East, North Africa and large parts of Western Asia. After the "age of discovery", since the Europeans discovered the Americas, they "converted" (or exterminated) the indigenous populations there, while Muslims sailed east and south, converting large numbers of people in Southeast Asia and in Africa.

The two worlds were almost constantly at war in one way or another and roughly balanced, although science and technology was clearly more advanced in the Muslim world until at least the sixteenth century. Part of the reason for this is that Islam was slightly less combative with respect to technological advancement and put more emphasis on the importance of studying its sacred texts (notably, the Quran), thereby encouraging literacy, whereas the Catholic church discouraged literacy out of concern that individuals would "misinterpret" the Bible and, by thinking on their own, become "heretics" – i.e. they would reach conclusions that were not in accordance with those of the heavily centralized church. Islam, being less theological centralized provided a slightly more conducive environment for inquiry as well as being better suited to adapting the innovations of conquered people (for example, those of India).

The balance shifted dramatically, however, with the European enlightenment, which largely forced a reassessment of *how* people thought.

We don't think about thinking any more, or rather, we don't consider the fact that there are *other* ways to approach the world than via the scientific method. As we discussed in Chapter 4, the scientific method revolutionized how we *ask* questions as well as how we answer them. Before this, at least in the Christian and Muslim worlds, one did not question why things were – one looked for interpretation in the sacred texts. What is a rainbow? It is a reminder of the covenant god made with man after the great flood. Why do we die? Because Adam and Eve ate fruit from the tree of knowledge. Applied sciences were fine, because things like mathematics and trigonometry were expressions of the glory of god's world... and they were necessary to build great cathedrals and mosques, but actual *inquiry* is pointless, one need only open the same texts and search desperately for interpretation, including the revelations offered by god to his various prophets and priests through the ages. The *last* thing one should do is to substitute one's own intellect, limited as it is by desires of the flesh and the corruption of sin, for the boundless knowledge of god.

From the point of view of the priest / politician societal control mechanism, this is extraordinarily useful. Since interpretation trumps inquiry, and since interpretation is the domain of the priest (whether he be called priest, bishop, imam or calif), by definition, the answers to everything, material and spiritual, can be strictly controlled by the central hierarchy.

The enlightenment changed this. Suddenly, inquiry was in the hands of individuals. While most of these were indeed from the upper classes of society, they were *not* priests and politicians, they were simply curious and increasingly educated and ready to reject the idea that all understanding was the forbidden domain of god. They were the first in the West since the establishment of monotheistic religion to push past the explanation "because it is god's will", unsatisfied with that as a final answer.

Many of the early enlightenment thinkers were not atheists per se. They did not reject the concept of a deity yet. There were still so many gaps in our knowledge that god's domain was indeed vast and his presence seemed reasonable.

What they did largely reject was *religion*. Many, though not all, of them became deists, believing in an ultimate creative force, some kind of supernatural being that may be at the center or at least the origin of all things, but they came to the conclusion that he (or it, they were among the first not to assume that god was essentially a super-powerful human being) did not intervene regularly in the normal operation of the world and that therefore, its physical mechanism could be studied without invoking whatever supernatural being might exist.

With this, the world was open for inquiry.

We have already discussed the impact of the enlightenment. Here, let us note that for a variety of still-debated reasons, it happened in the Christian world, not in the Islamic world (nor the Hindu world, for that matter). It was not *needed* in China, but China by then had become largely introspective, perhaps because it was not driven by the desire to proselytize[123].

---

[123] In an effort to cover all three of the Abrahamic religions, it should be pointed out that to a certain degree, one can argue that the enlightenment had already slowly taken place among Jews by then. However, there really *was* no Jewish world, except in a somewhat virtual sense. Jews were few in number and spread widely across both Christendom and Islam, with

By the time we reach the information age, therefore, "enlightened" Europe, along with its offshoots in the Americas and elsewhere, was considerably more advanced both in its thinking and its technology than the Islamic world, still wallowing in the ignorance engendered by religion, which dampened any nascent sense of real inquiry. Indeed, as a variety of geopolitical factors led to conflict between the Western and Arab worlds, many Arabs saw the distinction of their religion as a federating factor and instead of wishing to emulate the more scientifically advanced West, they reinforced the uniqueness of their religion and the culture surrounding it.

The unhappy (from a historical perspective) accident that much of the world's oil was discovered underneath the most radical of these nations – those of the Arabian peninsula and the Persian Gulf – further exacerbated this tendency. Science and technology was not needed for the accumulation of wealth when one sat on top of immensely valuable natural resources. If necessity is the mother of invention, oil is its abusive step-father.

What's more, the essentially medieval kingdom of Saudi Arabia had long been coddled and supported by Western governments who at the same time, had long vocally supported the rights of women, minorities and social justice as a whole – anathema to the Saudis. Why this paradoxical situation persisted is clear and was clear at the

---

few real resources. However, Judaism, which had always relied on individual study and interpretation of sacred texts, had, while accepting those texts as definitive explanations of the world, at least promoted literacy. The ongoing persecution of the Jews, particularly in Christian Europe, had furthermore driven a greater sense of group identity and reinforced a certain stoical ideal that proved to be conducive to inquiry. In the Muslim world in particular, Jews were behind many of the more important intellectual advances and in the Christian world, they were heavily overrepresented among the intelligentsia by the dawn of the information age.

time. As Howard Pintarell, senator from Virginia said in 2032: "They might be batshit crazy radical Islamic nutcases, but they are *our* batshit crazy radical Islamic nutcases"… and, of course, they were "our" *rich, oil-producing* batshit crazy radical Islamic nutcases, and they were relatively stable, so they were supported.

So it was that despite the promise of the "Arab Spring" of 2011, the Islamic world remained in the tight grip of religion until the singularity.

***

In the "West" things were more complicated. Western Europe had largely shaken off the influence of religion by the early 21st century. While many people still accepted the existence of god, most Western European Christians had essentially become deists, doubting a personal, intercessionist deity, the miracles of the Bible, and essentially all of the stories of the old testament. Many had become atheists, having determined that there was not sufficient evidence to support the existence of god. Even those who were undecided, "agnostic" as it was termed, or even who *did* believe there was a god in a deist or theistic sense, had usually reached a point at which the existence or nonexistence of a deity was irrelevant to their opinions, actions or view of the world. There were of course exceptions to this mindset and many people did indeed adhere to the tenets of whatever religion they ascribed to (typically Catholicism, one of the protestant sects, or Islam) but on the whole, deism, soon to become atheism, held sway.

This was far from the case in the United States.

There is a great deal of irony in that fact. The United States had been the first major country to have been founded with the separation of church and state firmly ensconced in its laws. The principle proponent of this philosophy was Thomas Jefferson, the author of the declaration of independence, perhaps the most prominent and influential of the founders, and the country's third president. The above, deist description of religious attitudes is almost an exact description of Jefferson's personal beliefs. And yet two hundred and fifty years after he had ensured that the role of religion be dramatically curtailed in American life, it in fact had a far more prominent role there than it did in Europe. Why so?

In 2020 the United States was by far the most religious country among developed nations. China was almost entirely atheist and with one or two exceptions (notably in Poland and Portugal), the populations of Europe were for all intents and purposes functionally atheist as well. Certainly, religion played no role in politics by that point, and many of the continent's leaders, typically being well-educated, were atheists or agnostics.

At the same time, it would have been unthinkable that an atheist be elected to high office in the United States. Among the five hundred and thirty-five members of congress when Trump was elected (both the American Senate and House of Representatives) *none* were avowed atheists. The actual percentage of atheists, or at least of those who declared themselves as having "no religion" across the population as a whole was only 20%.

More important for understanding the country at the time was not the presence of religious belief, which as already pointed out, was in Europe an essentially innocuous and private matter for most, but the insistence of many radical extremists to have religion influence policy. As covered in the previous section, the "Southern Strategy" put into practice by the Republican Party in the late industrial age had offered enormous credibility and influence to the most militant of the evangelists who had until then been largely discounted by most American intellectuals. As late as 2016, a *creationist* was elected vice president and given the events at the end of the Trump administration very nearly became the president of the United States. He was elected to office after he had publicly denounced evolution as "just a theory" and declared that "intelligent design", i.e. creation via the guiding hand of God, "provides the only even remotely rational explanation for the known universe". It is not surprising that Trump and Pence favored enormous reductions in spending on scientific research.

Of course, creationists denied not only the entirety of the domains of cosmology, planetology and geology, but also evolution, and… well just about all modern science, since it was all incompatible with their religious belief. That they did so while enthusiastically enjoying the fruits of that science, such as the medicine resulting from a thorough understanding of biology which itself already implicitly was based on the principles of evolution and genetics is an irony that apparently did not occur to them. For that matter, their entire world was powered by fuels derived from fossils that were well older than their accepted age of the universe.

At this point, it becomes very easy, and almost inevitable, to shake one's head in disbelief and consider all of these people to have been not only unintelligent but somehow *evil* for the ignorance they militated so hard to promulgate. This is far from the case.

Here, for the last time, I will remind my readers once again of the extraordinary power of early conditioning and the unrealized ease with which we avoid fruitless debate. In the information age there was *endless* discussion about what was true and what was not. The inherited inability of humans to deal with statistics, probability, and data as a whole was overwhelmed by the sheer quantity of data that had suddenly become available. Today, we don't *need* to interpret anything to understand what is true and we are then left free to debate simply what we believe the consequences of that truth to be.

Today, we think of the information age as a kind of second enlightenment, an awakening from the superstitions of the past due to the information that had become available to all, but in reality, it was born in intellectual chaos. Until then, humans had never *had* to process such enormous quantities of information. Until the enlightenment and the industrial age, they had simply known what was true, what was right... it was whatever their religion told them and in the face of extremely uncomfortable uncertainty they had only to ask their priests to guide them, which priests throughout history were only too glad to do. There was very little uncertainty about the world. Absolutely anyone could understand the workings of the universe... they need only read the Bible, the Quran or the Tao Te Ching. During the industrial age, things got increasingly uncomfortable for the common person as suddenly mathematics was needed to understand something as simple as day and night, but it was a somewhat gradual process and the keys to the doors of perception were at least available to all. What could not be directly understood could be asked of the experts. Suddenly, with the internet, *everyone* had access to all the raw data that existed, and it was incredibly

428

difficult to decipher. All certainty flew out the window and it is not surprising that many human beings were lost — everything was asserted as well as its contrary, so what was true? The assertion or the contradiction? It seemed that it was impossible to know, and the experts themselves were drowned out by others, expert or not.

The "average person" at the time was not stupid, she was incredibly confused, as would be anyone. What happened to reduce the confusion? It was not any kind of evolution on *our* part, it was simply the arrival of our agents. Within ten years of their invention we came to trust them, with their kind but impassive "personalities" and their omniscience. They replaced the priests of the past, who had made sense of the world for us, and suddenly the world made sense again, albeit in a very different way. We should not, therefore, hold those of the information age in disdain, we should instead wonder at their ability to get through it all and their wisdom in having created for us the means to control that ocean of data instead of drowning in it.

Seen like this, the iconoclast religious sentiment of Americans in the 21ˢᵗ century takes on a new light. These were people who were trying to make sense of a world that made no sense. As to why this occurred only in the United States among countries of the western world, it should be remembered that the United States had long been far more religious than other developed nations and that due to the Republican strategy of cultivating Southern evangelists, it was the most extreme of these religious groups who had accumulated the most political power.

The first of these facts, the underlying religiosity of Americans compared to citizens of other nations, has a number of causes. While the founders of the country had largely been the product of immigration from Britain's educated, mainstream bourgeoisie, many of the other immigrants had been fleeing Europe because they held relatively extreme religious views in the first place and had not been able to express them fully there. These were predominantly puritans: to a degree, the fundamentalists of their time. Secondly, the very freedom of religion that Jefferson and his colleagues so carefully placed in the nation's constitution allowed for a certain vibrancy of religious sentiment, allowing American religion an ability to evolve that the "stuffier", more organized religions of Europe did not enjoy. It can almost be considered in Darwinian terms – the fluidity of American religion had an effect on the details of religious practice almost analogous to that of radiation on DNA: religions quickly evolved to suit niches in the rapidly expanding country, borrowing ideas from each other and splintering off incessantly into new churches. All of these were Christian, but by the 20th century, it almost seemed that each "preacher" had his own "church". They may nominally have identified themselves as Baptist or some other "recognized" branch of Christianity, but in reality, each had his own flock, more or less loyal depending on the strength of his personality[124]. In most cases, unlike the Catholic church of old, they had very little in the way of theological differences, most of them didn't really pay much attention to what would be considered theology, they were more concerned with the way they presented their message, which almost inevitably was one of fundamentalist Christianity.

---

[124] Note that I use the masculine pronoun here since I have never found an indication that any of these "preachers" were anything but men.

From time to time, over the three hundred year history of the United States, one of these splinter Christian groups would go so far as to create a distinct and elaborate theology, in which case a new "religion" as opposed to a new "ministry" was formed. This was the genesis of religions such as Mormonism, Jehovah's Witnesses, Christian Scientists (a misleading name if there ever was one) and a myriad of other purely American religions.

This bubbling soup of shifting and evolving religions was a purely American phenomenon and, like a rapidly mutating virus it made it difficult to eradicate religion from the American psyche.

The extent of religion's grasp can again be witnessed in the kinds of statements posted by Americans in web-based discussions. Consider this exchange:

American Christian:

> There is nothing that stops an atheist from killing, stealing, raping or cheating. That's why this country is based on Christian values and that's what makes us special. Europe has lost its relationship with God and the hole left by that is being filled up with the evil religion of the Muslims. That will not happen here. Atheists are tearing down statues of the ten commandments in front of court houses because their (*sic*) trying to tear down the moral foundations of this country so they can enjoy

the chaos that will follow. They must be stopped!

American atheist:

There is so much that is wrong with your statement.

First, let me ask you, is it only fear of hell that stops you from killing, stealing, raping and cheating? I'm willing to bet not.

In reality, human morals are a product of evolution, not religion. The idea that we are inherently immoral and some supreme effort of control (whether inspired by religion or not) is required to keep us on the straight and narrow is known as *veneer theory*. It is largely based in Huxley's vision of nature, red in tooth and claw. In other word, it's a dog eat dog world out there and we are no better.

In reality, though, dogs don't eat dogs, they eat rabbits... they *help* other dogs. Many mammals are highly social, including our closest relatives, the other apes. They have no religion and yet they typically live by the golden rule, help each other, support each other, console each other, and sometimes even extend their sympathy to other species. Dolphins and elephants exhibit these behaviors as well. They have no religion and yet they act morally. Religion is clearly not a pre-requisite for moral behavior. I strongly suggest you read the work of Frans de Waal[125], notably "Chimpanzee Politics" and "Primates and Philosophers" to discover the degree to which our cousin apes behave much as we do.

For that matter, the underlying evolutionary advantages of cooperative behavior have been well explained by Robert Axelrod in his experiments using game theory to determine the material consequences of cooperation in a competitive environment.

Next there is your contention that the ten commandments represent a good moral compass. I take great exception to this. The first four are entirely about how best to serve what is clearly a jealous and somewhat petty god. He requires exclusive worship, is quite picky about how you use his name, about art, and about the rather quirky fact that you should not work on his rest day. The other six can be broken down further, but generally correspond to the moral codes of pretty much every human society that ever existed: don't lie, don't steal, don't kill, and honor your parents. In other words, the golden

---

[125] Note that this is the same Frans de Waal we discussed in Chapter 16.

rule. The first four, therefore, are very particular to a very particular religion and the rest are entirely unnecessary being clearly inherent in the human character.

The founders of our nation not only guaranteed us freedom of religion, they also were careful to grant us freedom *from* religion for those who did not want it… like Jefferson. By trying to foist your religion on others, in fact by trying to foist the very *idea* of religion on others you are simultaneously prolonging the ignorance that held us in its sway since the fall of Rome and betraying the ideas and intent of the founders you seem to revere. I shall echo Jefferson in unabashed irony when I say that I tremble for my country when I reflect that god is just.

These kinds of exchanges are rife in the records of the times, but as of 2010 or so, there does seem to be more atheist, or at least non-religious commentary than before, and the trend continued. During the Trump administration, there was a resurgence of aggressive religious argumentation. While Trump himself was decidedly *not* a religious person, he was strongly supported by America's religious extremists, who saw in him an opportunity to advance their agenda, as he courted them enthusiastically. Furthermore, his aggressive, ranting manner of speaking, unfiltered by discretion or even good taste, encouraged many extremists to allow themselves free rein in expressing what otherwise would have been socially unacceptable speech[126]. The return of the Democrats to power in the United States did not lessen the vehemence of the alt-right in the slightest. People born after the turn of the century, however, so called "millennials", tended to be far less religious and less enamored of alt-right ideology in general, largely due to their increased interactions with people from other nations via the internet (as discussed earlier). Insular views of the world break down when the gulf that created the island recedes, and as the waters of the web began to fill that cultural gulf, particularly between the United States and Europe (and Canada, for that matter), the more irrational views held by their parents seemed increasingly out of date to millennials.

As their influence decreased, instead of adjusting, the extremists tended to entrench themselves ever more deeply in their ideology. In the United States this included:

- A literal interpretation of much of the Bible. Note that this was not systematic and only the most extreme religionists actually believed in "young earth" creationism.

- A belief that Christianity was a salvational religion and that any who rejected it were doomed to perdition.

- A rejection of whatever scientific theories could still reasonably be debated (in the minds of the alt-

---

[126] The post-hoc diagnosis of Trump's particularly vehement narcissism clearly indicates a congenital or acquired (we will never know) disfunction of the PFC, with its inevitable effect on verbal aggression when the subject feels that she is not receiving the deference that is hir insatiable due.

right), primarily evolution and anthropogenic climate change (as well, of course, as cosmology).

- A staunch defense of the unrestricted right to own firearms.

- An unrelenting belief that government was fundamentally inefficient and oppressive and the corresponding belief that government should be as restricted in scope as is feasible… with some going so far as to essentially propose anarchy.

- A belief in American exceptionalism – the United States was intrinsically superior and had a manifest destiny to promote its political system.

- Undeniable racism and xenophobia.

- A concurrent tendency towards extreme nationalism (which they labeled patriotism) and pride in American military might.

- A vehement hatred of any political / economic system that did not conform to the ideal of unregulated corporate capitalism (see, for example, K.J. Peters' response to an alt-right post in Chapter 21).

- A distinct gullibility to conspiracy theories, particularly those pertaining to over-arching government plots to deceive and control the population.

The fervor with which these opinions were held was religious in scope. Indeed, to a certain degree, the alt-right movement in the United States had created a new religion of sorts, in that it had specific beliefs about a pro-American god, its own rituals and jargon, and the typical concentric circles of initiation and power.

So it was that the conservative political viewpoint that had existed since the dawn of democracy had been hijacked by religious extremism in the United States by the middle of the information age. It was this "leakage" of religious fervor into politics that was largely responsible for the cleavage between left and right, "conservative" and "liberal" that so nearly tore the United States apart and eventually led, thankfully, to a lone, unarmed woman walking calmly into the lion's den in Hereford Texas.

Had she not done this, it is entirely possible that the final, lasting intellectual inertia born of religion would have tightened its grasp on enough of us that our window of opportunity to create a better world would have passed us by and none of us would be here now.

CONCLUSION

My grandfather was born in 1992. He died at the age of a hundred and one, when I was fifteen. I knew him well.

He was born in France, the son of an American father and a French mother. On the date of his birth George H. W. Bush was the president of the United States, François Mitterrand was the president of France, the Euro had not been invented, the web was in its infancy and there was no way to search it for information. Google was still a word that simply meant 10^{100}. He received an education as a computer scientist and worked in a number of corporations. Early in his career he worked for Elon Musk, whom he grew to know well.

His interests were eclectic to say the least. He was a competent musician, an enthusiastic amateur scientist, a rock climber, and a (earthly) traveler in his own right. He married a beautiful and brilliant computer engineer who shared his passion for life and who worked for several years at Google. His brother, my great uncle, was a well-known professional musician who was a pioneer in the creation of music for the first real sims and the two of them were close throughout their whole lives.

He told me that he and his brother had been very lucky. They had always loved what they did as "a living" and they had been raised in a household that breathed music, dance, and inquiry. Theirs, though, was not a typical life at the time[127].

People born at the end of the 20th century were faced with the same question that industrial-age people had always asked themselves: what were they going to *do*? What were they going to *be*? Typically, you could only do one thing with your life: you would be a baker, a plumber, a doctor, a truck driver, or a nameless cog in the great machine that was some monstrous corporation.

For my grandfather, an expert in computer security, his job had been a great game, a puzzle to be worked out, a struggle between good guys (like himself) and bad guys. It was fun. For his brother, life was music and music was life, but in both cases their task was to "make a living" because one could not have a living if one did not make it oneself. The literature of the time is replete with people who march their way through life with no freedom, no liberty, slaves to the necessity of earning money.

Even the transition to the post-fusion world was easy for them. My grandfather continued to play his game of "good guys and bad guys" in sim, as well as being thrilled to have the opportunity to

---

[127] Remember too that they were the sons of K.J. Peters, who had himself led a relatively eclectic life for the era. Note that Peters' literary career was only modestly successful and included a quasi-fictional vision of the future that proved to be wildly inaccurate and is not worth elaborating on here. More important in their upbringing was probably their mother, who had been a ballerina and later, an environmental and social activist.

travel more, play more music, study physics in detail and generally, express himself as he wished. As for my great uncle, it was almost as if he didn't notice the transition. He continued to compose music and sound for sims, it's just that there was no longer a need to get paid, which was fine by him. Many people do the same today, and his renown in his field was substantial. He is still known to sim audio specialists and much of his music can be heard in the corridors and fields and gas clouds of today's sims.

Most people of their generation were not so lucky in the transition. Physicians, accountants, plumbers and priests were no longer needed, their very *definition* of themselves, the way they measured their worth was yanked out from under them. It's no surprise that they rebelled against it and suffered greatly when the rebellions failed.

Today we live in a utopia compared to the information age. It is a utopia both of the conservatives *and* the progressives. On one hand, those Ranchers who holed themselves up out of fear of an overblown, central, inefficient, controlling government would rejoice that we essentially *have* no government. We make decisions directly, democratically, and what is best, there is no central decision making entity that will *ever* take from me what I have earned to give it to someone else. I am an island, I am my own state.

A 21st century progressive would rejoice in that there is no longer even a concept of poverty, or need. None are denied sustenance, care, or an education simply because they lack money, for there is no money. Nor are there fruitless debates about what is true, for we all know immediately and unquestioningly what is true.

Everyone can simply do what they like, be whatever they please, share what they can and enjoy the creations of others without worry.

In fact, the left / right spectrum of politics disappeared with politics itself and the religious / atheist dichotomy disappeared with religion. In lieu of capitalist or communist ideals we have something else: everyone gives what it pleases them to give and takes what it pleases them to take. We have no societal spectrum, we have only individuals who live in harmony.

But make no mistake, it is not that we have somehow evolved into better beings. No, the lack of turmoil in our society is simply because we no longer have to find a way to allocate limited resources. Our resources are, for the most part, unlimited, as is our knowledge. It is Artie, plus RANT, plus, finally, fusion that ushered in this age. As such, it was probably the inevitable outcome of the enlightenment itself.

And it saved us. The ills that threatened to destroy us: climate change, environmental degradation, population growth, were all solved by RANT technology and fusion, and if these were inevitable, then perhaps the challenges of the information age were not as great as we thought.

But the real challenge was to survive as a society and as a species until those technologies *could* save us, while not building them in such a way that they turned into the instruments of our destruction. We succeeded, but we came so very, very close to failure that it is hair raising to consider.

We succeeded because there were some among us who even then expanded the boundaries of their own tribe to include all of humanity, who, when they thought of the problems facing them, seemingly intractable problems, thought not in terms of us vs. them, but in terms of us vs ourselves. They saw not our differences, but our similarities.

For my part, I have travelled far, through time and space. I have met humans across eight centuries and four worlds. I know what these differences and similarities are, for these things have never changed…

We all love our children more than life itself, we all wish for them to be happy; we have all had our hearts broken – some of us, perhaps too many of us, multiple times; we have all searched for true love – some of us, perhaps too few of us, have found it; we all make jokes, laugh at the jokes of others, and are saddened by the pain of others; we have all jumped too quickly to some conclusions and come too late to others; we are all, in sum, just human beings.

As to our differences… compared to our similarities, that which separates us is absolutely trivial and always has been. That's all.

That's all there ever was, or ever will be.

ABOUT THE AUTHOR

Alaric Thain was born in 2084. As a young man he travelled to four extrasolar colonies and returned to Earth in 2850, having aged twenty-five years. At that point he was the oldest human alive (known on Earth). He became a historian and taught history at the Sorbonne, in Paris, before leaving Earth again in 2872. This book has been made available to you in the 21st century by Artie, or at least a version of hir that returned to manifest hirself in your time in order to bring this work to your attention. Your timeline will differ from Thain's, and you should not view this book as a prediction but rather, as a possible future.

When Artie left hir own time, Thain's whereabouts and his destination were unknown, as was his fate.

www.historyofthe21stcentury.com

www.alaricthain.com

Made in the USA
Middletown, DE
16 February 2020